Familiar
and
Haunting

Familiar and Haunting

Collected Stories

by PHILIPPA PEARCE

GREENWILLOW BOOKS

An Imprint of HarperCollins*Publishers*

Familiar and Haunting: Collected Stories contains new stories first published in Great Britain in 2001 as *The Rope and Other Stories*, as well as stories from three collections previously published in the United States as *What the Neighbors Did and Other Stories* (Thomas Y. Crowell, 1973); *The Shadow Cage and Other Tales of the Supernatural* (Thomas Y. Crowell, 1977); and *Who's Afraid? And Other Strange Stories* (Greenwillow Books, 1987). The stories appear in this collection in the same order they did in their original collections, except that "Mrs. Chamberlain's Reunion" has been moved so that it could be included with the supernatural tales in "Part Two: The Haunting Stories," and "Black Eyes" and "Who's Afraid?" have been moved so that they could be included with the reality-based tales in "Part One: The Stories."

Familiar and Haunting: Collected Stories
Text copyright 1959, 1967, 1969, 1972, 1976, 1977, 1980, 1981, 1982, 1983, 1984, 1985, 1986, 1989, 2000 by Philippa Pearce
Collection copyright © 2002 by Philippa Pearce
Pages 391–392 constitute an extension of the copyright page.

The text of this book is set in Electra.

Library of Congress Cataloging-in-Publication Data
Pearce, Philippa.
    Familiar and haunting : collected stories / by Philippa Pearce.
      p. cm.
    "Greenwillow Books."
    Summary: A collection of thirty-seven stories previously published in magazines or books, including tales of animals, ghosts, and everyday life.
    ISBN 0-06-623964-8 (trade).   ISBN 0-06-623965-6 (lib. bdg.)
    1. Children's stories, English. [1. Short stories.] I. Title.
PZ7.P3145 Co 2002   [Fic]—dc21   2001040400

1 2 3 4 5 6 7 8 9 10   First Edition

Contents

Part I ❖ *The Stories*

Part II ❖ The Haunting Stories

Familiar and Haunting

Part I ❖
The Stories

The Rope ❖

*T*he rope hung from top to bottom of his dream. The rope hung softly, saying nothing, doing nothing. Then the rope began to swing very softly, very gently, at first only by a hair's breadth from the vertical . . . Toward him.

Mike could not see the swing of it, but he knew that it was happening.

The rope swung a little wider, a little wider . . . Toward him.

The rope had no noose at the end of it, but Mike knew it was a hangman's rope, as surely as if the rope had told him so, and he knew it was for him.

The rope swung a little wider, a lot wider. . . .

Wide, wide it swung . . . Toward him, toward him . . .

Mike shrieked and woke himself and found that he had only squeaked, after all. He had woken nobody, for he was sleeping alone, downstairs, on the couch in his granny's sitting room. That was because Shirley and his mother were occupying the spare room upstairs, and of course, Gran herself was in her own bedroom.

Thankfully he lay awake, but gradually thankfulness left him. He got out of his couch bed, went to the window, and drew back the curtains to look out at the early-morning weather.

Please, please, let there be rain . . . or at least a heavy sky that promised—that faithfully promised—rain later.

But the sky was blue and cloudless, and there was sunshine already in Gran's little garden and sunshine on the meadow beyond and on the trees that grew along the riverbank. The river bounded the meadow, and on the far bank several very tall trees grew. One of them was Mike's gallows, his gibbet.

He got back into bed. He didn't sleep again; he didn't want to. He didn't want the morning's happenings to begin earlier than need be. He dozed, until he had to get up because everybody else was up and about.

At breakfast Shirley said, "Can we go to the rope this morning?"

"Of course," said their grandmother. "You can both swim well, can't you? If necessary, that is. When I was your age—"

It always seemed that Gran had been a bit of a tomboy at their age, a *successful* tomboy. You could see that Shirley liked to think she resembled her granny in this. Perhaps, thought Mike, she really did.

Their mother—Gran's daughter-in-law, not her daughter—said uneasily, "We're here on such a short visit, and there are other places to go to besides the river and that rope. . . ." The river was not deep or fast-flowing or even very wide, but it was certainly very muddy. "If either of them fell in . . ."

Their gran said, "Nonsense! What's a little river water in summer to them, at their age?"

So, altogether, it had to be taken for granted that they would go to the river, to the rope.

And it certainly wasn't going to rain this morning, but oh! Mike thought, it just possibly could in the afternoon. So he must maneuver and contrive. He said, "We can go to the river this morning and to Brown's this afternoon. I expect there'll still be a few comics left." Brown's was the newsagent's in the village.

"*Left?*" said Shirley. "A few comics *left?*"

"They go very quickly," said Mike.

"Oh!" said Shirley. Then: "No, let's do Brown's this morning, the rope this afternoon."

"If you say so," said Mike. He also shrugged his shoulders.

Their grandmother had given them money to buy comics, enough money to buy at least one each. When they reached Brown's, Shirley was businesslike in her examining and choosing; Mike mooned around, flipping pages, dissatisfied. Here, in this one, was the kind of story he usually enjoyed. Mighty-righty—that was the hero's name—was tough and fearless. He also had magic powers. In an emergency, he just pressed a button on his chest and little luminous wings sprouted from his shoulders to carry him anywhere. (The wings could be retracted by the same device.) Moreover, if he clenched his right hand once, it became a fist to knock out a champion boxer; twice, and he could knock down trees and walls. (It was possible that he could clench it a third time and so acquire even superior power, but that was only hinted at in the story.)

"I saw you yesterday," said a voice at Mike's elbow. "Yesterday evening. By the river." A ginger-haired boy of about Mike's age; he sounded friendly.

"Oh," said Mike.

"Have you come to live in one of those houses beyond the meadow?"

"No," said Mike. "Only staying. With our gran. Two days."

"Have you seen the rope?" asked the ginger-haired boy.

"Yes," said Mike.

"We're going there later," said Shirley eagerly.

"See you then," said the ginger-haired boy. He left the shop with a packet of sweets that he had just bought.

Mike put Mighty-righty back on the display shelf. "I don't want any of them," he said. "They're rubbish."

Shirley, not really expecting any luck, asked if she could use Mike's share of the money they had been given, and to her amazement, he said that she could. He was very quiet as they walked back from Brown's, but Shirley was dipping into her comics as she went and noticed nothing. He was silent over their midday meal with the others, but no one noticed because Gran was hurrying everything today. She wanted the children to have plenty of time by the river, with the rope.

Mike offered to stay and help with the washing up, but his granny told him that she and his mother would do it. He must go off with his sister—no time like the present, for their age. So Mike and Shirley went alone across the meadow, in blazing sunshine, to the river and the trees on the riverbank.

There it hung: the rope.

A tall tree leaned over the river, and one end of the rope had been attached to a high branch of it, so that the rope hung down over the river. It hung to within a hand's breadth of the surface of the water, almost exactly over the middle of the river.

That was how it had hung yesterday evening, when Mike and Shirley had first seen it, but already today someone had waded or swum out to the rope and caught the end of it and brought it back to the far bank—the far bank, as far as Mike and Shirley were concerned. They looked across and saw the boy who must have taken the rope in this way. He was dripping with river water and shivering, and at the same time, he was laughing and talking with the friends gathered round him. Mike recognized him, in spite of the fact that his curly ginger hair was plastered down straight and dark over his wet head: Ginger.

And now Ginger saw them and recognized them. "Hi!" he shouted across the river, in his friendly way, and prepared to swing across to them on the rope.

He carried the operation out to perfection.

Four knots had been made in the rope at intervals, to suit the users of it. Ginger grasped the rope just above the third knot from the bottom, drew back from the edge of the riverbank in order to take a running leap, then ran—pushed off with both feet—and leapt forward over the water. His feet pushed and leapt and then clamped themselves about the rope just above the lowest knot, tied at the very end of it.

He came floating through the air on the rope, across the river, with the ease and grace of talent and practice. He landed faultlessly on the near bank, just beside Mike and Shirley. He steadied himself for an instant and then stood there, holding the rope.

He smiled directly at Mike; he really was a friendly boy. He said, "Like a go?"

Mike was still able to think, to speak. He said, "The others had better have their turns first. . . ."

"Everyone's had a turn. It's all yours."

Mike was rooted to the ground; his voice had vanished. But Shirley had moved forward hopefully, and Ginger, noticing her, said, "You first, then?"

He showed her exactly where to hold on to the rope, above the particular knot that suited her height, and reminded her of the position of her feet above the lowest knot. He made her draw back from the edge of the bank, so that she could get a good run and push before swinging out and over. And he pointed out earnestly that she would need as much push from the other side to get back again. "It's very important," he said. "If you miss your proper push from the bank—well, you've had it."

"Yes," said Shirley, again and again. "Yes—yes—I know!" And she really did seem to understand, without more explanation. She held on to the rope just as she should and made her little run and push and leap and, gripping the rope with her feet, swung right across the river to land among Ginger's friends, who raised a mild cheer in her honor. Then she turned to swing back but had not forgotten any of Ginger's instructions: Holding the rope, she drew back, ran, and pushed off across the river to land where Ginger and Mike stood on the other bank.

"That's it!" said Ginger, but before he could say more, she was off again toward the far bank.

And then, expertly, back again. This time Ginger caught her and held her, while he took the rope from her. Mike watched and knew what would happen next.

"Your turn," Ginger said to him, and he had the same truly friendly smile as before.

Mike knew that everyone was looking at him; they were interested, but casual, knowing what they were expecting from him, not doubting they would have it from him. Only Shirley was perhaps looking at him in a different way, because she was his sister and she knew him: she knew what he might be thinking, feeling; she knew what he might do, what he might not do.

He tried to say aloud, "No, I don't want to do it. I won't do it." But he could not.

And Shirley watched his fear, his fear within fear.

Ginger was still holding the rope out toward him. Mike took it and stretched his hands up above the knot that Ginger said was for him. Blindly, he was about to set off on his swing at once, but Ginger pulled him back to make the necessary run up, leap, and push.

So now he was away, swinging out from the near bank toward the far one, and one of his feet had come loose from its correct position above the bottom knot. The foot fumbled for its place again, and the rope tried to twist away from it, teasing it. And meanwhile he had left the near bank a long, long way behind and was over the middle of the river, and here came the far bank, taking him by cruel surprise. He still hadn't got both feet into the correct position, and that almost stupefied him with anxiety. He forgot the need to land properly on the far bank before starting his return swing. He remembered only the need to push off from it. His free foot touched the bank, and at once, with all the strength of his one foot, he pushed and swung away again, rather unevenly, back toward the near bank. There was a wasteful twirl to his swing, and when he reached the other bank, where Ginger and Shirley stood, his toes only just touched it. With his toes he managed a push backward, but too weakly to carry him the whole way back; at the end of his swing, his feet never touched the far bank at all. From that far bank, the automatic swing of a pendulum movement took him back toward the near bank, but with no possibility of his even touching it with his toes, far less of making a landing.

Now he swung toward the far bank, then back toward the near. To and fro he swung across the river, with no hope of making a landing on either bank.

Each time the swing became a little narrower. Narrower and narrower.

The rope, satisfied, now swung lazily and narrowly over the middle part of the river. Soon it would be hanging still, vertical, with Mike on it.

The swinging had narrowed to nothing. Stopped.

Mike was hanging on the rope over the middle of the river, and there was only one way in which he could stop hanging there and go home from this rope and river and meadow and hateful village. He must let go. His hands—and his remaining foot—must let go of the rope. He must fall into the river, which, after all, was not deep or swift-flowing, and he could swim.

He would not mind being in the river—oh, no!—but his hands would not let go of the rope. He whimpered to them to let go, but they would not. They gripped and clung and clutched in spite of the pain in the palms and an intolerable stretching of the muscles of his arms and a feeling as if his shoulders would split open.

He hung there on the rope, twirling slowly round over the middle of the river. Now he could see the people on the far bank; there were quite a lot of them, Ginger's friends and acquaintances, and they were all looking at him and giggling among themselves. Oh, yes! They were laughing all right! Now he couldn't see them anymore, because he had rotated further, so that now he was facing the near bank, from which Ginger and Shirley were watching him. They watched in silence. And beyond them, coming across the meadow toward the rope, he saw two more people: his mother and his grandmother. They had finished the washing up and were coming to see how Mike and Shirley were enjoying themselves.

Suddenly, hanging there helplessly, he saw; he knew. He knew that nothing and nobody could save him now—unless he could save himself. He must do it immediately. At once. Now—now, before his mother and his grandmother reached the riverbank. His grandmother particularly.

One foot was already dangling; he detached the other from the rope, so that both feet hung free, although that made the agony in his hands and arms and shoulders even worse. He concentrated his will on letting go with his hands—of his own free will, before he was made to let go by pain and exhaustion. His will was prizing open the fingers of his hands and achieved it, and in the split second of his falling, he also achieved the shout he willed himself to make. It came out partly as a scream, but it was also quite distinctly a word: "Whoops!"

He was in the river. He was choking and drowning, but he surfaced, and it didn't matter that he was crying because he was all over water, anyway, or that he was sobbing, too, because he had to gasp for breath. Then he was swimming clumsily toward the near bank, and then wading, and finally clambering out to where his mother and grandmother and Shirley and Ginger waited for him.

His mother began fussing at once about his wetness and coldness and muddiness. But his grandmother boomed through it all: "Well done, Mike! It doesn't matter a scrap that you didn't manage it first time! You were keen to have a go—that's the spirit! That's what I was like at your age! Well done!"

Ginger said nothing.

Shirley said nothing. She was looking at Mike, and Mike knew that because she was his sister, she knew things about him that nobody else did.

He just wanted to go home—to his own home. But that was impossible; he had to go back with the others to Gran's home, with his mother promising a hot bath and dry clothes, and his grandmother promising a tea with a very special summer treat. Apparently, while he and Shirley had been in the village buying comics, their grandmother and mother had been to a pick-your-own strawberry farm. There were strawberries and cream for tea. (The thought of it made Mike feel sick.)

Surprisingly, Ginger was coming, too. Mike supposed that his grandmother had bullied Ginger into that, or perhaps Ginger really wanted to come. Anyway, arrangements had been made about dry clothes and shoes or sandals or flip-flops for Ginger as well as for himself.

So they went home together. Shirley danced ahead in the triumph of her performance on the rope; then Gran, holding Ginger by her side in conversation; then Mum, trailing a little behind, to encourage Mike; lastly, Mike — miserable Mike.

Later Mike and Ginger were in the bath together. This had not been their idea, but by now Gran spoke of them together as "the boys." Because of her, they lay one at either end of her large bath, relaxing into the kindliness of hot, clean water. (They needed only to rinse off the river water, they had been told.) Now and then they shifted their limbs a little to start the ripples; they did not speak to each other.

Then, slyly, Ginger splashed at Mike, and Mike splashed back, and then they fooled around with the bathwater, until Mike sat up and looked over the side of the bath and wondered whether his grand-mother would be pleased at the mess. Ginger also sat up to look and said that his mother would have been furious.

Now they sat up at either end of the bath, facing each other, and Ginger said, "Your mum said you were going home tomorrow."

"Yes."

"Will you come again?"

"Maybe."

"I thought it was really good, that 'Whoops!' when you fell in. I fell in once, when I was caught in the middle, early on. I wish I'd thought of 'Whoops!' then."

Mike said, "If we come again, I shan't go on the rope again. . . . I don't want to. . . . I didn't want to, this afternoon. . . ." He repeated fiercely, "I tell you, I didn't want to!"

"You could have said," said Ginger.

"No. I couldn't. I just couldn't."

Ginger accepted this in silence, but thoughtfully.

The bathwater was cooling. Ginger, who sat at the tap end,

refreshed it with more hot water. Then he said, "I'll tell you something about my dad."

"Yes?"

"He's got a chain saw. He cuts up wood. And once he nearly cut his thumb off. He had to go to hospital."

"Oh, yes?"

"He nearly cut his thumb off." Ginger began giggling uncontrollably. He was rocking with laughter, backward and forward in the bathwater, making waves that hit against Mike with a splash. He was almost screaming with laughter, and tears were running down his cheeks. He gasped out: "There was an awful lot of blood everywhere, and when I saw it, I—I *fainted*." On the last word, he became quite still and quiet, staring at Mike. He said, "I haven't told anyone. You don't live here, and you're going away tomorrow."

"We'll be coming back someday," said Mike, "because of our gran."

"You won't tell," said Ginger.

"No," said Mike. He pondered. "Blood—that's funny. Shirley fell out of a tree once and cut her head. She howled a lot, but she didn't mind the blood, nor did I."

"Much blood?"

"Quite a bit. But I didn't mind."

Ginger patted the surface of the bathwater with his hand. "Funny . . ." he said.

Mike fished around in his mind for something his mother often remarked—nothing very witty or original, but just true. "People are different," he said.

Shirley came hammering on the door to tell them the tea was made and the strawberries were on the table and she wanted to begin.

So they got out of the bath and dried and dressed as best they could and went downstairs together, to the kitchen. Tea was laid in the kitchen, on a table with a white cloth, and in the middle of the cloth was a huge bowl piled high with strawberries, ripe and red and shiny;

there was cream in a jug, and sugar in a basin; and the sight did not make Mike feel sick.

Gran was sitting behind the teapot, and she was calling to them: "Come in—come in, to a feast for heroes!"

So they went in to tea.

Early Transparent ❖

A gray squirrel impudently ran on the Chapmans' lawn—skipped and ran and then suddenly froze in attention. Then, as suddenly, it streaked toward a fruit tree and up into its invisibility.

The old man glared out on the scene from his invalid chair in the glassed-in veranda. His mouth had made a sound which was not intelligible to his wife or to his grandson standing by. But they recognized it as some word, and a word of rage.

"Why's Grandpa so angry?" whispered the boy.

His grandmother whispered back: "They're thieves. They steal the fruit. Soon they'll be digging holes in the lawn for their nuts—*our* hazelnuts—against the winter. Then, after all that, they forget where they've hidden them! Your grandfather has never had any patience with them."

"Oh . . ."

"And that old war wound troubles him more than ever. That puts his nerves on edge."

She bent over the old man and kissed the top of his head so lightly that probably he did not know it.

So Nicky thought. He was on only a short visit to his grandparents. The last time he had stayed, his grandfather had been well and strong in spite of his age and in spite of the war wound that people were always going on about. He had not needed a wheelchair; he had been clear in his speech—often bitingly clear when he complained or objected. In excuse for his short temper, the old lady would murmur yet again about his having been so badly wounded in the war—and, if he happened to overhear, he would blow up in scorching fury.

Now he was different, and Nicky was uneasy with the change.

But anyway, Nicky would be home again soon. For his birthday. That looming event determined the longest he could possibly be expected to stay. His mother had said, "Granny so loved having you visit—you remember the expeditions she used to take you on? And now she hardly gets out at all, because of Grandpa's being—well, because of Grandpa's being as he is. You could cheer her up, perhaps help her a bit. Go to the shop for her, for instance. Garden. Odd jobs here and there. You're old enough."

Nicky didn't like the idea of that, but he supposed that he could help a bit. Now they were moving back into the house from the veranda, leaving old Mr. Chapman in his chair, still sitting in the sun. The veranda took most of the light from the living room against which it had been built. The room was already shadowy and a little musty-smelling—but with a thin, fresh sweetness through the mustiness. A bowl of fruit stood in the middle of the big table.

Nicky said, "Shall I go to the shop for you, Granny?"

She smiled at him delightedly. "What a kind thought!" (Nicky shuffled his feet, knowing that the thought was only secondhand.) "But everything's shut by now. And anyway, you've come to enjoy yourself while you're here. Perhaps with Jeremy Gillespie? You get on so well, don't you? He's on holiday, too, of course, and at home."

"Oh, Jeremy . . . Yes . . ." Jeremy was the boy of about Nicky's age and only two houses along that his grandmother had decided would make the ideal holiday friend.

"But you'll have to wait until tomorrow for Jeremy. Then, after breakfast, there's a job for you both, to pick Early Transparents before the squirrels get them all. There's a bumper crop this year." She took the bowl of fruit from the table, and the sweetness moved in the air as the fruit moved. She held the bowl under Nicky's nose. "Smell them. Then, before you eat one, try it against the light."

Then came the little speech on the so-called transparency of these greengages, a speech always before made fretfully by his grandfather. But now his grandmother spoke it gently, almost laughing: "Of course, they're not really *transparent*; you can't see right through them, as if they were made of glass. They're only *translucent*; you can see the light through the ripe ones. You should be able to see the darkness—the shadow—of the stone in the middle, against the light."

Nicky held up one of the greengages against the sunset light from the veranda. He peered. "I can't see any shadow."

"You need to hold it against a better light. Tomorrow morning, perhaps."

Neither of them mentioned the possibility of switching on the electric light. Artificial light was not what you used in testing an Early Transparent.

Nicky turned and turned the fruit, then gave up and popped it whole into his mouth. The resistance of the skin to his teeth, and then the almost liquid rush of softness and sweetness! For those few seconds he was dazed by Early Transparency.

He had even closed his eyes, and when he opened them again, his grandmother—to his astonishment—was in tears. She recovered herself instantly. "I was just thinking of a child—of your mother as a child—of her picking Early Transparents."

Nicky couldn't see the point of crying over a thing like that, but his grandmother was briskly going on: "Now, if you and Jeremy find squirrels at the tree before you, don't try any tricks with them. They can be very vicious with those teeth!"

"Of course not, Granny," said Nicky. His mind, however, was not on the squirrels but on Jeremy. The thought of sharing the picking of the first Early Transparents with Jeremy Gillespie depressed him. As his mother always pointed out, there was absolutely nothing wrong with Jeremy. Yet the idea of him lowered Nicky's spirits.

Cheerily now old Mrs. Chapman promised him: "You two can start picking straight after breakfast tomorrow morning. If it's fine."

But it wasn't fine. Rain began in the night and continued most of the next day. Even before Nicky was down for breakfast, a new plan had had to be made on the telephone with Jeremy Gillespie's mother: the Early Transparents were postponed until tomorrow, and meanwhile Nicky and his grandmother would go shopping in the town center. And no, Jeremy would not come with them because he wanted to work on his Holiday Project ("Oh," said Nicky as neutrally as he could), and yes, all this meant old Mr. Chapman would have been left alone in the house, but Mrs. Chapman could get a friend to sit with him and give him his lunch.

In town they shopped, and Mrs. Chapman bought Nicky his birthday present—something he wanted and something of which she could approve. There was a craze for poster making at the moment, so Nicky chose a set of colored crayons, the rather expensive sort with brilliant, deep colors. Back home again, his grandmother first of all checked that his grandfather was all right and thanked the friend and said goodbye to her; then, enjoying herself, she set to wrapping the crayon pack in birthday paper. "You mustn't open the parcel until your birthday morning," she told Nicky, and she put it inside his holiday suitcase to take home with him.

For the rest of that wet afternoon Nicky and his grandmother played board games and Nicky watched TV with his grandfather. (His grandmother said that she disliked what they showed on television nowadays.) In any fine interval they could glimpse the squirrels toward the bottom of the garden, where the greengage tree grew just out of sight. "They'll be at the Early Transparents." His grandmother sighed. "Well, at least, this year, there's plenty for all."

That night, at sunset, the sky was red, which gave old Mrs. Chapman much satisfaction. "Shepherd's delight," she said, meaning a fine day to come. And her husband, who had apparently heard and understood her, gave a loud exclamation unmistakably of scorn, so that she whispered to Nicky, "He means I talk *poppycock*—that's always been his word. I irritate him," she added humbly.

But the evening's weather forecast bore out Mrs. Chapman's hopes, and she telephoned the Gillespies to remake arrangements for the next day.

As he listened to her on the telephone, Nicky found a wild resolve forming in his mind. His grandmother had always stressed that they could start picking only after breakfast. But saying nothing to anybody, Nicky would begin picking *before* breakfast—well before breakfast and before Jeremy Gillespie could possibly be turning up. That meant getting up really early, but after all, these were *Early* Transparents, weren't they? So the early morning seemed right.

Moreover, quite alone, he would be able to eat morning fruit fresh from the tree.

After supper, Granny had to get Grandpa to bed, and she was already tired by the morning's shopping. So they were all in bed in very good time—Nicky much earlier than he would have been at home. He did not mind that, because he supposed he would wake earlier, and so he did.

He lay in bed, listening carefully. From his grandparents' bedroom, two snores: one a regular, gentle sighing sound; the other rasping and deep with an occasional snuffling exclamation—old Mr. Chapman suffered from dreams of the war in which he had fought years ago. Sometimes he used actually to scream aloud and wake himself—and his wife—from a nightmare. But not tonight.

And the night was really over by now. Cautiously Nicky got out of bed and dressed to let himself out into the garden.

There he found himself in a hushed time between birdsong and the start of human activity. He did not wish to disturb this quiet. He trod measuredly over the wet grass. He saw no raiding squirrels as he went. He reached the end of the garden, where the Early Transparent tree grew in a corner where garden fencing met hedge.

The branches of the tree were bowed down with the fruit as he had never seen them before. Last year there had been only a very poor crop, the year before that he had not even been here at the right time, and before that—well, he could not certainly remember. But this year! His grandmother had said "plenty"—and oh! the plenitude of it, the brimming abundance, the *munificence*! The morning sunshine lit up the fruit everywhere—larger than ordinary greengages and plump, with the lightest of blooms breathed on the skins and a freckling of red. Ripe, ready, and so many—so many!

As he gazed, one particular fruit seemed to present itself to him, to invite him. He stretched out his hand and touched it, and at his touch, it fell into the palm of his hand. He held it up between finger and thumb toward the sun, and the morning sunlight shone through it, and—yes, this time he saw clearly the shadow of the stone at the very heart of the fruit.

And, out of the corner of his eye, saw something else. Hardly a movement—a *presence*. And looked past the fruit he was holding and met the fixed gaze of eyes. Not the eyes of any wild creature, but wild all the same, with a stare of terror. He saw—how could he have missed it earlier?—a child who stood absolutely still among the leaves and branches and looked at him and also through him and beyond him with that stare of horror. The child was clutching a handful of Early Transparents to its chest.

Their gaze was locked, without wink or blink, until Nicky drew breath. Then: "You're stealing!" he accused. "Stealing!" he repeated in a shout, because he was somehow frightened by the child. The child's mouth opened as if it might speak, but did not, and the mouth remained open, a little black hole of silence. And the eyes still stared and stared.

As though his shout had raised an alarm, a door banged distantly from the direction of the house and his grandmother's voice was call-ing his name—calling to him again and again and (he realized) coming swiftly closer. He turned his head toward the sound, and when he turned his gaze back, the child had gone. Where it had been, the leaves were still moving, but the child had gone.

"What are you doing? Oh, what are you doing?" his grandmother was calling, and now he saw her. She was still in her nightdress, and running barefoot over the wet grass toward him, her gray hair uncombed, unarranged.

She reached him; she clutched him. "Nicky, what have you *done?*"

"There was someone stealing your Early Transparents."

"The child—only the child. Only a little girl." His grandmother began to weep, just as she had wept so unexpectedly on the day of his arrival. "She thinks nobody knows that she comes. But I know, and I don't mind—no, I'm glad for her, poor child."

"But, Granny—"

His grandmother was rushing on. "She's come to stay with some cousin who lives down the road. There's no one else where she comes from; her family all dead, all killed. Nicky, she was found underneath them all, the only one left alive, and since then she doesn't speak. She can't speak. And she stares. . . ."

His grandmother's headlong, sobbing speech bewildered Nicky. But now they both heard from the house the irregular ringing of a bell—the bell that always stood within close reach of Mr. Chapman, in case he needed anything or anyone. The ringing sounded impatient, angry.

"I must go to him," said Mrs. Chapman, calming herself. Without another word, she turned and ran back to the house. Nicky followed her. He had no more thought of the Early Transparents. He found the one he had picked to eat still in his hand when he reached the house. Violently he flung it toward the bottom of the garden for the squirrels to find.

Old Mr. Chapman's getting up and dressed and to the breakfast table was a slow and difficult business. He was cantankerous and kept his wife busy until the very end of breakfast. By then Jeremy Gillespie had arrived, which seemed to annoy the old man further. (Fortunately Jeremy Gillespie did not notice.)

The picking was to begin at once. Mrs. Chapman gave each boy a basket, and Jeremy set off immediately toward the bottom of the garden. She held Nicky back for a moment, while she put a finger to her lips. He nodded.

All the same, while they were picking, he said casually, "My granny says there's a funny girl staying down this road—I mean, she's strange. So my gran says."

"She's foreign," said Jeremy. "Quite young. Staying with some distant relative. Nobody sees her. She doesn't go out. She's too scared."

"What's she scared of?"

"She's a refugee," said Jeremy, as though that explained everything.

"But where's she a refugee from? Why's she one?" asked Nicky.

Jeremy was growing impatient of this conversation. "Some war zone abroad—civil war. It was all on telly ages ago."

Nicky didn't quite disbelieve his grandmother, but she could get things muddled. He asked, "But what *happened*?"

"Soldiers. They burnt the village. They shot everybody. They killed all this girl's family. There was a pile of dead bodies, but the girl was underneath everybody, so she wasn't killed. People rescued her, and she was brought to this country because of the relative here. Don't you ever follow the news?"

"Not really," said Nicky.

"We do Current Affairs at my school," said Jeremy Gillespie.

When they had filled their baskets, they went back to the house. Mrs. Chapman weighed her share of the fruit and prepared to make greengage jam. Jeremy Gillespie took his share home, but Nicky said he would stay with his grandmother and help her with the jam. Jeremy Gillespie did not seem to mind; he said that at home he could begin to finalize his project.

Nicky would have enjoyed the jam making, but he and his grandmother worked almost in silence. She refused absolutely to talk about what had happened that morning at the greengage tree. When he tried her with even one question, she wept again. He had only been wondering whether the little girl might ever come again. He would like to have said he was sorry. He would like to have said something that perhaps would make things better for her. He would like to have *done* something.

He could have given her something, as a present. Perhaps even his own birthday crayons. But he knew that a present was a stupid idea—stupid! A present wouldn't make up for not having a mother or a father or anyone else anymore. All your family killed and lying dead on top of you, you underneath them all, alive. Oh, a present was a stupid idea—stupid—stupid!

He tried not to think of the little girl. He thought of the greengage jam he was helping to make. There would be a pot of it to take home to his family. And when he got home, there would be planning for his birthday the next day. And the next day would *be* his birthday. . . .

He was going home tomorrow. This was his last night in his grandmother's house. Later, in bed, he thought of being at home again and of his birthday and his birthday party and all the presents. And suddenly he was thinking again of the little girl at the Early Transparent tree and of her stare that looked at him and through him and far beyond him. It was true that nothing could ever make up for what had happened to her in that country where she had once lived. Nothing.

In the quietness of the night he lay listening to the snoring of his grandparents in their bedroom.

After a while he slipped out of bed and rummaged in his case until he found the birthday crayons. He decided to unwrap them, so that it would be quite plain what they were and that at least they were harmless. The rustling of his unwrapping sounded so loud that he was afraid it might waken the sleepers, but they snored on.

Carrying the crayons, he crept downstairs and out of the house. This was truly nighttime, but by starlight he could still see his way down to the Early Transparent tree. He reached the tree and set the crayons on the grass at its foot, then thought that they might look accidental—left there by mistake. So he picked fruit from the tree and heaped it on top, then thought the squirrels would take the fruit, anyway. So he reversed the heap, with the crayon pack balanced on top of the fruit.

Then he went back to the house and to bed. There was still the same snoring from his grandparents' bedroom, one snore gently sighing, the other seeming to snatch at each rasping breath as though it were its last. As he listened, it seemed to him that probably, after all, he had just done a stupid, stupid thing. He fell asleep, half wishing that he had not done what he had done.

The next morning, after breakfast, the usual friend came to be with old Mr. Chapman, so that Mrs. Chapman could see Nicky off on the train.

Nicky positioned himself in front of his grandfather and said his good-bye. The old man looked at him, and it seemed to Nicky that his grandfather also looked through him and beyond him. But at least he spared his grandson a wintry smile. That done, and at the last moment: "I'd like to take an Early Transparent for the journey," said Nicky.

"Take several from the bowl," said his grandmother. "Hurry!" But Nicky was already on his way down to the tree itself. When he had almost reached it, he stopped. He daren't look. He so wanted this to be all right. Just this one little thing.

He looked. And there was nothing at the foot of the Early Transparent tree. She had come, after all, and she had taken his gift.

He picked his Early Transparents for the journey and rushed back to the house.

Later, in the train, he thought of the crayons and their intense colors and what you could do with them, and he thought that perhaps—just perhaps—she really would use them, and enjoy them, as he would have done. He hoped so.

The Fir Cone ❖

*T*he door of what was now Charlie's cupboard would not shut.

Not a crisis, you might think. Not even a tricky situation, really.

Certainly absurd for a mother to think of a *trap* of any kind. So Mrs. Waring reassured herself, controlling her breathing. She had to deal only with a cupboard overfull of old toys.

She dragged forward her huge, empty cardboard box (the carton in which a new school TV had been delivered). She had supposed that she and her carton and—of course—Charlie himself would be alone together in front of the cupboard. But here were her two elder children as well. Sandra and Bill had drifted downstairs quite separately, it appeared, but as though both expected something interesting. Sandra leaned against one doorjamb, attending minutely to a fingernail; Bill leaned on the other side, staring and chewing in the way that particularly irritated Mrs. Waring.

She decided to ignore the onlookers.

"Now, Charlie," she said. "Let's just see."

She laid her hand flat on the cupboard door and pressed steadily.

The door went back; it even seemed to click shut for a moment. Then, the hand pressure released, it sprang open again, gaping wider than before. Something small fell lightly from the cupboard to the floor and rolled a little.

"There!" said Mrs. Waring. "You see what I mean? An old fir cone that one of you was hoarding. Absolute rubbish. The door won't shut because of all the stuff in the cupboard, and most of it rubbish!"

She had stepped forward to pick up the fir cone, but Charlie was before her—picked it up and put it into his pocket. "Mine," he said. His hand remained in his pocket, around the fir cone, feeling its broken tips, its age. Long ago he had picked it up under the great green tent of its parent tree. There were ducks quacking at a little distance; they had a whole lake to swim about on. And he had picked up his fir cone and kept it ever since.

Charlie was now standing between his mother and the cupboard, and the cupboard door was slowly swinging open to its widest.

The inside of the cupboard became visible to them all. It was crammed. Along the front edge of the top shelf lay an exhausted doll, one arm dangling down toward the next shelf; lower, a fire engine, unmanned; a skipping rope frayed almost to a thread in the middle; some seashells in a see-through raffia bag; a climbing monkey with the remains of his ladder; a dirty Halloween outfit crammed into a shoebox; several My Pretty Ponies. . . .

"Such old, old stuff!" Mrs. Waring was saying. "Outgrown, all of it! Now, Charlie, I promised I wouldn't throw out anything that belonged to you, without your permission. But wouldn't you like some of your better things—say, the fire engine that you never play with now—to go into the jumble sale?" (The school jumble sale was being held that afternoon.) "Wouldn't you like some other, younger child to enjoy one of your old toys? Wouldn't you, Charlie?"

"No," said Charlie, "I wouldn't. I just hate other younger children."

Mrs. Waring sighed. She braced herself again and took a firmer grip of her carton. "All right, then. We'll just get rid of the rubbishy stuff that belonged to Sandra and Bill years ago."

"No," said Charlie.

"But Sandra and Bill don't want any of it now," said Mrs. Waring. She turned sharply on them. "You don't, do you?"

"Oh, no," said Sandra, and Bill said, "No concern of ours at all now." There was something about the way Bill said that last word, something in the way they both *watched* that made Mrs. Waring feel uneasy.

She turned back to Charlie. "So we'll just get rid of their stuff, anyway." She had the doll in mind. She stepped toward the cupboard.

Charlie sprang in front of it, his arms spread wide in its defense. "No!"

Mrs. Waring remained reasonable. "Remember, Charlie, I've promised I won't get rid of anything that belongs to you." (Mrs. Waring prided herself on her *straightness* with her children; she always said that a promise was a promise.) "Only Sandra's old stuff and Bill's will go—"

"No," said Charlie. "You can't take anything. You haven't my permission. And it *all* belongs to me—all of it."

"That's not true," said Mrs. Waring.

"Yes, it is," said Charlie. "Because they've given me all of their stuff. So it does all belong to me." He added, "Since last night." He glanced at Sandra and Bill.

Bill said, "Yeah. It was last night."

Mrs. Waring tried to speak but could not.

Sandra looked almost sorry for her mother. She said, "Charlie just asked us to give him all the old toy cupboard stuff that was ours, and we did. So you see . . ."

There was what seemed a long silence, a stillness, in which they were all looking at their mother.

Then Mrs. Waring groaned; she knew that she had been beaten. Charlie was saying, over and over again, loudly, "You've promised— you've promised—you've promised—"

Sandra said, "You needn't be so mean about it, Charlie." And to her mother: "I think I might make us some tea."

Bill said, "I'll look after the box." He began to drag it from the room.

Their mother said faintly, "It might as well go out with the dustbins."

The three of them left Charlie kneeling in front of his toy cupboard, alone in his triumph.

For a while he gloated.

He had wanted everything—or rather, he had wanted everything to stay there. To stay there for always.

He remembered the fir cone in his pocket and thought of putting it back in the cupboard, but the fir cone—the feel of it under his fingers in his pocket—made him think back to the ducks and the lake and the tent tree. Across the grass to the great tree his mother and father had danced him between them. They were all three breathless from laughing. And he had picked up his fir cone and kept it ever since.

This very afternoon his father would be saying to him, "What shall we do? Where shall we go?" and he could answer that he wanted to go back—back to the tree and the lake and the ducks and the happiness. His father had been there, so he would know the place.

This afternoon his mother would be at the school jumble sale, organizing.

He could hear his mother in the kitchen, talking to Sandra, but Sandra was doing most of the talking, in a soothing sort of voice.

He began to wish that he hadn't, perhaps, been so hard—yes, perhaps, so *mean*—to his mother, but on the other hand, it had, perhaps, been necessary. And anyway, perhaps, it wasn't too late. Thoughtfully he took the shoebox out of the cupboard and removed the Halloween kit. Then he began to put into the box a few of the things he could, after all, most easily spare, perhaps: certainly the doll, and a couple of the Ponies, several of the less attractive seashells from their bag. . . .

The voices from the kitchen continued. They had been joined by Bill.

Bill was laughing, chuckling away.

Charlie heard his name and began to listen intently, his hands still over the partly filled shoebox.

Bill was saying, "What a kid! You have to hand it to him!"

Sandra said, "It was childish—childish!"

His mother, steady-voiced by now, said, "Partly I blame myself. For he is still a child, after all—very young for his age, too. . . ."

Charlie scooped everything out of the shoebox and thrust it back into the cupboard. His hands were trembling with anger. He left the box and the Halloween stuff on the floor and the cupboard door wide open and stamped his way out of the room and up the stairs.

They heard him; they could not have failed to. The voices from the kitchen stopped. Then his mother called, "Charlie, remember, you're not to go to meet your father without Sandra." And Sandra said something about being ready soon. She spoke in that soothing voice that Charlie hated.

He went on hating his sister, with fervor but in sullen silence.

Later that morning, sitting in the tube going across London, with Sandra beside him as escort, Charlie still hated his sister, but he was thinking ahead to the meeting with his father. Would he be there? Once he hadn't been—missed the coach, he said. Then Charlie would have been stranded if Sandra or Bill hadn't been with him. That's what his mother had said afterward to his father on the telephone. And his father had said back—

Oh, Charlie thought, he was sick of them both. And of Sandra and Bill.

All the same, he did want to be with his father again. And he thrust his hand into his pocket and felt the fir cone there and remembered the ducks and the lake and the happiness.

And anyway, at the coach station his father was there, just descended from the coach and looking about him and saw Charlie and then Sandra with him. "Sandy!"

But Sandra said hurriedly, "Sorry, Dad—" and then about some friends she was due to go out with. Charlie could tell that his father was really disappointed, and he asked after Bill (who was at his Saturday afternoon match). Then Sandra said good-bye and left Charlie and his father to their afternoon together.

It was beginning to rain, and his father said they might as well start with something to eat, and Charlie chose Chinese. When the noodles and the bamboo shoots and all the rest were eaten, Charlie sat back in his chair and smiled at his father, and his father smiled back at him. The moment seemed just right, so Charlie said that what he'd *really* like to do next was go somewhere they'd been before, a special place, and (feeling for the fir cone in his pocket) he mentioned the tree and the lake and the ducks.

"I don't know what it was called, but we went there by train. You and me and—and Mum." Casually he brought the fir cone from his pocket and trundled it among the bottles of soy sauce and other things.

"By train?" said his father. "So it was outside London?"

"I don't know, really," said Charlie. "And when we got there, we had to pay to get in. But we didn't have to stand in a line, although you kept saying we'd have to queue. Oh, and there were animals—strange beasts. In a row."

"It sounds like Whipsnade Zoo, if there were wild animals and it was outside London. But I don't remember us ever taking you to Whipsnade. . . ." His father frowned, pondering.

Charlie said, "And there was a gapoda."

"A *what?*"

Charlie repeated, but in a fluster, "A gappy-something." In his fright he gestured aimlessly with his hand and knocked over the soy sauce bottle, and that sent flying a little bunch of wooden toothpicks. "A gadopa. As tall, as high as a house, and with sticky-out bits all the way up, like—like fins."

Suddenly his father was angry. "What rubbish you talk! A boy of your age! I only hope it isn't something your mother—"

He broke off with the same suddenness. "Look, Charlie, we've only got the afternoon, and it's raining hard. We can't go far, and it might be better not to get too wet. Right?"

Shakily Charlie said, "All right."

"So what about a cinema?"

"All right."

"And I'll get us some popcorn."

"All right—I mean, thank you," said Charlie.

So they went to the cinema and ate popcorn and watched a horror film that Charlie chose, and afterward they had quite a large snack in a snack bar. By then Charlie was rather enjoying his afternoon, after all, but by now his father was saying it was time to deliver Charlie back home and get himself back to the coach station.

They went home by way of the school, because Charlie said his mother might still be at the jumble sale.

"All right," said his father.

And so she was.

They went in through the school gate as the last of the jumble sale shoppers were coming out. One or two said, "Hello!" to Charlie, but nobody greeted his father. It was so long ago that he used sometimes to be at the school gate.

As soon as they entered the assembly hall, Charlie remembered the smell of other jumble sales. There was a dustiness and an *oldness* and a kind of undersmell that Mrs. Waring always said angrily was the smell of unwashed clothes. (The clothes that her children had grown out of were always washed and even ironed before she allowed them to go as jumble.)

All the chairs usually in the hall had been packed away, replaced by big trestle tables on which the jumble—mostly clothes, some china, and books and toys—had been laid out. People had queued to be first into the sale when the doors opened. Then they had stormed in and rushed at the tables and scrabbled and clawed to get whatever was worth getting before someone else reached it.

So by now—the end of the afternoon—very little was left, and a good deal of that was on the floor and trampled on. The only person still sorting through and still haggling to buy this or that for a very few pence was the old ragwoman.

The jumble sale helpers were still there, of course, fed up but at least satisfied because the sale was over and it was only a matter of counting the money taken. And centrally among the trestles stood

Charlie's mother, who was the organizer. Her arms and hands dangled as though their muscles were exhausted with the battle against snatch-and-grab. Her hair was all over the place, and her face was tired.

She saw Charlie and she smiled, and then abruptly stopped smiling, and Charlie knew that she had caught sight of his father standing behind him.

"Well?" she called.

Charlie edged past the trestle tables to reach her.

"Well?" she repeated.

"We went to the pictures," said Charlie, "and we ate Chinese. I had sweet-sour and fried noodles and—and"—he knew he would get it wrong, because now he was nervous—"and—you know—shampoo boots—"

"*What?*" said his mother.

Charlie knew that he could not speak again. If he tried, then he might begin to cry.

"Bamboo shoots," said his father from behind him. He said nothing else at all, but his hand touched the back of Charlie's neck, and Charlie knew that meant, Good-bye until next time. And Charlie did not turn to see him go.

"Charlie," said his mother, "I can't come away at once, but I shan't be long. You can go the rest of the way home by yourself, can't you? It's only a step. Sandra will still be there, and she'll let you in."

"Yes," said Charlie. "All right." But he did not move; he stood there, his hands in his pockets.

"Is something wrong?" asked his mother. "What is it, Charlie?"

"Nothing," said Charlie in a choked voice. "Nothing."

Nothing in either pocket, where his hands had searched for comfort.

Nothing, and in his mind's eye he saw the Chinese tablecloth and the muddle of empty dishes and the toppled soy sauce bottle and the scatter of toothpicks, and somewhere in that confusion he had left his fir cone.

Because of the fuss about the gapoda, because his father had shouted at him, he had lost his head and forgotten all about his fir cone. Forgotten it. Left it. *Lost it.*

"Charlie—" his mother began, but Charlie had already turned away—was gone. He ran headlong for home. It seemed to him that he reached it only in the nick of time, for the sobbing was beginning. He put his finger on the bell and kept it there, so that the bell rang and rang and rang through the house.

Sandra, in the bathroom, had just finished washing her hair for her evening out. The screaming of the bell irritated her, for she was late— oh! she was always late—and it could only be Charlie down there. She wrapped her hair in a towel turban and sailed downstairs to open the door. By now the ringing had ceased, but only because someone was hammering at the door—hammer—hammer—hammer with bare fists.

"*What on earth,*" she cried as she flung open the door, but then she staggered back, speechless, as Charlie flung himself inside in a storm of weeping. He landed up in his sister's arms, for she was too startled to remember her irritation, and he was too distraught to care about anything.

Clutching him in alarm, Sandra said, "What is it, Charlie? What's happened? Was it Dad? Did he say something awful?"

"I've lost it!" Charlie sobbed. "Now I shall never go there!'

"Lost what? Go where? Oh, Charlie, what's the matter?"

"They'll say we never went there. They'll say there's no such place. They'll say I made it all up. Dad thinks that. Mum will, too. But there was such a place. There was—there was!"

"What place, Charlie? Try not to cry, and then you can tell me properly. Tell me about it—just tell me, Charlie!"

Charlie calmed himself enough to tell her. About the lake and the ducks and the tent tree and the gapoda building and the stone monsters. "And we went there by train and all the time Dad was singing a little song he'd just made up about queuing to get in and Mum was laughing—and we didn't have to wait in a line, anyway. We just paid some money and walked straight in."

Sandra had been listening very attentively. Now she asked, "Were there greenhouses, Charlie? Big ones—enormous?"

"Yes, I forgot about those. We went into one, but it was too steamy-hot and full of huge plants right up to its roof. I liked it better outside."

"Charlie, this is important. Think carefully about the song Dad made up about queuing. What *exactly* did he sing?"

Rather fretfully, Charlie said, "I've just told you."

"Try to remember the exact words. The *exact* words, Charlie."

"Well . . . He sang over and over again: 'We'll be queueing—queueing—queueing—' No, it wasn't quite that. He sang: 'We'll have to queue—to queue—to queue—' Something like that."

"You're sure it wasn't. 'We're going to . . .' instead of 'We'll have to . . . '?"

"That's it," agreed Charlie. "It's easier to sing, isn't it? 'We're going to queue—to queue—to queue—' " He broke off suddenly. "But it doesn't *matter*, all that." His tears began to fall again.

Sandra clutched him and shook him, to make him listen. "It does matter, Charlie; it does! Because on the other side of London there's a place called Kew, with gardens—the most enormous gardens, with huge trees and huge glasshouses and a lake with ducks and a Chinese pagoda—not a gapoda, Charlie!—and you get to Kew Gardens by a special railway, the North London Railway. Oh, and the stone monsters are from the queen's coronation, ages ago. And that's where you went; that's what Dad was singing: 'We're going to Kew—to Kew—to Kew—' "

Charlie stared at her, angrily. "How do you know all that? You've just made it up. It's not true."

"It is true. Because I went. There was a school expedition for the Infants. Just to Kew Gardens."

"Why didn't Bill ever go with a school expedition to Kew?"

"He did, when he was an Infant."

"Then why didn't I go when I was an Infant?"

"Because you were having chicken pox. They didn't tell you what you were missing. But when you were all right again, I suppose Mum and Dad thought they'd take you, anyway, all on your own."

"So the place is really there. . . ." He believed her now. "So I could go with them again someday."

"Well, no," said Sandra.

"No?"

"Charlie, you know perfectly well they wouldn't take you, not the two of them together. Dad would take you, or Mum would. But not both of them together. Not now. Never again."

"Never again . . ." said Charlie.

While they were speaking, the front gate had clanged, and footsteps hurried to the front door, which Charlie had not closed behind him. Bill now flung it wide as he rushed in, disheveled, excited by his afternoon, and roared up the stairs. He shouted back to them that he'd only come to collect something, then he was off again with his mates. They must tell Mum what he was up to.

"Up to!" Sandra murmured satirically as she began to unwind her turban to shake out her damp hair. "Charlie, I must go. I'm late already. Mum'll be back any minute now. Then you'll be all right." She went upstairs again.

Charlie was left standing by the front door, while upstairs buzzed with blithe preparations for departure.

He was still grieving at loss: he had lost his fir cone. . . . (Bill roared past him again on his way out: "Eer chup, Misery! It may never happen!" Charlie easily worked out what that was supposed to mean. Only the stale old tease.)

But at least he had gained knowledge. There was a song, only a little song, but now it made sense: the Kew song. And it had power in it, too. A chant, an incantation, a spell . . . (Sandra swept down the stairs: "You okay now?" She did not wait for an answer but was through the hall and out through the front door, calling back to him: "Wait in for Mum, remember!" The front door clicked shut behind her.)

Abruptly the house was silent. Empty except for Charlie.

He stood there, thinking for a while. Then he shut his eyes and opened his mouth to whisper: "I'm going to Kew—to Kew—to Kew."

He stood on soft green turf, and the gardens lay before him: the glasshouses (he did not forget them this time) and the queen's beasts and the Chinese pagoda and the lake and the ducks and the great green tent trees. And the people—all visitors to the gardens, and among them a little boy being jumped along between his parents. All three were laughing, and when the child was set down, he stooped and picked up a fir cone and put it into his pocket. . . .

"That's me," said Charlie aloud, and was amazed to think how small, how very *young* he had been. He might go to Kew again, but he could never be that age again and do those things again that a little boy could do with his mum and his dad. With his mum and his dad, who had been happy to be together with him. Sandra had said, "Never again." And he saw now why she had said that.

He opened his eyes and stood for a moment, thinking. His mother would be back any moment; he hadn't much time. He moved swiftly from the hall into the kitchen and then out by the back door to where the dustbins stood.

When Mrs. Waring walked in, the hall was empty. She called anxiously up the stairs: "Charlie?"

"Here!" The answer was from downstairs. She pushed open a door, and there he was, kneeling in front of his old toy cupboard with the big TV carton beside him. He was packing it with objects from the cupboard.

"Oh, Charlie!" His mother sounded as if she might begin to cry.

He couldn't bear more of that. Without turning round, he said in a voice that he made cruel: "Of course, you realize it's all far too late for your jumble sale? You realize that?"

"Oh, no, it isn't, Charlie. At least, it's too late for the school one, but there are lots of jumble sales going on all the time, every Saturday. I can always take good jumble somewhere useful."

Still packing the carton, still not looking at his mother, he asked lightly: "Mum, do you remember when I was very little I had chicken pox?"

"Of course. Why?"

"Afterward you took me to Kew Gardens. You and Dad. We had a lovely time."

The expression on her face had changed; she said coldly, "Oh?"

"A *really* lovely time. Don't you remember?" He had turned around to search her face with his gaze.

"With your father?" Mrs. Waring would have liked to deny any such memory, but—just as a promise is a promise—truth is truth. She sighed. "Yes, just the three of us—I do remember, and we did have a lovely time. But that's in the past, Charlie, and—"

He interrupted her impatiently: "I know all that stuff about you and Dad nowadays. You've explained before. But I just wanted to know that you remembered that time. Because at least it really happened. It did."

"Of course it did," said his mother, and had the feeling—which she did not always have—that she had said a good thing as well as a correct one.

"So that's all right," said Charlie. He got up from his knees. "I can finish the cupboard after tea." With a deep sigh he stretched his arms to their utmost, as though he had been cramped for a long, long time.

Then, comfortingly: "What's for tea, Mum?"

Nutmeg ❖

The little black dog called Peppercorn died of old age at last, and the children of the family—Lydia and Joe and little Sam—buried him. The first that their neighbors the Copleys knew of all this was the doleful sound of "Abide with Me" coming in through Margaret Copley's bedroom window. She urged her husband to go out into the garden to see what the Tillotsons were up to.

The Tillotsons' garden had a neglected patch at the bottom, overrun with ivy, where snowdrops came up at the end of winter. Here the children had buried the body and were just setting up a homemade wooden cross, with "Pepper" scratched on its horizontal. ("Peppercorn" was too long, and anyway, the little dog had always been called Pepper for short.)

George Copley peeped cautiously over the fence, but the children's father, also a spectator, spotted him at once. He waved his hand toward the little group of mourners. "All the fun of a funeral!" he whispered.

Mr. Copley was elderly. He and his wife had no children. He stared over the fence, wonderingly. "You mean, they don't really care?"

"Oh, Lyddy does—just for now. The other two are too young, anyway."

Lydia had heard him. She had been crying. Now she turned and shouted at her father: "It's not just for now! And I hate you!"

"Temper!" said Mr. Copley from over the fence, and then, alarmed at his own boldness, withdrew and went indoors to tell his invalid wife about the strange customs of the Tillotson family.

Meanwhile Mrs. Tillotson was calling everyone in for tea. The children ran in ahead of their father. As Lydia passed him, she said savagely: "And you needn't think I'll ever want another dog after Pepper. Ever."

Her father laughed, amused, tolerant.

Lydia had loved Pepper.

But later that same year old Mr. Copley observed Lydia and the others playing in their garden with a new puppy. Mr. Copley was no more used to dogs than to children, so only one question seemed safe over the fence. He asked, "What are you going to call it?"

"Not *it*," said Joe. "Him. This is a boy dog, Mr. Copley."

"And we haven't decided what to call him," said Lydia. She picked up the puppy, soft and plump, and cuddled him almost under her chin. At the sight, Mr. Copley was reminded of many years ago, of the child—the only child—he and his wife had had. He remembered how his wife had held the baby against her breast, bending her head low and lovingly. Their child had died in infancy.

"Let me have him!" clamored Sam, and Lydia lowered the puppy into the little boy's arms. There he wriggled and bit with needle teeth until Sam squeaked with pain, but he would not give the puppy up. "I want to call him Cuddles," he said.

"Salt," said Joe. "To match Pepper."

"No!" cried Lydia, and then: "He's not the color of salt, anyway." The puppy was a rather unusual brown color.

"Cuddles," said Sam.

"We'll let you know, if you like, when we've decided," Lydia told Mr. Copley.

Later, indoors, their father explained to Sam: "You have to choose a dog's name that you can *call*. You couldn't really call 'Cuddles.' " He raised his voice, deliberately comic: "Cuddles! Cuddles! Come here, Cuddles!" Lydia and Joe laughed; Sam sulked, but he knew he was beaten.

It was their mother who had the brain wave. "He's just the color of ground nutmeg. Why not call him Nutmeg? It's a kitchen name, like Peppercorn."

The two boys liked the idea; Lydia hesitated

"Meg for short," said Joe, and Sam agreed.

"That's really a girl's name," objected Lydia.

"Come on, Lyddy!" said her father. "Why on earth should that matter, for a dog?"

So Lydia gave way, and the Tillotsons began training their new dog, Nutmeg—house-training him and training him to come when he was called. Their garden rang with the new name: Meg—Meg—Meg.

Margaret Copley, in her invalid's bedroom, managed a weak laugh as she listened to the children's voices distantly calling. George Copley did not even smile, because his wife's illness frightened him; he suspected that she was dying. His wife knew that she was.

Before the end of that summer Margaret Copley had died.

Mr. Copley's niece came to the funeral and afterward tried to persuade the old man to come and live with her family. He would not budge.

"He simply won't budge," Mrs. Tillotson reported to her husband. She had been chatting with Mr. Copley's niece. "Well, he's lived all his married life in that house. Nearly fifty years."

"It's a big change for him to get used to," agreed Mr. Tillotson. "He'll just have to put the past behind him. Forget."

Lydia noticed that her mother said nothing but looked doubtful.

The Tillotson children, out in the garden all day with their new puppy, spared hardly a thought for their bereaved neighbor. These were the school holidays; there was all the time in the world for playing with Nutmeg—playing with him and training him. "Meg! Meg! Meg!" they called, getting him really used to his name.

One afternoon when they had been calling, scolding and coaxing, Mr. Copley stuck his head over the fence to address them. He was white-faced and wild-haired. "Would you mind, please—I'm sure you wouldn't—not calling your dog all the time? Just don't use that name over and over again. Please."

All three of them stopped what they were doing; even Nutmeg stopped racing round; they stared at the old man. Then Lydia said, "But we need to call him, Mr. Copley. We're training him to come when he's called."

"There's no need about it!" said Mr. Copley, suddenly loud-voiced. He struck the top of the fence with his walking stick. "*Stop that calling, I say! Stop it!*"

Then, astonishingly, the walking stick came sailing over the fence toward them, unmistakably thrown with ill will. It missed the little group, but the Tillotson children snatched up their puppy and scurried indoors to safety and to report what had happened.

Sam was crying, but Lydia and Joe were more startled than frightened.

Their mother was startled and also alarmed for Mr. Copley himself. "The poor man sounds half out of his mind," she said, and resolutely made a Victoria sponge and took it round to his house. She rang the front doorbell, but Mr. Copley saw her through a side window and would not come to the door. As she had seen him seeing her, Mrs. Tillotson left the sponge cake on the front doorstep, hoping that he would recognize it as a peace offering.

The children's father, when he heard the story, was furiously angry about the walking stick. He hurled it back over the fence and shouted in the same direction that he would call the police if there were more trouble. Meanwhile he told the children to play in the garden with their puppy whenever they wanted and make as much noise as they liked. After a certain timidity, they began playing with Nutmeg again, and "Meg—Meg—Meg!" resounded as before.

The sponge cake stayed on the Copley front doorstep until the birds had pecked it into ruin. Mrs. Tillotson watched with disappointment and increased misgiving. She hesitated but at last telephoned Mr. Copley's niece. The niece came down a second time to urge Mr. Copley to leave. "But he won't," she told Mrs. Tillotson. She had dropped in to return the cake plate and found Mrs. Tillotson in the middle of cooking and Lydia mixing the puppy's tea. "He won't leave that house, yet he can't bear living there. Everything, every minute of the day, reminds him of Auntie Margaret. Things prey on his mind—drive him crazy. He says he hears voices—voices calling. . . ."

When she went, Mr. Copley's niece left a spare key to his house. "Just in case," she said to Mrs. Tillotson. "I'd be so grateful. In case Uncle gets worse in some way . . ." Rather unwillingly (as Lydia saw), Mrs. Tillotson took the key. She put it on the top shelf of the kitchen dresser, out of sight.

In what way could Mr. Copley be expected to get worse? There was no more banging or throwing of walking sticks over the fence, although the children still played outside with Nutmeg, calling to him constantly by name. Lydia paused sometimes to listen by the fence, she was aware of someone treading the paths in the Copley garden next door. Someone who never spoke.

Mrs. Tillotson listened to her children playing in the garden and thought of things that Mr. Copley's niece had told her—of one thing in particular. Perhaps it was an unimportant thing; perhaps her family would laugh at her for speaking of it. Yet she did speak of it at last, beginning in a rather roundabout way.

"Do you know what the name was—the first name—of poor Mrs. Copley?"

They all looked blank, until Lydia said, "When we were new here, Mrs. Copley—she was nice—asked me what my name was, and I said Lydia, and then I asked her what she was called, and I think she said Margaret."

"Margaret!" said Mr. Tillotson. "Of course, that was it! It was said at the funeral."

"Yes, Margaret," said Mrs. Tillotson. "I just wondered if you'd realized: Margaret. All her family—and his family—called her that, except for Mr. Copley. His niece told me he had a pet name for her. He always called her Meg." Mrs. Tillotson repeated, "He always called her Meg."

"So?" asked Mr. Tillotson, as though puzzled, but Lydia thought he knew what her mother was driving at. He must remember, as they all remembered, that name—Meg—being called and shouted over and over again in the Tillotson garden. It would have been heard all over the Copley garden and even in the house of mourning itself.

"So?" Mr. Tillotson repeated, angrily this time, but his wife would say no more. Joe and Sam looked confused and rather scared; Lydia was not confused. She stroked Nutmeg and wished that they had given him another name.

Nothing more was said on the subject.

At about this time there must have been a great deal of telephoning between old Mr. Copley and his niece. One day the Tillotsons heard that after all, he had decided to move; he had agreed to live with his niece's family.

So one Sunday morning there was old Mr. Copley, white-faced and wild-eyed, waiting at his own front gate with a small suitcase. When his niece's car at last drew up, he bundled himself and his suitcase into it at once. The Tillotsons could see that there was some kind of quite violent argument in the car between uncle and niece that delayed their departure. In the end, they drove off, and that was the last that the Tillotson family ever saw of old Mr. Copley.

Later, on the telephone, the niece explained that Mr. Copley had been adamant about leaving the house at once and for good, there and then, and never going back inside it. That was what the argument in the car had been about. Of course, the niece would have to come down again in a week or so to clear the house of its contents and put it up for sale. (That was when she would call on the Tillotsons to reclaim the spare key.)

Meanwhile the Tillotson family had its own worries: the puppy had disappeared. He had a dog-sized cat door from the house into the garden, so that he could come and go as he pleased. The garden itself, including the front garden, had been completely dog-proofed against escape. Yet he had gone.

Nutmeg had vanished between their all going to bed—rather late—on Saturday night and their coming down for breakfast on Sunday morning. That was the very Sunday of Mr. Copley's going, so for a short time, suspicion fell on him. "Mr. Copley's stolen our Nutmeg!" Joe had cried. "He's taken him with him."

"Don't be ridiculous!" Mrs. Tillotson said. "He got into that car with a suitcase, nothing else."

"Perhaps Nutmeg was inside the suitcase," suggested Sam, who seemed to think this possibility would cheer everyone up.

"Alive or dead?" their father inquired sarcastically.

Sam burst into tears, and their mother forbade them to say or think anymore about Mr. Copley and his suitcase.

One thing was certain: if Nutmeg had not escaped, he must have been taken. That would have been quite easy if the family were not about. For the puppy would always come, wagging his tail, to anyone who appeared at the front gate. A thief had only to lean over and scoop the puppy up.

The Tillotsons told the police of their loss and put LOST notices (with mention of "REWARD") all around the neighborhood. But nobody brought news of Nutmeg.

That was on Monday, and by Monday night the Tillotson family were grieving as if for the puppy's death. Mrs. Tillotson tried to cheer them: "He may still be brought back, you know." Everyone tried to believe that.

Everyone except Lydia. She went to bed without feeling the hope that her mother had suggested and fell into a blackness of sleep. She did not exactly dream, if dreams are seen. In blackness she saw nothing, only heard voices: Tillotson voices shrieking, "Meg—Meg—Meg!" and old Mr. Copley's frantic voice when he threw the walking stick and then another voice, very quiet and calm, that she thought at first was the voice of Mrs. Copley talking pleasantly to a little girl. But no, it was not that. It was not a particularly pleasant—or unpleasant—voice; it was just an extraordinarily *close* voice. A voice that seemed to come from inside herself, to be herself. The voice, calm, unhurried, told her that there was no time to be lost. She knew what she had to do.

Lydia woke.

She switched on the light and saw from her clock that there was plenty of time yet before her parents would rouse. She got out of bed and drew back the curtains; outside was dark, but she knew that that was probably the effect of the electric light. She turned out the light and looked again; sure enough, outside was now a gray half dark that would gradually become the dawn. There was already just enough light outside to see by.

She dressed and crept downstairs. In the kitchen she reached up to the top shelf of the dresser where she had seen her mother hide the Copley front door key and took it. Very quietly she let herself out of the house and then out through the Tillotson front gate, and then in through the Copley front gate and up to the Copley front door, and then a turning of the key in the lock and she stepped into the Copley hall.

Here she paused, half frightened, half triumphant at what she had already achieved so easily. And what did she mean to do next?

She was going to do what her parents would certainly not have approved of: she would search the house from top to bottom for Nutmeg, and she must begin at once. Ahead of her were the stairs, and she must climb them to search bedroom after bedroom. She would come to the bedroom where Mrs. Copley had died; she must search that, too.

She had set off across the hall toward the stairs before she noticed the stair cupboard. Its door stood open, and there was a muddle of something lying on the hall floor that seemed to have come from inside the cupboard. It looked perhaps like *someone* lying there, half inside and half outside the cupboard, and swathed or piled with clothing. That was a horrid idea, so Lydia very quickly and firmly went closer, and there was enough daylight by now to see that the muddle was of clothing only, clothing that came from inside the cupboard.

She peered inside the cupboard.

It was very dark inside, and she wished she had brought a torch with her. But if this stair cupboard were like their own cupboard—and all the houses were built alike—it had its own electric light. But would the electricity have been cut off by old Mr. Copley before he left? She felt up and down just inside the door, where their own light switch would have been. She found a switch, pressed it, and the inside of the cupboard was glaring at her.

Lydia found that she was standing at the foot of a mountain of clothes, all women's clothes, as far as she could see: blouses and jerseys, and a sparkly party dress that glittered in the bright light, and underwear and tights, and a dressing gown, and skirts, and high-heeled shoes, and a lacy nightdress, and silk scarves—all piled high in an enormous heap of garments that someone had hurled higgledy-piggledy into this stair cupboard, not managing to get quite everything in, anyway, leaving some half outside, and then perhaps rushing away.

Surely the only person who could have done this strange thing must have been old Mr. Copley himself?

Lydia gazed in wonder, then was about to turn away to begin her proper search when she heard a tiny sound like a mouse scratching the floorboards. It came from inside the cupboard.

She stood quite still. Listened.

Dared to hope.

The feeble sound came again. She whispered: "Meg?" and saw the slightest movement among the clothing toward the edge of the heap.

Then she was on her knees, scrabbling at the pile, burrowing into it, her fingers tangling in folds of clothing and the snares of ribbons and belts. She fought her way through everything until her fingers found something small and warm—and also bony—that moved, although feebly. "Meg!"

The little dog had been tied by someone with a string to one of the pipes at the back of the stair cupboard, and then that same someone—old Mr. Copley, two days ago—had frenziedly thrown over the puppy all the contents of dead Mrs. Copley's wardrobe and chest of drawers.

Lydia untied the string and, with both hands round the puppy's body, picked it up gently and cuddled it to her. It still lived. She carried it into the kitchen and ran a teaspoonful of water into the palm of her hand. She held her hand under the puppy's muzzle, and it licked.

"Darling Nutmeg," she whispered, "you're safe now. You're all right now."

She was beginning to cry, her tears falling on the puppy's head and settling among the hairs of his fur.

She heard, without bothering, the sound of footsteps hesitating at the open front door and then coming into the hall and then stopping again. "Lydia?" Her father's voice sounded anxious and at the same time angry.

She could not answer him, but he heard some sound from the kitchen and found her there. Now he was truly furious—until he saw the puppy.

"What on earth!"

She told him about the stair cupboard, the burial mound of Mrs. Copley's clothes, the string tied to the pipe.

Her father said, "No—oh, no!" as though he could not bear to believe what he was hearing. He covered his face with his hands.

"But, Dad," said Lydia, "Nutmeg's going to be all right. I'm sure he is. There's no need to tell the police or anything." She was remembering her father's rage at the time of the thrown walking stick. "We can take him to the vet just to make sure he's going to be all right. But he is going to be."

Her father took his hands from his face and said: "Poor, poor creature . . ." At first Lydia thought he meant the puppy, but he went on, always to himself: "Poor crazy old man . . . poor crazy old creature . . ."

He pulled himself together. "Come on, Lyddy. Your mum's already worried to death about where you might be. Bring the dog, and we'll go home."

Lydia held the puppy close, and her father put an arm round them both. So they left the Copley house together, locking up behind them as they went.

Only a little later that morning the whole Tillotson family took

Nutmeg to the vet. Lydia had been sure that Nutmeg was going to be all right, and the vet confirmed that. He gave them exact instructions on how they should feed him and exercise him: at first, very carefully, until he was strong again.

In due course, Mr. Copley's niece came to clear the house. (The Tillotsons said nothing about what had happened.) The house was sold to a young couple with a baby, with whom the Tillotsons were immediately on first-name terms. The baby would love playing with Nutmeg when it was older.

Nutmeg kept his full name, but Mr. Tillotson did not want him to be called Meg anymore. He forbade it. He would not discuss his reasons, and Mrs. Tillotson stayed out of any argument.

So the puppy's name was shortened in the opposite direction, to Nuts, or Nutter, or Nutty. This was confusing for the puppy at first, but he soon got used to his new name. And after all, as Lydia said, the new name suited him very well. He was a little dog easily excited to madness, barking at the top of his voice, quite crazy with the joy of being alive.

Bluebag ❖

*M*y great-aunt—Aunt Carrie—simply loved our washing machine. She'd sit by it while it hummed and thundered and tell stories of her youth, when there weren't such things. In those days there were huge coppers for boiling clothes and tubs for lesser washes and also dollies and mangles and great bars of yellow soap and bluebag.

The story of bluebag and Spot was one of my Aunt Carrie's favorites. Spot had been her dog when she was a girl, and bluebag— well, it almost describes itself. It was the size of a very large lump of sugar, solid blue, and you bought it tied up in a white cotton rag. It was dipped into the water when white things were being washed; the blueness seeped out into the water, and so the white things washed whiter. Aunt Carrie's mother always kept bluebag for laundry work, and for a second purpose, "to which"—my Aunt Carrie liked mysteriously to say—"I will come later in my story."

One sunny summer's day, long ago, Aunt Carrie was at a loose end. She looked thoughtfully at Spot, who was one of those dogs mostly white but with a few spots of brown and black. He was a small dog and usually very fond of my aunt Carrie.

My aunt addressed him: "Now, Spot, you'd like to be nice and clean and white and fluffy, wouldn't you? Of course you would!"

If Spot could have spoken, he would have answered, "Carrie, *no!*"

He disliked water, except for drinking. He was suspicious even of the fishpond at the bottom of the garden, and that was what a dog might call *natural* water, clear at the top and deep mud at the bottom, where the waterweeds rooted themselves. As for a large quantity of clean tap water gently steaming in an old tin bath out on the lawn, that horrified him. He knew what it meant.

And that was exactly what my aunt Carrie had in mind. She chose the longest dog lead, clipped it to Spot's collar, and then tied the other end to an apple tree on the edge of the lawn. Escape for Spot became impossible.

My aunt Carrie fetched the tin bath and filled it with warm water, transported in jug after jug from the house. Spot sat and watched her. His ears drooped.

She fetched the soap and a scrubbing brush, also the bluebag. My aunt's reasoning was that people used bluebag to wash white clothes white, so why not use it in washing Spot?

The sun was hot, but it's always best to give a dog a brisk rubbing down immediately after a bath. My aunt needed some kind of towel. Her mother was fussy about the family towels, so her father, who occasionally washed Spot if he was muddy or smelly, always made do with a clean sack. There were plenty of those, my aunt said. Her father used them in the apple room in the old part of the house; in winter, he spread them over the harvested apples to keep the frost off. As the family ate its way through the apples, the sacks were taken up, one by one, shaken, folded loosely, and stored on top of each other in a neat pile.

So Aunt Carrie went along to the apple room to fetch a sack. By now, of course, all the apples were eaten and the apple room was empty except for the mound of sacks in one corner. The room, so cold in winter, was now stuffily hot. The one window had jammed shut long ago, and the only ventilation was through a broken pane of glass. A wasp—obviously the apple room was a pleasant place for them, even empty—sailed out through the hole as Aunt Carrie was looking, and another sailed in.

The topmost sack of the pile looked newish and clean, but to be on the safe side, my aunt Carrie decided to shake it to get rid of any leafy apple stalk dust there might be. She took a good grip of the sack, yanked it off the pile, and, with the same movement, gave it a quick, strong shake.

At this point my aunt Carrie, who prided herself on her grasp of *suspense* in storytelling, would pause to ask:

How long does it take to give a quick, strong shake to a folded sack? One second?

Two seconds? Perhaps three?

For one of those seconds she had turned her head away, to avoid getting any apple dust into her eyes. But something warned her—there was something odd, perhaps, in the *feel* of the sack—even before the end of that second. She turned her head quickly to look and, even as she looked, flung the sack from her.

For the shaking open of the folded sack had in one instant both shown and shattered a *thing* that had been built within the concealment of the folds—a rounded dun-colored structure about the size of a child's head. As the sack shot from her fingers across the apple room, torn pieces of papery walls and roofings broke from it, and in the ruined chambers and passageways she glimpsed living things no longer than her thumbnail—some smaller—moving and squirming and crawling. And some had wings and began to fly. . . .

Yellow and black-barred, they began to fly, and she knew them. Wasps and wasps and more wasps—more and more wasps than she had ever seen together before in her whole life.

Never before or since (said my aunt in a kind of horrified wonder) had she seen a *lived-in* wasps' nest so close, so open to her inspection, and she hoped never to see one so again. Within the seconds of revelation the sack went flying, she went flying, and the wasps came flying after her. Before she was fairly out of the apple room—and she was moving fast, *fast*—two or three of the quicker-witted wasps had caught up with her and stung her. She was wearing only a sleeveless dress, and her legs were bare, so it was easy for them.

My aunt was running at top speed, with amazing acceleration from standstill, but wasps seemed to catch up with her (she said) quite effortlessly. She tore from the apple room down the passage to the main part of the house. She must have been shrieking, for she could already hear Spot in the distance barking in a frenzy of reply. Her family roused to the alarm, of course. But she was down the stairs and through the hall so fast that she never saw her father. Apparently he had stepped forward toward my aunt Carrie in her flight, then noticed the wasps hot in her pursuit and, with great common sense, as my aunt admitted, drew back. Apparently he had shouted to her to make for the fishpond, but my aunt never heard him.

My aunt Carrie tore down the hall, through the open garden door, and out onto the lawn. There was the tin tub and the yellow soap and the bluebag that hundreds of years before, it seemed, she had intended using, and there was Spot jumping about at the end of his lead and barking so continuously and shrilly that he was almost screaming, too. He had—again with great good sense—rushed to the furthest extent of his lead, well clear of the route that the wasps were taking.

Meanwhile my aunt never stopped running. Across the lawn and down the length of the garden and the orchard, and suddenly there was the fishpond. My aunt ran straight off the ground and into the water.

Into the water and down—down—so that the water closed over her head, and my aunt said she could have laughed for joy, except that you don't laugh underwater. When she came up, there were a few wasps trying to swim—they must have floated off her clothes and hair and skin—and a good many others were flying around, much taken aback.

My aunt thought it wise to submerge again at once. She did so again and again and again. At the last coming up to snatch air, she observed that there were no more wasps hanging around on the off chance (as she put it). In the distance they could be seen straggling homeward, disgruntled.

My aunt Carrie crawled out of the fishpond. From the top of her head downward she was covered with mud and waterweed. She staggered to her feet and began squelchily to walk back to the house. She was careful not to catch up with any wasps as she went.

Her mother came hurrying—but, equally, on a *careful* route—to meet her. When she saw the state my aunt was in, she turned back, crying that she would start to run a bath for her at once. In the meantime her father was preparing to untie Spot from his tree and tidy away the tin bath, the scrubbing brush, the soap, and the bluebag. He paused as my aunt drew level with him. He said, "You'll need this, my girl," and handed her the bluebag.

At this point in her story my aunt Carrie became triumphant. Above the roar of the washing machine, she would shout, "I said I'd let you into the secret of the bluebag—its second use. You don't know? You haven't guessed? In those days bluebag was used against bites and stings. My mother always dabbed it, wet, on a wasp sting to soothe the pain and the swelling.

"So, after my bath, there was I with runny blue blotches all over my face and arms and legs. My little dog came to see me, and my father— who always thought he had a great sense of humor—said he couldn't tell us apart for the spots. He called us Spot the Dog and Spot the Daughter."

My aunt Carrie would laugh heartily, then sometimes would add thoughtfully: "But I remember that it didn't seem funny at the time."

The Nest Egg ❖

School was dreary for William Penney. He was no good there. He was no good at lessons or at games, and he was no good at making new friends. Teachers, privately warned to make allowances for him, found him difficult in a dull way. His worst stroke of luck turned out to be his name. Nothing wrong with William, you might think, but another—and better-liked—boy in the class had the same name. Everybody said he had first claim to it, since William Penney was the newcomer. So what was William Penney to be called?

Someone, with a snigger, suggested Willy, and then everybody sniggered. William did not mind much; as long as they left him alone, he could bear sniggerings.

But then someone said, "Well, he's got a second name, hasn't he? W. H. Penney—he wrote his name once like that. I saw it. Come on, Willy! If you don't want to be called Willy, what does *H* stand for?"

"I don't mind being called Willy," said William.

"What does *H* stand for?"

"It's just my father's name."

"Well, what *is* your father's name?"

He didn't want to tell them. He didn't want them to know his father's name, because his father was all he had now, and even he was away somewhere. His mother had died.

"I'd rather be called Willy, please."

But now they knew he did not want to tell them, they tormented him. "Come on, what is it? Is it Hugh? Or Hubert? Or Herbert?"

"Or Halibut!" suggested a wit, and the same boy went on: "Or is it Halgernon? Or Hebenezer?"

So, after all, he was trapped by his own anger into telling them. Stammering in anger and haste, he cried, "It's not a stupid name, it's not! It's just Hen—Hen—"

Then they shouted with joyous laughter and called him Hen-Hen-Henny-penny and clucked at him and asked him what he had had for breakfast and, before he had time to answer, answered for him: "A hegg!"

If they had only known, their teasing came near the truth. William Henry Penney really did have an egg for breakfast, whether he liked it or not, nearly every day of the week, because now he was living with his aunt Rosa, who kept hens. She ran her garden—almost as big as a smallholding—as a business. She grew all the usual outdoor vegetables and had a greenhouse for cucumbers and early tomatoes. At the bottom of the garden and in the orchard, she kept hens, not very many, but good layers. William helped with the hens, feeding them in the morning before he went to school, filling their drinking bowl with fresh water, and letting them out of their run to roam in his aunt's orchard. He also collected the eggs in the evening, but this was only under Aunt Rosa's supervision. He had once broken an egg.

Until now Aunt Rosa had lived by herself, with her dog, Bessy. Aunt Rosa was middle-aged and sharp; Bessy was old and cantankerous. Neither of them was used to having children about the place.

When William's father had brought him here, he explained to his son that this was only until he could find another job in another place and a new home for them both. "Until then Rosa has said she'll put up with you—I mean, put you up. Very kind of Rosa," said William's father. He did not usually think his sister was particularly kind.

"Why's she wearing that scarf of Mum's?" asked William.

His father frowned. He said, "She's being very helpful in a bad time, and she asked if she could have it. It was one of the things she wanted."

"I don't like her having things," said William.

"Oh, come on, William!" his father said angrily. But William was not deceived; really, his father was angry with Aunt Rosa for wanting things that had so recently belonged to her dead sister-in-law, his own wife, William's mother. He was also angry with himself for having to give in to her.

William's father saw William settled in Aunt Rosa's house. Then he said good-bye, leaving William with Aunt Rosa and Bessy.

In Aunt Rosa's house William had a bedroom to himself, but it was big and bare and lonely after his own old room crammed with his ancient toys and his collections and gadgets and oddments, all in a friendly muddle. He could not feel at home here, in Aunt Rosa's house. Deliberately, he did not unpack his suitcase into the drawers left empty for him.

Nowadays William was always watched; he knew that. In Aunt Rosa's house he was watched by Aunt Rosa and by Bessy, in case he did anything silly, wasteful, or damaging. At school he was watched by those whose fun was to tease him. His only really safe and private time was in bed, at night. Every night he cried himself to sleep—but quietly, so that Aunt Rosa should not hear him and despise him for crying. He had sad dreams that woke him to real sadness. Then he cried for his father, who was far away, and for his mother, who was dead.

One day, in the early evening, Aunt Rosa came down from her bedroom dressed with unusual care. Besides her good clothes, she was wearing a thin gold chain. William recognized it at once. He had saved up to buy it for his mother on her last birthday.

He couldn't help himself; he said, "That's my mum's gold chain."

"Yes," said his aunt. "It was hers. It's not real gold, of course. I wouldn't have taken anything valuable from your father, when he pressed me to choose, after the funeral. The chain's not worth anything—just rubbish. But it does for the odd occasion."

William said nothing aloud, but to himself he said, "I hate Aunt Rosa. I hate having to live in her house."

His aunt was dressed up to attend a parish meeting. Before she left, she said to William, "You should be able to help more on your own by now. Go down to the henhouse and see if there are any eggs. Probably not; the hens are all going off lay. But if there is an egg, for goodness' sake, don't break it! And don't bring out the nest egg, as you did last time!" The nest egg was only an imitation egg; it was left in a nest to encourage the hen to lay other eggs there and nowhere else.

Aunt Rosa went off on her bicycle, Bessy settled herself in her basket in the kitchen, and William went down the garden to the henhouse.

He was still thinking of his mother's gold chain. Of course, he had known that it wasn't made of real gold, but his mother had loved to wear it. He remembered buying it and keeping it a secret until her birthday. In secret he had played with it, and he could still remember the way the thin links had poured and poured between his fingers. He remembered the way his mother had looked when she wore it, and now he hated to remember how it had looked around the neck of his aunt Rosa.

Still thinking of the gold chain, he reached the henhouse.

The henhouse was a low, wooden, homemade affair, very simple and rather ramshackle. It had a door at the back through which the egg collector could reach in. At the front was a pophole through which the hens and the cockerel went out into the run. The run had high chicken wire walls and a chicken wire door that let into the orchard. The door was open, as usual in the summer daytime; William had already seen the cockerel and his hens pecking about in the grass of the orchard.

He unlatched the henhouse door and peered in. It was always dim inside the henhouse, but there was not much to see, anyway. Just an earth floor with straw over it, in which the hens hollowed their nests; a perch across from side to side, for the fowls to roost on at night; and the daylight coming in through the pophole on the opposite side of the henhouse.

For the first time, William was here without Aunt Rosa nagging him to hurry. He let his eyes accustom themselves to the twilight of the henhouse, and then he saw the eye watching him. It belonged to the one hen that, after all, had not gone out with the others into the orchard. She was crouching in a corner of the henhouse, deep in the straw, absolutely still, absolutely quiet, staring at him.

The henhouse was not large, but it was quite big enough for a boy of William's size to creep inside. He did so now, for the convenience of looking more thoroughly for any eggs. But he kept away from the hen sitting in her corner.

The henhouse smelled of hens. There was a line of hen droppings in the straw under the perch; the straw would need changing soon. There was also the smell, brought out by the summer heat, of creosote in the wood. All the same, William rather liked being in the henhouse. It was a real house, in its way, and it was just his size. It fitted him; he felt at home in it.

Being careful where he put his feet down in the straw, he searched for eggs. But as his aunt had prophesied, there were none.

His search brought him to the sitting hen. Surely she must be sitting on something? As he had seen his aunt do, he slid his hand underneath her body to feel for any eggs, but at once she began to fluster and flounder and squawk. Her cries were immediately heard and answered from the orchard by the cockerel, who came running at a great pace and so appeared within seconds at the pophole, confronting William with furious enmity.

Once, recently, Aunt Rosa had remarked in scorn that William couldn't possibly be afraid of an ordinary *cockerel*, but Aunt Rosa was ignorant of a great many of life's possibilities. In this present emergency, William withdrew from the henhouse very quickly indeed, latching the door shut behind him. He heard the cockerel and the hen conferring crossly inside.

Meanwhile William had an egg in his hand—the only egg that had been under the hen. He opened his hand, and it was the nest egg, after all! A good thing that Aunt Rosa was not with him! By himself, he had time to look at the nest egg properly. It was made of earthenware, almost as smooth-surfaced as a real egg, and the same size and weight as a real egg. There were differences: the stamp of the maker's name made an unevenness of surface in one place, and there was an airhole in the side, about the size of a hole down a drinking straw. And the nest egg was hollow.

William handled the nest egg. He liked it, as he had liked being inside the henhouse. He liked the innocent trickery of it; he liked the neat little hole in its side, which was also the entry to its hollow interior. And as he studied the nest egg, an idea began to grow in his mind. . . .

He pocketed the nest egg and went back indoors. The kitchen door was open, and Bessy watched him suspiciously from her basket, but she could see nothing wrong that he was doing. He went upstairs and into his bedroom and shut the door. He took the nest egg from his pocket and hid it at the bottom of his suitcase.

He was in bed, waiting for sleep, when his aunt came back from her meeting. He heard her lock up, see to Bessy, and then come upstairs to her bedroom. Bessy came with her, because she slept at the foot of her bed at night. Aunt Rosa, with Bessy, went into the bedroom, and the door was shut behind them.

Now Aunt Rosa would be getting ready for bed. She would take her best coat off and hang it in the wardrobe. She would take her shoes off. She would take her dress off—but no! Before she did that, she would take off William's gold chain. She took it off and—well, where did she put it? Had she a jewel box for necklaces and brooches? Or did she put them into some special drawer? Or did she leave them on top of her dressing table, at least for the time being?

Worrying at uncertainties, William fell into an uneasy sleep. He dreamed sad dreams, as usual, and the saddest—and the silliest, too— was that the nest egg had grown little chicken legs and climbed out of his suitcase and was running to catch his mother's gold chain to eat it, as though it were a worm. But the nest egg never caught up with the gold chain.

The next morning William was woken by his aunt's calling from downstairs; his breakfast was ready. He dressed quickly and then went straight from his bedroom to his aunt's room. Her door was open, and even from the doorway he could see that his mother's gold chain lay coiled on the top of his aunt's dressing table.

Oh! He was in luck! He had only to cross the bedroom floor and pick up the chain, and it would be his.

He took one step inside the bedroom doorway, and—he was out of luck, after all. He had forgotten that Bessy slept in his aunt's room every night, and here she still was. She lay at the foot of the bed, watching him, and as he made that quick, furtive movement to enter the bedroom, Bessy growled. He knew that if he went any further, she would begin to bark—to shout to Aunt Rosa the alarm: "Thief! Thief!"

He was bitterly disappointed, but he had no choice but to withdraw and go on downstairs. Just as usual he had his breakfast and then fed and watered the fowls and let them out of their run. When he got to school, just as usual, the boys called him Henny-penny and enjoyed their joke. The witty boy of the class sacrificed a small chocolate and marshmallow egg by putting it on William's chair just before he sat down. School was hateful to William—as hateful as Aunt Rosa's house.

After school, Aunt Rosa had Willam's tea ready for him.

"I'll just wash my hands upstairs in the bathroom," he said.

"No, you can do it at the kitchen sink. And after your tea, I've a job for you."

And after his tea, she said, "Today you can change the straw in the henhouse for me."

"Now?"

"Yes, now!"

"Shouldn't I go and change out of my school clothes first?" asked William.

Aunt Rosa stared at him suspiciously. "You're not usually so fussy. . . ."

William waited.

"All right then," said his aunt. "Change, but be quick about it. I'll be getting you the barrow and the shovel out of the shed."

She went into the garden, followed by Bessy, and William went swiftly upstairs. The door of his aunt's room was shut, but he opened it without hesitation. He knew he was safe, for he could hear the rattle of the wheelbarrow down the garden as his aunt maneuvered it out of the shed, and Bessy would be there with her, too.

The gold chain had not been put away; it lay just as before on the top of the dressing table. He felt like crying as he picked it up; he had so longed to have it.

He disturbed nothing else and shut his aunt's bedroom door as he left. Then he went into his own room. One hand held the gold chain; he would not put it down for an instant. With the other hand he burrowed into his suitcase and brought out the nest egg. He turned the egg so that its airhole was uppermost. Then, with the fingers of his other hand, he found the free end of the gold chain and held it exactly above the airhole. He began to lower it toward the airhole, to feed it through, and it went through! He had foreseen correctly; the size was right.

He went on dropping the gold chain, link by link, through the airhole of the nest egg. The links fell and fell and fell until there were no more, and the whole chain had disappeared inside the nest egg, and still the egg was not full. He shook the nest egg, and he could hear the supple chain shifting and settling inside its new home.

"William!" his aunt shouted from the garden. He put the nest egg into his pocket and then had to take it out again, because he had forgotten that he was supposed to be changing into rough clothes. He changed quickly and, with the nest egg in a pocket, went down to the job in the henhouse. "For goodness' sake, boy!" said his aunt. "I thought you were never coming! Here's the barrow and shovel. Clean the shed right out, and barrow the soiled straw to the compost heap. Then fresh straw from the shed. I want to see the job well done. Oh! And mind the nest egg!"

She left him to his work. The restrawing took some time, but

William did well. His aunt had grudgingly to admit that when she inspected the inside of the henhouse. She also noted the presence of the nest egg, just where it should be.

And William left it there.

Aunt Rosa's discovery of the loss of the gold chain was not made until the following morning. William was woken by his aunt shaking him. "I know you've taken it!" she was crying. "You've stolen my gold chain!" Bessy stood in the doorway of the bedroom watching the scene and growling softly.

William managed to say, "I haven't stolen it."

Of course, she did not believe him. She turned out all the pockets of his clothes. She unpacked his suitcase all over the floor. She took the mattress and all the bedding off the bedstead and searched them. She searched everywhere, and all the time she ranted at him and cuffed him and slapped him.

It was all no more than William had expected, but it was hard to bear. Doggedly he repeated, "I haven't stolen it."

He was late for school, of course, and he had to deliver a letter from his aunt to the headmaster. Later the headmaster summoned him. "William, do you know what was in the letter from your aunt?"

"About me?" said William. "I can guess."

The headmaster sighed. He said, "I have written a note in reply to your aunt. I have suggested a time when she can call on me to discuss . . . things. William, you must be sure to deliver this note to your aunt; she is expecting to hear from me. . . ."

The other boys were curious about William's interview with the headmaster. He told them nothing. The witty boy suggested that the head had noticed feathers beginning to sprout on Henny-penny's legs. This boy found two sparrow feathers in the playground and stuck them in William's hair when he was not looking.

At the end of the school day, William took the headmaster's note with him back to Aunt Rosa's house, but Aunt Rosa was out. There was a message for him on the kitchen table saying that there was no tea for him today and that she would be back during the evening.

He did not mind about the food, but—later—he did mind about not being able to get into his bedroom. Bessy lay along the threshold, watching him and growling. She would not let him pass. He said aloud, "You don't want me here, but I don't want to be here. So we're quits." That made him feel better about Bessy.

He took the headmaster's note from his pocket, put it on the floor, and pushed it with his foot toward Bessy. She seized it angrily in her teeth and tore it into shreds.

He went downstairs and into the garden, to the bottom of it. All the hens were out in the orchard, and he could see the cockerel among them. He went to the henhouse, opened the door, and looked in. The fresh straw smelled pleasantly, and there was his dear nest egg. . . .

He stooped and crept inside the henhouse and pulled the door after him as closely shut as possible. He fumbled in the straw for the nest egg and found it and shook it gently, to hear the comforting sound of the chain moving inside.

He settled in the fresh straw on the far side of the henhouse from the roosting perch. At first he sat there; then, beginning to feel drowsy, he lay down in the straw. He fell asleep with the nest egg up to his cheek.

He slept deeply, dreamlessly, and better than he had ever slept in Aunt Rosa's house.

So he never noticed the fading of daylight and the hens and cockerel that came stooping in through their pophole, into the henhouse for the night. They saw William there and were disturbed at the sight, but he made no movement or sound, and they reassured themselves. One by one they flew up on the perch, and roosted there, and slept.

He never heard later the voice of his aunt Rosa calling distractedly up and down the garden and in the orchard, as she had already done inside the house. Neighbors were consulted and gave advice; at last the police were summoned; there was a great deal of telephoning. William slept through it all, his nest egg to his face.

With the first of daylight the hens and cockerel left the henhouse for the run and then—since no one had thought of shutting them up last night—for the orchard. The cockerel often stopped to crow, but William did not hear him. He slept on.

The sun was high in the sky before William woke. At first he did not remember where he was. In his own old room at home? In Aunt Rosa's cold house? Neither. He was in a *henhouse*; he had slept there, the whole night through, with the hens and with his old enemy, the cockerel. He laughed aloud. He felt lighthearted, as he had not done for many weeks. He also felt very hungry.

The hens and cockerel had gone; it was time for him to go, too. He did not know what was going to happen next, but at least he had had a long night's sleep in freedom, and he had his precious nest egg safe in his pocket.

He let himself out of the henhouse. He began walking up the garden path toward the house—toward Aunt Rosa's house. As he came nearer, his spirits sank lower; he was walking toward a prison.

Aunt Rosa would be waiting for him. And there she was, a figure standing on the garden doorstep, and—but no! It was not his aunt Rosa. It was his father.

With a wild cry William ran into his father's arms, and his father picked him up and hugged him safe. "William! William!" he repeated, over and over again.

It was some time before any scolding began: "Why on earth did you run away? You bad boy, you silly boy! Where did you go? Your aunt was out of her mind with worry, so she telephoned me, and I drove all through the night to come. William, you should never, never have run away like that!"

"But I didn't run away," said William. "I was here all the time."

"Where?"

"Just in the henhouse at the bottom of the garden."

William's father began to laugh. "And you've straw all over your clothes!"

He took his son indoors to Aunt Rosa—Aunt Rosa, sleep-starved, haggard with many fears, and by now, fortunately, speechless with fatigue. He explained that William was back. ("But I've never been away," protested William. "The henhouse isn't away.")

William's father said that now he was here, he might as well take William off Aunt Rosa's hands. She nodded. It wasn't that he wasn't grateful to her—Aunt Rosa nodded again—but he needed his son to be with him, after all. William was all he had now. "And somehow we'll manage," said William's father. "I'm not sure how, but we shall manage."

Then Aunt Rosa said she was going to bed, and she went, with Bessy following her. Bessy had had an extraordinarily disagreeable night, with upsets and unwanted visitors.

William's father telephoned the police and told the neighbors about William's return. Then he took over Aunt Rosa's kitchen and made an enormous breakfast for himself and William. After that, they packed everything into William's suitcase, got into the car, and drove off. They did not wake Aunt Rosa to say good-bye, but William's father left a note on the kitchen table.

When the car had taken them well away from Aunt Rosa's house, William said, "I liked her henhouse and her hens."

His father said, "But Rosa said you were frightened of the cockerel."

"I was afraid of him," said William, "but I liked him, too. He was only fierce when he was defending his hens, his family."

His father glanced down at something William had just taken out of his pocket. "Did Rosa give you that dummy egg?"

"No," said William. "I took it."

His father frowned. "That's stealing."

"I just *needed* it."

"It's still stealing. You'll have to send it back."

"It might break in the post. Couldn't we send the money instead?" William had a brilliant idea. "You could stop it out of my pocket money, and you could tell Aunt Rosa that. That would really please her."

So it was settled. But after a while, hesitantly, William asked, "Did Aunt Rosa ever say I'd stolen anything?"

"No," his father said, quite positively. "But then, she didn't know about this egg, did she?"

William thought: She'd tell the headmaster, but she wouldn't dare tell my dad about the chain. Because he knew it was my mum's, and I'd given it to my mum. I wasn't stealing. I just took back.

He tilted the egg in his hands, to feel the movement inside it. He said, "I shall always keep this egg. On my mantelpiece."

"You do that," said his father. "Only we shall have to find somewhere to live with a room with a mantelpiece in it."

"We'll manage somehow," William said comfortably. "You said so."

Inside Her Head ❖

*I*t was a hot, hot afternoon, and for once Elm Street was empty of children. A good many of the Elm Street lot had gone away on summer holidays; the rest had gone round the corner to the Lido to splash and swim and eat ice cream with their toes in the water. Except for one.

Except for Sim Tolland.

Sim Tolland was at home having chicken pox. He lay in bed with the window down as far as possible: the heavy, still air lay—so he thought—like an enormous plank balanced across the top sash. Only a sheet covered his sweaty, spotty body. He felt awful. The chicken pox made him feel awful, and the heat of the bedroom—which was the heat of the bedroom plus the heat of the downstairs rooms which had risen to join it—also made him feel awful. And he felt particularly awful when he thought of the others at the Lido or by the sea or in a cool green countryside.

His mother poked her head round the bedroom door, gave a quick glance to check that his lemonade jug was full, and said, "Mrs. Crackenthorpe to see you." She went away again.

Old Mrs. Crackenthorpe, from the other end of Elm Street, was known to have a soft spot for Sim Tolland. Sim groaned. This was even more awful than awful.

He heard the slow, heavy tread on the stairs, the little gasps of effort. Mrs. Crackenthorpe eased herself into the room and onto a chair. She perspired gently.

"I've had chicken pox, dear," she said. She took something from a brown paper bag. "Jelly babies to cheer you up. You *need* jelly babies."

"Thanks," said Sim. "But just now I couldn't . . ."

"It's the heat, dear."

"Yes," said Sim.

"And the chicken pox."

"Yes," said Sim.

They fell silent, while Mrs. Crackenthorpe tried carefully to think of some other way of cheering up Sim Tolland. At last she said, "I didn't bring any comics or anything for you to look at. I thought you wouldn't want to read."

"I don't," said Sim, and then added quickly, "And I don't want to watch any more telly. Or listen to things."

Mrs. Crackenthorpe was still following her own train of thought. "I didn't want to read, either. When I had chicken pox. And it was very hot weather, too, just like now. Here, in Elm Street."

It was, after all, unexpectedly soothing to listen to old Mrs. Crackenthorpe rabbiting on.

"Nobody much ever came to see me," Mrs. Crackenthorpe was saying sadly, "because of the chicken pox. It was dull. I was an only child—just about your age, or younger—and I'd never really had friends, anyway." (Sim thought of *his* friends, all the Elm Street lot, coolly enjoying themselves elsewhere; he could have wept.) "I didn't have friends because my mother liked to keep herself to herself. You know. She was very particular about me. So it was dull for me that summer."

In the silence that followed, Sim could see that Mrs. Crackenthorpe was pondering something difficult. She came to a decision. She began: "When you're in bed, you think a lot." She tapped the side of her head just above her ear. "Inside your head. I mean, *right* inside your head. Oh, you'd be surprised!"

"Yes?" said Sim.

"In the middle of the night, when you can't sleep for the heat and the chicken pox, and it's so dull . . ."

"Go on," said Sim.

"Well, to begin with, there was the elm tree—"

"The elm tree stump," corrected Sim. It was well known in the Street as the meeting place for the Elm Street lot—always had been. It had always been there: a stump.

But Mrs. Crackenthorpe was surprisingly firm. "A tree," she said. "In those days, when I was a child in Elm Street, it was a tree—not a cut-down stump. A tree, taller than the houses, reaching from side to side of the street. Green leaves. When there wasn't a breath of wind anywhere else, there was always a breath up among those leaves. The leaves—" She searched for a word. "The leaves *rustled.* It sounded cool up there, where the leaves rustled. So I thought."

Sim thought of green leaves and cool breezes. Greenness; coolness . . . "Yes . . ."

"So one night I decided to go up there."

"You *what?*"

"Decided to climb up there," said Mrs. Crackenthorpe. "And I did."

"Decided or climbed?"

"Both."

There was a disbelieving silence from Sim's bed.

"I was a little girl then," said Mrs. Crackenthorpe. "Plump, of course, but light, small, neat. Do you know, I'd never even thought of climbing a tree before?"

This was another extraordinary thing for Sim to have to believe.

"My mother always liked me to keep my clothes clean, you see. She insisted. But that particular night they'd gone to bed, and I lay awake, too hot and chicken poxy to sleep. I could see the elm tree from my window. I could see the leaves at the top moving in the breeze that was always there. The moon shone through the leaves. Bright moonlight, or I don't think I'd have dared. . . ."

"Dared . . ." repeated Sim Tolland. He looked at Mrs. Crackenthorpe sitting there, overflowing the bedroom chair; then he closed his eyes for a moment to try to imagine her a plump, small, neat little girl, *daring*. . . .

"Just in my nightie," said Mrs. Crackenthorpe. "Not even bedroom slippers. I went downstairs and into the street, all moonlit, and to the tree and up it—"

"How 'up it'?" interrupted Sim. "A tree like that doesn't have branches near the ground. They start high up—too high for you to reach, if you were a little girl."

"Let me think, then," said Mrs. Crackenthorpe. "A ladder?"

"No," said Sim. "You couldn't have lugged a ladder out. Not if you were just a little girl."

"You're right, of course," said Mrs. Crackenthorpe, dashed. Then she brightened: "How about this, then? There happened to be one of those very tall vans with a sort of roof rack and sort of rungs up the side of the van to the roof rack—you know! And this van—well, it happened to be parked just under the elm tree."

"Well . . ." said Sim.

"A real bit of luck for me, that van," said Mrs. Crackenthorpe, overriding any possible objection or doubt from Sim. "So I just climbed up the side of this van to its roof. From there I could easily reach the lowest branch of the tree and climb onto it. Then up and up, from branch to branch. I turned out to be a natural climber. From branch to branch," Mrs. Crackenthorpe repeated dreamily, "up and up, breezier and breezier, cooler and cooler . . ." She was fanning herself deliciously with the brown paper bag from which she had taken the packet of jelly babies.

She stopped suddenly, as a thought occurred to her. "Oh, dear! Do you think I ought to have taken a cushion with me?"

"Whatever for?" said Sim.

"To sit on, of course. The branches would have been uncomfortable without a cushion. So I did take a cushion. And do you know how high I climbed with that cushion?"

"No. How high?"

"To the top. To the very top. I wasn't afraid—not one bit. I climbed to where the branches grew quite thin and whippy. I settled that cushion in the elbow of a branch, and I settled myself on it, and I was comfortable and cool—so cool. All night long I stayed there. Do you think I might even have dozed off up there? I wasn't a bit afraid, you know."

"No," said Sim. "Too risky. You might have fallen."

Mrs. Crackenthorpe was only a little disappointed. "Oh, well . . . So I stayed awake all night, but cool and comfortable. I suppose I saw the dawn from that treetop." She sighed. "Oh, the dawn was so beautiful. . . ."

"What happened when your mother . . ."

"Let's see. Yes, I think they all came rushing out of the house. They shouted and cried and tried to get me to come down. But I was like a cat caught up a tree; I'd gone too high. My dad came up the tree after me, but he was a big, heavy man—it runs in the family. He got scared when he got really high and the branches began to be thin and whippy, as I've said. So he climbed down again."

"And did no one else try?"

"All the neighbors had come out by then and were calling up the tree to me. So—let's see. . . . Yes, some young fellow thinner than my dad came climbing up the tree, but even he daren't come right to the top, where I was. All he could do was reach up and tickle the sole of my foot. I shrieked, and everyone shouted to him to leave me alone and come down again. So he did."

"I like that bit," said Sim.

Mrs. Crackenthorpe smiled and bobbed her head in acknowledgment and went on. "Then my mother fetched all the blankets out of the house and made everybody hold the corners of them, drawn taut, all round the tree, close in. In case I fell. And they waited. . . ."

"Did you fall?"

"Of course not."

"Then how on earth *did* you get down?"

"There was a clanging and a rushing up," said Mrs. Cracken-thorpe, "and they'd sent for the fire brigade."

Sim couldn't help being impressed. "I say!"

"The first I knew of it was one of those shiny brass helmets coming up through the leaves at the top of the tree."

"You hadn't seen the firemen below, on the ground?"

"No," said Mrs. Crackenthorpe. Then, anxiously: "Why?"

"Well, how come you could see the people with the blankets, if you couldn't see the firemen?"

"Oh, dear!" said Mrs Crackenthorpe, taken aback. Then she pulled herself together. "I just *couldn't*. The leaves must have shifted in the breeze, I suppose. Anyway, as I've told you, there was this fire-man's helmet coming through the leaves at me. The fireman was on one of those special ladders they have that go straight up into the air. You know." Mrs. Crackenthorpe waved a hand vaguely.

"Go on."

"He called to me, all jolly, as if I were a cat caught up there. 'Kitty! Kitty! Kitty!' he called. I let him help me off my branch, and he carried me down the ladder to the bottom."

"What about the cushion?"

"That fell."

"You could have carried it down, if you carried it up."

"Have it your own way," said Mrs. Crackenthorpe. "I carried it down."

There was a long pause.

"That's the end of the story," said Mrs. Crackenthorpe.

"Not a story," said Sim. "It happened. You said."

"Oh, yes," said Mrs. Crackenthorpe. "Yes, yes, yes!"

"It was true," said Sim.

"It happened," said Mrs. Crackenthorpe.

"But there's no proof," said Sim, suddenly discontented.

"Well," said Mrs. Crackenthorpe slowly, "what about this? Ever after that, people have called me Kitty, as a joke. They still do. Kitty Crackenthorpe."

"Everybody?"

"Yes."

"Mr. Crackenthorpe calls you Kitty, too?"

Mrs. Crackenthorpe flinched, but, "Yes," she said.

Exactly at that moment Sim's mother called from downstairs: "Mrs. Crackenthorpe, Mr. Crackenthorpe's here asking if you're coming home to tea."

"Oh, yes, yes, yes!" cried Mrs. Crackenthorpe, gathering her flesh together, flustered. All Elm Street knew that Mr. Crackenthorpe was not a good-tempered man.

"Are you coming, then?" shouted Mr. Crackenthorpe from below.

"Oh, yes, yes, yes!" gasped Mrs. Crackenthorpe, now up from her chair and waddling toward the bedroom door.

"Elsie, do you hear me?"

"*Elsie* . . ." said Sim reproachfully. "But you definitely said—"

From the doorway Mrs. Crackenthorpe spoke hurriedly over her shoulder: "Lying in bed, you can think a lot of things. Inside your head. You can make things *happen* inside your head. Happenings. Real adventures . . ." She was gasping for words and for breath.

From below: "ELSIE!"

Mrs. Crackenthorpe's last wheezy whispers reached Sim from just outside his bedroom door: "You shut your eyes, Sim Tolland. You try it. Remember, inside your head." Then a slow thumping down the stairs, and Mrs. Crackenthorpe was gone.

Thoughtfully Sim collected the packet of jelly babies from the sheet where Mrs. Crackenthorpe had dropped it. He broke it open and popped a jelly baby into his mouth. But no, he'd lost his taste for jelly babies.

He spat the baby out onto a saucer by his bedside that already held some grape pips.

He was still thinking of what Mrs. Crackenthorpe had told him. She had climbed a tree. Well, he was pretty sure he could think of an even better, cooler thing to happen. Inside his head.

He settled himself as comfortably as possible. Then he shut his eyes.

What the
Neighbors Did ❖

*M*um didn't like the neighbors, although—as we were the end cottage of the row—we only had one, really: Dirty Dick. Beyond him, the Macys.

Dick lived by himself; they said there used to be a wife, but she'd run away years ago, so now he lived as he wanted, which Mum said was like a pig in a pigsty. Once I told Mum that I envied him, and she blew me up for it. Anyway, I'd have liked some of the things he had. He had two cars, although not for driving. He kept rabbits in one, and hens roosted in the other. He sold the eggs, which made part of his living. He made the rest from dealing in old junk (and in the village they said that he'd a stocking full of pound notes which he kept under the mattress of his bed). Mostly he went about on foot, with his handcart for the junk, but he also rode a tricycle. The boys used to jeer at him sometimes, and once I asked him why he didn't ride a bicycle like everyone else. He said he liked a tricycle because you could go as slowly as you wanted, looking at things properly, without ever falling off.

Mrs. Macy didn't like Dirty Dick any more than my mum did, but then she disliked everybody, anyway. She didn't like Mr. Macy. He was retired, and every morning in all weathers Mrs. Macy'd turn him out into the garden and lock the door against him and make him stay there until he'd done as much work as she thought right. She'd put his dinner out to him through the scullery window. She couldn't bear to have anything alive about the place (you couldn't count old Macy himself, Dad used to say). That was one of the reasons why she didn't think much of us, with our dog and cat and Nora's two lovebirds in a cage. Dirty Dick's hens and rabbits were even worse, of course.

Then the affair of the yellow dog made the Macys really hate Dirty Dick. It seems that old Mr. Macy secretly got himself a dog. He never had any money of his own because his wife made him hand it over, every week, so Dad reckoned that he must have begged the dog off someone who'd otherwise have had it destroyed.

The dog began as a secret, which sounds just about impossible, with Mrs. Macy around. But every day Mr. Macy used to take his dinner and eat it in his toolshed, which opened on the side furthest from the house. That must have been his temptation, but none of us knew he'd fallen into it until one summer evening we heard a most awful screeching from the Macys' house.

"That's old Ma Macy screaming," said Dad, spreading his bread and butter.

"Oh, dear!" said Mum, jumping up and then sitting down again. "Poor old Mr. Macy!" But Mum was afraid of Mrs. Macy. "Run upstairs, boy, and see if you can see what's going on."

So I did. I was just in time for the excitement, for as I leaned out of the window, the Macys' back door flew open. Mr. Macy came out first, with his head down and his arms sort of curved above it, and Mrs. Macy came out close behind him, aiming at his head with a light broom—but aiming quite hard. She was screeching words, although it was difficult to pick out any of them. But some words came again and again, and I began to follow: Mr. Macy had brought hairs with him into the house—short, curly yellowish hairs—and he'd left those hairs all over the upholstery, and they must have come from a cat or a dog or a hamster or I don't know what, and so on and so on. Whatever the creature was, he'd been keeping it in the toolshed, and turn it out he was going to, this very minute.

As usual, Mrs. Macy was right about what Mr. Macy was going to do.

He opened the shed door, and out ambled a dog—a big, yellowy white old dog, looking a bit like a sheep, somehow, and about as quick-witted. As though it didn't notice what a tantrum Mrs. Macy was in, it blundered gently toward her, and she lifted her broom high, and Mr. Macy covered his eyes, and then Mrs. Macy let out a real scream—a plain shriek—and dropped the broom and shot indoors and slammed the door after her.

The dog seemed puzzled, naturally, and so was I. It lumbered around toward Mr. Macy, and then I saw its head properly, and that it had the most extraordinary eyes—like headlamps, somehow. I don't mean as big as headlamps, of course, but with a kind of whitish glare to them. Then I realized that the poor old thing must be blind.

The dog had raised its nose inquiringly toward Mr. Macy, and Mr. Macy had taken one timid, hopeful step toward the dog, when one of the windows of the house went up and Mrs. Macy leaned out. She'd recovered from her panic, and she gave Mr. Macy his orders. He was to take that disgusting animal and turn it out into the road, where he must have found it in the first place.

I knew that old Macy would be too dead scared to do anything else but what his wife told him.

I went down again to where the others were having supper.

"Well?" said Mum.

I told them, and I told them what Mrs. Macy was making Mr. Macy do to the blind dog. "And if it's turned out like that on the road, it'll be killed by the first car that comes along."

There was a pause, when even Nora seemed to be thinking, but I could see from their faces what they were thinking.

Dad said at last: "That's bad. But we've four people in this little house, and a dog already, and a cat and two birds. There's no room for anything else."

"But it'll be killed."

"No," said Dad. "Not if you go at once, before any car comes, and take that dog down to the village, to the police station. Tell them it's a stray."

"But what'll they do with it?"

Dad looked as though he wished I hadn't asked that, but he said: "Nothing, I expect. Well, they might hand it over to the Cruelty to Animals people."

"And what'll *they* do with it?"

Dad was rattled. "They do what they think best for animals—I should have thought they'd have taught you that at school. For goodness' sake, boy!"

Dad wasn't going to say any more, nor Mum, who'd been listening with her lips pursed up. But everyone knew that the most likely thing was that an old, blind, ownerless dog would be destroyed.

Still, anything would be better than being run over and killed by a car just as you were sauntering along in the evening sunlight, so I started out of the house after the dog.

There he was, sauntering along, just as I'd imagined him. No sign of Mr. Macy, of course; he'd have been called back indoors by his wife.

As I ran to catch up with the dog, I saw Dirty Dick coming home, and nearer the dog than I was. He was pushing his handcart, loaded with the usual bits of wood and other junk. He saw the dog coming and stopped and waited; the dog came on hesitantly toward him.

"I'm coming for him," I called.

"Ah," said Dirty Dick. "Yours?" He held out his hand toward the dog—the hand that my mother always said she could only bear to take hold of if the owner had to be pulled from certain death in a quicksand. Anyway, the dog couldn't see the color of it, and it positively seemed to like the smell; it came on.

"No," I said. "Macys were keeping it, but Mrs. Macy turned it out. I'm going to take it down to the police as a stray. What do you think they'll do with it?"

Dirty Dick never said much; this time he didn't answer. He just bent down to get his arm around the dog, and in a second he'd hoisted him up on top of all the stuff in the cart. Then he picked up the handles and started off again.

So the Macys saw the blind dog come back to the row of cottages in state, as you might say, sitting on top of half a broken lavatory seat on the very pinnacle of Dirty Dick's latest load of junk.

Dirty Dick took good care of his animals, and he took good care of this dog he adopted. It always looked well fed and well brushed. Sometimes he'd take it out with him, on the end of a long string; mostly he'd leave it comfortably at home. When it lay out in the back garden, old Mr. Macy used to look at it longingly over the fence. Once or twice I saw him poke his fingers through, toward what had once been *his* dog. But that had been for only a very short, dark time in the shed, and the old dog never moved toward the fingers. Then: "Macy!" his terrible old wife would call from the house, and he'd have to go.

Then suddenly we heard that Dirty Dick had been robbed; old Macy came round specially to tell us. "An old sock stuffed with pound notes that he kept up the bedroom chimney. Gone. Hasn't he *told* you?"

"No," said Mum, "but we don't have a lot to do with him." She might have added that we didn't have a lot to do with the Macys, either; I think this was the first time I'd ever seen one step over our threshold in a neighborly way.

"You're thick with him sometimes," said old Macy, turning on me. "Hasn't he told *you* all about it?"

"Me?" I said. "No."

"Mind you, the whole thing's not to be wondered at," said the old man. "Front and back doors never locked, and money kept in the house. That's a terrible temptation to anyone with a weakness that way. A temptation that shouldn't have been put."

"I daresay," said Mum. "It's a shame, all the same. His savings."

"Perhaps the police'll be able to get it back for him," I said. "There'll be clues."

The old man jumped—a nervous sort of jump. "Clues? You think the police will find clues? I never thought of that. No, I did not. But has he gone to the police, anyway? I wonder. That's what I wonder. That's what I'm asking you." He paused, and I realized that he meant me again. "You're thick with him, boy. Has he gone to the police? That's what I want to know. . . ."

His mouth seemed to have filled with saliva, so that he had to stop to swallow and couldn't say more. He was in a state, all right.

At that moment Dad walked in from work and wasn't best pleased to find that visitor instead of his supper waiting, and Mr. Macy went.

Dad listened to the story during supper, and across the fence that evening he spoke to Dirty Dick and said he was sorry to hear about the money.

"Who told you?" asked Dirty Dick.

Dad said that old Macy had told us. Dirty Dick just nodded; he didn't seem interested in talking about it anymore. Over that weekend no police came to the row, and you might have thought that old Macy had invented the whole thing, except that Dirty Dick had not contradicted him.

On Monday I was rushing off to school when I saw Mr. Macy in their front garden, standing just between a big laurel bush and the fence. He looked straight at me and said, "Good morning," in a kind of whisper. I don't know which was odder: the whisper or his wishing me good morning. I answered in rather a shout, because I was late and hurrying past. His mouth had opened as though he meant to say more, but then it shut, as though he'd changed his mind. That was all, that morning.

The next morning he was in just the same spot again and hailed me in the same way, and this time I was early, so I stopped.

He was looking shiftily about him, as though someone might be spying on us, but at least his wife couldn't be doing that because the laurel bush was between him and their front windows. There was a tiny pile of yellow froth at one corner of his mouth, as though he'd been chewing his words over in advance. The sight of the froth made me want not to stay, but then the way he looked at me made me feel that I had to. No, it just made me; I had to.

"Look what's turned up in our back garden," he said, in the same whispering voice. And he held up a sock so dirty—partly with soot—and so smelly that it could only have been Dirty Dick's. It was stuffed full of something—pound notes, in fact. Old Macy's story of the robbery had been true in every detail.

I gaped at him.

"It's all to go back," said Mr. Macy. "Back exactly to where it came from." And then, as though I'd suggested the obvious—that he should hand the sock back to Dirty Dick himself with the same explanation just given to me—"No, no. It must go back as though it had never been—never been taken away." He couldn't use the word *stolen*. "Mustn't have the police poking around us. Mrs. Macy wouldn't like it." His face twitched at his own mention of her; he leaned forward. "You must put it back, boy. Put it back for me, and keep your mouth shut. Go on. Yes."

He must have been half out of his mind to think that I should do it, especially as I still didn't understand why. But as I stared at his twitching face, I suddenly did understand. I mean, that old Macy had taken the sock, out of spite, and then lost his nerve.

He must have been half out of his mind to think that I would do that for him, and yet I did it. I took the sock and put it inside my jacket and turned back to Dirty Dick's cottage. I walked boldly up to the front door and knocked, and of course, there was no answer. I knew he was already out with the cart.

There wasn't a sign of anyone looking, from either our house or the Macys'. (Mr. Macy had already disappeared.) I tried the door, and it opened, as I knew it would. I stepped inside and closed it behind me.

I'd never been inside before. The house was dirty, I suppose, and smelled a bit, but not really badly. It smelled of Dirty Dick and hens and rabbits—although it was untrue that he kept either hens or rabbits indoors, as Mrs. Macy said. It smelled of dog, too, of course.

Opening straight off the living room, where I stood, was the twisty, dark little stairway—exactly as in our cottage next door.

I went up.

The first room upstairs was full of junk. A narrow passageway had been kept clear to the second room, which opened off the first one. This was Dirty Dick's bedroom, with the bed unmade, as it probably was for weeks on end.

There was the fireplace, too, with a good deal of soot which had recently been brought down from the chimney. You couldn't miss seeing that; Dirty Dick couldn't have missed it, at the time. Yet he'd done nothing about his theft. In fact, I realized now that he'd probably said nothing, either. The only person who'd let the cat out of the bag was poor old Macy himself.

I'd been working this out as I looked at the fireplace, standing quite still. Around me the house was silent. The only sound came from outside, where I could see a hen perched on the bumper of the old car in the back garden, clucking for an egg newly laid. But when she stopped, there came another, tiny sound that terrified me: the click of a front gate opening. Feet were clumping up to the front door. . . .

I stuffed the sock up the chimney again, any old how, and was out of that bedroom in seconds, but on the threshold of the junk room I stopped, fixed by the headlamp glare of the old blind dog. He must have been there all the time, lying under a three-legged washstand, on a heap of rags. All the time he would have been watching me, if he'd had his eyesight. He didn't move.

Meanwhile the front door had opened, and the footsteps had clumped inside and stopped. There was a long pause, while I stared at the dog, who stared at me, and down below Dirty Dick listened and waited; he must have heard my movement just before.

At last: "Well," he called, "why don't you come down?"

There was nothing else to do but go. Down that dark, twisty stair, knowing that Dirty Dick was waiting for me at the bottom. He was a big man, and strong. He heaved his junk about like nobody's business.

But when I got down, he wasn't by the foot of the stairs; he was standing by the open door, looking out, with his back to me. He hadn't been surprised to hear someone upstairs in his house, uninvited, but when he turned around from the doorway, I could see that he hadn't expected to see *me*. He'd expected someone else—old Macy, I suppose.

I wanted to explain that I'd only put the sock back—there was soot all over my hands, plain to be seen, of course—and that I'd had nothing to do with taking it in the first place. But he'd drawn his thick brows together as he looked at me, and he jerked his head toward the open door. I was frightened, and I went past him without saying anything. I was late for school now, anyway, and I ran.

I didn't see Dirty Dick again.

Later that morning Mum chose to give him a talking to, over the back fence, about locking his doors against pilferers in future. She says he didn't say he would, he didn't say he wouldn't, and he didn't say anything about anything having been stolen, or returned.

Soon after that, Mum saw him go out with the handcart with all his rabbits in a hutch, and he came back later without them. He did the same with his hens. We heard later that he'd given them away in the village; he hadn't even bothered to try to sell them.

Then he went around to Mum, wheeling the tricycle. He said he'd decided not to use it anymore, and I could have it. He didn't leave any message for me.

Later still, Mum saw him set off for the third time that day with his handcart, not piled very high even, but with the old dog sitting on top. And that was the last that anyone saw of him.

He must have taken very little money with him; they found the sooty sock, still nearly full, by the rent book on the mantelpiece. There was plenty to pay the rent due and to pay for cleaning up the house and the garden for the next tenant. He must have been fed up with being a householder, Dad said—and with having neighbors. He just wanted to turn tramp, and he did.

It was soon after he'd gone that I said to Mum that I envied him, and she blew me up and went on and on about soap and water and fecklessness. All the same, I did envy him. I didn't even have the fun with his tricycle that he'd had. I never rode it, although I wanted to, because I was afraid that people I knew would laugh at me.

Black Eyes ❖

*C*ousin Lucinda was coming to stay with Jane, just for the weekend.

Jane had never met Lucinda, but Jane's mother said she was a year younger than Jane, and they must all be very kind to her. Jane imagined the rest. She imagined a shy little girl with blue eyes and golden curls that bobbed about a round, rosy face. She would be rather cuddly, and they would play with their teddy bears together.

But Lucinda was not at all like that. She was thin, and her hair was black without any curl to it, and her eyes were black in a white face— eyes as black as the Pontefract cakes you find in a licorice assortment. Jane didn't like licorice.

And Lucinda's teddy bear had black eyes, too.

"He was exactly like your teddy bear, to begin with," said Lucinda, "with eyes exactly like yours. But then one day my teddy bear saw something so horrid—so *horrible*—that his eyes dropped out. Then my mother made black eyes for him, with black wool." She paused for a quick breath. "But his eyes aren't made of ordinary black wool, and they're not stitched in an ordinary way. The black wool is magic, and my mother is a witch."

Jane said feebly, "My mother says your mother is her sister, so she can't be a witch."

"That's what your mother would like to believe," said Lucinda.

The two little girls were in their nightdresses, in Jane's room, which Lucinda was sharing for two nights. They had been playing and talking before going to bed.

Jane's father came in to say good night. He caught sight of the two teddies lying side by side. Lucinda's teddy never wore any clothes, she said, and Jane had just undressed her teddy for the night, taking off the trousers and jersey and balaclava helmet, with holes for the ears, that her mother had once knitted for him. So the two teddies lay side by side, with nothing on, and Jane's father cried: "Twins! Twin teddy bears—as like as two apples in a bowl!"

(He did not notice the difference in their eyes; that was the kind of thing he would never notice.)

He darted forward, snatched up each teddy bear by a leg, and began juggling with them—throwing them up, one after the other, very quickly, and catching them as quickly, so that there were always two teddy bears whirling round in the air. He sometimes juggled with apples like this, until Jane's mother told him to stop before he dropped one and bruised it.

Both the little girls were jumping about and shouting to him to stop, as he meant them to. But Lucinda's shouts turned into screams and then into long, screeching sobs. Jane's father stopped at once and thrust both teddy bears into her arms and tried to hug her and kiss her and talk to her gently, saying over and over again that he hadn't hurt the teddies one bit—they'd *liked* it—and he was very, very sorry. But Lucinda wriggled away from him and threw Jane's teddy bear away, hard, so that it hit the bedroom wall with a smack, and she went on sobbing.

In the end Jane's father left them. You could see that he was really upset.

Lucinda stopped crying. She said, "Sorry! He'll be sorry!"

"What do you mean?" asked Jane.

"Didn't you see the look my teddy gave your father out of his magic black eyes?"

"No," said Jane. "My teddy bear likes my father, even when he throws him up into the air. And my teddy can look at him better than your teddy, because my teddy has *real* teddy eyes. I don't believe your teddy can look at all with woolwork eyes. Not as well as my teddy, anyway."

"Your teddy has silly eyes," said Lucinda. "Yours is a silly teddy. Silly Teddy, Silly Teddy—that's your teddy's name now."

"No, it isn't," said Jane.

"Yes, it is," said Lucinda. "And my teddy is called Black Teddy. And your father will be sorry that he threw Black Teddy up into the air, so that Black Teddy had to look at him with his magic eyes."

Jane wanted to say something back, but her mother came in, rather anxiously, having heard about the juggling. She made the little girls get into their beds at once, and then she tucked them in, and kissed them good night, and went out, turning out the light.

They did not speak again. Perhaps Lucinda went quickly to sleep; Jane did not know. Jane herself burrowed under the bedclothes and then whispered in her teddy's ear, "I don't like Black Teddy, do you? But he's not staying long. . . ."

The next morning, after breakfast, Jane's father was washing up when he broke a cup.

"Oh, really!" said his wife.

"It's only one of the cheap ones," he said.

"There isn't such a thing as a cheap cup," she retorted. "If you go on breaking cups, I can't let you wash up."

"I'm planning to break the whole set," said Jane's father.

And no more was said, but Lucinda whispered to Jane, "Black Teddy did that."

"Did what?"

"Made him break that cup. Black Teddy ill-wished him to do it, with a look from his magic eyes."

"I don't believe it."

"Oh, Black Teddy can easily do that. He's ill-wished my father so that he's broken something, and my mother's got angry, and then my father's got angry, and then they've both screamed and screamed at each other and broken more things, and Black Teddy ill-wished it all with his magic eyes. Just as he ill-wished your father."

Jane wanted to shout, "I don't believe it!" But she was afraid of what Lucinda might say back. She was afraid of Lucinda or of Black Teddy. So she just turned away.

That Saturday morning Jane's mother took the little girls out with her when she went shopping. Jane said it would be better if they left their teddy bears at home, each on a separate bed. So they did.

When they got home, Jane went to her room to make sure that her teddy bear was all right. He sat exactly as she had left him, she thought, fully dressed, but then she saw that his balaclava helmet was on back to front. She trembled with anger as she put it right.

Lucinda had come into the room just behind her. "You did that!" said Jane. "You turned his balaclava round so that he couldn't see."

"He can't see, anyway, with those silly eyes," said Lucinda. "And I didn't touch him. Black Teddy just ill-wished it to happen to him, and it did."

"It wasn't Black Teddy; it was you!" said Jane. "And my teddy can see, except when his balaclava's on back to front."

"Your silly teddy can't see, ever. But Black Teddy, if he wanted to— Black Teddy could see through the back of a balaclava helmet, and through doors, and through walls; he can see through everything when he wants to ill-wish with his magic eyes."

Jane stamped her foot and shouted, "Go away!"

Lucinda said, "I'm going away tomorrow morning, and I'm never coming back. You hate me."

Jane said, "Yes, I hate you!"

At that moment Jane's mother came to call them to dinner, and she overheard what Jane had said. She was very angry with her, and she petted Lucinda, who allowed herself to be petted. Jane saw Lucinda staring at her with her Pontefract eyes from under Jane's mother's chin.

They sat down to dinner, but Jane's father was not in his place. "We've run out of orange squash," said Jane's mother. "He's just gone to the corner shop to get some."

"Is it far?" asked Lucinda.

"Just along our street and across the road," said Jane's mother. "You can start eating, Lucinda."

"Does he have to cross a busy road?" asked Lucinda.

"What?" said Jane's mother. "Oh, yes, busy on a Saturday. But that won't delay him. He's only to wait to cross the road."

Five minutes later Lucinda asked if she could have a drink of water, as there still wasn't any orange squash. Jane's mother got some from the tap and looked at the clock. "Where can he have got to?"

"I hope he's all right," said Lucinda.

"What do you mean, child?"

"I hope he's not been run over," said Lucinda, looking at Jane as she spoke.

"What rubbish!" said Jane's mother, and sat down suddenly with her hands clasped tightly in her lap.

At that moment Jane's father walked in with the orange squash. He was surprised that his wife was angry with him for having been so long. He explained that he'd met a friend in the corner shop, and they'd got talking. The friend wanted him to go to a darts match that evening, and he'd said yes.

"Leaving me to baby-sit?" said Jane's mother.

Jane's father said he hadn't thought of that, but he offered to take Jane and Lucinda to the playground in the park that afternoon. So it was agreed.

Again, the teddy bears were left at home. Just before they set out for the park, Lucinda said she wanted to wear her knitted hat, after all, and ran back into Jane's room to get it. Jane wondered, but her father was holding her fast by the hand, so she couldn't follow Lucinda.

When they came back from the park, Jane went straight into her bedroom, and—sure enough—there was her teddy with his balaclava on back to front. She put it right. Lucinda, smiling in the doorway, said, "How naughty of Black Teddy!" Jane glared at her.

That evening, after Jane's father had gone off to his darts match, they watched television. At bedtime there was Jane's teddy with his balaclava on back to front again, but this time Jane didn't bother to put it right, until she was in bed and her mother was just going to turn out the light. Then she took off the balaclava and the other clothes, and she took her teddy bear right down under the bedclothes and whispered: "Black Teddy is only staying until tomorrow morning. Then he's going home with Lucinda on the coach." She fell asleep with her teddy bear in her arms.

She woke because Lucinda was shaking her. Lucinda had drawn back the curtains so that moonlight streamed into the room. She stood by Jane's bed, and in the moonlight Lucinda's face looked whiter and her eyes looked blacker than by daylight. She was holding Black Teddy right up to the side of her face.

She said softly to Jane, "Don't make a noise, but listen! Can you hear someone crying?"

"Crying?"

"Sobbing and sobbing. It must be your mother sobbing."

Jane was frightened. "I don't think I can hear her. Why should she be sobbing?"

"Because Black Teddy ill-wished your father with his magic eyes."

"She wouldn't cry because of that," said Jane firmly. And she was certain now that she couldn't hear anything.

"Ah, but she would cry, when she heard what happened to your father on his way home from the darts match, after dark."

"What happened to him?" asked Jane. She hadn't meant to ask; she didn't want to ask; she didn't believe what Lucinda was going to say.

Lucinda turned Black Teddy so that he was facing Jane. She brought him forward so that his black eyes were looking into Jane's eyes. "Listen to what Black Teddy ill-wished," said Lucinda. "You remember that corner of the park where we took a shortcut? You remember that slimy pond that your father said was very deep? You remember that thick bush that grows just beside that pond? You remember?"

"Yes," said Jane faintly.

"Your father decided to take a shortcut home in the dark, after the darts match. He was crossing that corner of the park by the pond and the bush. It was very dark; it was very lonely. There was someone hiding behind the bush, waiting for your father."

"Oh, no!"

"He jumped out at your father from behind and hit him on the head, hard, and then he dragged him toward the pond—"

"No, no, no!" With what seemed one movement Jane was out of bed and into the sitting room, and there was her mother dozing in front of the television set. She woke up when Jane rushed in, and Jane rushed into her arms. What Jane said was such a muddle and so frantic that her mother thought she had been having nightmares. While she was trying to calm her, Jane's father walked in, very pleased with his darts evening and perfectly safe and sound.

They tried to understand what Jane tried to tell them. They looked into Jane's bedroom, but there was Lucinda in bed, apparently sound asleep, with Black Teddy clasped in her arms. Even the curtains were drawn close.

They were cross with Jane when she said she wasn't going to sleep in the same room as Lucinda's Black Teddy, but in the end, they gave way. They wrapped her in rugs, and she slept on the couch in the sitting room, and Lucinda and Black Teddy had Jane's room to themselves.

"And I don't want to play with her tomorrow morning, and I don't want to see her off at the coach station, or be with her and her Black Teddy *at all*!" said Jane, when they said a last good night to her.

On Sunday morning they all had breakfast together, but the little girls spoke not a word to each other. After breakfast Jane's mother said that she would help Lucinda get ready to go home, and Jane's father said he would take Jane to the playground while she was doing that. In the playground Jane's father often looked at his watch, and they didn't stay there very long. When they got back, Jane's mother and Lucinda had gone. Probably only just gone—Jane's father had timed their return very carefully.

He said, "Well, that's that! Poor little girl!"

Jane said, "She was horrible, and she had a horrible Black Teddy."

"She's very unhappy at home," said her father. "We must make allowances. Her mother and father fight like cat and dog. She suffers. That's why your mother asked her for a weekend, but it didn't work."

"Oh," said Jane, but she didn't feel sorry for Lucinda at all. She went off to her bedroom, her own bedroom that she wouldn't have to share with Lucinda and Black Teddy anymore. And there sat her own dear teddy bear on her bed, waiting for her. He had his balaclava helmet on back to front, as Lucinda must have arranged it before she left, but that was for the very last time. No more of Black Teddy and his ill-wishing, ever again . . .

She gazed happily at her teddy bear, but as she gazed, her happiness seemed to falter, to die in her. She gazed and thought that her teddy bear seemed somehow not his usual self. There was something odd about the way he sat, something odd about his paws, something odd about his ears.

She snatched him up and pulled off the balaclava helmet: a pair of black woolen eyes stared at her.

She rushed back to her father, crying, "She's taken the wrong teddy! Lucinda's stolen my teddy bear!" She gabbled and wept together.

Her father acted instantly. "Come on!" he said. "Bring him with you, and we're off. They've got ten minutes' start on us to the coach station, but we might be in time. We must catch them before the coach leaves with Lucinda and Lucinda's suitcase with your teddy in it. Come on—*run!*"

They tore out of the house, Jane's father gripping Jane's hand and

Jane gripping Black Teddy. They ran and ran; they had to wait at the main road for a gap in the traffic, and then across, and past the corner shop, and by the shortcut across the park—there was that dreadful bush beside that dreadful pond, only it was all bright and busy this Sunday morning—and on, down another street, and then another, and Jane was quite breathless, and there was the coach station! They went rushing in, and Jane's father seemed to know where Lucinda's coach would be, and there it was! There it was, with Jane's mother talking to the driver, no doubt about putting Lucinda off at the right place, where she would be met. And there was Lucinda herself, already sitting in the coach, with her suitcase in the rack above her head.

"Stay there!" said her father to Jane, and he took Black Teddy from her and climbed into the coach. He hadn't time to say anything to Jane's mother, who stared in amazement, so Jane explained to her mother— and to the coach driver—while she watched what her father was doing.

Once he was in the coach, Jane's father stopped being in a hurry and being excited. He walked to the empty seat next to Lucinda and sat down in it and spoke to her, showing her Black Teddy. (Jane could see all this very clearly through the window of the coach.) He talked to her, and while he talked, he took the trousers and jersey off Black Teddy and stuffed them into his pocket. Then he put Black Teddy into Lucinda's arms, but she just let him fall into her lap. Jane's father went on talking, and still he didn't take the suitcase from the rack and snatch Jane's teddy from it, as Jane expected every minute.

At last Jane's father took a handkerchief from his pocket and began dabbing Lucinda's cheeks with it. So Lucinda was crying.

And at last Lucinda stood up on her seat and reached for her suitcase in the rack and brought it down and opened it and took Jane's teddy from it and gave it to Jane's father. Then he put the suitcase back for her and tried to put his arm around her and kiss her good-bye, but she wouldn't let him. Then he got off the coach with Jane's teddy bear.

Jane's father thanked the coach driver for delaying those few minutes, and he handed Jane her teddy bear, and she hugged him.

Then the coach was off. It moved out of the station toward the

Great London Road. They were all waving good-bye to Lucinda, even Jane, but she never waved, never looked back.

The coach stopped at the lights before the Great Road. They couldn't see Lucinda anymore, because of the sun's dazzling on the glass of her window. But they could see the window beginning to crawl down; Lucinda must be winding it down from the inside. And Black Teddy appeared at the gap at the top of the window.

The lights changed, and the coach moved on again, into the traffic on the Great Road, gathered speed with the rest of the traffic. . . .

And Black Teddy fell from the window—no, he was *thrown* from the window. Thrown into the middle of the rushing, crushing, cruel traffic.

That was his end.

And the coach went on, out of sight.

Of the three watchers, no one moved; no one spoke. Jane hugged and hugged her own dear teddy to her, and the yellow fur on the top of his head began to be wet with tears. Against her will, she was weeping for what had happened—for all that had happened. She wept for Black Teddy. She wept for Lucinda, too. Now, at last, she felt sorry for Lucinda, and the sorrow was like a pain inside her.

In the Middle
of the Night❖

*I*n the middle of the night a fly woke
Charlie. At first he lay listening, half asleep, while it swooped about
the room. Sometimes it was far; sometimes it was near—that was what
had woken him—and occasionally it was very near indeed. It was very,
very near when the buzzing stopped; the fly had alighted on his face.
He jerked his head up; the fly buzzed off. Now he was really awake.

The fly buzzed widely about the room, but it was thinking of Charlie all the time. It swooped nearer and nearer. Nearer . . .

Charlie pulled his head down under the bedclothes. All of him
under the bedclothes, he was completely protected, but he could hear
nothing except his heartbeats and his breathing. He was overwhelmed
by the smell of warm bedding, warm pajamas, warm himself. He was
going to suffocate. So he rose suddenly up out of the bedclothes, and
the fly was waiting for him. It dashed at him. He beat at it with his
hands. At the same time he appealed to his younger brother, Wilson,
in the next bed: "Wilson, there's a fly!"

Wilson, unstirring, slept on.

Now Charlie and the fly were pitting their wits against each other,

Charlie pouncing on the air where he thought the fly must be, the fly sliding under his guard toward his face. Again and again the fly reached Charlie; again and again, almost simultaneously, Charlie dislodged him. Once he hit the fly or, at least, hit where the fly had been a second before, on the side of his head; the blow was so hard that his head sang with it afterward.

Then suddenly the fight was over: no more buzzing. His blows—or rather, one of them—must have told.

He laid his head back on the pillow, thinking of going to sleep again. But he was also thinking of the fly, and now he noticed a tickling in the ear he turned to the pillow.

It must be—it *was*—the fly.

He rose in such panic that the waking of Wilson really seemed to him a possible thing and useful. He shook him repeatedly. "Wilson—Wilson, I tell you, there's a fly in my ear!"

Wilson groaned, turned over very slowly like a seal in water, and slept on.

The tickling in Charlie's ear continued. He could just imagine the fly struggling in some passageway too narrow for its wingspan. He longed to put his finger into his ear and rattle it around, like a stick in a rabbit hole, but he was afraid of driving the fly deeper into his ear.

Wilson slept on.

Charlie stood in the middle of the bedroom floor, quivering and trying to think. He needed to see down his ear or to get someone else to see down it. Wilson wouldn't do; perhaps Margaret would.

Margaret's room was next door. Charlie turned on the light as he entered. Margaret's bed was empty. He was startled and then thought that she must have gone to the bathroom. But there was no light from there. He listened carefully; there was no sound from anywhere, except for the usual snuffling moans from the hall, where Floss slept and dreamed of dog biscuits. The empty bed was mystifying, but Charlie had his ear to worry about. It sounded as if there were a pigeon inside it now.

Wilson asleep, Margaret vanished; that left Alison. But Alison was bossy, just because she was the eldest, and anyway, she would probably only wake Mum. He might as well wake Mum himself.

Down the passage and through the door always left ajar. "Mum," he said. She woke, or at least half woke, at once. "Who is it? Who? Who? What's the matter? What?"

"I've a fly in my ear."

"You can't have."

"It flew in."

She switched on the bedside light, and as she did so, Dad plunged beneath the bedclothes with an exclamation and lay still again.

Charlie knelt at his mother's side of the bed, and she looked into his ear. "There's nothing."

"Something crackles."

"It's wax in your ear."

"It tickles."

"There's no fly there. Go back to bed, and stop imagining things."

His father's arm came up from below the bedclothes. The hand waved about, settled on the bedside light, and clicked it out. There was an upheaval of bedclothes and a comfortable grunt.

"Good night," said Mum from the darkness. She was already allowing herself to sink back into sleep again.

"Good night," Charlie said sadly. Then an idea occurred to him. He repeated his good night loudly and added some coughing, to cover the fact that he was closing the bedroom door behind him, the door that Mum kept open so that she could listen for her children. They had outgrown all that kind of attention, except possibly for Wilson. Charlie had shut the door against Mum's hearing because he intended to slip downstairs for a drink of water—well, for a drink and perhaps a snack. That fly business had woken him up and also weakened him; he needed something.

He crept downstairs, trusting to Floss's good sense not to make a row. He turned the foot of the staircase toward the kitchen, and there had not been the faintest whimper from her, far less a bark. He was passing the dog basket when he had the most unnerving sensation of something being wrong there—something unusual, at least. He could not have said whether he had heard something or smelled something; he could certainly have seen nothing in the blackness. Perhaps some extra sense warned him.

"Floss?" he whispered, and there was the usual little scrabble and snuffle. He held out his fingers low down for Floss to lick. As she did not do so at once, he moved them toward her, met some obstruction—

"Don't poke your fingers in my eye!" a voice said, very low-toned and cross. Charlie's first, confused thought was that Floss had spoken. The voice was familiar, but then a voice from Floss should *not* be familiar; it should be strangely new to him.

He took an uncertain little step toward the voice, tripped over the obstruction, which was quite wrong in shape and size to be Floss, and sat down. Two things now happened. Floss, apparently having climbed over the obstruction, reached his lap and began to lick his face. At the same time a human hand fumbled over his face, among the slappings of Floss's tongue, and settled over his mouth. "Don't make a row! Keep quiet!" said the same voice. Charlie's mind cleared; he knew, although without understanding, that he was sitting on the floor in the dark with Floss on his knee and Margaret beside him.

Her hand came off his mouth.

"What are you doing here, anyway, Charlie?"

"I like that! What about you? There was a fly in my ear."

"Go on!"

"There was."

"Why does that make you come downstairs?"

"I wanted a drink of water."

"There's water in the bathroom."

"Well, I'm a bit hungry."

"If Mum catches you . . ."

"Look here," Charlie said, "you tell me what you're doing down here."

Margaret sighed. "Just sitting with Floss."

"You can't come down and just sit with Floss in the middle of the night."

"Yes, I can. I keep her company. Only at weekends, of course. No one seemed to realize what it was like for her when those puppies went. She just couldn't get to sleep for loneliness."

"But the last puppy went weeks ago. You haven't been keeping Floss company every Saturday night since then."

"Why not?"

Charlie gave up. "I'm going to get my food and drink," he said. He went into the kitchen, followed by Margaret, followed by Floss.

They all had a quick drink of water. Then Charlie and Margaret looked into the larder: the remains of a joint; a very large quantity of mashed potato; most of a loaf; eggs; butter; cheese. . . .

"I suppose it'll have to be just bread and butter and a bit of cheese," said Charlie. "Else Mum might notice."

"Something hot," said Margaret. "I'm cold from sitting in the hall comforting Floss. I need hot cocoa, I think." She poured some milk into a saucepan and put it on the hot plate. Then she began a search for the cocoa. Charlie, standing by the cooker, was already absorbed in the making of a rough cheese sandwich.

The milk in the pan began to steam. Given time, it rose in the saucepan, peered over the top, and boiled over onto the hot plate, where it sizzled loudly. Margaret rushed back and pulled the saucepan to one side. "Well, really, Charlie! Now there's that awful smell! It'll still be here in the morning, too."

"Set the fan going," Charlie suggested.

The fan drew the smell from the cooker up and away through a pipe to the outside. It also made a loud roaring noise. Not loud enough to reach their parents, who slept on the other side of the house—that was all that Charlie and Margaret thought of.

Alison's bedroom, however, was immediately above the kitchen. Charlie was eating his bread and cheese, Margaret was drinking her cocoa when the kitchen door opened, and there stood Alison. Only Floss was pleased to see her.

"Well!" she said.

Charlie muttered something about a fly in his ear, but Margaret said nothing. Alison had caught them red-handed. She would call Mum downstairs; that was obvious. There would be an awful row.

Alison stood there. She liked commanding a situation.

Then, instead of taking a step backward to call up the stairs to Mum, she took a step forward into the kitchen. "What are you having, anyway?" she asked. She glanced with scorn at Charlie's poor piece of bread and cheese and at Margaret's cocoa. She moved over to the larder, flung open the door, and looked searchingly inside. In such a way must Napoleon have viewed a battlefield before the victory.

Her gaze fell upon the bowl of mashed potato. "I shall make potato cakes," said Alison.

They watched while she brought the mashed potato to the kitchen table. She switched on the oven, fetched her other ingredients, and began mixing.

"Mum'll notice if you take much of that potato," said Margaret.

But Alison thought big. "She may notice if some potato is missing," she agreed. "But if there's none at all, and if the bowl it was in is washed and dried and stacked away with the others, then she's going to think she must have made a mistake. There just can never have been any mashed potato."

Alison rolled out her mixture and cut it into cakes; then she set the cakes on a baking tin and put it in the oven.

Now she did the washing up. Throughout the time they were in the kitchen, Alison washed up and put away as she went along. She wanted no one's help. She was very methodical, and she did everything herself to be sure that nothing was left undone. In the morning there must be no trace left of the cooking in the middle of the night.

"And now," said Alison, "I think we should fetch Wilson."

The other two were aghast at the idea, but Alison was firm in her reasons. "It's better if we're all in this together, Wilson as well. Then, if the worst comes to the worst, it won't be just us three caught out, with Wilson hanging on to Mum's apron strings, smiling innocence. We'll all be for it together, and Mum'll be softer with us if we've got Wilson."

They saw that, at once. But Margaret still objected. "Wilson will tell. He just always tells everything. He can't help it."

Alison said, "He always tells everything. Right. We'll give him something *to* tell and then see if Mum believes him. We'll do an entertainment for him. Get an umbrella from the hall and Wilson's sou'wester and a blanket or a rug or something. Go on."

They would not obey Alison's orders until they had heard her plan; then they did. They fetched the umbrella and the hat, and lastly they fetched Wilson, still sound asleep, slung between the two of them in his eiderdown. They propped him in a chair at the kitchen table, where he still slept.

By now the potato cakes were done. Alison took them out of the oven and set them on the table before Wilson. She buttered them, handing them in turn to Charlie and Margaret and helping herself. One was set aside to cool for Floss.

The smell of fresh-cooked, buttery potato cake woke Wilson, as was to be expected. First his nose sipped the air; then his eyes opened; his gaze settled on the potato cakes.

"Like one?" Alison asked.

Wilson opened his mouth wide, and Alison put a potato cake inside, whole.

"They're paradise cakes," Alison said.

"Potato cakes?" said Wilson, recognizing the taste.

"No, paradise cakes, Wilson," and then, stepping aside, she gave him a clear view of Charlie and Margaret's entertainment, with the umbrella and the sou'wester hat and his eiderdown. "Look, Wilson, look."

Wilson watched with wide-open eyes, and into his wide-open mouth Alison put, one by one, the potato cakes that were his share.

But as they had foreseen, Wilson did not stay awake for very long. When there were no more potato cakes, he yawned, drowsed, and suddenly was deeply asleep. Charlie and Margaret put him back into his eiderdown and took him upstairs to bed again. They came down to return the umbrella and the sou'wester to their proper places and to see Floss back into her basket. Alison, last out of the kitchen, made sure that everything was in its place.

The next morning Mum was down first. On Sunday she always cooked a proper breakfast for anyone there in time. Dad was always there in time, but this morning Mum was still looking for a bowl of mashed potato when he appeared.

"I can't think where it's gone," she said. "I can't think."

"I'll have the bacon and eggs without the potato," said Dad, and he did. While he ate, Mum went back to searching.

Wilson came down and was sent upstairs again to put on a dressing gown. On his return he said that Charlie was still asleep and there was no sound from the girls' rooms either. He said he thought they were tired out. He went on talking while he ate his breakfast. Dad was reading the paper, and Mum had gone back to poking about in the larder for the bowl of mashed potato, but Wilson liked talking even if no one would listen. When Mum came out of the larder for a moment, still without her potato, Wilson was saying: ". . . and Charlie sat in an umbrella boat on an eiderdown sea, and Margaret pretended to be a sea serpent, and Alison gave us paradise cakes to eat. Floss had one, too, but it was too hot for her. What are paradise cakes? Dad, what's a paradise cake?"

"Don't know," said Dad, reading.

"Mum, what's a paradise cake?"

"Oh, Wilson, don't bother so when I'm looking for something. . . . When did you eat this cake, anyway?"

"I told you. Charlie sat in his umbrella boat on an eiderdown sea and Margaret was a sea serpent and Alison—"

"Wilson," said his mother, "you've been dreaming."

"No, really—really!" Wilson cried.

But his mother paid no further attention. "I give up," she said. "That mashed potato, it must have been last weekend . . ." She went out of the kitchen to call the others. "Charlie! Margaret! Alison!"

Wilson, in the kitchen, said to his father, "I wasn't dreaming. And Charlie said there was a fly in his ear."

Dad had been quarter listening; now he put down his paper. "What?"

"Charlie had a fly in his ear."

Dad stared at Wilson. "And what did you say that Alison fed you with?"

"Paradise cakes. She'd just made them, I think, in the middle of the night."

"What were they like?"

"Lovely. Hot, with butter. Lovely."

"But were they—well, could they have had any mashed potato in them, for instance?"

In the hall Mum was finishing her calling. "Charlie! Margaret! Alison! I warn you now!"

"I don't know about that," Wilson said. "They were paradise cakes. They tasted a bit like the potato cakes Mum makes, but Alison said they weren't. She specially said they were paradise cakes."

Dad nodded. "You've finished your breakfast. Go up and get dressed, and you can take this"—he took a coin from his pocket—"straight off to the sweetshop. Go on."

Mum met Wilson at the kitchen door. "Where's he off to in such a hurry?"

"I gave him something to buy sweets with," said Dad. "I wanted a quiet breakfast. He talks too much."

The Tree in the Meadow ❖

*T*here were buildings on three sides of Miss Mortlock's meadow; on the fourth, the river. In the middle of the meadow stood the elm. There were other trees in the meadow: sycamore, ash, horse chestnut. The elm was giant among them. It had always stood there. Nobody remembered its being younger than it was; nobody remembered it less than its present immense height. Nobody really thought about it anymore. They saw it, simply.

Then one day a branch fell from the elm tree. It seemed just to tear itself off from the main body of the tree. There was nothing to show why, except for a discoloration of wood at the torn end.

At its thickest, the branch that fell was almost the thickness of a man's body.

The fall caused some surprise in the houses overlooking the meadow, but nobody thought more about the incident until—no, not the next year, but the year after that—another branch dropped. The meadow had been cut for hay, and the Scarr children had been making hay houses. They had just gone in to tea when the branch—quite as big as the previous one—fell. It fell where they had been playing, smashing and scattering their hay houses. Mrs. Scarr was very much upset at what might have happened—at what *would* have happened if the children had still been playing there. Mr. Scarr agreed that the possibilities were upsetting, and he now pointed out that the rooks no longer nested in the elm. *They* knew. Someday—one day before too long—the whole tree would fall. It would fall without warning, and the damage could only be guessed at. The elm might fall on Miss Mortlock's house; it might fall on the Scarrs' house; it might fall on the buildings the other side—old Mortlock stables and outhouses, no great loss if they were smashed, but a mess. Or if everyone had great good luck, the elm might fall harmlessly away from all buildings, across the meadow toward the river.

Miss Mortlock was now told that she ought to have the elm taken down.

Miss Mortlock said that the elm had been there long before she was born and she hoped and expected that it would be there after she was dead. She wanted no advice on the subject.

Another branch fell from the elm tree, partly squashing a farm trailer. The farmer whose trailer it was had been renting the meadow from Miss Mortlock for his cows. He tried to make Miss Mortlock pay the value of the trailer. Miss Mortlock replied that he had left his trailer in a particularly foolish place. She could not be held responsible. Everyone knew what elm trees were like, especially when they were getting old and rotten. No doubt he had heard of previous branches falling.

Mr. Scarr had another conversation with Miss Mortlock about having the elm tree felled. She said that these tree surgeons, as they called themselves, used fancy equipment so that they could charge fancy prices. She could not afford them.

Mr. Scarr said that he knew two handymen, pals, with a crosscut saw, ax, wedges, and good rope. They could fell any tree to within six inches of where it should go. Miss Mortlock was surprised and delighted to hear that there was anybody who would come and do anything well nowadays. Through Mr. Scarr, a bargain was struck between Miss Mortlock and the handymen.

Mr. Scarr told his family about the arrangement at supper. Mrs. Scarr sighed with relief and thought no more of it—until later. The little girls were too young to understand. Only Ricky was interested. He said: "What will happen to the tree?"

His father stared at him. "It'll be felled. Didn't you hear me?"

"I mean, what will happen to the tree after that?" He had once seen a truck passing through the village carrying an enormous tree trunk, lopped of all its branches, chained down.

"It won't be a tree when it's felled," said Mr. Scarr. "Timber. Poor timber, in this case. Not sound enough even for coffins. Not worth cartage."

That night Ricky looked out of his bedroom window over the meadow to the elm. It stood, a tree. It was leafless, at this time of year, and the outer twigs on one side made what you could think of as the shape of a woman's head with fluffed-out hair, face bent downward. He had seen that woman from his window ever since he could remember.

He tried to imagine the elm tree cut down, not there. He tried to imagine space where the trunk and branches and twigs were—the whole great shape missing from the meadow. He tried to imagine looking right across the meadow without the interruption of the tree, looking across emptiness to the stables on the other side. He could not.

The next day, on his way to school, Ricky called as usual for Willy Jim, his best friend, who lived at the top of the lane. They went on together, and Ricky said: "Our elm's being cut down."

"So what?" said Willy Jim, preoccupied. He was still Ricky's best friend, perhaps, but he was also in with a new gang at school. Ricky wanted to get into the same gang. He meant to try, anyway.

In the playground later, Ricky said to Bones Jones, who was leader of the gang: "Our elm tree's going to be cut down. It's hundreds of years old; it's hundreds of feet high."

"Didn't know you owned an elm."

"Well, the elm in our meadow."

"Didn't know you owned a meadow."

"Oh, well—Miss Mortlock's meadow. She lets us play in it. Shall I let you know when they're going to cut the elm down?"

"If you like."

Later still that day, Toffy, a friend of Bones Jones's, spoke to Ricky, which he did not often bother to do. He said: "I hope they cut that tree down after school, or on a Saturday. Otherwise we'll miss it." So Bones Jones had told Toffy and the others.

And when they were all going home from school, Bones Jones called to Ricky: "Don't forget to find out about what you said. Might be worth watching."

Surprisingly Ricky had difficulty in getting his piece of information. His father was vague, even mysterious, about when exactly the elm would be felled. He glanced several times at his wife, during Ricky's questioning. She listened in silence, grim.

So Ricky first knew when, looking out of his window just after getting up one morning, he saw a truck in the meadow, with a ladder on its roof, and two men unloading gear that would clearly turn out to be saw, ax, wedges, and rope.

At breakfast his mother said to his father: "If they start now, they'll have finished before the afternoon, won't they?"

"Likely," said Mr. Scarr.

"So that wicked tree'll be safely down by the time you get home from school," his mother said to Ricky. Ricky scowled.

But there was still one chance, and Ricky thought it worth taking.

On the way to school he told Willy Jim; in the playground he told Bones Jones, Toffy, and the two others who made up the gang. "They're starting on the elm this morning. If we go to the meadow between the end of school lunch and the beginning of afternoon school, we might be lucky. We might see the fall."

The older children were allowed out of school after lunch to go to the sweetshop. The six boys would need only to turn right toward the lane, instead of left toward the sweetshop, when they set off at the permitted time. They would have about twenty minutes.

So, between one o'clock and a quarter past, the whole gang,

including Ricky, were tearing down the lane to Miss Mortlock's meadow. They halted at the meadow gate, surprised; Ricky himself felt abashed. The truck and handymen had gone, although wheel tracks showed they had been there. The elm still stood. At first sight, nothing had happened or was going to happen.

Then they noticed something about the base of the tree. They climbed the gate and went over. A wide gash had been chopped out of the trunk on the side toward the river. On the opposite side, at the same level, the tree had been sawed almost half through.

Ricky, remembering his father's talk, said: "They'll drive the wedges in there, where they've sawed. When the time comes."

It now occurred to them to wonder where *they* were—the handymen, the tree fellers. Toffy recollected having noticed a truck going up the village in the direction of The Peacock. The handymen, having done most of the hard work, had probably gone to get a beer at The Peacock. After that, they would come back and finish the job.

Meanwhile the boys had the elm tree to themselves.

They were examining the saw cut, all except for Ricky. He had gone round almost to the other side of the tree. Clasping the trunk with his arms, he pressed his body close against it, tipped his head back, and let his gaze go mountaineering up into the tree—up—up.

Then he saw it and wondered that he had not noticed it at once: the rope. It had been secured to the main part of the tree as near to the top as possible. Its length fell straight through the branches to the ground, passing near the fingertips of one of his hands. It reached the ground, where more of it—much more of it—lay at the foot of the tree, coiled around and ready for use.

"Look!" said Ricky.

The others came round the tree and gathered where the rope fell, staring at it, then staring up into the tree, to where the end was fastened, then staring across the meadow toward the river.

Bones Jones said: "We could take the rope out over the meadow. That wouldn't do any harm."

Toffy said: "Not with us not pulling on it."

Willy Jim said: "And not with the wedges not in."

Ricky said nothing.

All the same they were very careful to take the loose end of the rope over the meadow toward the river, keeping as far as possible from the buildings on either side. They walked backward toward the river, dragging the rope. At first, it dragged slackly through the rough grass of the meadow. Then, as they walked with it, it began to lift a little from the ground. They still walked, and the deep, floppy curve of it began to grow shallower and shallower—nearer and nearer to a straight line running from the boys to the top of the elm tree. They pulled it almost taut and paused.

Toffy said: "This is about where they'll stand."

Bones Jones said: "And pull."

They arranged themselves in what seemed to them a correct order along the rope, with the heaviest at the end. That was Bones Jones himself. Then came Toffy, then the other two and Willy Jim, and lastly Ricky, the lightest of all, nearest to the tree.

"And pull," repeated Bones Jones, and they pulled very gently, slightly tautening the rope, so that it ran from their hands in that straight, straight line to the top of the elm tree.

The cows that were grazing in the meadow had moved off slowly but intently to the farthest distance, against the old stables.

"Only the pulling would have to be in time," said Bones Jones. "You know, one, two, three, *pull*, rest; one, two, three, *pull*, rest. Feeling the sway of the tree, once it started swaying. Before it falls."

Miss Mortlock's dog, a King Charles spaniel, appeared at the gate into the meadow and stared at the boys. He was old, and he didn't like boys, but this was his meadow. He came through the gate and toward what was going on. He stood between the tree and the boys, but some way off, watching. After a while he sat down, with the regretful slowness of someone who has forgotten to bring his shooting stick.

They were getting the rhythm now, slow but strong: "one, two, three, and *pull*, rest; one, two, three, and *pull*, rest. . . ." They were chanting in perfect time under their breaths; in perfect time they were pulling, gently, well.

Mrs. Scarr, looking up from her sink and out through the kitchen window, might have seen them, but the sweetbriar hedge was in the way.

Miss Mortlock did see them, from an upper window. She had gone up to take an after-lunch nap on her bed and was about to draw the curtains. She looked out. Her eyesight was not good nowadays, but she knew boys when she saw them, and she knew at once what they must be doing. She saw that the elm tree was beginning a slow, graceful waving of its topmost branches. Very slightly: thisaway; thataway. Only each time it swayed, the sway was more thisaway, toward the river, than thataway, toward the house.

Thisaway, thataway . . .

Miss Mortlock knocked on the windowpane with her knuckles, but the boys could not hear the distant tapping. She called, but they could not hear her old woman's voice. She tried to push open the window, but that window had not been opened at the bottom for twenty years, and it was not going to be rushed now.

Thisaway, thataway; *this*away, thataway—

"Pull . . ." the boys chanted, ". . . and *pull* . . . and *pull*. . . ."

They did not hear the sound of the truck driving up to the meadow gate again. The two handymen saw. They began to shout even before they were out of the truck: "No!"

The cows lifted their heads to look toward the elm.

"Oh, no!" cried Miss Mortlock from the wrong side of the window glass.

The King Charles spaniel stood up and began to growl.

". . . and *pull* . . . and *pull* . . ."

"No!" whispered Ricky to himself.

For the rope they pulled on was no longer taut, even when they pulled it. It came slackly to them. There was a great, unimaginable creak, and then the elm began to lean courteously toward them. They stood staring, and the tree leaned over—over—reaching its tallness to reach them, and they saw what only the birds and the airplanes had ever seen before—the very crown of the tree—and it was roaring down toward them.

"NO!" screamed Ricky, who was nearest to it, seeing right into those reaching topmost branches that only the birds and the airplanes saw, and the other boys were yelling and scattering, and Miss Mortlock's window shot up suddenly, and she was calling shrilly out of it, and the handymen were vaulting the gate and shouting, and the King Charles spaniel was barking, and the elm tree that had stood forever was crashing to the ground, and Ricky was running, running, running from it, and then tripped and fell face forward into the nettles on the riverbank and staggered to his feet to run again, but suddenly there was nothing to run on, and fell again. Into the river this time.

The river was not deep or swift-flowing, but muddy. He wallowed and floundered to the bank and clawed a hold there and stood, thigh-deep in water, against the bank, still below visibility from the meadow. He listened. There were the mingled sounds of boys shouting and men shouting and a dog barking. He guessed that the men were chasing the boys, and the dog was getting in the way.

But he didn't stay. He waded along the river, in the shelter of the vegetation on its bank, until he reached the end of the meadow. The boundary of the meadow, on this side, was a sweetbriar hedge that, farther up, became the hedge of the Scarrs' garden. He crept out and crept home.

His face tingled all over and had already swollen—even to the eyelids—with nettle stings, and he was dripping with river water and with river mud that stank. His mother, meeting him at the door and having—at last; who could miss it now?—realized what had happened in the meadow, dealt with him.

No question of his going back to afternoon school; he ended up in bed. His mother rattled the curtains together angrily and told him to stay exactly where he was until his dad came home.

When she had gone, he slid out of bed and laid a hand on the curtains to part them. But he did not. There was no sound of voices from the meadow now, and he didn't really want to see. He had thought he wanted to, but he did not. He went back to bed.

His father, home for tea, was far less angry than his mother. He liked the idea of half a dozen schoolboys felling the elm tree by accident—and Ricky among them. "Didn't think you had it in you," he said to Ricky.

As for punishment, the state of Ricky's face was about as much as was needed, in Mr. Scarr's opinion.

And anyway, said Mr. Scarr, nobody had expressly told the boy not to fell the tree. Then Mrs. Scarr became very angry with Mr. Scarr, as well as with Ricky.

Next day at school there was a row, but not too bad. It was over quickly. The rest of the gang had had theirs yesterday. In the playground, Willy Jim said to Ricky, "You can go around with us, Bones says. We call ourselves Hell Fellows now—Hell Fellers—*fellers*, get it?"

"Oh," said Ricky, "you're one?"

"Yes," said Willy Jim, "and you can be one, too."

So that was all right, of course. Ricky had what he wanted.

Bones Jones decided that after school the Hell Fellers would go and look at the tree they had felled. No use going straight from school, however, as Ricky said, because the men would be there, lopping and sawing. So they all went home first to their teas and then reassembled, singly, carefully casual, at the top of the lane—all except for Ricky, of course, who had his tea and then hung over his front gate, waiting.

When daylight began to fail, the handymen stopped work, packed everything into the truck, shut the meadow gate, and drove away. They drove out of the top of the lane, and behind them, the boys converged on the entrance to the lane and poured down it. They collected Ricky as they passed his house, then over the meadow gate and across the meadow to the elm.

Most of its branches had already gone, so that they could clamber up it and along it fairly easily. Bones Jones, Willy Jim, Ricky—all of them—they clambered, climbed on and jumped off, ran along the trunk. They fought duels along the trunk with lopped-off branches and nearly put each other's eyes out, played a no-holds-barred King of the Castle on the tree stump, carved their initials in the thickness of the main bark. All they did, they did quietly—with whispers, gasps, grunts, suppressed laughter—for they did not wish to call attention to themselves. There was little fear, otherwise, of their being noticed in the half-light.

Now they gathered together in a line along the trunk. Ricky was in the middle. They linked arms and danced, stamping and singing softly together a song of victory, of Hell Fellers, hell-bent, of victors over the vanquished. The stamping of their feet hardly shook the massive tree trunk beneath them.

The meadow was almost dark now. Like ghosts, they danced along the long ghost of what had once been a tree.

Oblongs of yellow light had appeared in the houses overlooking the meadow. The dancers began to waver. They shivered at the chill of night and remembered their homes. They stopped dancing. They left the tree trunk, climbed the gate, went home.

Ricky went home. He was still humming the tune to which they had danced. "You seem pleased with yourself," his mother said grumpily. She had not got over yesterday.

Ricky said, "Yes."

When he was going to bed, he looked out of his window, across the meadow. It was quite dark outside, but you could still see which was sky and which was not. He could make out the blackness of the old stables against the sky. There was nothing between him and them. He stared till his eyes watered.

He got into bed thinking of tomorrow and the Hell Fellers at school, pleased. He fell asleep at once and began dreaming. His own tears woke him. He could not remember his dream and knew that it had not lasted long because the same television program was still going on downstairs.

In the middle of being puzzled at grief, he fell asleep again.

Fresh ❖

*T*he force of water through the river gates scoured to a deep bottom; then the river shallowed again. People said the pool below the gates was very deep. Deep enough to drown in, anyway.

At the bottom of the pool lived the freshwater mussels. No one had seen them there; most people would not have been particularly interested in them, anyway. But if you were poking about among the stones in the shallows below the pool, you couldn't help finding mussel shells occasionally. Sometimes one by itself; sometimes two still hinged together. Gray-blue or green-gray on the outside; on the inside, a faint sheen of mother-of-pearl.

The Webster boys were fishing with their nets in the shallows for minnows, freshwater shrimps—anything that moved—when they found a freshwater mussel that was not just a pair of empty shells.

Dan Webster found it. He said: "Do you want this shell? It's double." While Laurie Webster was saying, "Let's see," Dan was lifting it and had noticed that the two shells were clamped together and that they had unusual weight. "They're not empty shells," he said. "They've something inside. It's alive."

He stooped again to hold the mussel in the palm of his hand so that the river water washed over it. Water creatures prefer water.

Laurie had splashed over to him. Now he crouched with the river lapping near the tops of his Wellington boots. "A freshwater mussel!" he said. "I've never owned one." He put out fingers to touch it—perhaps to take it—as it lay on the watery palm of Dan's hand.

Dan's fingers curled up into a protective wall. "Careful," he said.

Together, as they were now, the Webster boys looked like brothers, but they were cousins. Laurie was the visitor. He lived in London and had an aquarium on his bedroom windowsill, instead of a river almost at his back door as Dan had. Dan was older than Laurie; Laurie admired Dan, and Dan was kind to Laurie. They did things together. Dan helped Laurie to find livestock for his aquarium—shrimps, leeches, flatworms, water snails variously whorled; whatever the turned stone and scooping net might bring them. During a visit by Laurie they would fish often, but—until the last day—without a jam jar, just for the fun of it. On the last day they took a jam jar and put their more interesting catches into it for Laurie's journey back to London.

Now they had found a freshwater mussel on the second day of Laurie's visit. Five more days still to go.

"We can't keep it," said Dan. "Even if we got the jam jar, it couldn't live in a jam jar for five days. It would be dead by the time you got it back to the aquarium."

Laurie, who was quite young, looked as if he might cry. "I've never had the chance of a freshwater mussel before."

"Well . . ." said Dan. He made as if to put it down among the stones and mud where he had found it.

"Don't! Don't! It's my freshwater mussel! Don't let it go!"

"And don't shout in my ear!" Dan said crossly. "Who said I was letting it go? I was just trying it out in the river again, to see whether it was safe to leave it there. I don't think the current would carry it away."

He put the mussel down in the shelter of a large, slimy stone. The current, breaking on the stone, flowed past without stirring it. But the mussel began to feel at home again. They could almost see it settling contentedly into the mud. After a while it parted the lips of its shells slightly, and a pastrylike substance crowded out a little way.

"What's it *doing?*" whispered Laurie. But this was not the sort of thing that Dan knew, and Laurie would not find out until he got back to his aquarium books in London.

Now they saw that they had not merely imagined the mussel to be settling in. There was less of it visible out of the mud—much less of it.

"It's burying itself. It's escaping," said Laurie. "Don't let it!"

Dan sighed and took the mussel back into the palm of his hand again. The mussel, disappointed, shut up tight.

"We need to keep it in the river," said Dan, "but somewhere where it can't escape."

They looked around. They weren't sure what they were looking for, and at first they certainly weren't finding it.

Still with the mussel in his hand, Dan turned to the banks. They were overhanging, with river water swirling against them and under them. The roots of trees and bushes made a kind of very irregular lattice fencing through which the water ran continually.

"I wonder . . ." said Dan.

"You couldn't keep it there," Laurie said. "It'd be child's play for a freshwater mussel to escape through the roots."

Dan stared at the roots. "I've a better idea," he said. "I'll stay here with the mussel. You go back to our house—to the larder. You'll find a little white plastic carton with Eileen's slimming cress growing in it." Eileen was Dan's elder sister, whose absorbing interest was her figure. "Empty the cress out onto a plate; I'll square Eileen later. Bring the plastic carton back here."

Laurie never questioned Dan. He set off across the meadows toward the house.

Dan and the freshwater mussel were left alone to wait.

Dan was holding the freshwater mussel as he had done before, stooping down to the river with his hand in the water. It occurred to him to repeat the experiment that Laurie had interrupted. He put the mussel down in the lee of the slimy stone again and watched. Again the current left the mussel undisturbed. Again the mussel began to settle itself into the mud between the stones.

Down—gently down—down . . . The freshwater mussel was now as deep in the mud as when Laurie had called out in fear of losing it, but now Laurie was not there. Dan did not interfere. He simply watched the mussel ease itself down—down. . . .

Soon less than a quarter of an inch of mussel shell was showing above the mud. The shell was nearly the same color as the mud embedding it; Dan could identify it only by keeping his eyes fixed continuously upon its projection. That lessened, until it had almost disappeared.

Entirely disappeared . . .

Still Dan stared. As long as he kept his eyes on the spot where the mussel had disappeared, he could get it again. He had only to dig his fingers into the mud at that exact spot to find it. If he let his eyes stray, the mussel was lost forever; there were so many slimy stones like that one, and mud was everywhere. He must keep his eyes fixed on the spot.

"Dan—Dan—Dan!" Laurie's voice came over the meadows. "I've got it!"

He nearly shifted his stare from the spot by the nondescript stone. It would have been so natural to lift his head in response to the calling voice. He was tempted to do it. But he had to remember that this was Laurie's mussel and it must not be lost; he did remember. He kept his gaze fixed and dug quickly with his fingers and got the mussel again.

There he was standing with the mussel in the palm of his hand, and water and mud dripping from it, when Laurie came in sight. "Is it all right?" he shouted.

"Yes," said Dan.

Laurie climbed down the riverbank into the water with the plastic carton in his hand. Dan looked at it and nodded. "It has holes in the bottom, and we can make some more along the sides with a penknife." He did so, while Laurie held the mussel.

"Now," Dan said, "put the mussel in the carton with some mud and little stones to make it comfortable. That's it. The next thing is to wedge the carton between the roots under the bank at just the right level, so that the water flows through the holes in the carton, without flowing over the whole thing. The mussel will have his flowing river, but he won't be able to escape."

Laurie said, "I wish I could think of things like that."

Dan tried fitting the plastic carton between the roots in several different places, until he found a grip that was just at the right height. Gently he tested the firmness of the wedging, and it held.

"Oh," said Laurie, "it's just perfect, Dan. Thank you. I shall really get it back to the aquarium now. My first freshwater mussel. I shall call it—well, what would *you* call it, Dan?"

"Go on," said Dan. "It's your freshwater mussel. You name it."

"I shall call it Fresh then." Laurie leaned forward to see Fresh, already part buried in his mud, dim in the shadow of the bank, but absolutely a captive. He stood up again and moved back to admire the arrangement from a distance. Then he realized a weakness. "Oh, it'll never do. The plastic's so white. Anyone might notice it and come over to look and tip Fresh out."

"We'll hide him then," said Dan. He found an old brick among the stones of the shallows and brought it over to the bank roots. He upended the brick in the water, leaning it in a casual pose against the roots, so that it concealed the white plastic carton altogether.

"There," he said.

Laurie sighed. "Really perfect."

"He should be safe there."

"For five days?"

"I tell you what," said Dan, "we could slip down here every day just to have a check on him. To make sure the level of the water through the carton isn't too high or hasn't sunk too low."

Laurie nodded. "Every day."

The daily visit to Fresh was a pleasure that Laurie looked forward to. On the third day it poured with rain, but they put on anoraks as well as boots and made their check as usual. On the fourth day they reached the riverbank to find a man fishing on the other side of the pool.

The fisherman was minding his own business and only gave them a sidelong glance as they came to a stop on the bank above Fresh's watery dungeon. (They knew its location exactly by now, even from across the meadow.) The man wasn't interested in them—yet. But if they clambered down into the river and began moving old bricks and poking about behind them, he would take notice. He would ask them what they were up to. When they had gone, he would perhaps come over and have a look for himself. He was wearing waders.

"Not now," Dan said quietly. "Later." And they turned away, as though they had come only to look at the view.

They went back after their tea, but the fisherman was still there. In the meantime Laurie had worked himself into a desperation. "All that rain yesterday has made the river rise. It'll be washing Fresh out of the carton."

"No," said Dan. "You've just got Fresh on the brain. The river's hardly risen at all. If at all. Fresh is all right."

"Why can't that man go home?"

"He'll go home at dusk, anyway," said Dan.

"That'll be too late for us. I shall be going to bed by then. You know your mum said I must."

"Yes." Dan looked at him thoughtfully. "Would you like *me* to come? I mean, Mum couldn't stop my being out that bit later than you, because I am that bit older."

"Oh, would you—*would* you?" cried Laurie. "Oh, thanks, Dan."

"Oh, don't thank me," said Dan.

Everything went according to plan, except that Dan, getting down to the river just before dark, found the fisherman still there. But he was in the act of packing up. He did not see Dan. He packed up and walked away, whistling sadly to himself. When the whistling had died away, Dan got down into the river and moved the brick and took out the plastic container. It had been at a safe water level, in spite of the rains, and Fresh was inside, alive and well.

Dan took Fresh out of the carton just to make sure. Then he put him among the stones in the river for the fun of seeing his disappearing act. As he watched, Dan reflected that this was what Fresh would have done if the fisherman *had* spotted the carton and taken him out of it for a good look and then by mistake dropped him into the water. The fisherman would have lost sight of him, and Fresh would have buried himself. He would have been gone for good—for good, back into the river.

The only signs would have been the brick moved, the plastic container out of place. And Fresh gone. That was all that Dan could have reported to Laurie.

But it had not happened, after all.

Dan picked up Fresh and put him back in the carton and put the carton back and then the brick, and then walked home. He told Laurie, sitting in his pajamas in front of the TV with his supper, that everything had been all right. He did not say more.

On the fifth day, the day before Laurie's return to London, they went together to the riverbank. There was no fisherman. The brick was exactly in place, and behind it the plastic carton, with the water flowing through correctly. There was Fresh, safe, sound, and apparently not even pining at captivity.

"Tomorrow," said Laurie. "Tomorrow morning we'll bring the jam jar, ready for me to take him home on the train."

That night was the last of Laurie's visit. He and Dan shared Dan's bedroom, and tonight they went to bed at the same time and fell asleep together.

Dan's father was the last person to go to bed at the end of the evening. He bolted the doors and turned out the last lights. That usually did not wake Dan, but tonight it did. Suddenly he was wide-awake in the complete darkness, hearing the sound of his parents going to bed in their room, hearing the sound of Laurie's breathing in the next bed, the slow, whispering breath of deep sleep.

The movements and murmurs from the other bedroom ceased; Laurie's breathing continued evenly. Dan still lay wide-awake.

He had never really noticed before how very dark everything could be. It was more than blackness; it seemed to fill space as water fills a pool. It seemed to fill the inside of his head.

He lay for some time with the darkness everywhere; then he got up very quietly. He put trousers and sweater on over his pajamas, bunchily. Laurie's breathing never changed. He tiptoed out of the bedroom and downstairs. In the hall he put on his Wellington boots. He let himself out of the house and then through the front gate. There was no one about, no lights in the houses, except for a night-light where a child slept. There was one lamp in the lane, and that sent his shadow leaping horribly ahead of him. Then he turned a corner and the lamplight had gone. He was taking the shortcut toward the river.

No moon tonight. No stars. Darkness . . .

He had been born here; he had always lived here; he knew these meadows as well as he knew himself, but the darkness made him afraid. He could not see the familiar way ahead; he had to remember it. He felt his way. He scented it. He smelled the river before he came to it, and he felt the vegetation changing underfoot, growing ranker when he reached the bank.

He lowered himself into the water, from darkness into darkness. He began to feel along the roots of the bank for the upended brick. He found it quickly; he had not been far out in the point at which he had struck the bank.

His hand was on the brick, and he kept it there while he tried to see. In the darkness and through the darkness he tried to see what was going to happen—what he was going to make happen. What he was going to do.

Now that he was no longer moving, he could hear the sound of other movements in the darkness. He heard the water flowing. He heard a *drip* of water into water somewhere near him, a long pause, another *drip*. He heard a quick, quiet birdcall that was strange to him; certainly not an owl—he used to hear those as he lay snug in bed in his bedroom at home. And whatever sound he heard now, he heard beneath it the ceaseless watery whispering sound of the river, as if the river were alive and breathing in its sleep in the darkness, like Laurie left sleeping in the bedroom at home.

It was within his power to move the brick and take hold of the plastic carton and tip it right over. Fresh would fall into the water with a *plop* so tiny that he might never hear it above the flow of the river. In such darkness there would be no question of finding Fresh again, ever.

If he meant to do it, he could do it in three seconds. His hand was on the brick.

But did he mean to do it?

He tried to see what was in his mind, but his mind was like a deep pool of darkness. He didn't know what he really meant to do.

Suddenly he took his hand from the brick and stood erect. He put his booted foot on one of the lateral roots that extended behind the brick. He had to feel for it with his toe. Having found it, he pressed it slowly downward, then quickly took his foot off again. He could feel the root, released from the pressure, following his foot upward again in a little jerk.

That jerk of the root might have been enough to upset or at least tilt the carton. It might have been enough to tip Fresh out into the river.

On the other hand, of course, it might not have been enough.

Dan flung himself at the bank well to one side of the brick and clambered up and began a blundering run across the meadows. He did not slow up or go more carefully until he reached the lamplight of the lane and the possibility of someone's hearing his footsteps.

He let himself into the house and secured the door behind him. He left his boots in the hall and his clothes on the chair in the bedroom. He crept back into bed. Laurie was still breathing gently and regularly.

Dan slept late the next morning. He woke to bright sunshine flooding the room and Laurie banging on the bedrail. "Fresh! Fresh! Fresh!" he was chanting. Dan looked at him through eyes half shut. He was trying to remember a dream he had had last night. It had been a dream of darkness—too dark to remember or to want to remember.

But when he went downstairs to breakfast and saw his boots in the hall with mud still drying on them, he knew that he had not dreamed last night.

Immediately after breakfast they went down to the river. Laurie was carrying his jam jar.

They climbed down into the shallows as usual. Laurie made a little sound of dismay when he saw the brick. "It's lopsided; the current's moved it!"

Dan stood at a distance in the shallows while Laurie scrabbled the brick down into the water with a splash. There behind it was the white plastic carton, but at a considerable tilt, so that water flowed steadily from its lowest corner. "Oh, Fresh, Fresh!" Laurie implored in a whisper. He was peering into the carton.

"Well?" said Dan, from his distance, not moving.

"Oh, no!" Laurie exclaimed, low but in dismay.

"Well?"

Laurie was poking with a finger at the bottom of the carton. Suddenly he laughed. "He's here after all! It's all right! It was just that burying trick of his! Fresh is here!"

Laurie was beaming.

Dan said, "I'm glad."

Laurie transferred Fresh from the carton to the jam jar, together with some mud and stones and a suitable amount of river water. Dan watched him.

Then they both set off across the meadows again, Laurie holding the jam jar carefully, as he would need to do—as he *would* do—during all the long journey to London. He was humming to himself. He stopped to say to Dan, "I say, I did thank you for Fresh, didn't I?"

"Don't thank me," said Dan.

Who's Afraid? ❖

"**Will** my cousin Dicky be there?"

"Everyone's been asked. Cousins, aunts, uncles, great-aunts, great-uncles—the lot. I've told you: it's your great-grandmother's hundredth birthday party."

"But will Dicky Hutt be there?"

"I'm sure he will be."

"Anyway, Joe, why do you want to know?"

Joe's mother and father were staring at Joe. And Joe said, "I hate Dicky."

"Now, Joe!" said his mother, and his father asked, "Why on earth do you hate Dicky?"

"I just do," said Joe. He turned away, to end the conversation, but inside his head he was saying: I'd like to kill Dicky Hutt. Before he tries to kill me.

When the day of the birthday came, everyone—just as Joe's mother had said—was there. Relations of all ages swarmed over the little house where Great-grandmother lived, looked after by Great-aunt Madge. Fortunately, Great-grandmother had been born in the summer, and now—a hundred years later—the sun shone warmly on her celebrations. Great-aunt Madge shooed everyone into the garden for the photograph. The grown-ups sat on chairs or stood in rows, and the children sat cross-legged in a row in the very front. (At one end, Joe, at the other, Dicky, and Dicky's stare at Joe said: "If I catch you, I'll kill you. . . ." There was a gap in the center of this front row for a table with the tiered birthday cake and its hundred candles.

And behind the cake sat Great-grandmother in her wheelchair, with one shawl over her knees and another round her shoulders. Great-aunt Madge stood just behind her.

Great-grandmother faced the camera with a steady gaze from eyes that saw nothing by now; she had become blind in old age. Whether she heard much was doubtful. Certainly, she never spoke or turned her head even a fraction as if to listen.

After the photograph and the cutting of the cake, the grown-ups stood around drinking tea and talking. (Great-grandmother had been wheeled off somewhere indoors for a rest.) The children, if they were very young, clung to their parents; the older ones sidled about aimlessly—aimlessly, except that Joe could see Dicky always sidling toward him, staring his hatred. So Joe sidled away and sidled away. . . .

"Children!" cried Great-aunt Madge. "What about a good old game? What about hide-and-seek? There's the garden to hide in, and most of the house."

Some of the children still clung to their parents; others said yes to hide-and-seek. Dicky Hutt said yes. Joe said no, but his father said impatiently, "Don't be soft! Go off and play with the others."

Dicky Hutt shouted, "I'll be He!" So he was. Dicky Hutt shut his eyes and began to count at once. When he had counted a hundred, he would open his eyes and begin to search.

Joe knew whom he would search for with the bitterest thoroughness: himself.

Joe was afraid, too afraid to think well. He thought at first that he would hide in the garden, where there were at least grown-ups about, but then he didn't trust Dicky not to be secretly watching under his eyelashes, to see exactly where he went. Joe couldn't bear the thought of that.

So, after all, he went indoors to hide, but by then some of the best hiding places had been taken. And out in the garden Dicky Hutt was counting fast, shouting aloud his total at every count of ten. "Seventy!" he was shouting now, and Joe had just looked behind the sofa in the front room, and there was already someone crouching there. And there was also someone hiding under the pile of visitors' coats— "Eighty!" came Dicky Hutt's voice from the garden—and two children already in the stair cupboard, when he thought of that hiding place. So he must go on looking for somewhere—anywhere—to hide—and "Ninety!" from outside—*anywhere* to hide—and for the second time he came to the door with the notice pinned to it that said: KEEP OUT! SIGNED: MADGE.

"A hundred! I'm coming!" shouted Dicky Hutt. And Joe turned the handle of the forbidden door and slipped inside and shut the door behind him.

The room was very dim, because the curtains had been drawn close, and its quietness seemed empty. But Joe's eyes began to be able to pick out the furnishings of the room, even in the half-light: table, chair, roll-top desk, and also—like just another piece of furniture, and just as immobile—Great-grandmother's wheelchair and Great-grandmother sitting in it.

He stood, she sat, both silent, still, and Dicky Hutt's thundering footsteps and voice were outside, passing the door and then far away.

He thought she did not know that he had come into her room, but a low, slow voice reached him: "Who's there?"

He whispered, "It's only me—Joe."

Silence, and then the low, slow voice again: "Who's there?"

He was moving toward her, to speak in her very ear, when she spoke a third time: "Who's there?"

And this time he heard in her voice the little tremble of fear; he recognized it. He came to her chair and laid his hand on hers. For a second he felt her weakly pull away, and then she let his hand rest but turned her own, so that his hand fell into hers. She held his hand, fingered it slowly. He wanted her to know that he meant her no harm; he wanted her to say: "This is a small hand, a child's hand. You are only a child, after all."

But she did not speak again.

He stood there, she sat there, and the excited screams and laughter and running footsteps of hide-and-seek were very far away.

At last, Joe could tell from the sounds outside that the game of hide-and-seek was nearly over. He must be the last player not to be found and chased by Dicky Hutt. For now Dicky Hutt was wandering about, calling, "Come out, Joe! I know where you're hiding, Joe, so you might as well come out! I shall find you, Joe. I shall find you!"

The roving footsteps passed the forbidden doorway several times, but—no, this time they did not pass. Dicky Hutt had stopped outside.

The silence outside the door made Joe tremble. He tried to stop trembling, for the sake of the hand that held his, but he could not. He felt that old, old skin-and-bony hand close on his, as if questioning what was happening, what was wrong.

But he had no voice to explain to her. He had no voice at all.

His eyes were on the knob of the door. Even through the gloom he could see that it was turning. Then the door was creeping open—not fast, but steadily; not far, but far enough.

It opened far enough for Dicky Hutt to slip through. He stood there, inside the dim room. Joe could see his bulk there. Dicky Hutt had always been bigger than he was; now he loomed huge. And he was staring directly at Joe.

Joe's whole body was shaking. He felt as if he were shaking to pieces. He wished that he could.

His great-grandmother held his shaking hand in hers.

Dicky Hutt took a step forward into the room.

Joe had no hope. He felt his great-grandmother lean forward a little in her chair, tightening her grip on his hand as she did so. In her low, slow voice she was saying: "Who—" And Joe thought, He won't bother to answer her; he'll just come for me. He'll come for me. . . .

But the low, slow voice went on: "Whooooooooooooooo—" She was hooting like some ghost-throated owl, and then the hooting raised itself into a thin, eerie wailing. Next, through the wailing, she began to gibber, with effect so startling—so horrifying—that Joe forgot Dicky Hutt for a moment and turned to look at her. His great-grandmother's mouth was partly open, and she was making her false teeth do a kind of devil's dance inside it.

And when Joe looked toward Dicky Hutt again, he had gone. The door was closing, the knob turning. The door clicked shut, and Joe could hear Dicky Hutt's feet tiptoeing away.

When Joe looked at his great-grandmother again, she was sitting back in her chair. Her mouth was closed; the gibbering and the hooting and the wailing had ceased. She looked exhausted—or had she died? But no, she was just looking unbelievably old.

He did not disturb her. He stood by her chair some time longer. Then he heard his parents calling all over the house for him; they wanted to go home.

He moved his hand out of hers; the grasp was slack now. Perhaps she had fallen asleep. He thought he wanted to kiss her good-bye, but then he did not want the feel of that century-old cheek against his lips.

So he simply slipped away from her and out of the room.

He never saw her again. Nearly a year later, at home, the news came of her death. Joe's mother said, "Poor old thing . . ."

Joe's father (whose grandmother Great-grandmother had been) said, "When I was a little boy, she was fun. I remember her. Jokey, then; full of tricks . . ."

Joe's mother said, "Well, she'd outlived all that. Outlived everything. Too old to be any use to herself—or to anyone else. A burden, only."

Joe said nothing, but he wished now that he had kissed her cheek, to say good-bye and to thank her.

Still Jim and
Silent Jim ❖

*O*ld James Heslop came to live with his daughter-in-law when young Jim was still a baby. By then Mrs. Heslop was a widow with four children, young Jim being the last. She was glad to take in old Jim to live with the family. It was true that he overcrowded an already crowded little house, and since he could not get up and down stairs, he had to have the downstairs room which had the television set in it. On the other hand, he gave his daughter-in-law nearly all his old age pension, as his share of the housekeeping expenses. Besides, Mrs. Heslop, hard-worked and harassed and sharp-tongued even to her children, had a kind heart. "When you're old, you need a real home," she said. "This is Granddad's as long as he wants it."

Old Jim was less trouble than might have been supposed. Take the television set, for instance. He was not at all interested in watching television, but as he was stone deaf, he did not mind the rest of the Heslop family having it on in his room. Indeed, as long as his chair was turned so that he need not look directly at the screen, he enjoyed it. "That makes a flickering on the walls, like firelight," he would remark.

"And you don't always get the chance of an open fire to sit by these days."

Another convenience of old Jim's deafness was that he did not mind the noisiness of the three elder Heslop children, and of young Jim, who never said much, anyway, he was very fond. It was a mutual affection. As soon as he could crawl, young Jim crawled around his grandfather's chair, and he first stood upright, rocking on unsteady legs, the better to listen to the deep, booming voice that was all the louder for old Jim's never hearing it himself. Young Jim listened before ever he could have understood what was being said; even later he very rarely attempted a word in reply. In summer, old Jim's chair was put out into the front garden, and he sat in the sun, with his hands motionless on the rug over his knees, statuelike except for his jaw, which moved when he spoke, and young Jim roamed about the flower borders, listening but silent. That was how the pair got their nickname from the neighbors: Still Jim and Silent Jim.

Young Jim was so silent that the neighbors said privately that he must be simpleminded, but when he went to school, he proved otherwise. He still spoke as little as possible, but he learned as well as anyone.

Even before young Jim had learned to read properly, he began bringing books home to show to his grandfather. The old man's eyesight was still good, and he read the text and looked at the pictures and told Silent Jim what he thought. Old Jim enjoyed books of history especially. He sighed and shook his head over them. "Ah! Those days!" he said, and it cannot always have been very clear to young Jim whether those days had been his grandfather's or days of long, long before his grandfather's birth. Old Jim pored over illustrations of the earliest motorcar and the penny-farthing bicycle, and before that the stagecoach, and the packhorse, and the Roman chariot. "Ah! Those days, those days! And the men that lived then! Why, they were giants on the earth in those days!" The neighbors, overhearing the old man, would smile and tap their foreheads, for they were sure that if Silent Jim were not simpleminded, Still Jim had become so—at least a little.

The rest of the Heslop family did not believe it of their grandfather, but they paid no attention to him—that is, all except for young Jim. He listened closely, staring with eyes just the blue of his grandfather's but not yet faded with extreme age.

Old Jim had been over eighty when he moved into the Heslops' television room, so he must have been over ninety when young Jim was about ten. By then young Jim would occasionally—if necessary—start a conversation. One day he planted himself in front of his grandfather and said: "If you're over ninety, Granddad, you must be over sixty as well." He did not shout—that would have been of no use—but he used an oddly still voice that seemed to creep into old Jim's ears in a way that no bawling could have done. Besides, he stood where the old man could watch his lips, and he shaped them very distinctly in speaking.

"Aye," said old Jim.

"Then you could belong to the Over Sixties' Club up the village," said young Jim, and cocked his head at him. Old Jim cocked his head back, and they stared at each other for a while.

"There's a boy at school," said young Jim, "his granddad goes. They play dominoes, they do, and whist. They have cups of tea, they do, and birthday parties. It's in the Church Hall."

"How'd I get there?" said old Jim.

"Oh!" said young Jim, and stared and pondered, and at last wandered away. This was before the time that the eldest Heslop girl took up with nice young Steve from the garage, who could hire a car very cheaply for his friends.

A day or two later young Jim came to his grandfather and said: "There's wheelchairs that belong to the Over Sixties' Club."

Old Jim nodded, as though to congratulate young Jim on a fine piece of investigation.

"They cost nothing," said young Jim.

Old Jim nodded and stared at young Jim. This time young Jim nodded back.

No more was said on the subject, but the following Friday young

Jim pushed a wheelchair up to the Heslops' house and as near to the front doorstep as it could be got. Then he went in to fetch his grandfather. Mrs. Heslop came running, in agitation. "Whatever are you thinking of, Jim!" she cried. "You're never going to get your granddad into that chair—not with his heart, not with his joints, not at his age!"

"I'm going to the Over Sixties' Club," said old Jim. He threw aside his rug, and with a stick in one hand and the other hand on his grandson's shoulder, he struggled up out of his armchair.

When old Jim stood up, you saw that he was a tall old man—"six foot, even allowing for shrinkage," he always said, and then would add: "And my father was well over six foot, and my grandfather—that lies in the churchyard over in Little Barley—he was seven foot. You can see his tombstone there, like a giant's. Ah! Those days!"

Now, seeing him determinedly on his feet, Mrs. Heslop cried: "And look at yourself, Granddad! You're a big, heavy man, even if you are skin and bone! Young Jim can never push you all through the village to the Over Sixties' Club!"

"I can," said young Jim.

Old Jim reached the wheelchair and let himself down into it; young Jim lifted his legs in after him and put the rug over them. Then they set off.

"Anyway, you're to be careful!" Mrs. Heslop called after them. "You're to mind all that traffic on the London road!"

Great Barley, where the Heslops lived, was a busy, built-up village, with a main stream of traffic running through it on the way to London. "Not like the old days," said old Jim. "Great and Little Barley, they were both quiet then." Little Barley, being several miles away and quite off the main road, was still quiet. Hardly anyone went there.

Fortunately, to reach the Over Sixties' Club at the other end of Great Barley village, Silent Jim and Still Jim never had to cross the main road at all. They arrived safely.

The chief organizer welcomed them. She smiled in a kindly and congratulatory way at young Jim. "That must have been a long, hard push for a boy of your size. Now you must run off, and come back at five o'clock to take your grandfather home again. Children can't attend the club."

Young Jim stared at the chief organizer, answered nothing, and stood his ground. She said in a low voice to the other organizers, "I don't think he can understand." She turned to old Jim. "Your grandson . . ." she began.

Slowly he moved his hand up to cup it around his ear and looked inquiring. "I'm deaf," he explained, "deaf as a post, deaf as a stone."

"Your grandson . . ." shouted the chief organizer.

Old Jim shook his head. "No, I shall never hear." He looked at her pleasantly. "But you mustn't think I'm unhappy. I'm very happy. If I have young Jim with me, I'm all right. Never you mind us."

The chief organizer gave up, and young Jim remained with his grandfather—the only child regularly to attend the Over Sixties' Club. He sat by old Jim, watching him play at dominoes, holding his saucer for him when he drank tea, and picking the cake crumbs off his waistcoat. Young Jim himself drank tea and ate cake, but old Jim always paid for both of them, so that you could not say that the club was cheated of anything. Moreover, young Jim kept the wheelchair (they always used the same one) in apple-pie order, brushing out the bottom, where old Jim put his feet, polishing the metalwork, and oiling the little wheels in a vain attempt to get rid of their squeak. After a while the chief organizer said the wheelchair might be kept in the Heslops' outhouse, which was done.

At about this time Maisie Heslop began her friendship with young Steve from the garage. He suggested that one summer Sunday he should take the family on a day's outing to the seaside; he would hire the car and drive.

All the Heslops went. Mrs. Heslop sat at the front with Steve, and Maisie sat between them; she did not seem to mind being squeezed up a little. The other three children traveled at the back, and right across the backseat, underneath them all, traveled old Jim. It seemed hard on the old man—it was hard for them, too, because he was very bony—but he found it was the only way he could go in a car at all. "That's not a patch on a wheelchair," he whispered to young Jim, but what old Jim thought to be a whisper was something quite loud and clear. Everyone heard it, and Steve laughed, and Maisie went red with indignation.

Old Jim had to get into the car before the others, because he had great difficulty in bending his back and legs. First of all, he sat backward onto the seat, and some of the Heslops went around to the other side and leaned into the car and pulled him, and the remainder of the Heslops stayed at his legs' end and pushed him from there.

Old Jim puffed and groaned. "That's not worth it," he said. " 'Tisn't the way to travel, hemmed in"—he knocked his head against the roof of the car—"boxed down! That was different in the old days: carriages, and horses; room to move, fresh air! A wheelchair, now; that's a kind of carriage."

"You may like a wheelchair for some things," said Steve, "but it can't go as fast as a car."

"I've heard you say to young Jim that you wish sometimes he could push your wheelchair faster," said Mrs. Heslop.

"You'll never go anywhere farther than your old club, just in a wheelchair. In Steve's car we shall get to the seaside and back in a day," said Maisie.

Young Jim said nothing, because he never did, and the other two Heslop children were too busy pulling and pushing.

Old Jim said nothing because he had heard nothing.

By now old Jim was completely in the back of the car, but crosscorneredly, with his right elbow against the window of the right-hand door, his left elbow against the back window, and his toes turned up against the bottom of the left-hand door. He was in—just.

Having made sure that the door could be shut on him, the three younger Heslop children opened it again and climbed in on top of their grandfather. They sat where they could. Young Jim sat on old Jim's stomach, because someone had to sit there, and he was the lightest. Also, he was his grandfather's favorite.

So they set off. When they reached the seaside, old Jim was pulled out of the car and put into a deck chair. He was so breathless from the journey and so exhausted from getting in and out of the car that he dropped into sleep at once. He woke up for the picnic and again to be put back into the car. When they got home and they were all thanking Steve and saying what a good driver he was and what a nice car and what a pleasant trip, old Jim said loudly: "Never again!"

"Granddad!" said Mrs. Heslop reproachfully. "And after such a lovely day!"

"And Steve's having taken such trouble!" cried Maisie.

"Don't mind me," said Steve, for he really did not mind.

"They talk about modern improvements, I believe," said old Jim. "Some things are improvements; some aren't. Especially for people too old for them—or too big. I daresay I'm an old-fashioned size for traveling in a modern motorcar. What my grandfather would have done—he that was seven feet tall, broad, too . . ."

"It's not kind to Steve!" Maisie cried. "And I don't believe your old grandfather was seven feet high, so there!" And she burst into tears.

"What's she crying for?" asked old Jim. They all looked at young Jim to explain. He was silent, and Maisie went on crying.

"What did she say?" asked old Jim. "Nobody tells me anything nowadays; for some reason nobody speaks to me—except young Jim. Come on, Jim; you tell me what she said."

Young Jim looked uncertain, but he said: "She says it's not kind to Steve." Old Jim looked dumbfounded. "And she says she doesn't believe your grandfather was seven feet high, so there."

Old Jim put his head back, closing his eyes, as though he were too tired to speak. At last he said: "So that's what's behind it. They've never believed me. Everything's modern nowadays, and everybody's young and small, and they all believe that's the right thing, and the only thing, and that it was never any different. They don't believe in those old days."

"Oh, Granddad!" said Maisie, and began crying in a different way. "I didn't mean that. Young Jim, tell him I didn't really mean that."

"Granddad!" said young Jim, and took the old man's hand and

shook it gently until he opened his eyes. "Granddad, she says she didn't mean it."

"They don't mean me to know what they think," said old Jim, "but they think it all the same."

There was nothing more to be said. Maisie went on crying for some time, but on her mother's advice, she did not speak of the subject again.

The next time that Steve brought the car around to take the Heslops on a jaunt—to Whipsnade Zoo this time, to see the animals—old Mr. Heslop said he would stay at home. Maisie made him egg sandwiches for his tea and kissed him good-bye remorsefully. Silent Jim stayed with him, although he, too, loved to see strange animals.

The summer advanced. Every Friday young Jim pushed his grandfather's wheelchair through the village to the Over Sixties' Club. Then the organizers decided to close the club for the month of August because most people went on their holidays then. The Heslops could not really afford a holiday, but Steve from the garage took Maisie and the two middle children off to a seaside camp for a fortnight. Mrs. Heslop did not go; she said it would be holiday enough to be left in the house with three less children than usual. Old Jim did not go, because he said he didn't want to, and young Jim would not go, even at his mother's urging. He would not say why, but his grandfather looked at him sadly. "You'd have enjoyed the sea." Young Jim neither assented nor contradicted. "You shouldn't have stayed for me," said old Jim.

Young Jim thought that old Jim might be lonely, and old Jim worried that young Jim might be bored. Every day of that hot season the neighbors saw them out in the front garden of the Heslops' house in what shade there was: Silent Jim busy with some job of his own making and Still Jim talking to him. Since the time of his unhappy return from the day by the sea, the old man had not referred again to "those days." Now, however, alone with young Jim, he felt free to go back into his memory for stories to interest and amaze. He would always end by saying: "And that was true, for all there's nothing left to prove it and people disbelieve."

One late afternoon he had been talking in this strain for some time. They had finished their tea, and young Jim had got the wheelchair out and was cleaning the wickerwork with an old toothbrush. Mrs. Heslop came out to fetch their tea things and said: "It's a pity there's nowhere to take your granddad in the wheelchair, till the club opens again next month." She went in again to do the bit of washing up.

Old Jim had stopped talking, and he did not start again now. Young Jim looked up at him in surprise. His grandfather beckoned to him to come close. "If I speak like this," he said, "can anyone hear but you?"

Young Jim looked around carefully. There were no neighbors in the gardens, and his mother was in the kitchen with the taps running. He shook his head.

His grandfather put his hand up and pulled young Jim's head into such a position that the boy's ear was only a few inches away from his mouth when he spoke. "What would you say to a jaunt—a real pleasure jaunt?"

Silent Jim turned his face so that his grandfather could see his eyebrows going up.

Old Jim nodded. "Mind you, it's a long push with the wheelchair."

Silent Jim simply left his eyebrows up.

"It came to me just now, in a flash," said old Jim. "The whole plan. We'll go over to Little Barley, where I was born, where I was christened at the font in the church there, with my father and grandfather standing by, my grandfather that's buried in the same churchyard, he that was seven foot tall. I'll show it to you—all of it."

Young Jim said: "When?"

"The sooner the safer, before the weather thinks to break. Tomorrow, and very early in the morning, before the traffic's on the main road, at least for our first crossing of it, and before others are about. Before your mother wakes."

Silent Jim nodded emphatically.

"Sunrise is before five now," said old Jim. "I've often seen it, for at my age I sleep lightly and never late."

It was easy for old Jim to wake early, but a different matter for young Jim, and it would be impossible for his grandfather to call to him without waking Mrs. Heslop, too, or to get upstairs in order to wake him quietly.

Young Jim's bedroom upstairs, like old Jim's room on the ground floor, was at the front of the house. This gave young Jim his idea. That evening he made a very long length of string out of several shorter pieces knotted together. The string stretched from his bedroom, out through the window, down and in again at the window of his grandfather's room. The lower end was left within easy reach of old Jim's hand; the upper end was tied around young Jim's big toe. The device was put into working position after Mrs. Heslop had gone to bed, and the next morning—before morning seemed even to have come—it worked perfectly.

That summer dawn surprised young Jim by its stillness and grayness; he had expected at least reds and yellows in the sky, like a festival. He was surprised, too, at the chill in the air, even indoors, at this time of heat wave. He dressed his grandfather in his warmest clothes and gave him an extra rug for the wheelchair. They had not planned to have any breakfast at all, but now young Jim, who was a sensible boy, saw they would need something later to warm them. The most that he dared do was to boil a kettle and make a thermos of tea. He also put a handful of biscuits into a paper bag. "And," said old Jim, in his lowest voice, "we'll take your mother's tape measure." He would not say why.

With old Jim in the wheelchair, and the thermos and biscuits and the tape measure on his knees, they left the house. In all the houses they passed, the curtains were still drawn; none of the neighbors was up. Young Jim pushed the chair along with his heart in his mouth, for the squeak of the wheels sounded very loud in the morning silence. Perhaps, if anyone heard at all, the hearer thought it was only the early, monotonous call of some strange bird.

They left the housing estate and came out onto the main road. There was no traffic at all to be seen, until an all-night truck rumbled by. Then nothing again.

They crossed the main road unhurriedly and without the slightest danger and struck off down the road to Little Barley. Now that they were leaving the houses of Great Barley behind them, old Jim dared talk aloud, and young Jim, feeling that they were really on their way, relaxed his pace and looked around him as he went.

This was a country road, going always deeper into the country. There were wide verges where the grasses grew tall, yellowing and drying with the heats of August. There were few flowers left in bloom, but the plants in the ditches were fresh and green where they could still suck up refreshment and life from ditch water or ditch mud.

Dew lay on grasses and plants and hedges, a short-lived coolness before the sun should come again in its full strength. Already young Jim began to feel its warmth on his back, and wheelchair and wheelchair pusher together began to make a strange long shadow on the road ahead.

They came to a bridge over a river and crossed it. They skirted a high wall; old Jim made young Jim stop to look at a fading black mark on it. When he was a young man, old Jim said, that mark had been repainted yearly; it was the boundary sign between the parishes of Great and Little Barley. When he was a boy, the champion fighter of the two villages stood with a foot on either side of the mark and shouted:

Barley Little and Barley Great,
Here I stand and won't be beat.

They went on and crossed a railway track, where you opened the gate for yourself and had to look both ways for safety.

They reached the outskirts of Little Barley village—a cluster of cottages and a farmhouse, and the church beyond. They still saw no sign of anyone astir and heard no sound of life, except a clank of metal from a farm building—perhaps a bucket in a cowshed where the early milking was starting.

They came to the little gray church. Young Jim pushed the wheelchair up the path between the tombstones to the church door. The door might so easily have been locked, but it was not. Young Jim could have wheeled the chair right inside, but old Jim thought that it might not be respectful. He got out of the chair instead, and leaning on young Jim's shoulder, he hobbled inside.

Little Barley was such a small village that no rector or vicar lived in it, and services were held in the church only occasionally. You could feel that on entering. There was a silence that was surprised to be disturbed. Church spiders had spun threads across and across the aisles, from pew head to pew head. Young Jim felt them breaking across his body as he and his grandfather paced along.

Now they were facing the east end of the church and the altar. Behind and above it was a great window of pale greenish glass, through which streamed the light of the risen sun.

Old Jim blinked into the light, and his eyes filled with tears, and he sat down rather suddenly in the pew beside him and prayed.

When he had finished, he said to young Jim: "I was married to your grandmother at that altar. She died long before you were born." Then he took young Jim to the west end of the church, to the gray stone font. "I was christened here; my mother and father stood here for my christening. They're dead and gone, too."

"And your grandfather stood with them," said young Jim. "He that was seven foot high."

"Aye, and he's gone, too." But this reminded old Jim of something. "I'll show you outside," he said. "Toward the east end of the church, it would be—his grave."

They went outside again, and as old Jim was tired, he got back into the chair, and young Jim wheeled him along the narrow path that went round the outside of the church. Toward the east end of the churchyard, old Jim said, "Stop!" He looked around him. "You'll find it about here. James Heslop, his name was—like my name, like yours."

Young Jim began to look. The graves in this part of the churchyard were very old, overgrown, and weatherworn. The inscriptions were hard to read.

Old Jim saw his grandson's difficulty. "Look for a big tombstone—the biggest. Seven foot tall he was, and his tombstone was to match."

"This is the longest tombstone," said young Jim at last. He scraped away the ivy tendrils from the head of it. "There's an O here—no, it's a cherub's face. But there's writing below. I can't read the first letters, but here's an S, and an L, and this really is an O. . . ."

" 'Tis Heslop," said old Jim. "It's his. Wheel me close, boy."

Young Jim brought the chair alongside the tombstone. Old Jim leaned forward with the tape measure he had brought. He placed one end at the head of the tombstone and, with difficulty, stretched the length of it out. It was only a five-foot tape measure, and it did not reach. Young Jim had to measure the remainder separately.

"Five feet," he said, "and another two feet nine inches."

"Nearly eight foot," said old Jim, and lay back in his chair and closed his eyes. "You must tell your sister that; you must tell them all that. Nearly eight feet his tombstone had to be, because in his life he was seven foot tall. There's his tombstone to prove it. Seven foot tall—they were giants in those days."

Then he opened his eyes again and said briskly: "What about the tea?"

Young Jim set the thermos and the biscuits out on the tombstone, as his grandfather told him. "He would never have minded," said old Jim, "any more than I should mind if you did it to me, when I'm gone. No, I should take it kindly."

They took turns at drinking out of the cup top of the thermos and ate biscuits. The time was still not yet half past six, but there was no doubt that the day was going to be another scorcher. The sun warmed them as they breakfasted, and old Jim spread his handkerchief over the top of his head for protection. Bees came out and began work among the tall weeds of the churchyard. A robin suddenly appeared at the far end of the tombstone, and young Jim threw him some crumbs.

Unexpectedly a car passed; they just saw its roof over the top of the churchyard wall and then—for a second—the whole of it as it passed the gap that was the churchyard gate. Then they heard brakes go on; the car seemed to stop abruptly, and then it backed until it was by the gate again, and then it stopped again. After a moment two policemen got out and stared at them.

"Who's got a better right than we have?" said old Jim indignantly. "It's my grandfather's tombstone."

The policemen opened the churchyard gate and began walking up the path.

Old Jim and young Jim watched them.

The policemen left the main path and, in single file, came along the narrow path by the church directly toward the Heslops.

When he was still some way away, the policeman in front called out, in an arresting voice: "James Heslop!" That he knew their name seemed ominous.

He did not go on at once; it was as if words failed him, but the second policeman burst out: "Whatever are you doing here, James Heslop, with your daughter-in-law and your mother off her head looking for you?"

The policemen now began to talk both at once.

"Running around the village looking for you," said the first policeman.

"In her dressing gown," said the second policeman.

"Came to us in despair," said the first policeman.

"In her bedroom slippers," said the second policeman.

"And here we've been looking for you ever since," said the first policeman. "Now what were you two up to?"

Both policemen waited for an answer to this. Neither old Jim nor young Jim said anything, so the second policeman said, "Eh?"

Old Jim smiled and shook his head, and young Jim cast his eyes down, putting himself out of the conversation altogether.

The second policeman said suddenly: "The old un's deaf—you remember she said so—and she said the child couldn't be got to talk much."

"Deaf?" said the first policeman. He drew a deep breath into his great chest, so that the blue bulk of it advanced until the silver buttons, moving from sunlight to sunlight, twinkled. With his breath very slowly going out, in a voice that might have wakened seven-foot James Heslop under his tombstone, the policeman shouted: "We've come to take you home in the car, Mr. Heslop." He added, with less voice because he had less voice left: "The child can push the wheelchair back, empty." The policeman, when he had finished, looked tired and hollow-chested; old Jim smiled and shook his head.

"Deaf," said the second policeman.

Then the two policemen began to explain to old Jim by gestures what they intended. In dumb show they explained to him how they would help him into their car and how comfortable he would be; they acted to him how swiftly and smoothly they would drive off, how soon they would get him safely home. Then they stopped to make sure he had understood. Old Jim clapped his hands and smiled, but he also shook his head.

The policemen started all over again, but in the middle of their performance, one of them—perhaps losing patience—set his hands on the wheelchair as if to push it toward the car, with or without old Jim's permission. Then old Jim spoke, languidly, almost feebly: "I never like to be awkward, but I wouldn't like you to take on the responsibility of trying to get me into a car at my age. My joints are stiff, you know. And then there's my heart."

The policemen looked at old Jim carefully. He certainly appeared very frail, and he sounded very frail indeed. Yet they had promised Mrs. Heslop not only to find her father-in-law and her son but to bring the old man home at once.

"Yet I'd like to be home, too," said old Jim. "It's been a strain . . . at my age . . . so early in the morning . . . so far. . . ." He let his voice die away and closed his eyes.

"We should get him home somehow, quickly," said the first policeman, and the second nodded; they both looked anxious.

In the anxious silence, old Jim suddenly said, "Ah!" so that both policemen jumped. He had opened his eyes, and now he said: "You could tow me home."

"Tow you home?" repeated the policemen.

"Fasten my wheelchair to the back of your car with a towrope," said old Jim. "Pull me home on a towrope."

The policemen looked at each other, neither ever having been asked to tow anyone in a wheelchair before or heard of such a thing being done.

"It'd be a question for the Traffic Department, probably," said the first policeman.

"There'd be rules and regulations about it," said the second.

"For instance, he'd have to have his own number plate," said the first.

"Aye, he'd have been turned into a trailer."

Old Jim, not being able to follow the policemen's conversation but seeing their hesitation, became impatient. "If you haven't a towrope, handcuffs would do. You could handcuff the wheelchair to the back of the car. Surely you have handcuffs in a police car."

"But you'd be a trailer!" shouted the first policeman.

"I'd be *what*?" asked old Jim; it was not clear whether he had not heard or could not believe what he had heard.

The first policeman shook his head despairingly. "And it wouldn't be safe, anyway," he said.

"Unless, of course," said the second policeman, "we drove very slowly and carefully." He seemed to see possibilities in the idea after all.

"There is that," the first policeman agreed. "But, however you look at it, he'd be a trailer; I doubt it wouldn't be legal."

At this point, young Jim surprised them by speaking. "But nobody'd see."

It was quite true; the hour was still so early that there was small danger of anybody's being on the roads between Little and Great Barley. On the other hand, the likelihood of such an encounter increased with every minute that the day advanced. If they were to act at all, they must act quickly.

The second policeman persuaded the first. It turned out, anyway, that they always carried a good rope in the car. With this they fastened the front of the wheelchair—with old Jim still in it—to the back of the police car. Young Jim tucked his grandfather well into the chair and then got into the back of the car. One policeman sat with him, and the other drove.

They went very slowly—that is, for a car, but much more quickly than a wheelchair could ever have been pushed. From the beginning to the end of the journey young Jim and the policeman with him kept watch through the rear window. Young Jim pressed his nose against the glass until it went white like a piece of pastry, and his eyes were very anxious.

At first old Jim looked anxious, too, but the faster he went, the more confident he seemed to become. His white hair streamed in the wind, and he began to signal to the two at the back for the car to go faster still. They did not pass his message on to the driver. Already the wheelchair was traveling at a speed it had never dreamed of before; its whizzing wheels gave out an unbroken, high-pitched squeak. "There'll be an accident!" the wheels screamed. "An accident!"

There was no accident, nor were they observed by anyone—unless you counted a horse looking over a gate beyond Little Barley. He watched their coming, but when they were almost level with him, his nerve seemed to break, for he galloped off, with his back hooves wildly in the air. Old Jim waved to him with one hand, clinging to the side of the wheelchair with the other.

Not even in Great Barley were there people about or traffic.

They turned into the housing estate, and the only sign of life was a figure drooping over one of the front gates: Mrs. Heslop, waiting. The police car drew up beside her, and she looked at it, and at young Jim's face at the window, and at old Jim in the wheelchair behind. He was waving to her, and now that the car engine was turned off, they could hear that he was singing, had probably been singing all the way. "Hearts of Oak" it must have been, because he now broke off at "Steady, boys, steady!"

Young Jim got out of the car quickly and said: "Mum, I've come all the way from Little Barley in a police car!"

Mrs. Heslop shot out an arm, perhaps to catch him to her, perhaps to slap him, but instead of doing either, she suddenly put both hands up to her face and burst into tears.

Poor Mrs. Heslop! Already it had been a long and very trying morning for her. She had not been woken at dawn by the gentle sounds of their setting forth, but a little later, waking of her own accord, she had listened to the silence of the house, and it had suddenly seemed to her unnatural in a way that it had never seemed before. She told herself that she was being foolish, and she tried to sleep again, but in the end she had got up and looked into young Jim's bedroom and found him gone. Then she had found old Jim gone, and the wheelchair, too. Then she had started out wildly to look for them and had only been sent home by the comforting promises of the police. Since then she had waited at the gate.

One policeman unhitched old Jim's wheelchair while the other put his arm round Mrs. Heslop's shoulder and told her there was no need to cry now; everyone was safe and sound.

They all went indoors, and Mrs. Heslop recovered sufficiently to boil a kettle and make a pot of tea. The policemen stayed to drink a cup and then went off, and then Mrs. Heslop settled down to cooking a proper, hot breakfast for old Jim and young Jim. "*Biscuits!*" she snorted, and she served them with porridge and fried eggs and bacon and hot toast and marmalade, and more tea.

After breakfast, old Jim said that he was not really tired after all and that he would like to sit out in the shade, in his usual chair, at the front of the house, and young Jim made him comfortable there. Young Jim wanted to stay with him, but Mrs. Heslop put her foot down and made him go upstairs to bed, where sure enough, he was soon falling asleep.

Mrs. Heslop saw him into bed and drew his curtains against the bright sunlight and left him; it was never much use, she knew, to question young Jim. She went downstairs and into the front garden. She planted herself in front of her father-in-law, so that he could not but pay some attention to her.

"Granddad!" she shouted. "Why did you *do* it?"

Old Jim nodded at her and said: "And I hope they're having as good weather by the seaside. I've something to tell young Maisie, too, when she comes back. That reminds me. . . ." He reached into his pocket and brought out the tape measure. "Here's your tape measure that we borrowed, my dear."

He held it out to Mrs. Heslop, and she took it, but as in a dream of amazement and carelessly. She only held it by one end, so that the rest of the tape fell and rolled around her feet, encircling them.

Mrs. Heslop stared at the tape measure and then at old Jim. "But why, Granddad, why—why?"

"Aye," said the old man, "those days . . ." He laughed to himself. "But what my grandfather would have said to see me bowling along this morning! The best of both worlds—that's what I've had."

"You and young Jim . . ." said Mrs. Heslop wonderingly, still standing within her magic circle of tape, staring at him. No longer was she expecting or hoping to be heard, but oddly, this time old Jim must partly have heard her.

"Aye, he's a good boy." He blinked sleepily into the sunlight. "And you know, although he's not big for his age, maybe he has the makings of a big man in him." His eyelids drooped, then rose again. "Maybe he'll grow to be six foot, after all, like his grandfather." Old Jim settled himself into his chair; he was going to sleep, and he knew it. "Or even seven foot, maybe, like his great-great-grandfather." His eyelids fell again. He slept.

Upstairs in his bedroom, listening in his half sleep to the booming voice from outside, young Jim had begun dreaming of giants and police cars.

The Great Blackberry Pick ❖

*D*ad was against waste—waste of almost anything: electricity, time, crusts of bread. Wasted food was his special dread. Just after the summer holidays, nearing the second or third Saturday of term, "Sun now," he would say, "frost later, and pounds and pounds and pounds and pounds of blackberries out in the hedges going to waste. Good food wasted: bramble jelly"—their mother flinched, perhaps remembering stained bags hanging from hooks in the kitchen—"jelly, and jam, and blackberry-and-apple pies. . . ." He smacked his lips. Dad seemed to think he must mime enjoyment to make them understand.

Val said eagerly, "I love blackberries."

Her father beamed on her.

Chris said, "I don't. I don't like the seeds between my teeth."

"Worse under your plate," their mother murmured.

Like their mother, Dad had false teeth, but he did not acknowledge them. He said scornfully, "In *bought* jam the seeds are artificial. Tiny chips of wood. Put in afterward."

"Nice job, carving 'em to shape," said Chris.

Peter was not old enough to think that funny, and Val decided not to laugh, so nobody did.

Peter said, "Do we have to go?"

"Bicycles," said Dad. "Everyone on bicycles and off into the country, blackberry picking. Five of us should gather a good harvest."

"I'll make the picnic," Val said. She liked that kind of thing. She looked anxiously around her family. Their mother had turned her face away from them to gaze out of the window. Peter and Chris had fixed their eyes upon Dad. Peter would have to go, although much bicycling made his legs ache, but Chris, the eldest of them, as good as grown up, Chris said: "I'm not coming."

"Oh, Chris!" Val cried.

Dad said: "Not coming?"

"No."

"And why not?"

"I've been asked to go somewhere else on Saturday. I'm doing something else. I'm not coming."

No one had ever said that to Dad before. What would happen? Dad began to growl in his throat like a dog preparing to attack. Then the rumble died away. Dad said: "Oh, have it your own way then."

So that was one who wouldn't go blackberrying this year.

Nor did their mother go. When Saturday came, she didn't feel well, she said. She'd stay at home and have their supper ready for them.

Two fewer didn't matter, because Dad begged the two Turner children from next door. Mrs. Turner was glad to be rid of them for the day, and they had bicycles.

"Bicycles," said Dad, "checked in good order, tires pumped, brakes working, and so on. Then, the picnic." Val smiled and nodded. "Something to gather the blackberries in," went on Dad. "Not paper bags or rubbishy receptacles of that sort. Baskets, plastic carrier bags, anything like that. Something that will go into a bicycle basket or can be tied on somewhere. Something that will bear a weight of blackberries. Right?"

Val said, "Yes," so that Dad could go on: "All assemble in the road at nine-thirty. I'll have the map."

There they were on this fine Saturday morning in September at half past nine: Val and Peter and their dad and the two Turner children from next door, all on bicycles.

They had about four miles on the main road, riding very carefully, two by two or sometimes in single file, with Dad in the rear shouting to them. Then Dad directed them to turn off the main road into a side road, and after that it was quiet country roads all the way. As Chris had once said, you had to hand it to Dad: Dad was good with a map; he knew where he was going.

Country roads, and then lanes that grew doubtful of themselves and became mere grassy tracks. These were the tracks that in the old days people had made on foot or on horseback, going from one village to the next. Nowadays almost no one used them.

They were pushing their bikes now or riding them with their teeth banging in their gums. The Turner children each fell off once, and one cried.

"Quiet now!" Dad said severely, as though the blackberries were shy wild creatures to be taken by surprise.

They left their bicycles stacked against one another and followed Dad on foot, walking steeply through an afforestation of pines and then out into a large clearing on a hillside, south-facing and overgrown with brambles.

You had to hand it to Dad; it was a marvelous place.

The bushes were often more than a man's height and densely growing, but with irregular passages between them. The pickers could edge through narrow gaps or stoop under stems arched to claw and clutch. For most of the time they wore their anoraks with the hoods up.

The blackberries grew thickly. They were very big and ripe—many already overripe, with huge bluebottles squatting on them.

"Eat what you want, to begin with," said Dad. "Soon enough you won't want to eat anymore. Then just pick and go on picking." He smiled. He was good-tempered. Everything was going well.

They separated at once, to pick. They went burrowing about among the bushes, meeting each other, exclaiming, drawn to each other's blackberry clumps, because always someone else's blackberries seemed bigger, riper.

They picked and picked and picked and picked. Their teeth and tongues and lips were stained, but their fingers were stained the most deeply, because they went on picking—on and on and on—after they had stopped eating. Dad had been right about that, too. But himself, he never ate any blackberries at all, just picked.

The brambles scratched them. Val had a scratch on her forehead that brought bright blood oozing down into her eyebrow. "Nothing!" said Dad. He tied her head with a handkerchief to stop the bleeding. The handkerchief had been a present to him; it was red with white polka dots. When he had tied it round Val's head, he called her his pirate girl.

Then he looked into her plastic carrier bag. "Why, pirate girl, you've picked more blackberries than anyone else!"

When Dad had gone off again, Peter began to dance round Val. "Pirate girl! Pirate girl!" Val didn't mind; no, she really enjoyed it. She felt happy to have picked more blackberries than anyone else, and for Dad to have said so, and to be wearing Dad's handkerchief, and to be teased for what he had called her. The Turner children appeared round a bramble corner, and she was glad of the audience. Peter was good-humored, too. His legs had stopped aching, and he had forgotten that they would ache again. The children were in early-afternoon sunshine and blackberry-scented air, they had picked enough blackberries to be proud of, the picnic would be any time now, and Dad was in a good temper.

"Pirate girl!" Peter teased. He set down his basket of blackberries to pick a solitary stem of hogweed, dry and straight and stiff. With this he made cutlass slashes at Val.

There was no weapon near to hand for Val, so she used her carrier bag to parry him. She swung the bag to and fro, trying to bang his stem and break it. The weight in the carrier made it swing slowly, heavily, like a pendulum. Val was getting nowhere in the fight, but she was enjoying it. She hissed fiercely between her teeth. Peter dodged. The bag swung.

Dad came back around the bushes and saw them. Val couldn't stop the swinging at once, and at once an awful thing began to happen. The swinging was too much for the weight of the blackberries in the bag. The bottom did not fall out—after all, the bag was plastic—but the plastic where she gripped it began to stretch. The handle holes elongated swiftly and smoothly. Swiftly and smoothly the plastic around them thinned, thinned out into nothingness. No ripping, no violent severance, but the bag gave way.

The blackberries shot out at Dad's feet. They pattered impudently over his Wellington boots, nestled there in a squashy heap. Val, looking down at them, knew they were wasted. She had gathered them, and she had literally thrown them away. She lifted her eyes to Dad's face. His brows were heavy, his lips open and drawn back; his teeth showed, ground together.

Then he growled, in his way.

She turned and ran. She ran and ran, as fast as she could, to get away. Fast and far she ran; now, as she ran, there were pine trees on either side of her, an audience that watched her. Then she tripped and fell painfully over metal, and realized that she had reached the bicycles. She pulled her own bicycle from the heap and got on it and rode. The way was downhill and rough, and she was riding too fast for carefulness. She was shaken violently as though someone were shaking a wicked child.

She followed the track by which they had come, then diverged into another. The way grew smoother; she passed a farmhouse; the surface under her wheels was made up now. She took another turn and another and was in a narrow road between high hedges. She cycled on and came to a crossroads, two quiet country roads quietly meeting and crossing, with no signpost saying anything. Without consideration she took the turn toward the downward sloping of the sun and cycled on more slowly. She knew that she was lost, and she was glad of it.

She found that she had a headache. She was surprised at the headache and wondered if the tight-tied handkerchief had caused it. Then she connected the feeling in her head with a feeling in her stomach; she was hungry. They had all been hungry for the picnic even before the pirate fight, and she had ridden away without eating.

She was so tired and hungry that she cried a little as she pedaled along. She knew she had nearly twenty pence in the pocket of her anorak. She could buy herself some food.

But these were not roads with shops on them. Another farm, a derelict cottage, and suddenly a bungalow with a notice at the gate: FRUIT. VEG.

She leaned her bicycle against the hedge and went up the path toward the front door. But the front door had a neglected look, and a power mower was parked right against it, under the shelter of the porch. She turned and went around the side of the bungalow, following a path but also a faint, enticing smell. The smell grew stronger, more exciting. The side door she came to was also a kitchen door, and it stood ajar. From inside came a smell of roast meat and of delicious baking.

Val went right up to the door and peered in. The kitchen was empty of people. A meal had just been finished. A baby's high chair stood near the table, its tray spattered with mashed potato and gravy. There was no food left on the table except more mashed potato and the remains of a treacle tart in a baking tin.

And there was the smell, overwhelming now.

Val inhaled and looked.

A door opened, and a young woman came into the kitchen. She picked up the tin with the treacle tart in it, evidently to put it away somewhere. Then she saw Val's face at the crack of the door. She gave a gasp.

Val pushed the door wide open to show how harmless she was, and with the same intention said, "I saw the notice at the gate."

"Oh," said the woman, recovering, "that shouldn't be there still. Should have come down last week. We've not much stuff left, you see. What did you want?"

"Something to eat now," said Val. The woman had put the treacle tart down on the table again.

"Blackberries?" the woman suggested.

"No," said Val. "Not blackberries. Thank you."

The woman had been staring at her. "Why's your head tied up? Have you had an accident? You're very pale."

"No," said Val. "I'm all right really." The woman's hand was still on the treacle tart tin; she remained staring.

"You have had an accident."

"Not really." Val didn't want to think of what had happened among the brambles. "I fell off my bike."

The woman left the treacle tart and came across to Val. She slipped the handkerchief from her head and laid it aside. She examined Val's brow. "It's really only a scratch, but it's bled a lot. You sit down." She cleaned the wound and then bandaged it. Then, "You'd better have some tea. I was going to make a pot while the baby slept." She boiled the kettle and made the tea. She also cleared the kitchen table, taking the treacle tart away and shutting it into a larder. Val watched it go, over the cup of tea the woman poured for her.

Next the woman opened the oven door just a crack. A smell of baking, hot, dry, delicious, came out and made straight for Val. The woman was peering into the oven. "Ah," she said. "Yes." She opened the oven door wide and took out two tin trays of scones, done to a turn. She got out a wire rack and began to transfer the scones one by one from the trays to the rack. They were so hot that she picked each one up by the tips of her fingers and very quickly.

"Have another cup," she said hospitably to Val.

"I won't have any more to drink, thank you," Val said. The scones sat on their wire rack, radiating heat and smell. The woman finished with the trays and began washing up.

There were footsteps outside, and a young man appeared, carrying a pig bucket. He left it just outside and came in. "Hello!" he said to Val. "Where've you sprung from?"

"She fell off her bike. I've given her a cup of tea." The woman dried her hands. "You might like a scone, too?"

Val nodded. She couldn't say anything.

The woman slit a scone, buttered it, and handed it to her.

"What about me?" asked the man.

"You!" said the woman. From the rack she chose a scone misshapen but huge, made from the last bits of dough clapped together. She slit it, pushed a hunk of butter inside, and gave it to him.

"Would you like another?" she asked Val.

Val said she would. The woman watched her eating the second scone. "Haven't you had much dinner?"

Val didn't decide what she was going to say. It came at once. "The others all rode away from me when I fell off my bike. Rode off with the picnic."

The woman was indignant. "But didn't you try to catch up with them again?"

"I got lost."

The woman gave Val a third scone and her husband a second. She went to the larder and came back with the treacle tart, which she set before Val. "There's a nice surprise for you," she said.

They asked where Val lived, and when she told them, the man said, "Quite a way on a bike."

Val said, "If you could tell me how to get to the main road from here. All these lanes and not many signposts . . ."

"Tricky," said the man.

Then the woman said, "Weren't you taking the van to the garage sometime to get that part?"

"Ah," said the man. "Yes. I could set her on her way. Room for the bike in the back."

"No hurry," the woman said to Val. "You sit there."

Away somewhere a baby began to cry, and the woman went to fetch it. While she was out of the kitchen, the man helped himself to another scone and butter, winking at Val. The woman came back with the baby in her arms. "You!" she said to the man. He kissed her with his mouth full of scone and kissed the baby.

The woman said to Val: "You hold her while I finish the washing up." So Val held the baby, smelling of cream cheese and warm woollies and talcum powder. The baby seemed to like her.

"Well," the man said to Val, "I'll be back for you later."

His wife gave him the old mashed potato and other remains for the pig bucket. "It wasn't worth your coming for it specially," she said.

"No," he said. "But I remembered about the scones."

"You!" she said.

He laughed and went off with his pig bucket again.

Val nursed the baby, and gave it a rusk, and helped to change its nappies, and played with it. The mother cleared and cleaned the kitchen and washed out the nappies.

It all took some time. Then the man came again.

"Ready?" he said to Val. Val took her anorak, which the baby had been sucking, and went with him. He had already hoisted the bicycle into the back of the van. The woman came to the gate with the baby in her arms. The baby slapped at the notice saying FRUIT. VEG. "You never get around to taking that notice down," the woman said to her husband. He grunted, busy with the van. Val kissed good-bye to the baby, who took a piece of her cheek and twisted it.

Then Val got into the van, and they drove off. Val was not noticing the way they took; she was thinking of the warm, sweet-smelling kitchen they had left. As they drove along, she half thought they passed one of the two farmhouses she had noticed earlier when she was cycling, but that was all.

She began to think of what it would be like when she got home.

They reached the main road at last and drove along it a short way to the garage. Here the man lifted Val's bicycle out of the van, and she mounted it. He gave her clear directions to set her on her way, ending with "You should be home well before dusk."

So she was, and they were all waiting for her. Even Chris was there.

The Turner children had wanted to stay, too, but Dad had packed them off home.

There was a great explosion from Dad about what had happened at the blackberry pick and after. Val was given some supper, but the row from Dad went on during it and after it. Their mother started her ironing; Chris settled down to TV; Peter played a quiet but violent game with soldiers and tanks behind the couch. Dad went on and on.

"And what about that bandage?" he shouted suddenly. Their mother knocked the iron against the ironing board, almost toppling it. "Where's my red handkerchief that I lent you?"

In a flash of memory Val saw the red handkerchief laid aside on the dresser in that scone-smelling, baby-smelling kitchen. "A woman gave me a cup of tea," she said. "She took the handkerchief off and put the bandage on instead. I must have left the handkerchief there."

"My red handkerchief!" Dad shouted.

"Oh," muttered Chris, without taking his eyes off TV, "a red cotton handkerchief!"

"I'm sorry," Val said to Dad.

"Sorry!"

Then Dad cross-questioned her. Who was this woman, and where did she live? All Val could say was that she lived quite a way from the bramble patch and from the main road, in a bungalow with a notice at the gate saying FRUIT. VEG.

"Right," said Dad. "You'll come with me tomorrow. You'll cycle back the way you came. You'll help me search until we find that bungalow and the woman and my red handkerchief."

So the next day—Sunday—Val cycled with her father alone into the country. Just the two of them; once she would have loved that.

He led them systematically to and fro among the country lanes. ("Do you recognize this road? Could that be the bungalow? Look, girl, look!") Dad knew his map, and he was thorough in his crisscrossing of the countryside, but they saw few bungalows, and none with a notice at the gate saying FRUIT. VEG.

As they passed one bungalow, Val looked up the path to the front door. Against it, under the shelter of the porch, was parked a motor mower. Also a pole with a board at the top; the inscription on the board faced the front door. And behind the glass of a window Val thought she saw movement, the odd, top-heavy shape of someone carrying a child. But they were cycling past too quickly for her to be sure.

When they got home at last, Dad was too tired to go on with the row. He just said: "A day wasted!"

Val was even more tired, and she said nothing.

Lucky Boy ❖

*T*his was just about a perfect summer afternoon, with sunshine, flowers blooming, and birds singing, even to a cuckoo (only that happened to be Lucy next door, who was good at it), and it was Saturday into the bargain. Everything was in Pat's favor: jobs done and his family safely in the back garden. He strolled down the front garden to the front gate. Clicked open the gate . . .

Free . . .

And then: "Where are you going, Pat? Will you take me with you, Pat? Take me, too, Pat!" The cuckoo had stopped calling, because Lucy had given up mimicry to poke her face between the slats of the dividing fence. "Take me."

If he went through the gate and on, without her, Lucy would bawl. That was understood on both sides. The question was: would anyone from either house come in response to the bawling? And if they did, would they bother to get to the bottom of things: detain Pat for questioning, cross-examine him on his plans, ruin his perfect afternoon?

Of course, he could run for it—now, instantly. That was perhaps the only certain way of keeping his afternoon to himself. He would just

leave Lucy bawling behind him. What made him hesitate was that
once he used to take Lucy on expeditions even without her asking.
When Lucy had been a baby in a pram, he had helped to wheel her.
Later on, when she was old enough to walk, he had taken her to the
sweetshop, and he had even shared his pocket money with her. Not so
very long ago he had taken her regularly to the swings and the sandpit
and seesaw on the recreation ground.

So he paused, holding the gate open before him, to reason with
her. "I'm not going where I could take you," he said; "you're too little."

But she simply repeated: "Take me."

Pat had delayed, and Lucy's mother must have been watching from
the window. She opened the front door and came down the path
toward them, carrying a pair of red sandals. She had misunderstood
the situation. "Lucy," she said, "you put your sandals on if you're going
out of this garden." And then, to Pat: "Are you taking her to the shops
or to the swings?"

Pat was going to neither, so he said nothing.

Lucy's mother went straight on: "Because if it's the shops, she can
have fourpence."

"No," said Pat. "Not the shops."

"Well, then!" said Lucy's mother to Lucy. "You do as Pat tells you
now." She turned briskly back to the house. Lucy's mother was always
like that.

Lucy had been putting on her sandals. Now she went through her
front gate and waited for Pat to come through his. She held out her
hand, and he took it.

They walked to the recreation ground, toward the swings. The sun
still shone, flowers bloomed, birds sang—and Lucy with them—but
the afternoon was ruined for Pat.

They were within sight of the swings. "Will you push me high?"
Lucy was saying.

He made up his mind then. Instead of loosening his hold of her
hand, so that she could run ahead to the swings, he tightened it. He
gripped her attention. "Listen, Lucy. We could go somewhere much

better than the swings." Yes, he'd take Lucy, rather than not go at all. "We'll go somewhere really exciting—but secret, Lucy, mind. Just you and me, secretly."

"Secretly?"

"Come on."

They veered abruptly from the direction of the swings and scudded along the fencing that bounded the recreation ground on its far side. They left behind them the swingers, the sandpit players, and even the football kickers. Down to the lonely end of the recreation ground, where Pat had poked about a good deal recently. He had poked about and found a loose fencing stake that could be prized up and swung aside, to make a gap.

"No one's looking. Through here, Lucy—quickly. Squeeze."

Gaps in the fencing of the recreation ground were not unheard of, nor boys getting through them when they should not. But trespassing through such holes was disappointing. On the other side of this fence lay only a private garden. True, it ran down to the river, but what was the use of a riverbank neatly turfed and herbaceous-bordered and within spying distance of its house? And if one tried to go further along the riverbank, one soon came to another fence, and beyond it, another private garden, and so on. Trespassing boys looked longingly over to the other side of the river, which was open country—thin pasturage, often flooded in winter, with ragged banks grown here and there with willow and alder. They looked, and then they turned back through the gap by which they had come. And in due course the groundsman would notice the hole and stop it up.

Pat's hole had not yet been found by the groundsman, which was a bit of luck, but beyond it, in the garden, lay the best luck of all.

"Now," Pat said as Lucy emerged from the hole in the fence into the garden. "Keep down behind the bushes, because of being seen from the house, and follow me. This way to the riverbank, and now—look!"

Lucy gazed, bewildered, awed. The turf of the bank had been mutilated and the flower border smashed by a tangle of boughs and twigs that only yesterday had been the crown of an alder tree, high as a house, that grew on the opposite bank. For years the river had been washing away at the roots of the alder, dislodging a crumb of earth here and a crumb there, and in floodtime sweeping away the looser projections of its bank. For years the alder had known that its time was coming; no roots could hold out against it. In the drowsy middle of the day, on Friday, there had been no wind, no extra water down the river, but the alder's time had come. It slid a little, toppled a little, and then fell—fell right across the river, bridging it from side to side.

The people of the house were exceedingly annoyed at the damage done to their grass and flowers. They spent the rest of Friday ringing up the farmer from whose land the alder had fallen, but the farmer wasn't going to do anything about a fallen tree until after the weekend, and *they* certainly did not intend to, they said.

They did not know about Pat. After school on Friday, he found his hole in the fence and, beyond it, the new tree bridge to take him across to the far bank of the river.

Then he had had no time to explore; now he had.

"Come on!" he told Lucy, and she followed, trusting him as she always did. They forced a passage through the outer branches to the main trunk. The going was heavy and painful. Pat, because he was just ahead of Lucy, shielded her from the worst of the poking, whipping, barring branches, but still he heard from behind him little gasps of hurt or alarm. More complaint than that she would not make.

They got footholds and handholds on the main trunk, and now Pat began—still slowly and painfully—to work his way along it to the far bank. The last scramble was through the tree roots, upended at the base of the trunk, like a plate on its edge. From there he dropped onto the riverbank of that unknown, long-desired country.

And now he looked back for Lucy. She had not been able to keep up with him and was still struggling along the tree trunk, over the middle of the river. She really was too little for this kind of battling, too young, yet Pat knew she would never admit that, never consent to his leaving her behind.

As he watched her creeping along above the water, he was struck by the remembrance that Lucy could not swim. But she was not going to fall, so that did not matter. Here she was at the base of the trunk now, climbing through the tree roots, standing beside him at last. Her face, dirtied and grazed, smiled with delight. "I liked that," she said. She put her hand in his again.

They began to move along the riverbank, going upstream. "Upstream is toward the source of the river," said Pat. "We might find it. Downstream is toward the sea."

"But I'd like to go to the seaside," said Lucy, halting. "Let's go to the seaside."

"No, Lucy. You don't understand. We couldn't possibly. It's much too far." He pulled her again in the upstream direction.

A ginger-colored puppyish dog had been watching them from one of the gardens on the other side. They noticed him now. He stared and stared at them, then gave a bark. Before Pat could prevent her, Lucy had barked back—rather well and very provocatively.

"Hush!" said Pat, but he was too late, and Lucy had barked again. The dog had cocked his head doubtfully at Lucy's first bark; at the second, he made up his mind. He began to bark shrilly and continuously and as if he would never stop. He pranced along his section of the bank, shrieking at them as they went.

"Now look what you've done!" Pat said crossly. "Somebody will hear and guess something's up."

Lucy began to cry.

"Oh, I didn't mean it," said Pat. "No one's come yet. Stop it, do, Lucy. Please."

She stopped, changing instantly from crying to the happiest smiling. Pat ground his teeth.

The dog continued barking, but soon he could keep level with them no longer, for a garden fence stopped him. He ran up and down the length of it, trying to get through, banging his body against it. He became demented as he saw Lucy and Pat going from him, curving away with the riverbank beyond all possible reach. They heard his barking long after they had lost sight of him.

And now the nettles began. At first only a few, but at the first sting Lucy made a fuss. Then the clumps grew larger and closer together. They might have tried skirting them altogether, by moving in an arc from the riverbank, but in that direction they would have been stopped by another stream, flowing parallel to their own, and not much narrower. They could see that very soon the nettles were filling all the space between the two streams.

Pat considered. He had foreseen the possibility of nettles that afternoon and was wearing a long-sleeved sweater as well as jeans and socks and sandals. Lucy and Lucy's mother, of course, had foreseen nothing; Lucy was wearing a short-sleeved dress, and her legs were bare. Legs always suffered most among nettles, so Pat took off his sweater and made Lucy put it on like a pair of curiously constructed trousers, with her legs thrust through the sleeves. Then he found himself a stick and began beating a way for them both through the nettle banks.

Whack! and *whack!* Left and right, he slashed the nettle stems close to the ground, so that they toppled on either side and before him. Then he trampled them right down, first to one side, then to the other. Then again *whack! whack!* and trample, trample. From behind him Lucy called: "I'd like to do that."

"Oh, I daresay!" he said scornfully.

"Aren't you coming back for me?" she asked next, for his beaten path had taken him almost out of sight. So he went back to her and took her pickaback for some way, then decided that didn't help much and was too tiring, anyway. He put her down, and she waited behind him while he whacked. She kept her sleeved legs close together and hugged her bare arms close around her, against the nettles.

The nettles were always there—*whack! whack!* and trample, trample—until suddenly they stopped. There was an overflow channel from the river, man-made of brick and stone and cement patchings; it was spanned by a rather unnecessary bridge with a willow weeping over it. Lucy settled at once on the bridge under the willow to serve tea with leaves for plates and cups and scrapings of moss for sandwiches, fancy cakes, and jellies. She was very happy. Pat took off his sandals and socks and trod about in the thin film of water that slid from the upper river down the overflow channel into the lower stream. He climbed about on the stone stairs down which the overflow water ran, spattering and spraying, to its new, lower level. The wateriness of it all delighted him.

Then the barking began again. There, on the other side of the river, stood the gingery dog. By what violence or cunning he had got there, it was impossible to say. It was certain, however, that he would bark at them as long as he could see them. Some loose stones were lying in the overflow, and Pat picked up several and threw them at the dog. Those that did not fall short flew wide. The dog barked steadily. Lucy left her tea party and descended onto a slimy stone to see what was happening, and the sliminess of the stone betrayed her: she slipped and sat down in the inch of water that flowed to the lower stream and began to cry. Pat was annoyed by her crying and because she had sat down wearing—and wetting—his sweater and above all, because of the ceaseless barking on the other bank.

He hauled Lucy to her feet. "Come *on!*"

Beyond the overflow there were fewer nettles, so that they went faster, but the gingery dog still kept pace with them, barking. But Pat could see something ahead that the dog could not: a tributary that joined the main river on the dog's side and that would check him, perhaps, more effectively than any garden fence. They drew level with the tributary stream, they passed it, and now they were leaving the gingery dog behind, as well as the nettles.

They entered a plantation of willows, low-lying and neglected. Saplings had been planted here long ago for the making of cricket bats; then something had gone wrong, or perhaps the trees had been forgotten. Cricket was still played, and willow bats used for it, but these particular willows, full-grown and aging, had never been felled for the purpose. So, in time, like the alder downstream, many of them had felled themselves. Ivy, which had made the plantation its own, had crept up the growing trees and shrouded the fallen ones with loose-hanging swaths of gloomy green.

Lucy was charmed with the place and would have liked to resume the tea party interrupted under the weeping willow. Here were tree stumps for tables and—an improvement on the overflow—meadowsweet and figwort on the riverbank that could be picked for table decoration. But she would not be left behind if Pat were going on.

Pat saw his chance. "I won't leave you behind," he promised, "but you can play while I just have a look ahead at the way we must go. Then I'll be back for you." Lucy accepted that. He left her choosing a tea table.

So, for a very little while, the afternoon became as Pat had planned it: just for himself. He went on through the sad plantation and came to the end of it, a barbed-wire fence beneath which it would not be too difficult to pass. Beyond lay more rough pasture. Far to the right he saw the occasional sun flash of cars on a distant road. But he was interested only in the river. Looking, he caught his breath anxiously, for a punt was drifting downstream. The only occupant, however, was a man who had shipped his pole in order to drift and doze in the sun; his eyes were shut, his mouth open. He would not disturb Pat and Lucy, if they did not disturb *him*.

Shading his eyes against the sun, Pat looked beyond the punt, as far as he could see upstream. The river appeared very little narrower than at the fallen alder, so probably he was still far from its source. Still, the riverbank tempted him. He could see it curving away, upstream and out of sight. Even then he could mark the course of the river by the willows that grew along it. In the distance he could see the top of a building that seemed to be standing on the river, perhaps a mill of some kind, or the remains of one, perhaps a house. . . .

Anyway, he would soon see for himself.

He had actually stooped to the barbed-wire fencing when he remembered Lucy. Recollecting her, he had also to admit to himself a sound coming from where he had left her, and that had been going on for some time: a dog's furious barking. He sighed and turned back.

Back through the sad plantation to the part of the riverbank where he had left Lucy. "Lucy!" he called, and then he saw the dog on the opposite bank. Its gingeriness was darkened by the water and mud it had gone through in order to arrive where it was. For a wonder, it had stopped barking by the time Pat saw it. It sat there staring at Pat.

"Lucy!" Pat called, and looked round for her. There on a tree stump were her leaf plates, with crumbs of bark and heads of flowers, but no Lucy.

His eyes searched among the trees of the plantation, and he called repeatedly: "Lucy! Lucy! Lucy!"

There was no answer. Even the dog on the opposite bank sat silent, cocking its head at Pat's calling, as if puzzled.

It was not like Lucy to wander from where he had left her. He looked round for any sign of her beside the tea table. He noticed where she had picked meadowsweet and figwort; stems were freshly broken. A wasp was on the figwort. Lucy was afraid of wasps, but perhaps the wasp had not been there when she had picked what she wanted. The figwort with the wasp on it leaned right over the water.

"Lucy!" Pat called again. He went on calling her name while he slowly swiveled round, scrutinizing each part of the willow plantation as he faced it. He came full circle and was facing the river again.

The river flowed softly, slowly, but it was deep and dark. Every so often, perhaps at distances of many years, somebody drowned in it. Pat knew that.

He looked over the river to the dog and wondered how long he had been there and why he had barked so furiously and then stopped.

He looked at the bank where the figwort grew; it was crumbly, and now he noticed that some of it had been freshly broken away, slipping into the water.

He saw the flowing of the water, its depth and darkness. Speechless and motionless he stood there, staring.

The summer afternoon was still perfect, with sunshine, flowers blooming, birds singing, even to the cuckoo. . . .

Then suddenly: *the cuckoo*! He swung around, almost lost his balance on the edge of the riverbank, and with a shout of "Lucy!" started off in quite the wrong direction. Then he saw a hand that lifted a curtain of ivy hanging over a fallen tree trunk. He plunged toward it and found her. She was hiding in a green ivy cave, laughing at him. He pulled her out, into the open, and began smacking her bare arms, so that she screamed with pain and astonishment and anger. The dog began barking again. Pat was shouting, "You stupid little girl—stupid—stupid—stupid!"

And then another voice was added to theirs, in a bellow. The punt Pat saw earlier had come downstream as far as the plantation, and the man who had been dozing was now on his feet and shouting: "Stop that row, for God's sake! And you ought to be ashamed of yourself— beating your sister like that! Stop it, or I'll come on land and stop you myself with a vengeance!"

The two children stared, still and silent at once. Then Pat gripped Lucy and began to pull her away from the riverbank and the man and the dog. They blundered through the plantation and reached the barbed wire. They crept under it, and Pat set off again, pulling Lucy after him, across the meadows to the right, toward the distant road.

"We're going home," he said shortly when Lucy in tears asked where they were going.

"But why aren't we going back by the riverbank and over the tree? I liked that."

"Because we're not. Because I say so."

When they reached the road, they turned in the direction of home. There was a long way to go, Pat knew, and Lucy was already whining steadily. She hated to walk when she had to walk. There was not much chance of anyone they knew stopping to give them a lift, and if anyone did, there would be a lot of questions to be answered.

They passed a bus stop and plodded on. Lucy was crying like a toothache. Pat heard a car coming, and it passed them. Later a truck, and it passed them. Then there was a heavier sound behind them on the road, and Pat turned. "Lucy, quick! Back—run back!"

"Back?"

But Pat was already dragging her with him back to the bus stop, signaling as he ran. The bus drew up for them, and they climbed in and sat down. Pat was trembling. Lucy, who had needed a handkerchief for some time now, passed from sobbing to sniffing.

The conductor was standing over them. "Well?" he said.

Pat started. "Two halves to Barley," he said.

The conductor held out his hand.

Pat felt through all the contents of his trouser pockets, but before he reached the bottoms, he knew, he remembered: "I've no money."

The conductor reached up and twanged the bell of the bus, and the driver slowed to a halt, although there was no bus stop. "I've a heart of gold," said the conductor, "but I've met this trick before on a Saturday afternoon."

Pat could feel the other passengers on the bus were listening intently. Their faces, all turned in his direction, were so many pale blurs to him; almost certainly he was going to cry.

The conductor said, "You've some hard-luck story, no doubt, you and your little sister."

"She's not my sister," Pat muttered.

A voice from somewhere in the bus—the voice of Mrs. Bovey, who lived down their road—said: "I know him. He's Pat Woods. I'll pay the fare. But what his mother would say . . ."

"You're a lucky boy, aren't you?" the conductor said.

Pat did not look at Mrs. Bovey; he did not thank her; he hated her.

The conductor took Mrs. Bovey's money and twanged the bell again, so that the bus moved on. He held out two tickets to Pat but did not yet let him take them. "Latest fashion, I suppose?" he said. Pat did not know what he meant until he pointed, and then Pat realized that Lucy was still wearing his sweater as trousers.

"Take that off," Pat ordered Lucy. As she was slow, he began to drag the sweater off her.

The conductor interrupted to hand him the tickets. "You be gentle with your sister," he warned Pat, and from somewhere in the bus a passenger tutted.

"She's not my sister, I tell you."

"No," said Mrs. Bovey, "and what *her* mother will say I don't like to think."

"You'll grant you're in charge of her this afternoon?" said the conductor. "Speak up, boy."

In the silence, Lucy said: "You're making him cry. I hate you. Of course, he looks after me. I'm always safe with him."

Pat had turned his head away from them—from all of them—as the tears ran down his cheeks.

Return to Air ❖

*T*he Ponds are very big, so that at one end people bathe and at the other end they fish. Old chaps with bald heads sit on folding stools and fish with rods and lines, and little kids squeeze through the railings and wade out into the water to fish with nets. But the water's much deeper at our end of the Ponds, and that's where we bathe. You're not allowed to bathe there unless you can swim, but I've always been able to swim. They used to say that was because fat floats—well, I don't mind. They call me Sausage.

Only, I don't dive—not from any diving board, thank you. I have to take my glasses off to go into the water, and I can't see without them, and I'm just not going to dive, even from the lowest diving board, and that's that, and they stopped nagging about it long ago.

Then, this summer, they were all on to me to learn duck-diving. You're swimming on the surface of the water, and suddenly you upend yourself just like a duck and dive down deep into the water, and perhaps you swim about a bit underwater and then come up again. I daresay ducks begin doing it soon after they're born. It's different for them.

So I was learning to duck-dive—to swim down to the bottom of the

Ponds and pick up a brick they'd throw in and bring it up again. You practice that in case you have to rescue anyone from drowning--say, they'd sunk for the third time and gone to the bottom. Of course, they'd be bigger and heavier than a brick, but I suppose you have to begin with bricks and work up gradually to people.

The swimming instructor said, "Sausage, I'm going to throw the brick in." It was a brick with a bit of old white flannel round it, to make it show up underwater. "Sausage, I'm going to throw it in, and you go *after* it—go *after* it, Sausage, and get it before it reaches the bottom and settles in the mud, or you'll never get it."

He'd made everyone come out of the water to give me a chance, and they were standing watching. I could see them blurred along the bank, and I could hear them talking and laughing, but there wasn't a sound in the water except me just treading water gently, waiting. And then I saw the brick go over my head as the instructor threw it, and there was a splash as it went into the water ahead of me, and I thought: I can't do it; my legs won't upend this time; they feel just flabby; they'll float, but they won't upend; they *can't* upend; it's different for ducks. . . . But while I was thinking all that, I'd taken a deep breath, and then my head really went down and my legs went up into the air. I could feel them there, just air around them, and then there was water around them, because I was going down into the water after all. Right down into the water, straight down . . .

At first my eyes were shut, although I didn't know I'd shut them. When I did realize, I forced my eyelids up against the water to see. Because although I can't see much without my glasses, as I've said, I don't believe anyone could see much underwater in those Ponds, so I could see as much as anyone.

The water was like a thick greeny brown lemonade, with wispy little things moving very slowly about in it, or perhaps they were just movements of the water, not things at all; I couldn't tell. The brick had a few seconds' start of me, of course, but I could still see a whitish glimmer that must be the flannel around it; it was ahead of me, fading away into the lower water, as I moved after it.

The funny thing about swimming underwater is its being so still and quiet and shady down there, after all the air and sunlight and splashing and shouting just up above. I was shut right in by the quiet, greeny brown water, just me alone with the brick ahead of me, both of us making toward the bottom.

The Ponds are deep, but I knew they weren't too deep, and of course, I knew I'd enough air in my lungs from the breath I'd taken. I knew all that.

Down we went, and the lemonade look quite went from the water, and it became just a dark blackish brown, and you'd wonder you could see anything at all. Especially as the bit of white flannel seemed to have come off the brick by the time it reached the bottom and I'd caught up with it. The brick looked different down there, anyway, and it had already settled right into the mud; there was only one corner left sticking up. I dug into the mud with my fingers and got hold of the thing, and then I didn't think of anything except getting up again with it into the air.

Touching the bottom like that had stirred up the mud, so that I began going up through a thick cloud of it. I let myself go up—they say fat floats, you know—but I was shooting myself upward, too. I was in a hurry.

The funny thing was, I only began to be afraid when I was going back. I suddenly thought: perhaps I've swum underwater much too far; perhaps I'll come up at the far end of the Ponds among all the fishermen and foul their lines and perhaps get a fishhook caught in the flesh of my cheek. And all the time I was going up quite quickly, and the water was changing from brown-black to green-brown and then to bright lemonade. I could almost see the sun shining through the water, I was so near the surface. It wasn't until then that I felt really frightened; I thought I was moving much too slowly and I'd never reach the air again in time.

Never the air again . . .

Then suddenly I was at the surface; I'd exploded back from the water into the air. For a while I couldn't think of anything, and I couldn't do anything except let out the old breath I'd been holding and take a couple of fresh, quick ones and tread water—and hang on to that brick.

Pond water was trickling down inside my nose and into my mouth, which I hate. But there was air all around and above, for me to breathe, to live.

And then I noticed they were shouting from the bank. They were cheering and shouting, "Sausage! Sausage!" and the instructor was hallooing with his hands round his mouth and bellowing to me: "What on earth have you got there, Sausage?"

So then I turned myself properly around; I'd come up almost facing the fishermen at the other end of the Ponds, but otherwise only a few feet from where I'd gone down, so that was all right. I turned around and swam to the bank, and they hauled me out and gave me my glasses to have a good look at what I'd brought up from the bottom.

Because it wasn't a brick. It was just about the size and shape of one, but it was a tin—an old, old tin box with no paint left on it and all brown-black slime from the bottom of the Ponds. It was as heavy as a brick because it was full of mud. Don't get excited, as we did; there was nothing there but mud. We strained all the mud through our fingers, but there wasn't anything else there—not even a bit of old sandwich or the remains of bait. I thought there might have been, because the tin could have belonged to one of the old chaps that have always fished at the other end of the Ponds. They often bring their dinners with them in bags or tins, and they have tins for bait, too. It could have been dropped into the water at their end of the Ponds and got moved to our end with the movement of the water. Otherwise I don't know how that tin box can have got there. Anyway, it must have been there for years and years, by the look of it. When you think, it might have stayed there for years and years longer, perhaps stayed sunk underwater forever.

I've cleaned the tin up, and I keep it on the mantelpiece at home with my coin collection in it. I had to duck-dive later for another brick, and I got it all right, without being frightened at all, but it didn't seem to matter as much as coming up with the tin. I shall keep the tin as long as I live, and I might easily live to be a hundred.

Part II ❖

The Haunting Stories

The Shadow Cage ❖

 he little green stoppered bottle had been waiting in the earth a long time for someone to find it. Ned Challis found it. High on his tractor as he plowed the field, he'd been keeping a lookout, as usual, for whatever might turn up. Several times there had been worked flints; once, one of an enormous size.

Now sunlight glimmering on glass caught his eye. He stopped the tractor, climbed down, picked the bottle from the earth. He could tell at once that it wasn't all that old. Not as old as the flints that he'd taken to the museum in Castleford. Not as old as a coin he had once found, with the head of a Roman emperor on it. Not very old, but old.

Perhaps just useless old . . .

He held the bottle in the palm of his hand and thought of throwing it away. The lip of it was chipped badly, and the stopper of cork or wood had sunk into the neck. With his fingernail he tried to move it. The stopper had hardened into stone and stuck there. Probably no one would ever get it out now without breaking the bottle. But, then, why should anyone want to unstopper the bottle? It was empty, or as good as empty. The bottom of the inside of the bottle was dirtied with something blackish and scaly that also clung a little to the sides.

He wanted to throw the bottle away, but he didn't. He held it in one hand while the fingers of the other cleaned the remaining earth from the outside. When he had cleaned it, he didn't fancy the bottle any more than before, but he dropped it into his pocket. Then he climbed the tractor and started off again.

At that time the sun was high in the sky, and the tractor was working on Whistlers' Hill, which is part of Belper's Farm, fifty yards below Burnt House. As the tractor moved on again, the gulls followed again, rising and falling in their flights, wheeling over the disturbed earth, looking for live things, for food, for good things.

That evening, at tea, Ned Challis brought the bottle out and set it on the table by the loaf of bread. His wife looked at it suspiciously. "Another of your dirty old things for that museum?"

Ned said, "It's not museum stuff. Lisa can have it to take to school. I don't want it."

Mrs. Challis pursed her lips, moved the loaf further away from the bottle, and went to refill the teapot.

Lisa took the bottle in her hand. "Where'd you get it, Dad?"

"Whistlers' Hill. Just below Burnt House." He frowned suddenly as he spoke, as if he had remembered something.

"What's it got inside?"

"Nothing. And if you try getting the stopper out, that'll break."

So Lisa didn't try. Next morning she took it to school, but she didn't show it to anyone. Only her cousin Kevin saw it, and that was before school and by accident. He always called for Lisa on his way to school—there was no other company on that country road—and he saw her pick up the bottle from the table, where her mother had left it the night before, and put it into her jacket pocket.

"What was that?" asked Kevin.

"You saw. A little old bottle."

"Let's see it again—properly." Kevin was younger than Lisa, and she sometimes indulged him, so she took the bottle out and let him hold it.

At once he tried the stopper.

"Don't," said Lisa. "You'll only break it."

"What's inside?"

"Nothing. Dad found it on Whistlers'."

"It's not very nice, is it?"

"What do you mean, 'Not very nice'?"

"I don't know. But let me keep it for a bit. Please, Lisa."

On principle Lisa now decided not to give in. "Certainly not. Give it back."

He did, reluctantly. "Let me have it just for today, at school. Please."

"No."

"I'll give you something if you'll let me have it. I'll not let anyone else touch it; I'll not let them see it. I'll keep it safe. Just for today."

"You'd only break it. No. What could you give me, anyway?"

"My week's pocket money."

"No. I've said no, and I mean no, young Kev."

"I'd give you that little china dog you like."

"The one with the china kennel?"

"Yes."

"The china dog with the china kennel—you'd give me both."

"Yes."

"Only for half the day, then," said Lisa. "I'll let you have it after school dinner; look out for me in the playground. Give it back at the end of school. Without fail. And you be careful with it."

So the bottle traveled to school in Lisa's jacket pocket, where it bided its time all morning. After school dinner Lisa met Kevin in the playground, and they withdrew together to a corner which was well away from the crowded jungle gym and the Infants' sandpit and the rest. Lisa handed the bottle over. "At the end of school, mind, without fail. And if we miss each other then"—for Lisa, being in a higher class, came out of school slightly later than Kevin—"then you must drop it in at ours as you pass. Promise."

"Promise."

They parted. Kevin put the bottle into his pocket. He didn't know why he'd wanted the bottle, but he had. Lots of things were like that. You needed them for a bit, and then you didn't need them any longer.

He had needed this little bottle very much.

He left Lisa and went over to the jungle gym, where his friends already were. He had set his foot on a rung when he thought suddenly how easy it would be for the glass bottle in his trouser pocket to be smashed against the metal framework. He stepped down again and went over to the fence that separated the playground from the farmland beyond. Tall tussocks of grass grew along it, coming through from the open fields and fringing the very edge of the asphalt. He looked round. Lisa had already gone in, and no one else was watching. He put his hand into his pocket and took it out again with the bottle concealed in the fist. He stooped as if to examine an insect on a tussock and slipped his hand into the middle of it and left the bottle there, well hidden.

He straightened up and glanced around. Since no one was looking in his direction, his action had been unobserved; the bottle would be safe. He ran back to the jungle gym and began to climb, jostling and shouting and laughing, as he and his friends always did. He forgot the bottle.

He forgot the bottle completely.

It was very odd, considering what a fuss he had made about the bottle, that he should have forgotten it, but he did. When the bell rang for the end of playtime, he ran straight in. He did not think of the bottle then or later. At the end of afternoon school, he did not remember it, and he happened not to see Lisa, who would surely have reminded him.

Only when he was nearly home and passing the Challises' house, he remembered. He had faithfully promised—and had really meant to keep his promise. But he'd broken it and left the bottle behind. If he turned and went back to school now, he would meet Lisa, and she would have to be told. . . . By the time he got back to the school playground, all his friends would have gone home; the caretaker would be there, and perhaps a late teacher or two, and they'd all want to know what he was up to. And when he'd got the bottle and dropped it in at the Challises', Lisa would scold him all over again. And when he got home at last, he would be very late for his tea, and his mother would be angry.

As he stood by the Challises' gate, thinking, it seemed best, since he had messed things up, anyway, to go straight home and leave the bottle to the next day. So he went home.

He worried about the bottle for the rest of the day, without having the time or the quiet to think about it very clearly. He knew that Lisa would assume he had just forgotten to leave it at her house on the way home. He half expected her to turn up after tea, to claim it, but she didn't. She would have been angry enough about his having forgotten to leave it, but what about her anger tomorrow on the way to school, when she found that he had forgotten it altogether—abandoned it in the open playground? He thought of hurrying straight past her house in the morning, but he would never manage it. She would be on the lookout.

He saw that he had made the wrong decision earlier. He ought, at all costs, to have gone back to the playground to get the bottle.

He went to bed, still worrying. He fell asleep, and his worry went on, making his dreaming unpleasant in a nagging way. He must be quick, his dreams seemed to nag. *Be quick. . . .*

Suddenly he was wide-awake. It was very late. The sound of the television being switched off must have woken him. Quietness. He listened to the rest of his family going to bed. They went to bed and to sleep. Silence. They were all asleep now, except for him. He couldn't sleep.

Then, as abruptly as if someone had lifted the top of his head like a lid and popped the idea in, he saw that this time—almost the middle of the night—was the perfect time for him to fetch the bottle. He knew by heart the roads between home and school; he would not be afraid. He would have plenty of time. When he reached the school, the gate to the playground would be shut, but it was not high; in the past, by daylight, he and his friends had often climbed it. He would go into the playground, find the correct tussock of grass, get the bottle, bring it back, and have it ready to give to Lisa on the way to school in the morning. She would be angry but only moderately angry. She would never know the whole truth.

He got up and dressed quickly and quietly. He began to look for a flashlight but gave up when he realized that would mean opening and shutting drawers and cupboards. Anyway, there was a moon tonight, and he knew his way, and he knew the school playground. He couldn't go wrong.

He let himself out of the house, leaving the door on the latch for his return. He looked at his watch: between a quarter and half past eleven—not as late as he had thought. All the same, he set off almost at a run but had to settle down into a steady trot. His trotting footsteps on the road sounded clearly in the night quiet. But who was there to hear?

He neared the Challises' house. He drew level with it.

Ned Challis heard. Usually nothing woke him before the alarm clock in the morning, but tonight footsteps woke him. Who, at this hour—he lifted the back of his wrist toward his face, so that the time glimmered at him—who, at nearly twenty-five to twelve, could be hurrying along that road on foot? When the footsteps had almost gone—when it was already perhaps too late—he sprang out of bed and over to the window.

His wife woke. "What's up, then, Ned?"

"Just somebody. I wondered who."

"Oh, come back to bed!"

Ned Challis went back to bed but almost at once got out again.

"Ned! What is it now?"

"I just thought I'd have a look at Lisa."

At once Mrs. Challis was wide-awake. "What's wrong with Lisa?"

"Nothing." He went to listen at Lisa's door—listen to the regular, healthy breathing of her sleep. He came back. "Nothing. Lisa's all right."

"For heaven's sake! Why shouldn't she be?"

"Well, who was it walking out there? Hurrying."

"Oh, go to sleep!"

"Yes." He lay down again, drew the bedclothes round him, lay still. But his eyes remained open.

Out in the night, Kevin left the road on which the Challises lived and came into the more important one that would take him into the village. He heard the rumble of a truck coming up behind him. For safety he drew right into a gateway and waited. The truck came past at a steady pace, headlights on. For a few seconds he saw the driver and his mate sitting up in the cab, intent on the road ahead. He had not wanted to be noticed by them, but when they had gone, he felt lonely.

He went on into the village, its houses lightless, its streets deserted. By the entrance to the school driveway, he stopped to make sure he was unobserved. Nobody. Nothing—not even a cat. There was no sound of any vehicle now, but in the distance he heard a dog barking, and then another answered it. A little owl cried and cried for company or for sport. Then that, too, stopped.

He turned into the driveway to the school, and there was the gate to the playground. He looked over it, into the playground. Moonlight showed him everything: the expanse of asphalt, the sandpit, the big jungle gym, and—at the far end—the fence with the tussocks of grass growing blackly along it. It was all familiar, and yet strange because of the emptiness and the whitening of moonlight and the shadows cast like solid things. The jungle gym reared high into the air, and on the ground stretched the black crisscross of its shadows like the bars of a cage.

But he had not come all this way to be halted by moonshine and insubstantial shadows. In a businesslike way he climbed the gate and crossed the playground to the fence. He wondered whether he would find the right tussock easily, but he did. His fingers closed on the bottle; it was waiting for him.

At that moment, in the Challises' house, as they lay side by side in bed, Mrs. Challis said to her husband, "You're still awake, aren't you?"

"Yes."

"What is it?"

"Nothing."

Mrs. Challis sighed.

"All right, then," said Ned Challis. "It's this. That bottle I gave Lisa—that little old bottle that I gave Lisa yesterday—"

"What about it?"

"I found it by Burnt House."

Mrs. Challis drew in her breath sharply. Then she said, "That may mean nothing." Then: "How near was it?"

"Near enough." After a pause: "I ought never to have given it to Lisa. I never thought. But Lisa's all right, anyway."

"But, Ned, don't you know what Lisa did with that bottle?"

"What?"

"Lent it to Kevin to have at school. And according to her, he didn't return it when he should have done, on the way home. Didn't you hear her going on and on about it?"

"Kevin . . ." For the third time that night Ned Challis was getting out of bed, this time putting on his trousers, fumbling for his shoes. "Somebody went up the road in a hurry. You know—I looked out. I couldn't see properly, but it was somebody small. It could have been a child. It could have been Lisa, but it wasn't. It could well have been Kevin. . . ."

"Shouldn't you go to their house first, Ned, find out whether Kevin is there or not? Make sure. You're not sure."

"I'm not sure. But if I wait to make sure, I may be too late."

Mrs. Challis did not say, "Too late for what?" She did not argue.

Ned Challis dressed and went down. As he let himself out of the house to get his bicycle from the shed, the church clock began to strike the hour, the sound reaching him distantly across the intervening fields. He checked with his watch: midnight.

In the village, in the school playground, the striking of midnight sounded clangorously close. Kevin stood with the bottle held in the palm of his hand, waiting for the clock to stop striking—waiting as if for something to follow.

After the last stroke of midnight, there was silence, but Kevin still stood waiting and listening. A car or truck passed the entrance of the school drive; he heard it distinctly, yet it was oddly faint, too. He couldn't place the oddness of it. It had sounded much further away than it should have done—less really there.

He gripped the bottle and went on listening, as if for some particular sound. The minutes passed. The same dog barked at the same dog, bark and reply—far, unreally far away. The little owl called; from another world it might have been.

He was gripping the bottle so tightly now that his hand was sweating. He felt his skin begin to prickle with sweat at the back of his neck and under his arms.

Then there was a whistle from across the fields, distantly. It should have been an unexpected sound, just after midnight, but it did not startle him. It did set him off across the playground, however. Too late he wanted to get away. He had to go past the jungle gym, whose cagework of shadows now stretched more largely than the frame itself. He saw the bars of shadow as he approached; he actually hesitated, and then, like a fool, he stepped inside the cage of shadows.

Ned Challis, on his bicycle, had reached the junction of the by road with the road that, in one direction, led to the village. In the other it led deeper into the country. Which way? He dismounted. He had to choose the right way—to follow Kevin.

Thinking of Whistlers' Hill, he turned the front wheel of his bicycle away from the village and set off again. But now, with his back to the village, going away from the village, he felt a kind of weariness and despair. A memory of childhood came into his mind: a game he had played in childhood, something hidden for him to find, and if he turned in the wrong direction to search, all the voices whispered to him, "Cold—cold!" Now, with the village receding behind him, he recognized what he felt: cold . . . cold . . .

Without getting off his bicycle, he wheeled round and began to pedal hard in the direction of the village.

In the playground there was no pressing hurry for Kevin anymore.

He did not press against the bars of his cage to get out. Even when clouds cut off the moonlight and the shadows melted into general darkness, even when the shadow cage was no longer visible to the eye, he stood there, then crouched there, in a corner of the cage, as befitted a prisoner.

The church clock struck the quarter.

The whistlers were in no hurry. The first whistle had come from right across the fields. Then there was a long pause. Then the sound was repeated, equally distantly, from the direction of the river bridges. Later still, another whistle from the direction of the railway line or somewhere near it.

He lay in his cage, cramped by the bars, listening. He did not know he was thinking, but suddenly it came to him: Whistlers' Hill. He and Lisa and the others had always supposed that the hill had belonged to a family called Whistler, as Challises' house belonged to the Challis family. But that was not how the hill had got its name; he saw that now. No, indeed not.

Whistler answered whistler at long intervals, like the sentries of a besieging army. There was no moving in as yet.

The church clock had struck the quarter as Ned Challis entered the village and cycled past the entrance to the school. He cycled as far as the recreation ground, perhaps because that was where Kevin would have gone in the daytime. He cycled bumpily around the ground: no Kevin.

He began to cycle back the way he had come, as though he had given up altogether and were going home. He cycled slowly. He passed the entrance to the school again.

In this direction he was leaving the village. He was cycling so slowly that the front wheel of his bicycle wobbled desperately; the light from his dynamo was dim. He put a foot down and stopped. Motionless, he listened. There was nothing to hear, unless—yes, the faintest ghost of a sound, high-pitched, prolonged for seconds, remote as from another world. Like a coward—and Ned Challis was no coward—he tried to persuade himself that he had imagined the sound, yet he knew he had not. It came from another direction now: very faint, yet penetrating, so that his skin crinkled to hear it. Again it came, from yet another quarter.

He wheeled his bicycle back to the entrance to the school and left it there. He knew he must be very close. He walked up to the playground gate and peered over it. But the moon was obscured by cloud; he could see nothing. He listened, waited for the moon to sail free.

In the playground Kevin had managed to get up, first on his hands and knees, then upright. He was very much afraid, but he had to be standing to meet whatever it was.

For the whistlers had begun to close in slowly, surely, converging on the school, on the school playground, on the cage of shadows. On him.

For some time now cloud masses had obscured the moon. So he could see nothing, but he felt the whistlers' presence. Their signals came more often, and always closer. Closer. Very close.

Suddenly the moon sailed free.

In the sudden moonlight Ned Challis saw clear across the playground to where Kevin stood against the jungle gym, with his hands writhing together in front of him.

In the sudden moonlight Kevin did not see his uncle. Between him and the playground gate, and all round him, air was thickening into darkness. Frantically he tried to undo his fingers, which held the little bottle, so that he could throw it from him. But he could not. He held the bottle; the bottle held him.

The darkness was closing in on him. The darkness was about to take him, had surely got him.

Kevin shrieked.

Ned Challis shouted, "I'm here!" and was over the gate and across the playground and with his arms around the boy. "*I've got you.*"

There was a tinkle as something fell from between Kevin's opened fingers; the little bottle fell and rolled to the middle of the playground. It lay there, very insignificant-looking.

Kevin was whimpering and shaking, but he could move of his own accord. Ned Challis helped him over the gate and to the bicycle.

"Do you think you could sit on the bar, Kev? Could you manage that?"

"Yes." He could barely speak.

Ned Challis hesitated, thinking of the bottle, which had chosen to come to rest in the very center of the playground, where the first child tomorrow would see it, pick it up.

He went back and picked the bottle up. Wherever he threw it, someone might find it. He might smash it and grind the pieces underfoot, but he was not sure he dared to do that.

Anyway, he was not going to hold it in his hand longer than he strictly must. He put it into his pocket, and then, when he got back to Kevin and the bicycle, he slipped it into the saddlebag.

He rode Kevin home on the crossbar of his bicycle. At the Challises' front gate Mrs. Challis was waiting, with the dog for company. She just said: "He all right then?"

"Ah."

"I'll make a cup of tea while you take him home."

At his own front door, Kevin said, "I left the door on the latch. I can get in. I'm all right. I'd rather—I'd rather—"

"Less spoken of, the better," said his uncle. "You go to bed. Nothing to be afraid of now."

He waited until Kevin was inside the house and he heard the latch click into place. Then he rode back to his wife, his cup of tea, and consideration of the problem that lay in his saddlebag.

After he had told his wife everything, and they had discussed possibilities, Ned Challis said thoughtfully, "I might take it to the museum, after all. Safest place for it would be inside a glass case there."

"But you said they wouldn't want it."

"Perhaps they would, if I told them where I found it and a bit— only a bit—about Burnt House. . . ."

"You do that, then."

Ned Challis stood up and yawned with a finality that said bed.

"But don't you go thinking you've solved all your problems by taking that bottle to Castleford, Ned. Not by a long chalk."

"No?"

"Lisa. She reckons she owns that bottle."

"I'll deal with Lisa tomorrow."

"Today, by the clock."

Ned Challis gave a groan that turned into another yawn. "Bed first," he said, "then Lisa." They went to bed not long before the dawn.

The next day and for days after that, Lisa was furiously angry with her father. He had as good as stolen her bottle, she said, and now he refused to give it back, to let her see it, even to tell her what he had done with it. She was less angry with Kevin. (She did not know, of course, the circumstances of the bottle's passing from Kevin to her father.)

Kevin kept out of Lisa's way and even more carefully kept out of his uncle's. He wanted no private conversation.

One Saturday Kevin was having tea at the Challises', because he had been particularly invited. He sat with Lisa and Mrs. Challis. Ned had gone to Castleford and came in late. He joined them at the tea table in evident good spirits. From his pocket he brought out a small cardboard box, which he placed in the center of the table, by the Saturday cake. His wife was staring at him; before he spoke, he gave her the slightest nod of reassurance. "The museum didn't want to keep that little old glass bottle, after all," he said.

Both the children gave a cry. Kevin started up with such a violent backward movement that his chair clattered to the floor behind him; Lisa leaned forward, her fingers clawing toward the box.

"No!" Ned Challis said. To Lisa he added: "There it stays, girl, till *I* say." To Kevin: "Calm down. Sit up at the table again and listen to me." Kevin picked his chair up and sat down again, resting his elbows on the table, so that his hands supported his head.

"Now," said Ned Challis, "you two know so much that it's probably better you should know more. That little old bottle came from Whistlers' Hill, below Burnt House—well, you know that. Burnt House is only a ruin now, elder bushes growing inside as well as out, but once it was a cottage that someone lived in. Your mother's granny remembered the last one to live there."

"No, Ned," said Mrs. Challis, "it was my great-granny remembered."

"Anyway," said Ned Challis, "it was so long ago that Victoria was the queen, that's certain. And an old woman lived alone in that cottage. There were stories about her."

"Was she a witch?" breathed Lisa.

"So they said. They said she went out on the hillside at night—"

"At the full of the moon," said Mrs. Challis.

"They said she dug up roots and searched out plants and toadstools and things. They said she caught rats and toads and even bats. They said she made ointments and powders and weird brews. And they said she used what she made to cast spells and call up spirits."

"Spirits from hell, my great-granny said. Real bad uns."

"So people said, in the village. Only the parson scoffed at the whole idea. Said he'd called often and been shown over the cottage and seen nothing out of the ordinary—none of the jars and bottles of stuff that she was supposed to have for her witchcraft. He said she was just a poor cranky old woman; that was all.

"Well, she grew older and older and crankier and crankier, and one day she died. Her body lay in its coffin in the cottage, and the parson was going to bury her next day in the churchyard.

"The night before she was to have been buried, someone went up from the village—"

"Someone!" said Mrs. Challis scornfully. "Tell them the whole truth, Ned, if you're telling the story at all. Half the village went up, with lanterns—men, women, and children. Go on, Ned."

"The cottage was thatched, and they began to pull swatches of straw away and take it into the cottage and strew it round and heap it up under the coffin. They were going to fire it all.

"They were pulling the straw on the downhill side of the cottage when suddenly a great piece of thatch came away and out came tumbling a whole lot of things that the old woman must have kept hidden there. People did hide things in thatches, in those days."

"Her savings?" asked Lisa.

"No. A lot of jars and little bottles, all stoppered or sealed, neat and nice. With stuff inside."

There was a silence at the tea table. Then Lisa said, "That proved it: she was a witch."

"Well, no, it only proved she *thought* she was a witch. That was what the parson said afterward—and whew! Was he mad when he knew about that night."

Mrs. Challis said, "He gave it 'em red-hot from the pulpit the next Sunday. He said that once upon a time poor old deluded creatures like her had been burnt alive for no reason at all, and the village ought to be ashamed of having burnt her dead."

Lisa went back to the story of the night itself. "What did they do with what came out of the thatch?"

"Bundled it inside the cottage among the straw and fired it all. The cottage burnt like a beacon that night, they say. Before cockcrow, everything had been burnt to ashes. That's the end of the story."

"Except for my little bottle," said Lisa. "That came out of the thatch, but it didn't get picked up. It rolled downhill, or someone kicked it."

"That's about it," Ned agreed.

Lisa stretched her hand again to the cardboard box, and this time he did not prevent her. But he said, "Don't be surprised, Lisa. It's different."

She paused. "A different bottle?"

"The same bottle, but—well, you'll see."

Lisa opened the box, lifted the packaging of cotton wool, took the bottle out. It was the same bottle, but the stopper had gone, and it was empty and clean—so clean that it shone greenly. Innocence shone from it.

"You said the stopper would never come out," Lisa said slowly.

"They forced it by suction. The museum chap wanted to know what was inside, so he got the hospital lab to take a look; he has a friend there. It was easy for them."

Mrs. Challis said, "That would make a pretty vase, Lisa. For tiny flowers." She coaxed Lisa to go out to pick a posy from the garden; she herself took the bottle away to fill it with water.

Ned Challis and Kevin faced each other across the table.

Kevin said, "What was in it?"

Ned Challis said, "A trace of this, a trace of that, the hospital said. One thing more than anything else."

"Yes."

"Blood. Human blood."

Lisa came back with her flowers; Mrs. Challis came back with the bottle filled with water. When the flowers had been put in, it looked a pretty thing.

"My witch bottle," said Lisa contentedly. "What was she called—the old woman that thought she was a witch?"

Her father shook his head; her mother thought. "Madge—or was it Maggy?"

"Maggy Whistler's bottle, then," said Lisa.

"Oh, no," said Mrs. Challis. "She was Maggy—or Madge—Dawson. I remember my granny saying so. Dawson."

"Then why's it called Whistlers' Hill?"

"I'm not sure," said Mrs. Challis uneasily. "I mean, I don't think anyone knows for certain."

But Ned Challis, looking at Kevin's face, knew that he knew for certain.

Miss Mountain ❖

*W*hatever else might be spring-cleaned in Grandmother's house, it was never her storeroom. Old Mrs. Robinson lived in a house with only two rooms upstairs, besides the bathroom. One was her bedroom; the other, the storeroom. This room fascinated her grandchildren, Daisy and Jim. It was about eight feet by six and so full of stuff that even to open the door properly was difficult. If you forced it open enough to poke your head round, you saw a positive mountain of things reaching almost to the ceiling: old suitcases, bulging cardboard boxes of all shapes and sizes, stringed-up parcels of magazines, cascades of old curtains, and a worm-eaten chair or two.

Grandmother was teased about the state of her storeroom. She retorted with spirit, "There isn't as much stuff as there seems to be, because it's all piled up on the spare bed. The room's really a guest room. I'm only waiting for a bit of time to clear it."

Then everybody would laugh: Daisy and Jim and their father, who was Grandmother's son, and their mother, who was her daughter-in-law. Grandmother would join in the laughter. She always laughed a lot, even at herself.

If they went on to suggest lending a hand in the clearing of the storeroom, Grandmother stopped laughing to say, "I'd rather do it myself, thank you, when I have a bit of time." But she never seemed to have that bit.

She was the nicest of grandmothers: rosy to look at, and plump, and somehow cozy. She liked to spoil her grandchildren. Daisy and Jim lived only just round the corner from Grandmother's little house, so they were always calling on her, and she on them.

Then suddenly everything was going to change.

The children's father got another job that would mean the whole family's moving out of the district, leaving Grandmother behind.

"Goodness me!" Grandmother said, cheerful about most things. "It isn't the end of the world! I can come and visit you for the day."

"Not just for the day," said young Mrs. Robinson, who was very fond of her mother-in-law. "You must come and stay—often."

"And the children shall come and stay with me," Grandmother said.

"Where shall we sleep?" Jim asked.

"You'll have to clear the guest room," Daisy said.

"Yes, of course," said her grandmother, but for a moment looked as if she had not quite foreseen that and regretted the whole idea. But really the clearing out of the storeroom ought to have been done years and years ago.

Grandmother said that she preferred to do all the work herself, but everyone insisted that it would be too much for her. In the end she agreed to let Daisy and Jim help her. Perhaps she thought they would be easier to manage than their parents.

How much the storeroom held was amazing, and everything had to be brought out and sorted carefully. A lot went straight into the trash; some things—such as the bundles of magazines and the curtaining— went to the church hall for the next rummage sale; the chairs went onto the bonfire. Grandmother went through all the suitcases and got rid of everything; the suitcases themselves were only fit for rummage. The cardboard boxes, Grandmother said, were going to be more difficult, so for the moment they were piled up in a corner of her bedroom.

They sorted and cleared for several days. Sure enough, under the mountain, there really had been a bed—narrow, but quite wide enough for Daisy (who was older and larger than Jim)—and there was a mattress on it, and pillows and blankets (only one moth-eaten enough for the dustbin). Grandmother made the bed up at once with sheets and pillowcases from her airing cupboard.

"There!" she said. "My guest room!"

Daisy and Jim loved it. The room seemed so small and private, with an old-fashioned wallpaper that must have been there before Grandmother moved in, all those years ago. The window looked over the garden and received the morning sun. (Of course, that meant that in the evening the room dimmed early.)

All that remained was to clear the cardboard boxes still in Grandmother's own bedroom. She said she could do this herself in the evening when the children had gone home. But Daisy thought her grandmother already looked tired. She made her sit down in a chair, and the two children began going through the boxes for her. "We'll show you everything as we come to it," Daisy said.

Grandmother sighed.

For the first half hour everything went into the wastebasket: the cardboard boxes themselves and their contents, which turned out to be certificates of this and that and old programs and views and other souvenirs. Then they came to boxes of photographs, some of them framed. These delayed the children.

"Look, Daisy!" said Jim. "What a fat little girl!"

"Here she is again," said Daisy. "Just a bit older and even fatter."

"It's me," said their grandmother, and leaned forward from her chair to dart a hand between the two children and take the photographs and tear them in halves as rubbish.

"Grandmother!" they protested, but it was too late.

They found a framed wedding group of long ago with gentlemen in high-buttoning jackets and ladies wearing long dresses and hats toppling with feathers and flowers and fruit and bows.

"Was this your wedding, Grandmother?"

Grandmother said, "I'm not as old as *that*. I wasn't thought of then. That was the wedding of my mother and father."

The children peered. "So that's our great-grandfather and our great-grandmother. . . ."

"And a couple of your great-great-aunts as bridesmaids," said their grandmother. She snorted. "I preferred not to go in for bridesmaids." She found them a photograph of her own wedding, with everybody still looking very strange and old-fashioned, but clearly their grandmother did not think so.

The children thought that the quaint wedding group of their great-grandparents would suit the little guest room. With their grandmother's agreement, they hung it there. Most of the other photographs went into the wastebasket.

The last of the cardboard boxes was a squarish one, from which Daisy now drew out a barrel-shaped container. The staves of the barrel and the bands encircling them, and the lid, were all of the same tarnished metal.

Grandmother said, "That's a biscuit barrel."

"Is it real silver?" asked Daisy.

"Yes," said Grandmother.

"How grand!" said Jim.

"Yes," said Grandmother. "Very valuable."

Daisy set the biscuit barrel respectfully on the floor, where they could all admire it.

"It was in our house when I was a child," said Grandmother. "I never liked it."

"There's a curly *H* on it," said Jim.

"For Hill," said Grandmother. "That was our surname. But I hated that biscuit barrel. I've always meant to get rid of it."

"Please, Grandmother!" cried Daisy. "You could stand it on the sideboard downstairs. It would look so nice. I'll polish up the silver." Their grandmother still stared unforgivingly at the barrel. "Think, Grandmother, you could keep biscuits in it for when we come to stay. Our favorite biscuits. I like custard creams best."

"I like pink sugar wafers," said Jim.

"Promise you'll keep it, Grandmother, to keep our biscuits in," said Daisy.

Grandmother stopped looking at the biscuit barrel and looked at her grandchildren instead. Suddenly she jumped up to hug them. "Oh, yes!" she said. "For after all, I'm lucky. Very, very lucky. I've a guest room and two grandchildren who want to come and stay with me!"

The little guest room, so small and private, was ready for its first guest.

The first guest was Jim. Perhaps by rights it should have been Daisy, because she was the elder, but Jim was the one likely to be a nuisance during the family's move. So the night before moving day and the first night afterward were spent by Jim in his grandmother's guest room. Then his father drove over and fetched him back to their new home.

In the new house, everyone was tired with the work of getting straight and might have been short-tempered with Jim's little-boy bounciness. But Jim was quieter than usual. They asked whether he had had a good time with his grandmother. Yes, he had gone shopping with her, and she had bought him a multicolored pen, and he had had sparklers in the garden after dark, and peaches for both his suppers, and Grandmother had had pink sugar wafer biscuits for him—his favorite.

"You're lucky to have a grandmother like that," said his mother.

"Reminds me of my own granny," said his father, "your grand-mother's mother. She was a good sort, too."

That night Daisy and Jim had to share a bedroom, because Daisy's room wasn't ready yet. Jim went to bed and asked his mother to leave the landing light on and the door ajar. "I thought you'd given that up," she said. "You're a big boy now." But she let him have his way.

Later, when Daisy came up, he was still awake.

Daisy said, "I'll be in my own room tomorrow night."

"I don't mind sharing."

Daisy got into bed.

"Daisy . . ."

"What?"

"I don't want to sleep here alone tomorrow night."

"But—but, Jim, you always sleep alone!" There was no reply from the other bed. "Jim, you're just being silly!"

Still no reply, and yet a little noise. Daisy listened carefully. Jim was crying.

She got out of bed and went to him. "What is it?"

"Nothing."

"It must be something."

"No, it's not. It's nothing."

Daisy knew Jim. He could be very obstinate. Perhaps he would never tell her about whatever it was.

"You'd feel better if you told me, Jim."

"No, I shouldn't."

He was crying so much that she put her arms round him. It struck her that he was shivering.

"Are you cold, Jim?"

"No."

"Then why are you shivering? You're not afraid of something?"

In answer, Jim gave a kind of gasp. "Let me alone."

Daisy was extremely irritated—and curious, too. "Go on—say something. I shan't let you alone till you say something."

Still, he did not speak, and Daisy amended, "If you say something, I won't argue; I'll go back to bed and let you alone. But you must say something—something that *is* something."

Jim collected himself, said carefully, "I don't want to stay the night in Grandmother's house again—ever." He turned over in bed with his back to Daisy.

Daisy stared at him, opened her mouth, remembered her promise, shut it, went back to bed, and lay there to think. She tried to think what might have happened during Jim's visit to make him feel as he did. It occurred to her that she might find out when her turn for a visit came. . . .

How odd of Jim. There could be nothing to be afraid of at night in the house of the coziest, rosiest, plumpest of grandmothers.

The moment she fell asleep, she was standing on her grandmother's front doorstep, her suitcase in her hand. She had already knocked. The door opened just as usual; there stood her grandmother, just as usual. But no, not as usual. Her grandmother peered at Daisy as if at a stranger. "Yes?" she said. "I'm Daisy Robinson," said Daisy. "I'm your granddaughter. I've come to stay the night." Without a word, her grandmother stood aside to let her enter. At once Daisy began to mount the stairs that led to that early-shadowed little guest room. She already saw the door ajar, waiting for her. Behind her, downstairs, she could hear her grandmother securing the front door for the night: the lock, the bolts, the chain. She shut the two of them in together for the night. Daisy could hear her grandmother's little laugh; she was chuckling to herself.

The rest of the dream—if there were any—had vanished by the time Daisy woke in the morning. All she knew of it was that she was glad she could not remember it.

Daisy told no one about Jim, chiefly because there was so little to tell. He seemed all right again, anyway. By that evening the bedrooms had been sorted out, so that Jim had his to himself. Without protest, he went to sleep alone. It's true that he screamed in the night, so that his mother had to go to him, but all children have nightmares sometimes. By the next night he had resumed his usual sound sleeping.

So Jim had been making a strange fuss about nothing, Daisy thought, or perhaps he'd got used to the idea of whatever there might have been, or—not the most comfortable idea for Daisy—he had been able to shut it from his mind because he was now a safe distance from Grandmother's little guest room.

Their grandmother came to stay. She was her usual cheerful self, and everyone enjoyed the visit; Jim seemed to enjoy her company as much as usual. At the end of her visit, Grandmother said, "Well, which of you two is coming to sleep in my guest room next?"

Jim said, "It's Daisy's turn."

"That's very fair of you, Jim," their mother said approvingly. Daisy looked at Jim, but Jim stubbornly looked past her. She knew that he would not have agreed to go under any circumstances.

Only a few weeks later Daisy went.

With her suitcase, she stood on her grandmother's doorstep. Twice she raised a hand to the knocker and twice let it fall. The third time she really knocked. She heard the patter of her grandmother's feet approaching. The door opened, and there was Grandmother, and all the uneasy feelings that Jim had given her vanished away. Her grandmother was laughing for joy at her coming, and the house seemed to welcome her. Even from the doorway Daisy could see into the sitting room, where the electric light had not yet been switched on: an open fire burned brightly, and by the fireplace stood a tea table with the china on it shining in the firelight, and beyond that glowed the polish of the sideboard with the objects on it all giving as much glow or glitter as they could.

They had tea with boiled eggs and salad, as time was getting on and this had to be tea and supper together.

"Anything more you fancy, Daisy, dear?"

Daisy looked over to the sideboard, to the biscuit barrel. "Pink sugar wafers?" she said.

"What an idea!" said her grandmother. "They're not *your* favorite biscuits!"

Daisy went over to the biscuit barrel, put her hand in.

"Go on, dear, take whatever you find, as many as you want. I like you to do that."

Daisy drew out a custard-cream biscuit. "Grandmother, you're wonderful! You never forget anything."

Grandmother sighed. "Sometimes I wish I were more forgetful."

Daisy laughed and munched.

Later they went to bed. They stood side by side looking into the little guest room. With the curtains drawn and the bedside light glowing from inside a pink shade, the room looked as cozy and rosy as Grandmother herself. "I hope you sleep well, my dear," said her grand-mother, and talked about the number of blankets and the number of pillows and the possibility of noise from neighboring houses. Some-times people had late parties.

"Did the neighbors disturb Jim?" Daisy asked suddenly.

"No," said her grandmother. "At least—he's a poor sleeper for such a young child, isn't he? He slept badly here."

Daisy glanced sideways to see her grandmother's expression when she had said this. She found her grandmother stealing a sideways glance at her. They both looked away at once, pretending nothing had happened.

"Remember," said Grandmother, "if you want anything, I'm just across the landing." She kissed Daisy good night.

Daisy decided not to think about that sideways glance tonight. She went to bed, slipped easily downhill into sleep, and slept.

Something woke her. She wasn't sure that it had been a noise, but surely it must have been. She lay very still, her eyes open, her ears listen-ing. Before going to bed, she had drawn the curtains back, so that she would wake to the morning sun; now it was night, without moon or stars, and all the lights of the surrounding houses had been extinguished.

She waited to hear a repetition of noise in the house, but there was none. She knew what she was expecting to hear: the creak of a stair tread. There was nothing, but she became sure, all the same, that someone was creeping downstairs.

It could be—it *must* be—her grandmother going downstairs for something. She would go quietly, for fear of waking Daisy. But would she manage to go so very, very quietly?

Whoever it was would have reached the foot of the stairs by now. Still no noise.

It must be her grandmother, and yet Daisy felt that it wasn't her grandmother. And yet again she felt it was her grandmother.

She must know. She called, "Grandmother!" pitching her voice rather high to reach the bottom of the stairs. The sound she made came out screamlike.

Almost at once she heard her grandmother's bedroom door open and the quick, soft sound of her feet bringing her across to the guest room.

"Here I am, dear!"

"I thought I heard—I thought you were going downstairs, Grandmother."

Grandmother seemed—well, agitated. "Oh, did you? Sometimes I need a drink of water in the night, and sometimes I do go downstairs for it."

"But it wasn't you. You came from your bedroom just now, not back up the stairs."

"What sharp ears you have, dear!"

"I didn't exactly *hear* anyone going downstairs, anyway," Daisy said slowly.

"So it was all a mistake. That's all right then, isn't it?"

Not a mistake, more of a muddle, Daisy thought. But she let herself be kissed good night again, and her light was switched off. Her grandmother went back to bed. There was quiet in the house: not only no unusual sound, but no feel of anything unusual. Daisy slept until morning sunshine.

The daytime was made as delightful for Daisy as her grandmother had made it for Jim. But evening came, and night, and this night was far worse than the previous one.

Daisy woke and lay awake, knowing that someone was creeping downstairs again. But it's my imagination, she told herself; how can I know, when I hear nothing?

Whoever it was reached the bottom of the stairs and crossed the hall to the sitting room door. Had Grandmother left that door shut or open when she went to bed? It did not matter. Whoever it was had entered the sitting room and was moving across to the sideboard.

What was happening down there in the dark and the silence?

Suddenly there was no more silence. From downstairs there was a shrill scream that turned into a crying and sobbing, both terrified and terrifying.

Hardly knowing what she was doing, Daisy was out of bed, through her bedroom door, across the landing to her grandmother's room. The door was shut; she had to pause an instant to open it, and in that instant she realized that the crying from downstairs had stopped.

She was inside her grandmother's bedroom. The bedside light was on, and Grandmother, flustered, had just sat up in bed. Daisy said, "That crying!"

"It was me," said her grandmother.

"Oh, no, no, no, no!" Daisy contradicted her grandmother with fury. She glared at her in fury and terror; the nicest grandmother in the world was concealing something, lying. What kind of grandmother was she then: sly; perhaps treacherous? Wicked?

At the look on Daisy's face, Grandmother shrank back among the pillows. She hid her face in her hands. Between the fingers Daisy saw tears beginning to roll down over the dry old skin. Grandmother was crying, with gasping sobs, and her crying was not all that different, but much quieter, from the crying Daisy had heard downstairs.

In the middle of her crying, Grandmother managed to say, "Oh, Daisy!" and stretched out her hands toward her, begging her.

Daisy looked searchingly at her grandmother, and her grandmother met her gaze. Daisy took the outstretched hands and stroked them. She calmed herself even while she calmed her grandmother. "I'll make us a pot of tea," she said. "I'll bring it up here."

"No," said her grandmother. "I'll come down. We'll have it downstairs, and I'll tell you—I'll tell you—" She began to cry again.

Daisy was no longer afraid. She went downstairs into the kitchen to boil a kettle. As she went, she turned the sitting room light on and switched on an electric heater. Everything was exactly as usual. The door had been shut.

From downstairs she heard her grandmother getting up and then coming out of her bedroom. She did not come directly downstairs. Daisy heard her cross the landing into the guest room, spend a few moments there, then come down.

Daisy carried the tea on a tray into the sitting room; she took the biscuit barrel off the sideboard and put it on the tray, in case Grandmother wanted something to eat with her tea. Grandmother was already waiting for her. She had brought downstairs with her the framed wedding photograph from Daisy's bedroom and set it where they could both see it. Daisy asked no question.

They sat together and sipped their tea. Daisy also nibbled a biscuit; her grandmother had shaken her head and shuddered when Daisy offered her the biscuit barrel.

"Now I'll tell you," said Grandmother. She paused, while she steadied herself, visibly. "I brought the wedding photo down so that I could *show* you."

Again she paused, for much longer, so Daisy said, "Your mother looked sweet as a bride."

"I never knew her," said Grandmother. "She died when I was very young."

Daisy said, "But Dad knew her! He talks about his granny."

"That was my stepmother, his stepgrandmother."

Now something seemed plain to Daisy. "A stepmother—poor Grandmother!"

"No," said Grandmother. "It wasn't like that at all. My stepmother—only I never really think of her as my stepmother, just as my mother—she was a darling."

"Then?"

"They're both in the group," said Grandmother. "My mother as the bride. My stepmother, as she later became, as one of the bridesmaids. The bridesmaids were my two aunts: one my mother's sister, whom my father married after my mother's death; the other, my father's sister."

Daisy studied the photograph. Now that she knew that one of the bridesmaids was the bride's sister, it was easy to see which; there was the same plumpness with prettiness.

The other bridesmaid was tall, thin, and rather glum-looking. There was a resemblance between her and the bridegroom, but not such a striking one.

"When my mother died," said Grandmother, "I was a very little girl, still babyish in my ways, no doubt. My father had to get someone to look after me and to run the house. He was in business and away at his office all day.

"He asked his sister to come—the other bridesmaid."

Daisy looked at the thin bridesmaid and wondered.

"She'd always been very fond of my father, I believe, and jealous of his having married. Perhaps she was glad that my mother had died; perhaps she would have been glad if I had never been born. She would have had my father all to herself then.

"She hated me."

"Grandmother!"

"Oh, yes, she hated me. I didn't fully understand it then. I just thought I had suddenly become stupid and disobedient and dirty and everything that—as it seemed to me—anyone would hate. I daresay I was rather a nasty little girl; I became so. One of the worst things was—"

Grandmother stopped speaking, shaded her face with her hand.

"Go on."

"It won't seem terrible to you. You may just laugh. Aunt used to sneer. When she sneered, that made it worse."

"But what was it?"

"I ate."

"Well, but . . ."

"I ate whenever I could. I ate enormously at meals, and I ate between meals. Aunt used to point it out to my father and put a tape measure round where she said my waist should be, as I sat at table. I've always been plump, like my mother's side of the family; I grew fat—terribly fat.

"Our surname was Hill. There were two Miss Hills in the house, my aunt and myself. But Aunt said there need be no confusion: she was Miss Hill; I was Miss Mountain. She called me Miss Mountain, unless my father was present. She would leave notes to me, addressed to Miss Mountain. Once my father found one and asked her about it, and she pretended it was just a little joke between us. But it wasn't a joke—or if it were, it was a cruel, cruel one."

"Couldn't you just have eaten less and grown thinner and spoiled her game?" asked Daisy.

"You don't understand. Her teasing of me made me eat even more. I took to stealing food. I'd slip out to the larder after Sunday dinner and tear the crisp bits of fat off the joint while it was still warm. Or I'd take sultanas out of the jar in the store cupboard. Or I'd pare off bits of cheese. Even a slice of dry bread, if there were nothing else. Once I ate dog biscuits from the shelf above the kennel.

"Of course, sooner or later, Aunt realized what was happening. She began to expect it and took a delight in catching me out. If she couldn't catch me at it, she would prevent me. She took to locking the kitchen door at night, because she knew I went down then to the store cupboard and larder.

"Then I found the biscuit barrel."

"This very biscuit barrel?"

"Yes. It always stood on the sideboard with cream crackers in it— just the plainest of biscuits, to be eaten with cheese. Well, I didn't mind that. I used to creep down for a cream cracker or two in the middle of the night."

"In this house?"

"Goodness, no! We lived a hundred miles from here, and the house has been pulled down now, I believe.

"Anyway, I used to creep down, as I've said. I daren't put on any light, although I was terribly afraid of the dark—I had become afraid of so many things by then. I felt my way into the room and across to the sideboard and along the sideboard. All kinds of rather grand utensils were kept on the sideboard: the silver cream jug, a pair of silver candlesticks, the silver-rimmed bread board with the silver-handled bread knife. I felt among them until I found the biscuit barrel. Then I took off the lid and put my hand in."

She paused.

"Go on, Grandmother."

"I did that trip once, twice, perhaps three times. The third or fourth time seemed just as usual. As usual, I was shaking with fright, both at the crime I was committing and at the blackness in which I had to commit it. I had felt my way to the biscuit barrel. I lifted the lid with my left hand, as usual. Very carefully, as usual, I slipped my right hand into the barrel. I had thought there would be crackers to the top, but there were not. I had to reach toward the bottom—down, down, down—and then my fingers touched something, and at once there was something—oh, it seemed like an explosion!—something snapped at me, caught my fingers, held them in a bitter grip, causing me pain, but far more than pain: terror. I screamed and screamed and sobbed and cried.

"Footsteps came hurrying down the stairs; lights appeared; people were rushing into the dining room, where I was. My father, my aunt, the maidservant—they all stood looking at me, a fat little girl in her nightdress, screaming, with her right hand extended and a mousetrap dangling from the fingers.

"My father and the servant were bewildered, but I could see that my aunt was not taken by surprise. She had been expecting this, waiting for it. Now she burst into loud laughter. I couldn't bear it. With my left hand I caught up the silver-handled bread knife from the sideboard and I went for her."

"You killed her?"

"No, of course not. I was in such a muddle with screaming and crying, and the knife was in my left hand, and my aunt sidestepped, and my father rushed in and took hold of me and took the knife from me. Then he pried the mousetrap off my other hand.

"All this time I never stopped crying. I think I was deliberately crying myself ill. Through my crying I heard my father and my aunt talking, and I heard my father asking my aunt how there came to be a mousetrap inside the biscuit barrel.

"The next day either I was ill or I pretended to be; there wasn't much difference, anyway. I stayed all day in bed with the curtains drawn. The maid brought me bread and milk to eat. My aunt did not come to see me. My father came, in the morning before he went to his office and in the evening when he got home. On both occasions I pretended to be asleep.

"The day after that I got up. The fingers of my right hand were still red where the trap had snapped across them, and I rubbed them to make them even redder. I didn't want to be well. I showed them to the maidservant. Not only were the fingers red, but two of the fingernails had gone quite black. The maid called my father in; he was just on his way to work. He said that the doctor should see them, and the maid could take me there that afternoon on foot. Exercise would do me good, and change. He looked at me as if he were about to say more, but he did not. He did not mention my aunt, who would have been the person to take me to see the doctor, ordinarily, and there was still no sign of her.

"The maid took me. The doctor said my fingers had been badly bruised by the blow of the mousetrap, but nothing worse. The fingernails would grow right. I was disappointed. I had hoped that my finger bones were broken, that my fingertips would drop off. I wanted to be sent into hospital. I didn't want to go home and be well and go on as before: little Miss Mountain as before.

"I walked home with the maid.

"As we neared our house, I saw a woman turn in at our gateway. When we reached the gate, she was walking up the long path to the front door. Now I've said I never knew my own mother, to remember, but when I saw the back view of that young woman—she *stumped* along a little, as stoutish people often do—I knew that that was exactly what my mother had looked like. I didn't think beyond that; that was enough for me. I ran after her, as fast as I could, and as she reached the front door, I ran into her. She lost her balance, she gave a cry between alarm and laughter and sat down suddenly on the front doorstep, and I tumbled on top of her, and felt her arms round me, and burrowed into her, among the folds of all the clothing that women wore in those days.

I always remember the plump softness and warmth of her body, and how sweet it was. I cried and cried for joy, and she hugged me.

"That was my other aunt, the other bridesmaid, my mother's sister. My father had telegraphed for her to come, from the other side of England, and she had come. My father had already sent my thin aunt packing; I never saw her again. My plump aunt moved in as housekeeper, and our house was filled with laughter and happiness and love. Within the year my father had married her. She had no child of her own by him, so I was her only child. She loved me, and I her."

"Did you—did you manage to become less stout?" Daisy asked delicately.

"I suppose I must have done. Anyway, I stopped stealing food. And the biscuit barrel disappeared off the sideboard; my new mother put it away, after she'd heard the story, I suppose. Out of sight, out of mind, I forgot it. Or at least I pretended to myself that I'd forgotten it. But whenever it turns up, I remember. I remember too well."

"I've heard of haunted houses," said Daisy thoughtfully. "But never of a haunted biscuit barrel. I don't think it would be haunted if you weren't there to remember, you know."

"I daresay."

"Will you get rid of it, Grandmother? Otherwise Jim will never come to stay again, and I—I—"

"You don't think I haven't wanted to get rid of it, child?" cried her grandmother. "Your grandfather wouldn't let me; your father wouldn't let me. But no, that was never the real explanation. Then I couldn't bring myself to give them my reasons, to tell the whole story, and so the memory has held me, like a trap. Now I've told the story; now I'm free; now the biscuit barrel can go."

"Will you sell it, Grandmother? It must be worth a lot of money."

"No doubt."

"I wonder how much money you'll get and what you'll spend it on, Grandmother. . . ."

Grandmother did not answer.

The next morning Daisy woke to sunshine and the sound of her Grandmother already up and about downstairs. Daisy dressed quickly and went down. The front door was wide open, and her grandmother stood outside on the doorstep, looking at something further up the street. There was the sound of a heavy vehicle droning its way slowly along the street, going away.

Daisy joined her grandmother on the doorstep and looked where she was looking. The weekly garbage truck was droning its way along; it had almost reached the end of the street. The men were slinging into it the last of the rubbish that the householders had put out for them overnight or early this morning. The two rows of great metal teeth at the back of the truck opened and closed slowly, mercilessly on whatever had been thrown into that huge maw.

Grandmother said, "There it goes," and at once Daisy knew what "it" was. "Done up in a plastic bag with my empty bottles and tins and the old fish finger carton and broken eggshells and I don't know what rubbish else. Bad company—serve it right." The truck began to turn the corner. "I've hated it," said Grandmother. "And now it's being scrunched to pieces. Smashed to smithereens." Fiercely she spoke, and Daisy remembered the little girl who had snatched up a bread knife in anger.

The truck had turned the corner.

Gone.

Grandmother put her arm round Daisy and laughed. She said, "Daisy, dear, always remember that one can keep custard creams and pink sugar wafers for friends in any old tin."

Guess ❖

*T*hat last day of October a freak storm hit the suburb of Woodley Park. Slates rattled off roofs, garbage cans chased garbage can lids along the streets, billboards were slammed down, and at midnight there was a huge sound like a giant breaking his kindling wood, and then an almighty crash, and then briefly the sound of the same giant crunching his toast.

Then only the wind, which died surprisingly soon.

In the morning everyone could see that the last forest tree of Grove Road—of the whole suburb—had fallen, crashing down onto Grove Road Primary School. No lives had been lost, since the caretaker did not live on the premises, but the school hamster had later to be treated for shock. The school buildings were wrecked.

Everyone went to stare, especially, of course, the children of the school. They included Netty and Sid Barr.

The fallen tree was an awesome sight, partly because of its size and partly because of its evident great age. Someone in the crowd said that the acorn that grew into *that* must have been planted centuries ago.

As well as the confusion of fallen timber on the road and on the

school premises, there was an extraordinary spatter of school everywhere: slates off the roof, bricks from the broken walls, glass from
the windows, and the contents of classrooms, cloakrooms, and
storerooms—books and collages and clay and paints and nature tables
and a queer mixture of clothing, both dingy and weird, which meant
that the contents of the lost property cupboard and the dressing-up
cupboard had been whirled together and tossed outside. Any passerby
could have taken his pick, free of charge. Netty Barr, who had been
meaning to claim her gym shoes from lost property, decided that they
had gone for good now. This was like the end of the world—a school
world.

Council workmen arrived with gear to cut, saw, and haul timber.
Fat old Mr. Brown from the end of the Barrs' road told the foreman
that they ought to have taken the tree down long ago. Perhaps he was
right. In spite of last season's leaves and next year's buds, the trunk of
the tree was quite hollow; a cross section revealed a rim of wood the
width of a man's hand, encircling a space large enough for a child or a
smallish adult. As soon as the workmen's backs were turned, Sid Barr
crept in. He then managed to get stuck and had to be pulled out by
Netty. An untidy young woman nearby was convulsed with silent
laughter at the incident.

"You didn't stay inside for a hundred years," she said to Sid.

"That smelled funny," said Sid. "Rotty." Netty banged his clothes
for him; the smell clung.

"Remember that day last summer, Net? After the picnic? When I
got stuck inside that great old tree in Epping Forest?" Sid liked to
recall near disasters.

"Epping Forest?" said the young woman, sharply interested. But no
one else was.

Meanwhile the headmaster had arrived, and that meant all fun was
over. School would go on, after all, even if not in those school buildings for the time being. The pupils of Grove Road were marshaled and
then sent off in groups to various other schools in the neighborhood.

Netty and Sid Barr, with others, went to Stokeside School: Netty in the top class, Sid in a lower one.

There was a good deal of upheaval in Netty's new classroom before everyone had somewhere to sit. Netty was the next to last to find a place; the last was a thin, pale girl who chose to sit next to Netty. Netty assumed that she was a Stokesider, yet there was something familiar about her, too. Perhaps she'd just seen her about. The girl had dark, lank hair gathered into a ponytail of sorts and a pale, pointed face with grayish green eyes. She wore a dingy green dress that looked ready for a rummage sale and gym shoes.

Netty studied her sideways. At last, "You been at Stokeside long?" Netty asked.

The other girl shook her head and glanced at the teacher, who was talking. She didn't seem to want to talk, but Netty did.

"A tree fell on our school," whispered Netty. The other girl laughed silently, although Netty could see nothing to laugh about. She did see something, however: this girl bore a striking resemblance to the young woman who had watched Sid being pulled from the hollow tree trunk. The silent laughter clinched the resemblance.

Of course, this girl was much younger. Of course.

"How old are you?" whispered Netty.

The girl said a monosyllable, still looking amused.

"What did you say?"

Clearly now: "Guess."

Netty was furious. "I'm just eleven," she said coldly.

"So am I," said the other girl.

Netty felt tempted to say, "Liar," but instead, she asked, "Have you an elder sister?"

"No."

"What's your name?"

Again that irritating monosyllable. Netty refused to acknowledge it. "Did you say Jess?" she asked.

"Yes. Jess."

In spite of what she felt, Netty decided not to argue about that Jess but went on: "Jess what?"

The girl looked blank.

"I'm Netty Barr; you're Jess something—Jess what?"

This time they were getting somewhere; after a tiny hesitation, the girl said, "Oakes."

"Jess Oakes, Jessy Oakes." But whichever way you said it, Netty decided, it didn't sound quite right, and that was because Jess Oakes herself didn't seem quite right. Netty wished now that she weren't sitting next to her.

At playtime Netty went out into the playground; Jess Oakes followed her closely. Netty didn't like that. Unmistakably, Jess Oakes wanted to stick with her. Why? She hadn't wanted to answer Netty's questions; she hadn't been really friendly. But she clung to Netty. Netty didn't like it—didn't like *her*.

Netty managed to shake Jess Oakes off but then saw her talking with Sid on the other side of the playground. That made her uneasy. But Jess Oakes did not reappear in the classroom after playtime; Netty felt relieved, although she wondered. The teacher made no remark.

Netty went cheerfully home to tea, a little after Sid.

And there was Jess Oakes sitting with Sid in front of the television set. Netty went into the kitchen, to her mother.

"Here you are," said Mrs. Barr. "You can take all the teas in." She was loading a tray.

"When did *she* come?" asked Netty.

"With Sid. Sid said she was your friend." Netty said nothing. "She's a lot older than you are, Netty."

"She's exactly my age. So she says."

"Well, I suppose with that face and that figure—or that no figure—she could be any age. Any age."

"Yes."

Mrs. Barr looked thoughtfully at Netty, put down the bread knife she still held, and with decision set her hands on her hips. "Netty!"

"Yes?"

"I don't care what age she is, I like your friends better washed than that."

Netty gaped at her mother.

"She smells," said Mrs. Barr. "I don't say it's unwashed body; I don't say it's unwashed clothes—although I don't think much of hers. All I know is she smells nasty."

"Rotty," said Netty under her breath.

"Don't bring her again," said Mrs. Barr crisply.

Netty took the tea tray in to the other two. In the semidark they all munched and sipped while they watched the TV serial. But Netty was watching Jess Oakes. The girl only seemed to munch and sip; she ate nothing, drank nothing.

A friend called for Sid, and he went out. Mrs. Barr looked in to ask if the girls wanted more tea; Netty said no. When her mother had gone, Netty turned off the television and switched on the light. She faced Jess Oakes. "What do you want?"

The girl's green glance slid away from Netty. "No harm. To know something."

"What?"

"The way home."

Netty did not ask where she had been living, or why she was lost, or any other commonsense questions. They weren't the right questions, she knew. She just said savagely, "I wish I knew what was going on inside your head, Jess Oakes."

Jess Oakes laughed almost aloud, as though Netty had said something really amusing. She reached out her hand and touched Netty, for the first time; her touch was cool, damp. "You shall," she said. "You shall."

And where was Netty now? If she were asleep and dreaming, the falling asleep had been very sudden, at the merest touch of a cool, damp hand. But certainly Netty must be dreaming. . . .

She dreamed that she was in a strange room filled with a greenish light that seemed partly to come in through two windows, of curious shape, set together rather low down at one side. The walls and ceilings of this chamber were continuous, as in a dome, all curved. There was nothing inside the dome-shaped chamber except the greenish light, of a curious intensity, and Netty. For some reason Netty wanted to look out of the two windows, but she knew that before she could do that, something was required of her. In her dreaming state, she was not at first sure what this was, except that it was tall—very tall—and green. Of course, green: green in spring and summer, and softly singing to itself with leaves; in autumn, yellow and brown and red, and its leaves falling. In winter, leafless. A tree, a forest tree, a tree of the forest, a tree of Epping Forest. A tree, a hundred trees, a thousand trees, a choice of all the trees of Epping Forest. She had been to the forest; she was older than Sid, and therefore she knew the direction in which the forest lay, the direction in which one would have to go to reach the forest. Her knowledge of the forest and its whereabouts was in the green-glowing room, and it passed from her in that room and became someone else's knowledge, too. . . .

Now Netty knew that she was free to look out of the windows of the room. Their frames were curiously curved; there was not glass in them, but some other greenish gray substance. She approached the windows; she looked through them; and she saw into the Barrs' sitting room, and she saw Netty Barr sitting in her chair by the television set, huddled in sudden sleep.

She saw herself apart from herself, and she cried out in terror, so that she woke, and she was sitting in her chair, and the girl who called herself Jess Oakes was staring at her with her gray-green eyes, smiling.

"Thank you," said Jess Oakes. "Now I know all I need to know." She got up, unmistakably to go. "Good-bye."

She went out of the sitting room, leaving the door open; Netty heard her go out of the front door, leaving that open, too. The doors began to bang in a wind that had risen. The front gate banged as well.

Mrs. Barr came crossly out of the kitchen to complain. She saw that Netty was alone in the sitting room. "Has she gone then?"

Netty nodded, dumb.

They went into the hall together. Scattered along the hall were pieces of clothing: one gym shoe by the sitting room door, another by the coat hooks; a dingy green dress, looking like something out of a dressing-up box, by the open front door. . . .

Mrs. Barr ran to the front gate and looked up and down the road. No one; just old Mr. Brown on the lookout, as usual. Mrs. Barr called to him, "Have you seen anyone?"

"No. Who should I have seen?"

Mrs. Barr came back, shaken. "She can't have gone stark naked," she said. Then, as an afterthought: "She can't have gone, anyway." Then, again: "But she has gone."

Netty was looking at the gym shoes in the hall. She could see inside one of them, and she could see a name printed there. It would not be JESS OAKES; it would be some other name. Now she would find out the true identity of the girl with the greenish eyes. She stooped, picked up the shoe, read the name: NETTY BARR.

"Those are the gym shoes you lost at school," said Mrs. Barr. "How did she get hold of them? Why was she wearing them? What kind of a girl or a woman was she, with that smell on her? Where did she come from? And where's she gone? Netty, you bad girl, what kind of a friend was she?"

"She wasn't my friend," said Netty.

"What was she then? And where's she gone—*where's she gone?*"

"I don't know," said Netty. "But guess."

At the River Gates ❖

*L*ots of sisters I had (said the old man), good girls, too, and one elder brother. Just the one. We were at either end of the family: the eldest, my brother, John—we always called him Beany, for some reason; then the girls, four of them; then me. I was Tiddler, and the reason for that was plain.

Our father, was a flour miller, and we lived just beside the mill. It was a water mill, built right over the river, with the mill wheel underneath. To understand what happened that wild night, all those years ago, you have to understand a bit about the working of the millstream. About a hundred yards before the river reached the mill, it divided. The upper river flowed on to power the mill, as I've said; the lower river, leaving the upper river through sluice gates, flowed to one side of the mill and past it; and then the upper and lower rivers joined up again well below the mill. The sluice gates could be opened or shut by the miller to let more or less water through from the upper to the lower river. You can see the use of that: the miller controlled the flow of water to power his mill; he could also draw off any floodwaters that came down.

Being a miller's son, I can never remember not understanding that. I was a little tiddler, still at school, when my brother, Beany, began helping my father in the mill. He was as good as a man, my father said. He was strong, and he learned the feel of the grain, and he was clever with the mill machinery, and he got on with the other men in the mill—there were only ten of them, counting two carters. He understood the gates, of course, and how to get just the right head of water for the mill. And he liked it all. He liked the work he did, and the life; he liked the mill, and the river, and the long riverbank. One day he'd be the miller after my father, everyone said.

I was too young to feel jealousy about that, but I would never have felt jealousy of Beany, because Beany was the best brother you could have had. I loved and admired him more than anyone I knew or could imagine knowing. He was very good to me. He used to take me with him when you might have thought a little boy would have been in the way. He took me with him when he went fishing, and he taught me to fish. I learned patience, then, from Beany. There were plenty of roach and dace in the river, and sometimes we caught trout or pike, and once we caught an eel, and I was first of all terrified and then screaming with excitement at the way it whipped about on the bank, but Beany held it and killed it, and my mother made it into eel pie. He knew about the fish in the river and the little creatures, too. He showed me freshwater shrimps and leeches—"Look, Tiddler, they make them-selves into croquet hoops when they want to go anywhere!"—and he showed me the little underwater cottages of caddisworms. He knew where to get good watercress for Sunday tea; you could eat watercress from our river, in those days.

We had an old boat on the river, and Beany would take it upstream to inspect the banks for my father. The banks had to be kept sound; if there was a breach, it would let the water escape and reduce the water-power for the mill. Beany took Jess, our dog, with him in the boat, and he often took me. Beany was the only person I've ever known who could point out a kingfisher's nest in the riverbank. He knew about birds. He once showed me a flycatcher's nest in the brickwork below the sluice gates, just above where the water dashed and roared at its highest. Once, when we were in the boat, he pointed ahead to an otter in the water. I held on to Jess's collar then.

It was Beany who taught me to swim. One summer it was hotter than anyone remembered, and Beany was going from the mill up to the gates to shut in more water. Jess was following him, and as Beany went, he gave me a wink, so I followed, too, although I didn't know why. As usual, he opened the gates with the great iron spanner, almost as long in the handle as he was tall. Then he went down to the pool in the lower river, as if to see the water level there. But as he went, he was unbuttoning his flour-whitened waistcoat; by the time he reached the pool he was naked, and he dived straight in. He came up with his hair plastered over his eyes, and he called to me, "Come on, Tiddler! Just time for a swimming lesson!" Jess sat on the bank and watched us.

Jess was really my father's dog, but she attached herself to Beany. She loved Beany. Everyone loved Beany, and he was good to everyone. Especially, as I've said, to me. Just sometimes he'd say, "I'm off on my own now, Tiddler," and then I knew better than to ask to go with him. He'd go sauntering up the riverbank by himself, except for Jess at his heels. I don't think he did anything very particular when he went off on his own. Just the river and the riverbank were happiness enough for him.

He was still not old enough to have got himself a girl, which might have changed things a bit, but he wasn't too young to go to the war. The war broke out in 1914, when I was still a boy, and Beany went.

It was sad without Beany, but it was worse than that. I was too young to understand then, but looking back, I realize what was wrong. There was fear in the house. My parents became gloomy and somehow secret. So many young men were being killed at the front. Other families in the village had had word of a son's death. The news came in a telegram. I overheard my parents talking of those deaths, those telegrams, although not in front of the girls or me. I saw my mother once, in the middle of the morning, kneeling by Beany's bed, praying.

So every time Beany came home on leave, alive, we were lucky.

But when Beany came, he was different. He loved us as much, but he was different. He didn't play with me as he used to do; he would sometimes stare at me as though he didn't see me. When I shouted, "Beany!" and rushed at him, he would start as if he'd woken up. Then he'd smile and be good to me, almost as he used to be. But more often than he used to, he'd be off all by himself up the riverbank, with Jess at his heels. My mother, who longed to have him within her sight for every minute of his leave, used to watch him go and sigh. Once I heard her say to my father that the riverbank did Beany good, as if he were sickening for some strange disease. Once one of the girls was asking Beany about the front and the trenches, and he was telling her this and that, and we were all interested, and suddenly he stopped and said, "No. It's hell." And walked away alone, up the green, quiet riverbank. I suppose if one place was hell, then the other was heaven to him.

After Beany's leaves were over, the millhouse was gloomy again, and my father had to work harder, without Beany's help in the mill. Nowadays he had to work the gates all by himself, a thing that Beany had been taking over from him. If the gates needed working at night, my father and Beany had always gone there together. My mother hated it nowadays when my father had to go to the gates alone at night; she was afraid he'd slip and fall in the water, and although he could swim, accidents could happen to a man alone in the dark. But of course, my father wouldn't let her come with him, or any of my sisters, and I was still considered much too young. That irked me.

Well, one season had been very dry and the river level had dropped. The gates were kept shut to get up a head of water for the mill. Then clouds began to build up heavily on the horizon, and my father said he was sure it was going to rain, but it didn't. All day storms rumbled in the distance. In the evening the rain began. It rained steadily; my father had already been once to the gates to open the flashes. He was back at home, drying off in front of the fire. The rain still drove against the windows. My mother said, "It can't come down worse than this." She and my sisters were still up with my father. Even

I wasn't in bed, although I was supposed to have been. No one could have slept for the noise of the rain.

Suddenly the storm grew worse—much worse. It seemed to explode over our heads. We heard a pane of glass in the skylight over the stairs shatter with the force of it, and my sisters ran with buckets to catch the water pouring through. Oddly, my mother didn't go to see the damage; she stayed with my father, watching him like a lynx. He was fidgeting up and down, paying no attention to the skylight, either, and suddenly he said he'd have to go up to the gates again and open everything to carry all possible floodwater into the lower river. This was what my mother had been dreading. She made a great outcry, but she knew it was no use. My father put on his tarpaulin jacket again and took his oil lamp and a thick stick—I don't know why, nor did he, I think. Jess always hated being out in the rain, but she followed him. My mother watched him from the back door, lamenting, and urging him to be careful. A few steps from the doorway, and you couldn't see him any longer for the driving rain.

My mother's lingering at the back door gave me my chance. I got my boots on and an oilskin cape I had (I wasn't a fool, even if I was little), and I whipped out of the front door and worked my way round in the shelter of the house to the back and then took the path my father had taken to the river, and made a dash for it, and caught up with my father and Jess, just as they were turning up the way toward the gates. I held on to Jess's tail for quite a bit before my father noticed me. He was terribly angry, of course, but he didn't want to turn back with me, and he didn't like to send me back alone, and perhaps in his heart of hearts he was glad of a little human company on such a night. So we all three struggled up to the gates together. Just by the gates my father found me some shelter between a tree trunk and a stack of driftwood. There I crouched, with Jess to keep me company.

I was too small to help my father with the gates, but there was one thing I could do. He told me to hold his lamp so that the light shone on the gates and what he was doing. The illumination was very poor, partly because of the driving rain, but at least it was better than nothing, and anyway, my father knew those gates by heart. Perhaps he gave me the job of holding the light so that I had something to occupy my mind and keep me from being afraid.

There was plenty to be afraid of on that night of storm.

Directing what light I could onto my father also directed and concentrated my attention on him. I could see his laborious motions as he heaved the great spanner into place. Then he began to try to rack up with it, but the wind and the rain were so strong that I could see he was having the greatest difficulty. Once I saw him stagger sideways nearly into the blackness of the river. Then I wanted to run out from my shelter and try to help him, but he had strictly forbidden me to do any such thing, and I knew he was right.

Young as I was, I knew—it came to me as I watched him—that he couldn't manage the gates alone in that storm. I suppose he was a man already just past the prime of his strength. The wind and the rain were beating him; the river would beat him.

I shone the light as steadily as I could and gripped Jess by the collar, and I think I prayed.

I was so frightened then that afterward, when I wasn't frightened, I could never be sure of what I had seen, or what I thought I had seen, or what I imagined I had seen. Through the confusion of the storm I saw my father struggling and staggering, and as I peered and peered, my vision seemed to blur and to double, so that I began sometimes to see one man, sometimes two. My father seemed to have a shadow self besides himself, who steadied him, heaved with him, worked with him, and at last together they had opened the sluice gates and let the flood through.

When it was done, my father came back to where Jess and I were and leaned against the tree. He was gasping for breath and exhausted and had a look on his face that I cannot describe. From his expression I knew that he had *felt* the shadow with him, just as I had seen it. And Jess was agitated, too, straining against my hold, whining.

I looked past my father, and I could still see something by the sluice gates: a shadow that had separated itself from my father and lingered there. I don't know how I could have seen it in the darkness. I don't know. My father slowly turned and looked in the direction that he saw me looking. The shadow began to move away from the gates, away from us; it began to go up the long riverbank beyond the gates, into the darkness there. It seemed to me that the rain and the wind stilled a little as it went.

Jess wriggled from my grasp and was across the gates and up the riverbank, following the vanished shadow. I had made no move, uttered no word, but my father said to me, "Let them go!" I looked up at him, and his face was streaming with tears as well as with rain.

He took my hand, and we fought our way back to the house. The whole house was lit up, to light us home, and my mother stood at the open back door, waiting. She gave a cry of horror when she saw me with my father, and then she saw his face, and her own went quite white. He stumbled into her arms, and he sobbed and sobbed. I didn't know until that night that grown men could cry. My mother led my father indoors, and I don't know what talk they had together. My sisters looked after me, dried me, scolded me, put me to bed.

The next day the telegram came to say that Beany had been killed in action in Flanders.

It was some time after that that Jess came home. She was wet through, and my mother thought she was ill, for she sat shivering by the fire and for two days would neither eat nor drink. My father said, "Let her be."

I'm an old man. It all happened so many years ago, but I've never forgotten my brother, Beany. He was so good to us all.

Her Father's Attic ❖

Rosamund was an only child and the apple of her mother's eye. She resembled her mother: pink-cheeked, golden-haired, blue-eyed. She was going to be like her mother: pretty.

Mrs. Brunning had faith in her daughter's looks. "She'll be picked out," she said. "She'll go up to London and be a model. Or go on TV. She'll make a name for herself, and money, and marry well. . . . What did you say, Geoff?"

But Mr. Brunning, who was hungry from working out-of-doors, had only grunted; his attention was entirely on his dinner. Besides, he knew the kind of thing that would come next.

"Anyway," his wife said, "she won't hang about here until some drudging clodhopper marries her, and she has to end her days where she began 'em."

This was a dig at her husband, who was a small farmer and an unsuccessful one; he worked hard on his land for very little return. He had inherited his father's farm and farmhouse only because none of his four elder brothers had wanted to; they had had higher ambitions and achieved them. He had been the runt of the family, small, sallow, timid; he had been teased and persecuted all his childhood. He had married—so his wife considered—above him, and he would be teased and persecuted for the rest of his married life.

"Rosamund has more of me in her than she has of you, thank goodness," said Mrs. Brunning. "She's all me, is Rosamund."

Rosamund, above whose head her mother wrangled, yawned inside her mouth and was glad that dinner was over. Her father got up and went back to his work outside, and Mrs. Brunning began washing up. There was no question of Rosamund's helping; she was the only child, spoiled, her mother's darling. Mrs. Brunning considered most of the local children unfit company for her, so as often before, Rosamund went off now to play alone indoors. Indoors, because her mother hated farm filth, as she called it, ever to be on her feet.

Brunning's was an old house, although without any particular history; Geoffrey Brunning could say only that his father knew that *his* father had been born there. It was not at all a grand house, but it had been built for a time of many children and of farm servants living with their masters. Nowadays there were shut rooms and unused passageways, away from the central, lived-in part of the house; such outlying parts suffered the erosions of neglect and time. Since Geoffrey Brunning's childhood, for instance, the highest attic, once a nursery, had been closed. Mr. Brunning said the floor was unsafe and, particularly to safeguard Rosamund, had locked the door that opened to the attic stairway.

So the door was already locked before Rosamund was old enough to roam the house on her own, and soon after that the woodworms had begun their invisible banquet upon the framework. Rosamund used regularly to bang at the closed door as she passed it, but without real curiosity. Perhaps her knock interrupted the woodworms' gnawing for a moment; then they resumed. Neither she nor they, after the passage of years, were at all prepared for the day—this very day—when their world exploded in a flurry of wood dust, as her casual blow sent the metalwork of the lock right through the decayed woodwork of the frame. Abruptly the door swung open as if to open wide. Then its hinges creaked to a rusty standstill, and Rosamund was left with a sliced-off view of wooden stairs powdered with old plaster and new wood dust.

Of course, Rosamund had always known of the existence of the attic, but the opening of the way to it was new. She must—she *must* go up and see it for herself. Circumstances were favorable: her father was out on the farm; her mother would still be in the kitchen, either finishing washing up or beginning to prepare for a genteel visitor that afternoon. Between the kitchen and the attic lay a wasteland of empty rooms and passages. Rosamund listened carefully, but she could hear no sound from anywhere.

She took a deeper breath than usual and pushed firmly against the door. It offered surprising resistance but finally opened wide enough to allow her body to pass through. She began going carefully up into the darkness of the stairway, feeling before her with her hands.

At the top of the stairs, she stubbed her fingers against another door. It had a small round hole at the level of a handle, but a spider had been at work, and her peeping eye could see only a mesh illumined from beyond by a dim lemon-colored light.

For the first time, with darkness round her, and the unbroken silence of years, she nearly felt afraid but would not allow the feeling to grow upon her. She pressed very softly at the door. At once, with a kind of overeagerness, the door swung right back.

She stood on the threshold of her father's attic nursery. Its bare length stretched uninterruptedly from her feet to a small window at the far end, where the afternoon sunlight shone weakly through dusty glass, greenish yellow where the last leaves of a creeper encroached upon the panes.

She was not afraid now. Being a practical child, she first considered the floor, which her father had said was unsafe. The bare boards looked firm, and she began to test them, one after another. They bore her weight. She knew that she was not as heavy as a grown-up person, yet she felt beneath her feet the solid assurance of timber that would outlast generations. The floor was sound, when her father had said it was not; she felt puzzled.

There was no other mystery to the room. It was quite empty, except for the low shelves and cupboards that had been built into the steep angle where the sloping roof met the floor. She examined the cupboards carefully; they were all quite empty, even the one with the door that appeared to be locked but was only jammed. Someone, at some time, had forced the door, and damaged it. Delicately she eased it open. She left that door standing ajar, because it had been so difficult. She might want to get in again. The cupboard was a roomy one, without shelves.

Rosamund went to the window next. With the stubbornness of disuse, it refused to open, but she cleared a pane of glass and could look through. She was charmed with the novelty of the view from here. She looked right across the roofs of the farm buildings to the fields and the spire of the parish church beyond. She thought that she could distinguish her father at work in one of the middle fields, but the light was failing. The setting sun stood in irregular red slices behind a thin copse of trees on the skyline.

Having gazed for so long into the last of the sun, she was surprised at the darkness of the room when she turned back to it. Shadows had gathered thickly at the far end, by the door, and inky blackness had settled in the depth of the one cupboard left open. She decided suddenly that it was time to leave the attic.

She started off across the safe, safe floor toward the stairway that led back to the peopled part of the house.

The attic was a long one, and Rosamund walked slowly—still with that careful, light step—because she could not quite put from her mind the idea that the place was dangerous. She drew level with the open cupboard, and looked deeply into it. She halted as it occurred to her—without surprise or pleasure—that this cupboard would make a good hiding place; it was large enough for a child of her age, crouching. Neither excitement nor pleasure; neither surprise nor speculation—she seemed to have remembered the possibilities of the cupboard rather than freshly to have thought of them.

There she stood, staring into the cupboard.

The sun had gone, and the shadows of the room moved up toward the window. They lapped round Rosamund like a sea, and she began to sink into them like a drowning person. She sank to the floor and lay along it, quite still. Her eyes were wide open, fixed upon the darkness in the cupboard. Darkness and fear flowed from the cupboard and filled the attic from doorway to window.

Outside in the field Geoffrey Brunning was still working in the afterlight. Now he stopped abruptly; he told himself he had forgotten that he must go in early today. He must go.

He had forgotten nothing, but it was as if something had remembered *him*. He did not know why he was going, why he was hurrying. As he neared the farmhouse, he broke into an awkward, anxious trot.

He went in by the back door as usual, leaving his boots there, and so into the kitchen. It was empty and almost dark except for the red glow from the old-fashioned stove that his wife was always complaining about.

"Ros!" he called. There was no answer.

He decided to have some common sense. He switched on the light, filled the kettle and put it on to boil, and began to cut bread for toast. He cut one slice, then laid the knife carefully down and went to stand out in the hall. It was dark there, with only a line of light from underneath the door of the sitting room. That was where his wife would be entertaining. He could hear voices, but not Rosamund's. He had not expected to hear it.

He turned away from the door of the sitting room, as he had turned away from the kitchen, and now he faced the main stairs. In the dark he could hardly see them. He stood peering, trying to make his mind work commonsensically, to think of the electric light switch that would banish darkness. But darkness increased moment by moment, filling his mind. Darkness and fear flowed round him like a sea, rose round him to drown him.

He gave a cry and turned quickly back to the light of the kitchen. Then, at the very door, he swerved aside and set off at a rush, but not firmly, stumbling and feeling like a blind man up the stairs, along walls, round corners. His course was directly up and toward the dis-used attic.

At the threshold of the attic he took a deep breath, like a man about to enter a smoke-filled room. He could see nothing, but he knew that Rosamund was there. He made one mistake, in thinking—in being sure—that she would be crouching in the cupboard with the jammed door. Even as his feet felt their way toward it, they met her body on the floor. He bent, took hold of her, and dragged her to the top of the attic stairway; then, having gathered her in his arms, he carried her down and away, to the kitchen. There he set her upon a chair, where she began to stir and blink in the bright light, like a dreamer waking, but she had not been asleep. She was very pale at first, but soon the pink began to reappear in her cheeks. She did not speak to her father, but her awakened gaze never left him.

Her father had collapsed upon another chair in the kitchen.

There Mrs. Brunning found them, having said good-bye to her visitor. Her daughter seemed as usual, but her husband was leaning forward in an attitude of exhaustion, his fingers dangling over the edge of his knees, his face white and sweaty.

"Don't say you're sickening for something, now!" Mrs. Brunning said sharply. "You're a sight! What do you feel like?"

"Oh . . . I feel . . ."

What did he feel like?

Long ago, when he was a child, he had felt like this, once. His brothers had shut him into one of the nursery cupboards, just for their fun, and the cupboard door had jammed. That was all it had been, except for the darkness inside the cupboard, and his fear. The darkness and the fear had lasted forever. They said afterward that his being shut in had all lasted only a short time and that he had been stupid to be so afraid. They'd been able to force the cupboard door open in the end, and then they'd dragged him out. But the darkness had stayed behind in the cupboard, and his fear.

"Well, what do you feel like?" his wife repeated irritably.

"Nothing special."

"Let's hope you pass nothing special on to Rosamund then. But at least she's not one of those easy-ailing children. Like me, in that."

Rosamund was staring at her father, paying no attention to her mother's refrain: "Yes, more of me in her than you, thank goodness. All me." Rosamund was staring at her father as at somebody strange to her and of the strangest importance.

The Running Companion ❖

*A*ny day, over the great expanses of the common, you can see runners. In tracksuits or shorts and running tops, they trot along the asphalted paths across the grass, or among the trees, or by the ponds. On the whole, they avoid London Hill, toward the middle of the common, because of its steepness. There is another reason. People climb the hill for the magnificence of the view of London from the top, but runners consider it unlucky, especially at dusk. They say it is haunted by ghosts and horrors then. One ghost; one horror.

In his lifetime, Mr. Kenneth Adamson was one of the daily runners. This was a good many years ago now. His story has been pieced together from what was reported in the newspapers, what was remembered by neighbors and eyewitnesses, and what may have been supposed to have been going on in the mind of Mr. Adamson himself.

Sometimes Mr. Adamson ran on the common in the early morning; more often he ran in the evening after work. He worked in an office. He was not liked there; he was silent, secretive, severe. People were afraid of him.

The Adamsons lived in one of the terrace houses bordering the common. There was old Mrs. Adamson, a widow, who hardly comes into this story at all, and her two sons, of whom Kenneth, or Ken, was the elder. There were only two people in the world who called Mr. Adamson by his first name: they were his mother and his brother. He had no wife or girlfriend, no friends at all.

Mr. Adamson ran daily in order to keep himself fit. The steady jogtrot of this kind of running soothed his whole being; even his mind was soothed. While his legs ran a familiar track, his mind ran along an equally familiar one. Ran, and then ran back, and then ran on again; his mind covered the same ground over and over and over again.

His mind ran on his hatred.

Mr. Adamson's hatred was so well grown and in such constant training that at times it seemed to him like another living being. In his mind there were the three of them: himself, and his hatred, and his brother, the object of his hatred.

Of course, Mr. Adamson's brother never ran. He could not walk properly without a crutch; he could only just manage to get upstairs and downstairs by himself in their own house. He had been crippled in early childhood, in an accident, and his mother had not only cared for him but spoiled him. To Mr. Adamson's way of thinking, she had neglected *him*. Jealousy had been the beginning of Mr. Adamson's hatred, in childhood; as the jealousy grew, the hatred grew, like a poison tree in his mind. It grew all the more strongly because Mr. Adamson had always kept quiet about it; he kept his hatred quiet inside his mind.

He grew up, and his hatred grew up with him.

For years now Mr. Adamson's hatred had been with him, not only when he ran but all day, and often at night, too. Sometimes in his dreams it seemed to him that his running companion, his hatred, stood just behind him or at his very elbow, a person. By turning his head, he would be able to see that person. He knew that his hatred was full-grown now, and he longed to know what it looked like. Was it monster or man? Had it a heavy body, like his own, to labor uphill only with effort, or had it a real runner's physique, lean and leggy? He had only to turn his head and see, but in his dreams he was always prevented.

"Ken!"

His mother's thin old voice, calling his name up the stairs, would break into his dreams, summoning him down to breakfast. Mr. Adamson breakfasted alone, listening to the sound of his brother moving about in his room above or perhaps beginning his slow, careful descent of the stairs. Listening to that, Mr. Adamson seemed to hear something else: a friend's voice at his ear, whispering a promise: "One day, Ken . . ."

One day, at last, Mrs. Adamson died of old age. The two brothers were left alone together in the house on the edge of the common. They would have to manage, people said. On the morning after the funeral, Mr. Adamson prepared the day's meals, then went off to his office. At this time of year, he ran in the evenings, never in the mornings. It was the beginning of autumn and still pleasant on the common in the evening, in spite of mist.

Mr. Adamson came home from work, and presumably the two brothers had supper, talked perhaps—although Mr. Adamson never spoke to his brother if he could help it—and prepared for bed. Just before bedtime, as usual, Mr. Adamson must have changed into his running shorts and top and training shoes and set off on his evening run.

Questioned afterward, the neighbors said that the evening seemed no different from any other evening. But how were they to know? The Adamsons lived in a house whose party walls let little noise through. Would they have heard a cry of fear: "Ken—no!" Would they have heard a scream? The sound of a heavy body falling, falling?

Sometime that evening Mr. Adamson's brother fell downstairs, fatally, from the top of the stairs to the bottom. Whether he fell by his own mischance (but no, in all his life, he had never had an accident on those stairs) or whether he was pushed, nothing was ever officially admitted. But the evidence examined afterward at least pointed to his already lying there at the foot of the stairs, huddled, still, when Mr.

Adamson went out for his evening run. Mr. Adamson must have had to step over his dead body as he came downstairs, in his running gear, to go out on the common.

It so happened that neighbors did see Mr. Adamson leaving the house. He left it looking as usual—or almost as usual, they said. One neighbor remarked that Mr. Adamson seemed to be smiling. He never smiled, normally. They saw no one come out of the house with him, of course. No one followed him.

Mr. Adamson set off across the common, as usual increasing his pace until it reached a jogtrot. This was the speed that suited him. Joints loosened; heartbeats and breathing steadied; the air was on his face, only the sky above him. His mind felt both satisfied and empty: free. This was going to be the run of his life.

He planned to run across the common to the ponds, then take the main exit route from the common, leading to the bus terminus and shopping center, but he would veer away just before reaching them, taking a side path that circled the base of London Hill, and so home.

When he got home, he would ring the doctor or the police, or both, to report his brother's accident. He had no fear of the police. No fear of anyone.

Now, as he ran, he began to get his second wind and to feel that he could run forever. No, the police would never catch up with him. No one could ever catch up with him.

Pleasantly he ran as far as the ponds, whose shores were deserted even of ducks. Mist was rising from the water, as dusk descended from the sky. Mr. Adamson wheeled round by the ponds and took the path toward the terminus and shopping center. He was running well, it seemed to him, superbly.

A runner going well is seldom aware of the sound of his own footfalls, even on an asphalted surface. But Mr. Adamson began to notice an odd, distant echo of his own footsteps: perhaps, he thought, an effect of the mist or of the nearness of London Hill.

Running, he listened to the echo. Unmistakably, running footsteps in the distance: a most curious effect.

Running, listening carefully, he began to change his mind. Those distant footsteps were neither his own nor an echo of his own after all. Someone behind him was running in the same direction as himself, trotting so exactly at his own pace that he had been deceived into supposing echoes. The footsteps were not so very far in the distance, either. Although the pace was so exactly his own, yet the footsteps of the other runner seemed all the time to be coming a little nearer. The impossibility of this being so made Mr. Adamson want to laugh, for the first time in many years. But you don't laugh as you run.

Very slightly Mr. Adamson increased the pace of his running, and maintained it, and listened. The runner behind seemed also to have very slightly increased his pace; the footsteps were a little more rapid, surely, and clearer. Clearer? *Nearer?* Mr. Adamson had intended to leave the main way across the common only just before it reached the terminus and shops; now he decided to take a side path at once. It occurred to him that the runner might just be someone hurrying to catch a bus from the terminus. That supposition was a relief.

He turned along the side path, and the feet behind, in due time, turned, too. They began to follow Mr. Adamson along the side path, never losing ground, very slightly gaining it.

Mr. Adamson quickened his pace yet again; he was now running rather faster than he liked. He decided to double back to the main path, across the grass.

The grass was soft and silent under his feet. He heard nothing of his own footfalls; he heard no footfalls behind him. Now he was on the main path again and still could hear nothing behind him. Thankfully he prepared to slacken his pace.

Then he heard them. The runner behind him must have crossed the soundless grass at a different angle from his own. The strange runner's feet now struck the asphalt of the path behind Mr. Adamson nearer than he could possibly have expected—much nearer.

The pace was still the same as his own, yet gained upon him very slightly all the time. He had no inclination to laugh now. He ran faster—faster. The sweat broke on him, ran into his eyes, almost blinding him.

He reached his intended turning off the main path and took it. The feet, in due time, followed him. Too late he wished that he had continued on the main path right to the bus terminus and the shops, to the bright lights of streets and buses and shops. But now he had turned back over the common, duskier and mistier than ever. He had before him the long path winding round the base of London Hill before it took him home. It was a long way, and a lonely, unfrequented one at this time of evening. The hill was straight ahead of him, and he knew there would be groups of people at the top, people who walked there in the evening to admire the view. Never before had he chosen to go where there were other human beings, just because they were other human beings, flesh and blood like himself. Now he did. He took the path that led directly to the summit of the hill.

The evening strollers on the top of the hill had been looking at the view, and one or two had begun to watch the runner on the slopes below. He was behaving oddly. They had watched him change course and then double to and fro—"like a rabbit with something after it," as one watcher said.

"He's coming this way," said another.

"Straight up the hill," observed someone else in the little crowd. Most of them were now peering down through the dusk. "Straight up the hill—you need to be young and really in training for that."

Straight up the hill he went, his heart hammering against his ribs, his breath tearing in and out of his throat, his whole body dripping with sweat. He ran and ran, and behind him came the feet, gaining on him.

On the hill, they were all staring now at the runner. "What's got into him?" someone asked. "You might think all the devils in hell were after him."

"He'll kill himself with running," said a young woman. But she was wrong.

Now he was laboring heavily up the steepest part of the slope, almost exhausted. He hardly ran, rather, staggered. Behind him the feet kept their own pace; they did not slow, as his had done. They would catch up with him soon.

Very soon now.

He knew from the loudness of the following feet that the other runner was at his back. He had only to turn his head and he would see him face to face, but that he would not do; that he would never do, to save his very soul.

The footsteps were upon him; a voice close in his ear whispered softly—oh, so softly!—and lovingly—oh, so lovingly! "Ken!" it whispered, and would not be denied.

The watchers on the hill peered down.

"Why has he stopped?"

"Why's he turning round?"

"What's he— Oh, my God!"

For Mr. Adamson had turned and seen what none of the watchers on the hill could see, and he gave a shriek that carried far over the common and lost itself in darkness and distance—a long, long shriek that will never be forgotten by any that heard it.

He fell where he stood, in a twisted heap.

When they reached him, he was dead. Overstrain of the heart, the doctor said later, but being a wise man, he offered no explanation of the expression on Mr. Adamson's face. There was horror there and— yes, something like dreadful recognition.

All this happened a good many years ago now, but runners on the common still avoid London Hill, because of Mr. Adamson and whatever came behind him. There may be some runners who fear on their own account—fear the footsteps that might follow *them*, fear to turn and see the face of their own dearest, worst wickedness. Let us hope not.

Beckoned ❖

*F*awcett's, as the house was called, stood alone. It was not very much older or very much larger than the pink-bricked houses that surrounded it in their rows and courts and crescents, but the unkemptness of its garden and its own dark, desolate aspect set it apart. No one lived there but old Mr. Fawcett, a widower, ailing. No one used its weedy front drive but the district nurse and Mrs. Pugh (who had cleaned and shopped and cooked for Mr. Fawcett for years) and the occasional baffled hawker. Mr. Fawcett never went out, never.

The play space for the children of the housing development extended to Fawcett's boundary, marked by a grim old brick wall, now broken or breaking in several places, but a formidable barrier still. Of the children, Peter was the one who went over oftenest, because he was the best at finding old tennis balls or footballs. He had a knack. He didn't mind looking for a lost ball, which most people hated doing, because of his special trick, but he didn't much like Fawcett's.

"Go on, Peter!" they said. "Find it for us!" And gave him a leg up over the wall.

Once over, Peter stood absolutely still among the brambles and the nettles. The voices on the other side of the wall had become indistinct to him, seemed unimportant. He let the playground and the game and the other children drift out of his mind. His mind emptied itself. All that was left was an intentness upon finding a certain old tennis ball.

Then, as always before, he began to move toward the ball. He dodged under a half-fallen tree; he circumnavigated a huge bramble bush; he had his eyes fixed now on a tangle of grass where the ball must be, when he was interrupted.

Something interfered with his reception of the message of the ball's whereabouts; something deflected his course. He hesitated, stopped, then turned aside and began to move along what, from the feel of the ground under his feet, might once have been a graveled path. The path took him through garden jungle until he found himself facing the back of Fawcett's itself, across the weedy rankness of a neglected lawn. He saw the house as a whole, almost black against the winter sunset. The windows were all blank and unlit, except for a weak glow from one upper room. But his attention focused on the ground floor and on the French windows that opened—if they could ever be forced over the weeds just outside—onto a little paved terrace. He became aware of a slight movement and a variation of darkness on the other side of the French windows. He realized that he was looking at someone on the other side of the glass, someone who was almost certainly looking at him. Whoever it was moved close up to the window and thereby became more distinct. He saw the tallness of a human figure, wrapped in some long dark striped garment, presumably a dressing gown; he saw the pallor of face and hands and the movement of the hands: one hand moved to the middle of the window, where the catch would be; the other hand was raised in a gesture which Peter guessed rather than clearly saw. The figure beckoned to him.

Peter knew that he was trespassing, but perhaps that was not all that frightened him. He felt his skin sweating, warm for an instant, then cold. The chill made him shiver, and the shiver set him free. Suddenly his mind was empty no longer: he was thinking of his own fear, and of his trespassing, and of the boys waiting in the playground, and of his own fear again.

He slued round and rushed back the way he had come, to the wall and over it, into the playground again.

"Where's the ball?" they cried, crowding round him.

"I couldn't find it."

"You always find it! Why couldn't you find it? We haven't another. Go back, Peter. Find it. You always find it. Go back."

"No," said Peter. "I shan't. I'm going home." He set off at a run, with the others jeering at him, saying they would go over in a body to find the ball.

In the end none of them went, either singly or in a group. No one quite liked going into Fawcett's after dark, and it was gloaming already.

When Peter reached home, he did not speak of his experience at Fawcett's, partly because he knew his parents would be sharp with him about his trespassing right up to the house, especially as he had been caught at it, partly, too, because the incident had been unimportant, and partly for the exactly opposite reason: that it had been important *to him*. He tried to recall what little he knew of Fawcett's: that the Fawcetts had always lived there, but old Mr. Fawcett was the last of them; he had once had a wife, but she had died, not so very long ago; he had once had a son, but he had died as a boy, and that had been a very long time ago indeed. And had there been a daughter, too?

"Yes," said Peter's mother, talking through the whisper of television and the sputter of fat in the pan. "Yes. A daughter—oh, yes. A good girl, but her father was one of these girls-are-worth-nothing men." Peter's mother tutted, and it was not because of hot fat spitting out onto her hand. "He cared nothing for her. Then the boy was born. He was the apple of his father's eye, of course. When he was killed—it was a car accident, I think—old Mr. Fawcett went nearly out of his mind. According to Mrs. Pugh, who's always helped there, he went around shouting that the wrong child had died. After that he couldn't bear to have the daughter about the house. In the end she had to go. She was just eighteen. A good girl—very like her mother, in some ways. I remember her mother well."

"I don't remember any of them," said Peter.

"You weren't born or too young to notice. The girl went to a job away, and then she married and had children, and then her husband died. She must have had a hard life. She never came back; she was never allowed back, even after her mother died. She could be keeping house now for her invalid father and making a proper home for her children, but no! Mrs. Pugh still does it, stone-deaf and one foot in the grave by now."

"What was the boy like?"

"Just a boy. He was about your age when he died. Your sort of boy, well grown, up to any mischief." Peter's mother eyed him sardonically. "I notice you don't ask about Mrs. Fawcett."

"Mrs. Fawcett?"

"I suppose you're one of those women-are-worth-nothing people. But Mrs. Fawcett was really worth ten of Mr. Fawcett, in spite of his loudmouthed cantankerousness and the fuss he made about getting his own way. Mrs. Fawcett was one of those quiet, big women; she was as tall as her husband. Quiet. Patient. Clever. Yes—" Peter's mother had surprised herself by her own conclusion. "Yes, she was a clever woman, I think. If she'd lived, she'd have got her daughter home again, by hook or by crook, in spite of that brute of a husband." She began dishing up the supper, having finished all she had to say.

But Peter's father, who had been drowsing in front of the television set, now entered the conversation. "And if she was so clever, and he was such a brute, why didn't she leave him?"

"Because some women are saints, and she still loved him." And Peter's mother triumphantly dashed a plate of fish and chips onto her husband's knees. He accepted it, and defeat, together.

Peter went on thinking about Fawcett's and old Mr. Fawcett prowling downstairs in his dressing gown. He made an excuse to himself to go back; he really must recover that tennis ball. He chose a time early in the morning, when nobody was about, to nip over the wall. There was no need to use his trick of mind emptying; he knew already where the ball was. He made his way to it, found it, and stood with it in his hand, irresolute. He would have liked to have gone on to the house, as he had done before, but yes, he was frightened of that. In the end he climbed back over the wall with his tennis ball.

When he was back outside Fawcett's again, he discovered that he felt disappointed, flat. Also somehow guilty, as though he had left something undone, as though he had failed someone.

So the next day he went again, very early, before school, with the deliberate intention of going far enough to see the back of the house.

By morning light the house looked less forbidding, but more obviously neglected; there was, of course, not even a light from the upstairs window.

Yet Peter saw that Mr. Fawcett was already up and about; from the deep shadows on the other side of the glass of the French windows the same tall figure in the dark striped dressing gown moved into view. There were the same gestures of opening the windows, of beckoning.

Peter's earlier fears and any remembrance of his parents' warnings against the acceptance of strange invitations all vanished. He obeyed the summons. As he crossed the roughness that had once been lawn, the figure behind the glass began to withdraw into the shadows of the interior, still beckoning.

Peter reached the French windows. He had expected to find them ajar for him, but they were not. Perhaps they had been left unlatched but not open. Sure of this, he pulled hard at them, but something resisted. Perhaps the resistance was from the tough grass clumps that sprang in the pavement crevices outside the windows and grew thickly against the frame and glass. He tugged harder, his mind set upon following where he had been beckoned; something gave sharply, and the windows opened to admit him.

By now the room inside—a dank, gloomy dining room—was empty: Peter did not doubt that old Mr. Fawcett had gone from it to lead the way he was to follow, and certainly the door at the other end of the dining room stood persuasively open. He followed into the hall.

Here he was taken aback, for the various doors round the hall were shut, and surely, if he had been meant to follow, a way would have been left open to him. Then he realized that the stairs lay open to him. He mounted them, and even before he reached the top, he could see another door open—to a bedroom, he supposed.

There were several doors from this upstairs landing, but there was only one open, inviting him. He went in.

Instantly he was aware that this must be the room that he had noticed on the first evening, because of its lighted window. Then the artificial light from inside had been dim; now the daylight from outside was largely cut off by half-drawn, heavy curtains. But even by the half-light he could see that the room was old Mr. Fawcett's, because there was old Mr. Fawcett himself in the big double bed.

It had not seemed to Peter that he had taken very long to enter the house and make his way upstairs, but already Mr. Fawcett was in bed again, lying there in an attitude of exhaustion, his head and shoulders against piled pillows, his arms outside the bedclothes, hands open with palms upward. His eyes were shut. The striped dressing gown, of some soft woolen material, had been discarded and lay rumpled over the bottom part of the bed, like an extra rug.

Peter stood at the foot of the bed, looking at Mr. Fawcett. Slowly Mr. Fawcett's eyelids went up, and he was looking at Peter. Neither spoke, but each regarded the other with the closest attention.

Peter's hands gripped the bedrail. If the other did not, he must speak. He opened his mouth, but no words suggested themselves. He closed his mouth again.

Barely, Mr. Fawcett spoke, his eyes never leaving Peter. He whispered a word or half a word: "Rob . . ."

Peter wanted to protest: No! I wasn't stealing anything. I came because you beckoned me; you *invited* me. I came straight to you. I've damaged nothing, taken nothing. Nothing.

But still something prevented his speaking.

Mr. Fawcett continued to stare at him—glare at him. He muttered a word that sounded like *robbery*. His eyelids closed then; he turned his head aside on the pillow, as if he had seen enough, spoken enough.

Peter remained where he was, staring. For seconds. For minutes. Would he have been there still an hour later perhaps—the figure of a boy at the foot of Mr. Fawcett's bed, waiting for Mr. Fawcett to reopen his old, blurred eyes and see him again?

The house was so quiet that even a slight noise from downstairs resounded: the fumble of a key in the lock of the front door. If he heard, old Mr. Fawcett paid no attention, but Peter heard and fled. But by the time he had reached the top of the stairs, he could already distinguish footsteps on the tiling of the hall floor; he realized that if he went down now, he would unavoidably come face to face with—whom?

He turned back, opened the first door he came to, and slipped inside; he was in a bedroom evidently long disused. He closed the door to a crack and then peeped through the crack. Somebody was now toiling up the stairs: Mrs. Pugh, in her apron and carrying her cleaning tools. Studying her through the crack, Peter saw what his mother meant by "one foot in the grave": Mrs. Pugh looked almost as old and tired as old Mr. Fawcett himself.

Once Mrs. Pugh had passed and gone into Mr. Fawcett's bedroom, Peter could escape. As he tiptoed down the stairs, he heard Mrs. Pugh dolefully asking Mr. Fawcett whether he'd used the commode in the night and telling him the weather was bad and so was her sciatica. He heard no more. Back downstairs and through the French windows he went, and across the garden, skulking behind shrubs as much as possible, in case either Mr. Fawcett or Mrs. Pugh might be looking through the bedroom window. So to the wall, and over it.

He was late for school that day.

For the rest of that day—and for many days after—Peter turned over in his mind what had happened at Fawcett's. He couldn't understand it; he couldn't even understand what there was to understand. Beckoned in and then: "robbery" . . . It didn't make sense. . . .

He wondered if Mr. Fawcett would tell Mrs. Pugh about his visitor,

Peter. He wondered if he *could* tell Mrs. Pugh, since his voice seemed so weak, and she was stone-deaf. He asked his mother.

"I believe the old man writes notes," she said. "Although that must be hard for him, because he's half blind by now, they say." She snorted. "The stone-deaf looking after the half blind! And that daughter willing and able to look after her father and not allowed into the house!"

Peter could hardly imagine Mr. Fawcett's writing a note to Mrs. Pugh about a visit as strange as his own, and he could certainly not imagine Mrs. Pugh's understanding it. He put anxiety about himself out of his mind.

Then, when Peter had begun to shelve the whole subject, the surprise came. He was fooling about as usual with his friends in the playground of the housing development, against Fawcett's wall. He had not been over that wall since his encounter with old Mr. Fawcett; he did not intend ever going again. But he sometimes looked speculatively at the wall, and today he saw a boy climbing it—climbing out of Fawcett's. He was the new boy, Davy Taylor, who had arrived at school in the middle of term. A small, quiet boy, pleasant enough, but he had climbed out of Fawcett's, and Peter, who had been in the playground nearly an hour, had not seen him climb in.

"Here!" said Peter. "Where've you been?"

"Home to tea," said Davy Taylor.

"Where?"

"Fawcett's."

"You don't live there; old Fawcett lives there."

"I know he does; he's my granddad."

Peter stared stupidly. "Old Fawcett lives alone."

"Not now. He sent for my mum to come and look after him, so we all live there now."

"Sent for you—*why?*"

"Dunno." Impatient of the conversation, Davy Taylor slid away into the game being played. Peter was left unanswered.

He believed Davy Taylor; he had to. Yet it was odd. . . .

Peter decided to get to know Davy Taylor better. That was easy, because Davy was new and wanted acquaintances and friends. It turned out that he kept gerbils. So did Peter. They swapped information and anecdotes, and they swapped a gerbil or two. Peter found that he liked Davy, anyway, so that he was in no hurry to press the friendship to a useful conclusion. In that, he turned out to be wrong; time was short after all. Peter asked Davy to his house to see his gerbils, and Davy came.

Then Davy asked Peter to Fawcett's to see *his* gerbils, and Peter was going, all agog, when old Mr. Fawcett died.

His dying was really no surprise to anybody, Peter discovered: Mr. Fawcett was nearly ninety, and the district nurse had expected him to pop off any day, she said. He made a good end: he had his daughter with him, and he was glad of it.

Sometime after the funeral, Davy renewed his invitation to Peter to come and see his gerbils. There was no longer the same point in the visit, of course, but Peter went.

They went from school together. When they reached Fawcett's, Davy led the way at breakneck speed through the front door, across the hall, up the stairs to his own room.

"No!" cried Peter, alarmed. Davy's hand was on the knob of the door of old Mr. Fawcett's bedroom. But of course, Davy paid no attention; he flung the door wide, and there was a room newly painted in buttercup yellow, with Davy's narrow bed pushed in one corner, and the rest of the floor space covered with trains and airplanes and gerbil cages and gerbils. And that was all.

Except that over the bed was spread something dark striped, silkily warm-looking, that Peter recognized.

"That," he said.

"What?"

"That stripy thing. That dressing gown."

"It's not a dressing gown. It's a bedspread, sort of."

"It's a dressing gown. It must be."

"It's not." Davy was cross. He picked the thing up; and Peter could see that it really was not a dressing gown. On the other hand, it was a very odd bedspread: not large enough, not rectangular, and made up of odd-shaped pieces, with the stripes going all ways. Davy said, "My granddad used it on his bed. Over the bottom, to keep his feet warm."

"He used it as a dressing gown, too," said Peter. "He must have, somehow. When he went downstairs, he wrapped it round him. Just a few weeks ago."

"Don't be silly. He never went downstairs. Not for years. And what do you know about my granddad, anyway? Honestly . . ." Davy was exasperated. "Honestly . . ."

Peter dropped the subject. They looked at the gerbils and took them out of their cages and played with them, and after a while Mrs. Taylor called them down to tea. The other Taylor children were there: Davy's elder brother and sister. Mrs. Taylor had toasted crumpets for everyone and made sausages and mashed potatoes and a big pot of tea. Mrs. Taylor had hardworking hands and a plain face with a nice smile. When the elder children had gone off to do their homework, she kept Peter at the table, asking about his gerbils and also about his family, whom she remembered a little from long ago. Then Peter and Davy helped her clear the tea things to the sink, after which Davy said, "Let's go to the playground, Pete. Everyone'll be there by now."

Peter cleared his throat. "You go," he said. "I'll come in a bit. I'll help your mother with the washing up first."

Davy goggled at him, and even Mrs. Taylor was too astonished to be able to look grateful.

"Honestly . . ." said Davy. "Honestly . . ."

"You go with Davy, Peter," said Mrs. Taylor. "I can manage. I always do. It's a pity to miss the last of the daylight."

"No," said Peter. "I'll help. But Davy can go."

Davy hesitated uneasily, then went. Mrs. Taylor began washing up; Peter began drying.

For the second time since tea, Peter cleared his throat. "That stripy thing on Davy's bed—it's nice, but it's a funny thing, isn't it?"

"Well," said Mrs. Taylor, "it was my mother's dressing gown—her winter dressing gown, of a beautiful warm stuff. When she died, it was too good just to let go, but my father wouldn't wear it—a woman's dressing gown, you know—although it would have fitted him. My mother was a big woman. Anyway, Mrs. Pugh was younger in those days, and she unpicked it all and made a half bedspread of it. It's odd-looking, but warm."

Peter said, "It was your mother's dressing gown. . . ."

"She was a remarkable woman," said Mrs. Taylor. "She could manage most things, and she was patient. She needed to be. My father was difficult. You'll have heard tales. . . ."

"Yes," said Peter. Then, as Mrs. Taylor did not go on, he added, "Mum said you had a brother, much younger, and he died, and then your father . . ."

"Yes. When he was killed—he was only a boy—my father turned me out of the house, I'm afraid. He swore that he'd not see me in this house again before he saw him, his dead son, I mean. My father prided himself on being a man of his word."

"He meant never to have you here?"

"Yes. My mother fought him, but it was no good. She said she'd never rest, in this life or the next, till her daughter could come home. It made no difference."

Peter did not contradict. Changing the subject a little, he asked, "What was your brother called, that died?"

"Robert."

"Just Robert?"

"We called him Rob for short. Or Robbie."

"Yes," said Peter. "I see. Now I see."

Gently Mrs. Taylor took the drying-up cloth from his hand. "You've been drying the same plate over and over again, Peter. You go now. I'll finish."

"Yes," said Peter. "Thank you—thank you very much."

"I'm glad Davy has such a good friend," said Mrs. Taylor. "Take our shortcut to the playground, Peter. Through the dining room—I use it for my dressmaking—and through the French windows and across the garden to the wall. That's the way Davy always goes."

Peter went that way. When he reached the far side of the lawn—hacked short by a mower, since the Taylors had moved in—he stopped to look back at the house. He half expected to see a tall figure through the French windows, with hand raised for the last time in salutation, in acknowledgment, in thanks.

But nobody.

He went over the wall, into the scrum of boys in the playground, with Davy Taylor in the middle of them.

The Dear Little Man with His Hands in His Pockets ❖

When I was little, our next-door neighbor was Mr. Porter. To begin with, we didn't know him very well; perhaps we never knew him very well. I still wonder about him sometimes.

Mr. Porter was a widower, with one married daughter who lived the other side of London. She wanted her father to live with them, but he wouldn't. He preferred to live alone. He wouldn't have even a dog or cat for company.

Mr. Porter didn't go out much because he had a bad leg. He said that a lion had chewed it long ago in Africa. He'd certainly spent nearly all his life in Africa—his skin was browned and dried with years and years of sun—but you never knew how much to believe of his stories. He had an eyelid that twitched fairly regularly, and you couldn't be sure whether he was winking or just twitching when he said certain things.

Sometimes his chewed leg was painful, and then he had to put it up to rest it. When my mother realized that, she offered to do his shopping for him. Mr. Porter accepted her offer very gratefully, and so we got to know Mr. Porter better. My mother and father liked Mr. Porter. He was always grateful to them, and when we were away on holiday, he fed Tibby, our cat, and kept an eye on the house. His married daughter, when she visited him, always called on us and said what a comfort it was to know we were just next door, and she used to give me the most enormous bags of sweets.

I was so little then that wherever my mother went, I went. I used to go with her when she called in to see how Mr. Porter was; he'd given her a house key so that he didn't need even to hobble to the door to let her in. The inside of Mr. Porter's house was rather dull, except for one or two African curios.

"Look, Betsy!" said my mother one day, when I'd been fidgeting at the time she was talking with old Mr. Porter to make out his shopping list. "Look, Betsy! A big dolly. Look, just behind the door!"

I looked into the shadows behind Mr. Porter's sitting room door, and someone was standing there, about two feet tall, silent and still.

"Not a dolly," I said.

My mother peered. "A dear little man with his hands in his pockets," she said.

"Bring him over here, Betsy," said Mr. Porter, who was sitting with his leg up on a stool.

I wouldn't touch the manikin, but my mother picked him up for me. Since he had his hands in his pockets, as she put it, his arms formed jug handles, one on each side of his body. Using one of these handles, my mother carried him over to Mr. Porter. He was easy to carry, but evidently quite heavy.

My mother left me with Mr. Porter while she went into the kitchen to see what vegetables he had and whether they were fresh enough.

Mr. Porter showed me the little man. I think he was made of wood, but the whole of his body, except for his head, was covered in a kind of closely knitted string, rather dirty. He had a face, of sorts, but the most remarkable thing about him was a crown—or perhaps it was meant to be a bush of hair—made of chicken feathers, also rather dingy and broken at the tips.

"Don't you like him?" asked Mr. Porter.

"No," I said.

"But he makes a true friend. A loyal and determined friend, Betsy. So they used to say in that part of Africa where I got him." And he said the name of a place so strange-sounding that I paid no attention to it at all; I rather wish now that I could remember it.

"You must realize, Betsy," said Mr. Porter, "that my friend's not quite as he should be. The shabbiness doesn't matter, but he should have a pair of goat horns, and if you wanted him to set off and do your work for you, you'd have to pour a special liquid into him through the feathers on top. See if you can find the hole among the feathers."

My curiosity got the better of my fear. I parted the feathers here and there and peered down among them but could see nothing. So I felt with one hand, and sure enough, there was a hole in the top of the head.

My mother had come back by now with the shopping list, to which she was adding some vegetables. She began to talk to Mr. Porter, and he answered her, but he kept his eyes on me.

My hand was still very small in those days, and I put it right into the hole that I had found. The hole went surprisingly deep, and then, at the bottom, my fingers touched a sticky wetness. I drew my hand up again quickly and began wiping it on my jacket.

Mr. Porter was watching me all the time, and now he said, "You never asked me, Betsy, what work such a friendly little chap can do when he gets his stuff inside him."

"What does he do?"

"Well, you can send him walking off to deal with any enemy you may have." His eyelid twitched, or he winked.

"What does he *do*?"

"He kills that enemy."

I stared at the fingers I had been scrubbing at. "Is it poison then — the liquid? Does he shoot it out of himself at the enemy?"

"Oh, no, no, no," said Mr. Porter. "The liquid is only like the petrol that makes a car go — although it's much more special and difficult to come by than petrol. No, there are more ways of killing an enemy than by poison, you know. . . ."

I think he might have been going to tell me exactly how the little man did his work, but my mother said briskly, "What a *very* interesting African curio, Mr. Porter. Come, Betsy, or we'll never get all the shopping done." I could tell from her voice that she didn't think Mr. Porter was being good for me.

Perhaps my mother was right, for that night I had a nightmare about Mr. Porter's little man. I saw him in the distance, walking toward me. I tried to escape him, but his walk broke into a run, swift and steady. In Mr. Porter's house I had seen that the little man's hands weren't really in pockets; they just disappeared into his body. But I supposed that he could pull them out of his body, and in the nightmare, coming toward me, he was going to pull them out. What would they be like? Would they be grasping some weapon or weapons? Would they be ordinary hands at all? Or would they be, say, paws, like a lion's paws, only smaller, with deadly claws sheathed in them? Just as he was close to me and pulling them out, I woke.

I didn't tell my mother about the nightmare, of course, and you might have thought I would have avoided Mr. Porter and his friend after that. But there was one way in which Mr. Porter—and only Mr. Porter—could reassure me about the little man, and so I went with my mother on several further occasions to Mr. Porter's house. At last it happened that for a few minutes my mother left us alone together.

I said baldly, "That man couldn't really kill anybody. He's too small. He couldn't even reach."

Mr. Porter understood me at once. "Reach? Consider your own cat, Betsy. I've seen Tibby at the foot of the garden wall, which is many times her own height—say, five or six feet high. I've seen her look up, crouch, and then spring vertically—vertically, Betsy—to the top. With ease. Right?" I nodded miserably, seeing what he was getting at. "Now imagine some enemy of mine as tall as six feet. His throat—a very vulnerable part—would be less than that from the ground. My friend has only to walk, or perhaps run, up to him—"

This was so like my nightmare that I closed my eyes. I had to hear Mr. Porter's voice going on, but at least I needn't listen to the words he was saying. Then there was another sound. I opened my eyes again, and my mother was reentering the room from wherever else in the house she had been.

"And so," Mr. Porter was saying, "just like your Tibby, my friend can easily do what he wants to do. His little job of work, I mean."

His eyelid twitched, or he winked. He also smiled at my mother in his grateful way.

I took care never to enter into conversation with Mr. Porter again on the subject of his friend. If I had to go into Mr. Porter's house, I never looked behind the sitting room door. But I was sure the little man was there. And I used to wonder about the hole among the chicken feathers: whether there was still a sticky wetness at the bottom or whether it had dried up. Or whether Mr. Porter renewed it sometimes. My hand was growing bigger, and I doubted that I could have squeezed it in, as I had done in the first place, to find out.

I don't know how many years passed before the time of the burglaries in our neighborhood. Certainly Mr. Porter seemed much, much older. There were several burglaries, and the burglary of Mr. Porter's house was the last.

Mr. Porter still lived alone. Although he wasn't exactly bedridden, he'd had his own bed moved downstairs into his sitting room, and he spent most of his time lying in it or on it. His married daughter made more fuss every time she came to see him. But Mr. Porter pointed out that he had the telephone by his bed, and he'd promised to ring us at once if he were taken ill or needed help in any way.

One night I was woken by the sound of voices, near and far. The near voice was my mother's in the bedroom next to mine, shouting at my father, who slept soundly: "Get up, get up! Can't you hear?"

I could hear. From further away, out in the street, came the sound of another voice — or other voices. There was a most terrible screaming and shouting — but not words, at least that one could distinguish — and a deep grunting. Once I did think the screaming was for help.

By now I was in my parents' room. They didn't notice my coming in because they had thrown the window up and were looking out of it. You couldn't see anything; it was one of those times when the street-lights were on all day and off all night, and there was no moon. (I believe that is the kind of night that burglars usually choose.)

My father said, "It's a fight."

"It's a murder!" said my mother. And she dashed at the telephone and began ringing the police.

What was going on out there sounded like a fight *and* a murder. And then, abruptly—just when my father had found his big flashlight, which was also heavy enough to be a weapon—whatever had been going on was over. There was the sound of running feet—one pair of running feet—and a kind of choking, howling crying that died away with the sound of the feet.

Through all this, by the way, I managed to avoid being noticed by my mother, who would have tried to send me back to bed. I stuck close to my father and was just behind him when he reached the front gate-way to our house and flashed his flashlight up and down the street. The whole street had been aroused by the screaming. Windows had been flung up. Many front doors were now open, and silhouetted fig-ures peered out or, like my father, shone flashlights.

The flashlights, crisscrossing over the street, showed nobody—and no body, either.

My mother came rushing out from the house behind us and brushed past my father, crying, "Mr. Porter! What about old Mr. Porter?" She had a sixth sense about things, sometimes.

My father turned his flashlight beam onto Mr. Porter's house. The front door had swung open, and we could see a gaping, jagged hole in the glass of the upper paneling, just above the lock. There was no sign of Mr. Porter.

My mother gave a little cry and came back to my father—she must have looked straight at me but never saw me—and he put his arm round her shoulder, and together they went quickly into Mr. Porter's house. I began to follow at a distance when out of the corner of my eye,

I thought I saw something lying in the darkness of the gutter. I hurried then to catch up closely with my parents. I was very scared indeed.

There was no light in the hall of Mr. Porter's house, but there was a light beyond, in the sitting room, where—as you may remember—Mr. Porter now slept. The sitting room door was open, but only just. (It had a spring on it, so that it was self-closing against drafts.) My father gave a push to the door, and we all walked into the sitting room.

And there was Mr. Porter sitting on the side of his bed in his pajamas, with the telephone receiver in his hand. He was glittering with excitement. Also in his expression was an eagerness, which I didn't at first understand.

As soon as he saw us, he called out, "Come in, come in! I've just been ringing the police, and then I was trying to ring my kind next-door neighbors, as I've always promised."

My mother said, "Oh, Mr. Porter! We thought you'd been murdered in your bed." Tears began to run down her cheeks.

"There, there!" said Mr. Porter. "Only a burglar—not even a very brave one. Didn't expect to find me in the first room he tried. Didn't expect to find me ready for him." His eyelid twitched, or he winked. "Shock of his life. Ran for it."

Behind us other neighbors had begun trickling into the house. Mr. Porter appealed eagerly to this little crowd: "Well, did he get right away, or did someone—I mean, one of you, of course—catch him? No? No sign of him?"

But everyone agreed that the burglar had got clean away, and according to Mr. Porter, he had taken nothing with him from the house.

"Except this." Another neighbor pushed through the rest of us to reach Mr. Porter. "Isn't this one of your African ornaments, Mr. Porter? It was lying in the gutter, just along the street." He held out the little man with the jug handle arms.

"Well, fancy a burglar taking my little man!" said Mr. Porter, staring. The little man was filthy with mud from the gutter, and with a lot of blood on him. My mother, returning from the kitchen with a cup of tea for Mr. Porter, exclaimed in disgust at the sight.

My father said, "The blood must be from the burglar's cutting himself on broken glass. He broke the glass in the front door so that he could reach in and open the door from the inside. The police will certainly want to see this thing."

He took the little man and, not realizing that he was able to stand on his own two feet, leaned him temporarily against the wall. I wondered if Mr. Porter would tell the police, when they came, that the little man usually stood behind the sitting room door, and whether they would think it odd that a burglar, coming in, should reach right round the door to take him.

But when the police came, very soon afterward, we heard nothing because we were all turned out of the house while they talked to Mr. Porter. We left Mr. Porter in bed, sipping his tea and looking as peaceful and contented as our cat, Tibby, when she suns herself on the top of the garden wall. A policeman sat by the bed with his notebook open, asking questions. I suppose you might say that Mr. Porter was helping the police with their inquiries.

My father said the police's best clue would be the blood. He said they would ask all the hospitals to look out for a man coming in with severe glass cuts on hands, wrists, or arms. They may have done so; but the burglar was never caught. Moreover, nobody was ever able to explain what all the screaming had been about in the street. Nor why there was blood in the gutter and in the street, but not by the front door where the glass had been broken.

When Mr. Porter's married daughter heard of the burglary, she said this settled it and her father was coming to live with them. Mr. Porter was surprisingly meek and agreed. So there had to be a big clearout of Mr. Porter's house because he couldn't take all his things with him to his daughter's home. And then one day Mr. Porter went off in his daughter's car, and we never saw him again, although my mother had a nice letter from him, saying how kind we'd been and how much he missed us. For several years we had Christmas cards, and then they stopped coming. I suppose he died. He was very old.

I don't know what happened to the little man with his hands in his pockets when the police had finished with him. He was so filthy with mud and blood that perhaps Mr. Porter's daughter burned him; the chicken feathers would have made a terrible smell. Or perhaps she cleaned him up and let Mr. Porter stand him behind the door of his new bedroom.

When my father said that about the hospitals looking out for a man with wrist cuts from broken glass, I thought they would have done better to look out for a man suffering from severe throat wounds. I know we were Mr. Porter's friends, not his enemies, but all the same, I was quite glad when we weren't next-door neighbors anymore.

The Dog Got Them ❖

When Captain Joel Jones retired from the sea, he was persuaded by his wife to buy a handy little bungalow in the middle of nowhere in particular. Here the two of them lived very quietly—but with a certain amount of mystery. At least, to Andy Potter, their grandnephew, there was mystery.

Andy knew Aunt Enid fairly well—really, she was Great-aunt Enid, of course: she used to visit her relations while the captain was at sea. She was kind but very prim. She liked to help with the washing up, mending of clothes, ironing—anything—but she and the captain had had no children, and she exclaimed a good deal at the noisiness of Andy's friends and the language that young people used nowadays.

Captain Joel was another matter altogether. Andy had met him only rarely, on his return from voyages: a big, red-faced, restless man with a loud voice. (Andy's mother complained privately about *his* language.) When he drank tea, he picked up and set down the cup with a good deal of rattling of china against china. In excuse, he said that he was rather unfamiliar with tea as a beverage. He liked to carry Andy's father off for an evening at the pub. He was always sociable and said that the Potters must all come and stay in the new bungalow when they had moved in. There would be two bedrooms: He and Aunt Enid would use one, of course, but Andy's parents could have the other, and Andy himself, being still a little boy, could sleep on the sofa in the sitting room. Andy could even bring his terrier puppy, Teaser, if he were careful about the Joneses' cat.

They moved in, but oddly, the invitation to the Potters was never renewed.

Mrs. Potter said, "It's not as if I particularly *want* to stay, but all the same I wonder they don't press us to go. Aunt Enid's so often stayed here, and the captain, too—and I could have done without the smell of whiskey in the bedroom cupboard afterward."

Mr. Porter said, "It'll take some time for them to settle down. Especially for Joel: no sea, no shipmates, no pub near, no company of any kind except Aunt Enid's."

"You make it sound a bad move for them."

"Well . . ."

Andy listened, without paying much attention.

Over a year later, on their way back from a holiday by car, the Potters found that they would be passing quite close to the new bungalow. They decided to drop in—and not to telephone ahead about the visit in case, as Mrs. Potter said, the answer was, "Not at home."

They parked the car outside the bungalow, and all got out—all except Teaser. He was left in the car, chiefly because of the Joneses' old tabby. In a harmless way, Teaser was always on the lookout for cats. He loved any chase—no doubt, would have loved any fight, too. He came of a breed once specialist in ratting.

They rang the doorbell. From inside they could hear some exclamation of dismay (was it Aunt Enid's voice?) and a much louder, violent exclamation, undoubtedly in the captain's voice. There was the sound of light footsteps, and the front door was opened.

"Oh, dear!" cried Aunt Enid, on seeing them. "Oh, dear, oh, dear! How very nice to see you all!"

She did not move from the doorway.

Mrs. Potter said, "We were just passing, Aunt Enid. We thought we'd call to see how you'd settled in. Just a very brief visit." As Aunt Enid said nothing, Mrs. Potter added for her, "Just time for a quick cup of tea, perhaps, and a chat."

"Of course!" said Aunt Enid. "How very nice! But it's not at all suitable, I'm afraid. The captain is in bed with influenza. Severe influenza."

There was a roar from inside the bungalow: "Enid! I say, Enid!"

"There's my patient calling!" cried Aunt Enid. "Perhaps another time, when he's stronger . . . But telephone first." To everyone's astonishment, she began to close the door.

Mr. Potter put his foot in the doorway. "Aunt Enid," he said, "we don't want to come where we're not wanted for any reason, but— you're all right, aren't you?"

"Oh, perfectly, perfectly!" cried Aunt Enid. "I'm perfectly all right, and so is the captain. He is in perfect health. It's just that, with infection in the house, I simply cannot—*cannot* risk having visitors. I admit only the doctor, ever." She stooped and put her hands round Mr. Potter's leg to lift it from the doorway. He withdrew it to save her trouble.

Aunt Enid was in the act of shutting the front door. Mrs. Potter said quickly, "Aunt Enid, promise to let us know at once if we can help you at any time, in any way."

Aunt Enid's face still showed in the gap of the doorway. Her eyes filled with tears. "My dear, you are truly kind," she said. Then: "But no help is required. I have the captain, you know." This time she finished shutting the front door. They heard her good-bye from the other side.

They went back to the car in silence. As they were driving off, Andy's mother said, "She looked so worried and miserable. It couldn't be just the captain's flu."

"She didn't even seem certain that he *was* ill," said Andy's father.

And Andy said, "He wasn't in bed. I looked past Aunt Enid when you were talking. I saw him. He wasn't even in pajamas."

"What was he doing?"

"Just walking about, in a wandery sort of way. Waving something about in the air."

"Waving what?"

"I think it was a bottle."

Later, when they got home, Mrs. Potter wrote to Aunt Enid, and then she began writing regularly, once a fortnight. Occasionally she had a reply. She would pass it to Andy's father to read but never read it aloud to them all. Andy wondered.

Then, after many months, Aunt Enid wrote to say that Captain Joel had died.

"What did he die of?" asked Andy.

His parents looked at him thoughtfully, sizing him up, Andy knew. Was he old enough to be told whatever it was?

"Yes," said his mother, "you're old enough to know, and it should be a warning to you all your life: Captain Joel drank."

"So does Dad," said Andy. "You mean, more than that?"

"He drank much more," said his father. "He drank much, much too much. He died of it."

"Oh," said Andy. There was a mystery gone, it seemed.

After the funeral, which Mr. and Mrs. Potter attended, Aunt Enid came to stay for a bit. She was pale, thin, and apt to burst into tears for no clear reason. Andy's mother gave her breakfast in bed during her stay and would not let her help as much as usual with the housework. She had long private talks with her, after which they both seemed to have been crying.

"Poor woman," said Andy's mother when Aunt Enid had gone. "It was a perfectly dreadful time when the captain was dying. Appalling."

"DTs?" asked Andy's father.

His mother nodded.

Andy asked what DTs were.

"Delirium tremens," said his mother. "A particularly awful kind of deliriousness, from drinking too much for too long. You see things. It's a waking nightmare, according to Aunt Enid." She shuddered. "Horrible."

In due course a letter arrived from Aunt Enid thanking them all for her stay and saying that she felt much better as a result. She had the energy now to start getting the house to rights again after the captain's death. She had already changed his sickroom back into a spare room. "But," she said, "I'm not sure that they've faded yet."

"They?" Andy's mother queried, passing the letter to her husband.

"Mistake for *it*, I suppose," said Mr. Potter, studying the letter. "*It* being the smell of booze, or something like that."

"Her letter says 'they' quite clearly," said Andy, also looking.

"Makes no sense," said his father, and the subject was dropped.

In the next letter Aunt Enid was very much upset because the cat had died. The cat had grown very old and poor in health, but mysteriously, Aunt Enid seemed to blame herself for its death. She said that it had had a shock which she ought to have been able to spare it, and she thought this shock had caused its death. She had not closely enough supervised where the cat had gone in the house. "But you don't supervise where a cat goes about indoors, to spare it shock," said Andy's father.

The next letter was written from hospital. Aunt Enid had fallen and broken her hip, running too fast on the polished floors in the bungalow. She explained briefly: "I was afraid of not getting the door shut in time."

"Why should she be running to *shut doors in time*?" Andy's father asked crossly. He foresaw upheavals, if Aunt Enid were in hospital.

He was right. Mrs. Potter telephoned to the hospital to suggest a visit, and they had an express letter from Aunt Enid to say that she was looking forward to seeing them at the weekend and suggesting that they stay overnight in the bungalow. Andy's father and mother could sleep in the double bed in Aunt Enid's room; Andy himself could sleep on the sofa in the sitting room. If they had to bring Teaser, she did not advise that he came indoors at all; could he not sleep in the car and be exercised from there? She was sorry that the spare room was not yet habitable; she did not think they had faded yet. The key to the bungalow would be in the milk box by the back door.

"This fading," said Andy's father. "*What is she talking about?*" He was exasperated. However, he agreed that they should all go down, as Aunt Enid had suggested, and they did.

The bungalow was neat and clean, as one would have expected of Aunt Enid's home, but it seemed empty and lifeless with even the cat dead. They decided to leave Teaser mostly in the car, as Aunt Enid had wished it. Andy's parents would sleep in Aunt Enid's own room, but what about Andy? It was all very well for Aunt Enid to suggest the sofa; she had forgotten how time had passed—how much older Andy was, how much bigger. So they discussed the suitability of Aunt Enid's spare room, after all.

Standing in the spare room, looking around, they could see nothing against its use. Like the rest of the bungalow, it was neat and clean, with a single bed and a bedside lamp that worked. The room had no special features. There was a chiming clock on the mantelpiece; at least, Andy's mother said that it used to chime, but it had stopped working altogether by now. (Andy tried to wind it, in vain.) There was a cactus in a pot on the windowsill, and a white china rabbit heading a procession of little white china rabbits on a dressing table.

"Why didn't she want us to use the room?" Andy's mother asked suspiciously. They had a good look round. Nothing odd, and absolutely no trace left of the late Captain Joel, except for an empty whiskey bottle that Andy spotted, poked up the chimney.

Andy decided for himself by unrolling his sleeping bag on the single bed.

After supper they all went to bed.

Andy woke up in what seemed the middle of the night, but the room was not really dark. He thought he had been woken by a noise, a squeaking, perhaps. Now he was almost sure there was a soft scrabbling sound from the floor beyond the bottom of the bed. Very quietly he raised himself on his elbow to look. Against the far wall, heads together as if conferring, were two rats. They must be rats, and yet they were much, much larger than any ordinary rat, and their color was a gray-white splotched with chestnut brown. He disliked their coloring very much. They seemed to have heard the slight creak of Andy's bedsprings, for now they turned their heads to look at him. They had pink eyes.

Then they began creeping to and fro against the wall and then running, in an agitated kind of way, almost as if they were getting their courage up. Each time they ran in the direction of the bed, they ran nearer than they had done the last time. Especially the bigger of the two rats, which Andy assumed to be the male. The female lagged behind a little, always, but still, she ran a little nearer to the bed every time.

The male rat was scurrying closer and closer, and suddenly the knowledge came to Andy that it was going to attack. He was appalled. Frantically he prepared to ward off its attack with his naked hand. The rat sprang, launching its heavy body through the air like a missile and sank its teeth into his hand.

Andy was already on his feet on the bed. He knew the female rat would attack next. The male hung from his hand as he slapped it violently, madly, repeatedly against the wall so that the body of the iron-teethed monster banged again and again and again against the wall. It seemed to him that almost simultaneously the body of the rat suddenly flew from its head, still teeth clenched in his flesh, and he himself flew from that dreadful bedroom. He slammed the door behind him against the female rat and rushed into his parents' room. They had already put on the light, roused by his screaming.

Andy was still screaming: "Look! The rat, the rat!" He held out his hand for them to see the horror hanging from it.

They all looked at his hand: Andy's brown right hand, just as it always had been, entirely unmarked except where he had once scarred himself with a saw long ago. No rat.

"You've been dreaming," said his mother. "You were asleep, and you had a nightmare."

"No," said Andy, "I was awake." And he told them everything.

They went back into the spare room with him. There were no rats of course, nor any sign of one.

Staring round, Andy's father said at last, "They weren't your rats, Andy; they were the captain's. And as your great-aunt said, they haven't faded yet."

They shut the door fast on the spare room and made up a bed of sorts for Andy in the sitting room, with cushions on the floor and his sleeping bag on top. Then they all went back to bed.

But—not surprisingly, perhaps—Andy could not get to sleep. He found that he was listening for sounds behind the door of the spare room. In the end he got up quietly and went out of the bungalow and brought Teaser in from the car for company. Teaser was delighted.

Andy had begun to fall asleep with the comforting weight of Teaser on his feet when the dog left him. He was slipping out of the sitting room, whose door had been deliberately left ajar. Andy called softly, but Teaser paid no attention. Andy got up and followed him. By now Teaser was across the hall and at the spare room door. His nose was at the bottom crack, moving to and fro along it, sampling the air there. His tail moved occasionally, stiffly, in pleasure or in pleasurable anticipation.

Andy thought he heard a squeak from the other side of the door, *two* squeaks, the squeaks of two different rat voices.

"No, Teaser," whispered Andy. "Oh, no!"

But Teaser looked over his shoulder at Andy, and his look spoke. On impulse Andy opened the spare room door a few inches, and at once Teaser had pushed past it into the room.

Instantly there was tumult—a wild barking and the rush of scuttering feet and objects falling and crashing and breaking and the clock that never went now chiming on and on in horological frenzy. Above all, the joyous barking of chase and battle.

Andy held the door to, without clicking it shut, in case Teaser might want to get out in a hurry. But Teaser did not want to get out; he was in a terrier's paradise.

By now Andy's father and mother were out of bed again, with Andy, and he explained what he had done. Mr. Potter was of the opinion that they should wait outside the room until Teaser had finished doing whatever he was doing. Mrs. Potter insisted that in the meantime Mr. Potter should fetch the poker from the sitting room. Then they waited until the barking and worrying noises grew less frequent. A kind of peace seemed to have come to the spare room.

Mr. Potter flung wide the door, at the same time switching the light on.

The room was in a terrible mess: the bedspread had been torn off the bed, and the floor rugs were in a heap in one corner; the china rabbit and its litter were smashed and scattered all over the room; the cactus stood on its head in the middle of the floor, with earth and potsherds widely strewn round it; and the clock had been hurled from the mantelpiece and lay face downward on the floor in a mess of broken glass, still chiming. On the bed stood Teaser, panting, his mouth wide open with his tongue hanging out, his tail briskly wagging, his eyes shining. He was radiant, triumphant. The night of his life.

After a silence, "*They* won't come back," said Mr. Potter, "ever."

They tidied the bedroom as best they could. They repotted the cactus and threw away the remains of the rabbits and put the clock back on the mantelpiece. It would need a new glass, of course, but it had stopped chiming and was ticking quite sensibly. Mrs. Potter set it to the right time—nearly breakfast time.

Later that day, visiting Aunt Enid in hospital, Andy apologized for Teaser about the rabbits and the clock glass. He did not explain things. His mother had said that it would be best not to burden the invalid with the whole story.

Aunt Enid was not as prim as she used to be. She was naturally confused about what had been going on in the bungalow, but pleased. "I'm pleased that you and the dog had such a nice romp, Andy dear," she said. "And when I'm home again, it'll be a great convenience that the clock really goes. I can easily get a new glass." She hesitated. "You had no trouble from—from *them*?"

Andy's father said quickly, "The dog got them."

Mrs. Chamberlain's Reunion ❖

*T*his is a tale of long ago. I was a little boy, and our family lived—no, *resided*—among other well-off families in a residential neighborhood. All those neighbors were people like ourselves, who thought well of themselves and also liked to keep themselves to themselves.

Except for one neighbor. That's where my story starts.

On one side of us had lived for many years the Miss Hardys, two spinster sisters, very ladylike. Our two gardens were separated by a trellis fence with rambler roses, a rather sketchy, see-through affair. So our family had at least an acquaintance with the Miss Hardys, and my sister, Celia, knew them quite well. As a little girl she had played with their cat, Mildred, until it died of old age.

Of course, we had neighbors on the other side, too, but on that side a thick laurel hedge grew so high that these neighbors—to us children, anyway—seemed hardly to exist.

In all the years that we lived in our house (and it had been bought by my father from a family called Chamberlain, just before my birth), neighbors may have come and gone beyond the laurel hedge, but we never noticed.

Then one day there was a new neighbor, and suddenly things were different. The new neighbor cut down the hedge—not to the ground, of course, but to shoulder level. He thus revealed himself to us: Mr. Wilfred Brown, retired and a widower.

He was a well-built man with an inquiring nose. His eyes, large and prominent, looked glancingly, missing nothing, yet his gaze could settle with close attention. My mother said he stared.

My mother snubbed Mr. Brown's attempts at conversation over what remained of the hedge. She had decided that he was what she called "common." She remarked to my father that Mr. Brown had been a *butcher*, and my father, in rare joking mood, pointed out that he had indeed butchered the hedge. But my father was no more ready than my mother for a friendly chat with Mr. Brown.

We three children, however, had been strictly taught to be attentive and polite to our elders. In the garden, therefore, we were at Mr. Brown's mercy. He hailed us, talked with us, questioned us. We had to answer. Thus Mr. Brown discovered that, in our well-ordered family way, we would be off on our fortnight's summer holiday, starting—as always—on the second Saturday of August.

The date was then the thirtieth of July.

The next time that my mother went into the garden, to cut flowers for an arrangement, Mr. Brown accosted her over the hedge. He begged to be allowed "to keep a friendly and watchful eye" on our house while we were away at the seaside.

My mother answered with instant refrigeration: "*Too* kind, Mr. Brown! But we could not possibly put you to such trouble. We shall make our usual arrangements."

Mr. Brown asked, "How good are these arrangements, Mrs. Carew? What are they exactly?" He gazed earnestly, and his inquiring nose seemed to quiver.

My mother was flustered by Mr. Brown's stare. She was forced into explaining in detail that the Miss Hardys would be left with the key to the house, as well as with our telephone number at the seaside. But all this was only for use in case of emergency.

Mr. Brown shook his head. "The Miss Hardys, you say? Oh, dear me! Ladies are prone to panic in an emergency."

By now my mother had recovered herself. She retorted quite sharply: "The Miss Hardys are never prone to anything, Mr. Brown."

Mr. Brown smiled and shook his head again. So there the matter was left. My mother could hardly forbid a neighbor to focus his eyes sometimes on our house, now so very visible over the low hedge. So, for the first time since we had lived there, our empty house would be overlooked not only by the Miss Hardys but also by our new neighbor on the other side, Mr. Brown.

Meanwhile that second Saturday in August was drawing nearer and nearer.

I was the youngest child and excited at the thought of the sea and the seaside. The other two were much calmer; they remembered so well other fortnights beginning with that second Saturday in August. Celia told me privately that Robert, the eldest of us, had said (but not in our parents' hearing, of course) that family holidays got duller and duller.

Celia herself would probably be too preoccupied with her white mouse, Micky, to be bored on the holiday. There was nothing at all remarkable about Micky, except that neither of our parents knew of his existence. They had never liked animals. They hadn't really approved of Celia's playing with the Hardys' cat; they were relieved when Mildred died. Disappointingly for Celia, the Hardys did not get another cat; Mildred had only been inherited from their old friend and neighbor Mrs. Chamberlain when she died. Celia missed a pet and at last—most daringly and, of course, secretly—had acquired Micky. She would take Micky on holiday with her, and his very private companionship would console her during her seaside fortnight.

At the seaside we always stayed in the same guesthouse and did the same things; that was one of Robert's complaints. My father played golf and did some sea fishing, and whatever the weather, he swam every morning before breakfast, taking Robert with him. Sometimes he shared with my mother the duty of supervising our play: we were allowed to paddle and trawl in rock pools with nets and to make sand castles and sand pictures. Sometimes we went for long walks inland, all five of us. Of course, there were wet Augusts, but my father never allowed rain to keep us indoors for even half a day. One could walk quite well in mackintoshes and Wellington boots, he said, and our landlady, Mrs. Prothero, was obliging about the drying out of wet clothes.

Our return from these holidays was always the same. As the car turned into our quiet, treelined street, there was our house, but first my mother had to collect the key from the Miss Hardys.

"All has been well, I hope, Miss Hardy?"

"Nothing at all for you to worry about, Mrs. Carew."

The younger Miss Hardy, from behind her sister in the doorway, would ask, "And you had a restful holiday, Mrs. Carew?"

"Restful and delightful," said my mother. "Perhaps a little rainy, but that never kept us indoors. And now it's good to be home."

Having recovered the key from the Miss Hardys, my mother would rejoin the family as we waited at our own front door. She handed the key to my father. He unlocked the door, and we entered. We brought with us the salty smell of the seaside rising from our hair and skin and clothing and from the collections of seashore pebbles and shells in our buckets. That saltiness, together with fresh air from newly opened windows, soon began to get rid of the stuffy, rather unpleasant smell of an empty house shut up for a whole fortnight. Soon our home was exactly as it had always been, and so it would remain for another year, until another second Saturday in August.

But this particular year our seaside holiday could not possibly have been described as restful and delightful, even by my mother, and our homecoming was to be very different.

From that second Saturday in August rain fell without stopping; this we had had to endure on holidays before now. What was new was Robert's sullen ill temper, as continuous as the rain and as damping.

He said nothing openly, for my father could be very sharp with a child of his ungrateful enough not to enjoy the holiday he was providing. My mother tried to soothe and smooth. She gave out that Robert was probably incubating some mild infection.

As if to prove her point, Robert developed a heavy cold after one of our wet walks and sneezed all over Mrs. Prothero's paying guests' sitting room. He had to borrow his father's linen handkerchiefs, and Mrs. Prothero had to boil them after use and dry them and iron them. Mrs. Prothero complained about the extra work, and we all caught Robert's cold. In spite of this, my father continued to play golf and to fish, until one morning he embedded a fishhook in the palm of his right hand. He came out of the local hospital with his hand bandaged and in a bad temper. No more golf or fishing for the rest of the holiday.

This all happened in our first week. We were still, however, expecting to remain at the seaside, enjoying ourselves, to the end of our fortnight.

Then came the telephone call.

We had returned from a moist morning's walk to be told that a Mr. Wilfred Brown had telephoned. He had urgently asked that Mr. or Mrs. Carew should telephone him back as soon as possible.

"What's the man on about?" my father demanded fretfully. "Telephone him back, indeed! Does he think I'm made of money?"

"Perhaps something's wrong at home," faltered my mother. She was remembering Mr. Brown's "watchful eye."

"Rubbish!" said my father. "One of the Miss Hardys would have telephoned us; not this Brown fellow."

He was so enraged with Mr. Brown that when during lunch, the telephone rang again for Mr. or Mrs. Carew, my mother had to deal with it. She went most reluctantly; she returned clearly shaken. "Mr. Brown was surprised that we hadn't rung back." My father snorted. "He thinks there's something wrong at home. He's been on the watch, and he's sure there are goings-on (as he puts it) inside our house. He's sure that 'something's up.' "

"Inside our house!" cried my father, throwing aside his napkin.

"Then why on earth hasn't the fool got the police? Burglars! And he just . . . Oh, the idiot, the juggins!"

"No," said my mother. "Nobody's broken in; he was quite positive about that. This is different, he says. Something wrong *inside the house.*"

My father stared in angry disbelief. Then he gave his orders. "Go and telephone the Miss Hardys." My father felt that as a general rule, ladies should communicate with ladies; men with men. "Tell them what Brown says, and find out—oh, just find out *something!*"

My father bade us all go on with our lunch, as he himself did, and my mother went to the telephone again. She came back after a while, still troubled. "I told them, dear, and they're sure there's nothing at all for us to worry about. They insist that's so. But they're upset by Mr. Brown's suspicions. I didn't tell you at the time, dear, but he asked me on the telephone whether we'd empowered—that was his word: *empowered*—the Miss Hardys to use the house in our absence. But they say they've never set foot over the threshold in our absence. Ever. It's all rather strange and horrid. . . ."

We three children listened, appalled—delightfully appalled. If the Miss Hardys were other than they had always seemed—if they were liars, trespassers, thieves—if all this, then houses might come toppling about our ears and cars take off with wings.

My father had risen from his carving chair. "There's only one thing to be done: we go home. Now. At once. We catch them red-handed."

"Red-handed?" my mother repeated faintly, thinking no doubt of the towering respectability of the two Miss Hardys, and: "Now? When we're only halfway through our holiday?"

"Damn the holiday!" cried my father, who never swore in the presence of his family. "We're going home. There are hours yet of daylight. If we leave now, we can be there before dark. Everyone pack at once."

There was trouble with Mrs. Prothero. At the time several of my father's handkerchiefs were simmering away soapily in one of her saucepans. Also, my father thought that the holiday charge should be reduced by more than Mrs. Prothero would agree to.

However, within the hour, ourselves and our belongings (including, of course, Celia's stowaway mouse) were packed into the car; Mrs. Prothero's account had been settled ("Shark!" said my father); and we were off. For once, my mother drove, as my father's injured hand would not allow him to.

Of course, Mr. Brown, having been at such pains to warn us, must have been on the lookout for our return. And if my father had hoped to catch the Miss Hardys unawares (let alone "red-handed"), he underestimated the alertness of elderly maiden ladies. We drove up under darkened skies and pouring rain, and my mother was about to get out of the car when the Miss Hardys, together under a huge umbrella, rushed down their front path to greet us.

My father had lowered the window on the passenger side and now called sternly, "Good evening. We need our front-door key, please."

Unmistakably the Miss Hardys were taken aback by our arrival; indeed, they seemed the very picture of guilt caught red-handed. "Oh, dear!" and "Oh, no!" they cried desperately. "So early back from your holiday!" and: "Surely you won't want to go into your house now, at once? Surely not! Oh, dear! Oh, dear!"

"The key!" said my father, and got it.

Quite a large party gathered in the shelter of our porch: my father in front with the key; the rest of his family behind him; behind us, again, the two Miss Hardys, still distraught; and behind them—although at first we were unaware of his having joined us— Mr. Wilfred Brown.

My father, left-handed but resolute, inserted the key in the lock, turned it, and pushed open the front door.

We had been expecting to enter or at least to peer forward, even if fearfully, into the hall. Instead, we found ourselves reeling back from a smell—a *stench*—which flowed out toward us. We knew when the tide had reached the last of our party because "Phew! What a stinker!" exclaimed Mr. Brown, thus declaring his presence through a handkerchief muffling nose and mouth.

But in spite of the smell, we could, of course, see into the hall.

(Surely my father saw *something*, however much he afterward preferred to deny that?) To me the hall seemed somehow darker than one would expect, even on an evening so overcast, darker in the way of having more shadows to it, and the shadows seemed to shift and flicker and move. They were just above ground level.

And I was almost sure that for a moment only I glimpsed a taller shadow whose shape I could interpret: it was human and surely female. I was not alone in this perception. The Miss Hardys had edged forward, and one now whispered, "Yes, it *is* dear Mrs. Chamberlain!" and the other, clearly in an agony of social embarrassment, murmured: "We are in the wrong. We are intruding upon the privacy of dear Mrs. Chamberlain's reunion!"

And then the shadowy figure had vanished.

Even before the Miss Hardys' whispering, I was aware that Celia was standing on tiptoe for a better view into the hall. With the keen eye of love, she recognized—or thought she recognized—one shape among the low-moving shadows. She became certain. "Mildred!" she cried. She took three eager steps past my father and across the threshold of the front door into the hall itself.

There she was halted abruptly by the behavior of someone whom, in the excitement, she had quite forgotten, her dear Micky. Up to now he had been in the concealment and safety of a pocket.

If the extraordinary smell from the house was sickening for us, it must have crazed with fear the poor mouse. He attempted to escape.

His small white face was already visible over the edge of Celia's pocket, and it was as if the shadowy house saw him. (If walls have ears, why not eyes, too? Eyes that stare, that glare, that stupefy.)

I suppose that if he were capable of planning at all, Micky must have meant to leap from Celia's pocket and instantly leave the house at greatest speed by the open front door. But the gaze of the shadowy hall was full upon him: he did not leap but fell helplessly from Celia's pocket onto the floor of the hall and lay there motionless.

("Oh!" moaned my mother, and there was a small clatter as she fainted away in her corner of the porch among the potted plants. She knew how a lady should react to the sight of a mouse.)

What followed is difficult to describe. It was as if the house—not the bricks and mortar, of course, but the inside of the house, the shadowy air itself—gathered together swiftly and with one ferocious purpose against a terrified white mouse—

And pounced!

Micky gave one heartrending squeak, a mouse shriek that rose to heaven, imploring mercy, and met none. He died in mid-squeak, and Celia fell on her knees by his body, babbling grief.

And the last of the slinking shadows melted away, every last one of them.

Only the smell remained, and later my intelligent nose would remember and make a connection between the present appalling stench of cat and the peculiar and rather repellent stuffiness of our house after every seaside holiday. In that stuffiness lurked the very last faint trace of this present horror of a smell.

As for my father, he would never, anyway, countenance any idea of the supernatural; he had always ridiculed it. The very idea of *evidence* put him into a fury. Now he was beside himself with indignation. "What is going on?" he shouted into the empty hall.

There was no reply—no sound at all except a slight scuffling from the back of the porch, where my mother was beginning to struggle among the potted plants; also Celia's quiet sobbing. He picked on that. He realized that the mouse had been Celia's rash secret. In this she had been, he said, deceitful, disobedient, and—oh, yes!—defiant and disloyal. Under the fury of her father's attack, Celia's weeping became hysterical. Her tears rained down upon the corpse clasped to her breast, and she was led away by the Miss Hardys to be given sal volatile and sympathy.

My father now turned to the plight of my mother in her porch corner. On regaining consciousness, she had opened her eyes to find Mr. Brown's gazing fully into them at a distance of about three and a half inches. And he was now gallantly assisting her with helping hands, one at her waist, another at her elbow. My father rushed down upon them, demanding that Mr. Brown remove himself instantly from his wife and his porch and the rest of his property. Without pause he went on to attack Mr. Brown's birth, breeding, appearance, character, and former occupation — "trade"! (Rage always inspired my father.)

Mr. Brown was neither foolhardy nor a fool. He retreated. Out into the drenching rain he went, and home. We all watched him go. That was really the last we saw of Mr. Brown. Within two days my father had caused a seven-foot-high solid fence to be built just our side of the laurel hedge.

Having dispatched Mr. Brown, my father became master again in his own house. He instructed us to go round opening all the windows to let what he called "this stale air" out and the fresh air in. Never mind the rain. Then we must unpack. "Our holiday is over; we are at home; we resume our routine."

In the long term, however, our routine had been undermined, and for this my father could not forgive the Miss Hardys. He suspected them of conniving at happenings which were all the more deplorable because they simply could not have occurred. He had known of the existence of the late Mrs. Chamberlain, of course, because he had bought our house from her heirs. He may even have heard of her mania for cats. ("She couldn't resist a stray," the Miss Hardys explained to Celia. "She tried to keep the numbers down. But, by the end — well, the house did begin rather to *smell*. Cats, you know . . .")

My father would never admit to what became obvious: that the ghosts of Mrs. Chamberlain and her cats had been returning regularly to haunts where they had been happy. They had been tempted by the absolute regularity of our holiday absences to hold a kind of annual old girls' reunion in our house, but there must have been old boys as well. Only the attendance of at least one tomcat could explain the strength of that smell.

The Miss Hardys had known what was going on every August but saw no harm in it. The ghosts came promptly after our departure for the seaside and had always vacated the house well before the date of our return. "It was all so discreetly done!" the Miss Hardys remarked plaintively to Celia as they administered the sal volatile. "Such a pity that it should have to stop!"

But it did. Before the next summer we had moved house, and I do not suppose that any family succeeding us could have had such a very dependable holiday routine. I only hope the ghosts were not too much disappointed.

After that summer my father became—and remained—jumpy about family holidays. We were never allowed to go at the same time for two years running. This meant, incidentally, that we no longer stayed in Mrs. Prothero's guesthouse. In a huff she had said that she could not be expected to be "irregularly available."

The Miss Hardys were seldom spoken of; Mr. Brown never.

The Strange Illness
of Mr. Arthur Cook ❖

*O*n a cold, shiny day at the end of winter
the Cook family went to look at the house they were likely to buy. Mr.
and Mrs. Cook had viewed it several times before and had discussed it
thoroughly; this was a first visit for their children, Judy and Mike.

Also with the Cooks was Mr. Biley, of the real estate agent's firm of
Ketch, Robb, and Biley in Walchester.

"Why's *he* come?" whispered Judy. (And although the Cooks were
not to know this, Mr. Biley did not usually accompany clients in order
to clinch deals.)

Her parents shushed Judy.

They had driven a little way out of Walchester into the country. The
car now turned down a lane which, perhaps fifty years before, had been
hardly more than a farm track. Now there were several houses along it.
The lane came to a dead end at a house with a FOR SALE notice at its
front gate. On the gate itself was the name of the house, Southcroft.

"There it is!" said Mr. Arthur Cook to his two children.

"And very nice, too!" Mr. Biley said enthusiastically.

But in fact, the house was not particularly nice. In size it was small to medium; brick-built, slate-roofed; exactly rectangular; and rather bleak-looking. It stood in the middle of a large garden, also exactly rectangular and rather bleak-looking.

Mike, who tended to like most things that happened to him, said, "Seems okay." He was gazing around not only at the house and its garden but at the quiet lane—ideal for his bike—and at the surrounding countryside. It would be all far, far better than where they were living now, in Walchester.

Judy, who was older than Mike and the only one in the family with a sharply pointed, inquisitive nose, said nothing—yet. She looked round alertly, intently.

"Nice big garden for kids to play in," Mr. Biley pointed out.

"I might even grow a few vegetables," said Mr. Cook.

"Oh, Arthur!" his wife said, laughing.

"Well," Mr. Cook said defensively, "I haven't had much chance up to now, have I?" In Walchester the Cooks had only a paved backyard. But anyway, Mr. Cook, whose job was fixing television aerials onto people's roofs, had always said that in his spare time he wanted to be indoors in an easy chair.

"Anyway," said Mr. Biley as they went in by the front gate, "you've lovely soil here. Still in good tilth."

"Tilth?" said Mr. Cook.

"That's it," said Mr. Biley.

They reached the front door. Mr. Biley unlocked it, and they all trooped in.

Southcroft had probably been built some time between the two wars. There was nothing antique about it, nor anything of special interest at all. On the other hand, it all appeared to be in good order, even to the house's having been fairly recently redecorated.

The Cooks went everywhere, looked everywhere, their footsteps echoing uncomfortably in empty rooms. They reassembled in the sitting room, which had French windows letting onto the garden at the back. Tactfully Mr. Biley withdrew into the garden to leave the family to private talk.

"Well, there you are," said Mr. Cook. "Just our size of house. Not remarkable in any way but snug, I fancy."

"Remarkable in one way, Arthur," said his wife. "Remarkably cheap."

"A snip," agreed Mr. Cook.

"Why's it so cheap?" asked Judy.

"You ask too many questions beginning with *why*," said her father, but good-humoredly.

It was true, however, that there seemed no particular reason for the house's being so cheap as it was. Odd, perhaps.

"Can't we go into the garden now?" asked Mike.

Mike and Judy went out, and Mr. Biley came in again.

There wasn't much for the children to see in the garden. Close to the house grew unkempt grass, with a big old apple tree—the only tree in the garden—which Mike began to climb very thoroughly. The rest of the garden had all been under cultivation at one time, but now it was neglected, a mass of last season's dead weeds. There were some straggly bushes—raspberry canes, perhaps. There had once been a greenhouse; only the brick foundations were left. There was a garden shed and behind it a mass of stuff which Judy left Mike to investigate. She wanted to get back to the adult conversation.

By the time Judy rejoined the party indoors there was no doubt about it: the Cooks were buying the house. Mr. Biley was extremely pleased, Judy noticed. He caught Judy staring at him and jollily, but very unwisely, said, "Well, young lady?"

Judy, invited thus to join in the conversation, had a great many questions to ask. She knew she wouldn't be allowed to ask them all, and she began almost at random: "Who used to live here?"

"A family called Cribble," said Mr. Biley. "A very *nice* family called Cribble."

"Cribble," Judy repeated to herself, storing the piece of information away. "And why—"

At that moment Mike walked in again from the garden. "There's lots of stuff behind the shed," he said. "Rolls and rolls of chicken wire, in an awful mess, and wood—posts and slats and stuff."

"Easily cleared," said Mr. Biley. "The previous owners were going to have bred dogs, I believe. They would have erected sheds, enclosures, runs—all that kind of thing."

"Why did the Cribbles give up the idea?" asked Judy.

Mr. Biley looked uneasy. "Not the Cribbles," he said, "the Johnsons. The family here before the Cribbles."

"Why did the Johnsons give up the idea then?" asked Judy. "I mean, when they'd got all the stuff for it?"

"They—" Mr. Biley appeared to think deeply, if only momentarily. "They had to move rather unexpectedly."

"Why?"

"Family reasons, perhaps?" said Mrs. Cook quickly. She knew some people found Judy tiresome.

"Family reasons, no doubt," Mr. Biley agreed.

Judy said thoughtfully to herself: "The Johnsons didn't stay long enough to start dog breeding, and they went in such a hurry that they left their stuff behind. The Cribbles came, but they didn't stay long enough to have time to clear away all the Johnsons' stuff. I wonder why *they* left. . . ."

Nobody could say that Judy was asking Mr. Biley a question, but he answered her all the same. "My dear young lady," he said, in a manner so polite as to be also quite rude, "I do not know why. Nor is it my business." He sounded as if he did not think it was Judy's, either. He turned his back on her and began talking loudly about house purchase to Mr. Cook.

Judy was not put out. She had investigated mysteries and secrets before this, and she knew that patience was all important.

The Cooks bought Southcroft and moved in almost at once. Spring came late that year, and in the continuing cold weather the house proved as snug as one could wish. When the frosts were over, the family did some work outside, getting rid of all the dog-breeding junk: they made a splendid bonfire of the wood and put the wire out for the garbage men. Mr. Cook took a long look at the weeds beginning to sprout everywhere and groaned. He bought a garden fork and a spade and hoe and rake and put them into the shed.

In their different ways the Cooks were satisfied with the move. The new house was still convenient for Mr. Cook's work. Mrs. Cook found that the neighbors kept themselves to themselves more than she would have liked, but she got a part-time job in a shop in the village, and *that* was all right. Mike made new friends in the new school, and they went riding round the countryside on their bikes. Judy was slower at making friends, partly because she was absorbed in her own affairs, particularly in investigation. In this she was disappointed for a time. She could find out so little about the Cribbles and the Johnsons: why they had stayed so briefly at Southcroft, why they had moved in so much haste. The Cribbles now lived the other side of Walchester, rather smartly, in a house with a large garden which they had had expensively landscaped. (Perhaps the size of the garden at Southcroft was what had attracted them to the house in the first place. In the village people said that the Cribbles had already engaged landscape garden specialists for Southcroft when they suddenly decided to leave.) As for the Johnsons, Judy discovered that they had moved right away, to Yorkshire, to do their dog breeding. Before the Cribbles and the Johnsons, an old couple called Baxter had lived in the house for many years, until one had died and the other moved away.

The Cooks had really settled in. Spring brought sunshine and longer days, and it also brought the first symptoms of Mr. Cook's strange illness.

At first the trouble seemed to be his eyesight. He complained of a kind of brownish fog between himself and the television screen. He couldn't see clearly enough to enjoy the programs. He thought he noticed that this fogginess was worse when he was doing daylight viewing, at the weekends or in the early evening. He tried to deal with this by drawing the curtains in the room where the set was on, but the fogginess persisted.

Mr. Cook went to the optician to see whether he needed glasses. The optician applied all the usual tests and said that Mr. Cook's vision seemed excellent. Mr. Cook said it wasn't—or, at least, sometimes wasn't. The optician said that eyesight could be affected by a person's state of general health and suggested that if the trouble continued, Mr. Cook should consult a doctor.

Mr. Cook was annoyed at the time he had wasted at the optician's and went home to try to enjoy his favorite Saturday afternoon program. Not only did he suffer from increased fogginess of vision, but— perhaps as a result, perhaps not—he developed a splitting headache. In the end he switched the set off and went outside and savagely dug in the garden, uprooting ground elder, nettle, twitch, and a great number of other weed species. By tea time he had cleared a large patch, in which Judy at once sowed radishes and mustard and cress.

At the end of an afternoon's digging, the headache had gone. Mr. Cook was also able to watch the late-night movie on television without discomfort. But his Saturday as a whole had been ruined, and when he went to bed, his sleep was troubled by strange dreams, and on Sunday morning he woke at first light. This had become the pattern of his sleeping recently: haunted dreams and early wakings. On this particular occasion, as often before, he couldn't get to sleep again, and he spent the rest of Sunday—a breezy, sunny day—moving restlessly about indoors from Sunday paper to television set, saying he felt awful.

Mrs. Cook said that perhaps he ought to see a doctor, as the optician had advised; Mr. Cook shouted at her that he wouldn't.

But as spring turned to summer, it became clear that something would have to be done. Mr. Cook's condition was worsening. He gave up trying to watch television. Regularly he got up at sunrise because he couldn't sleep longer and couldn't even rest in bed. (Sometimes he went out and dug in the garden, and when he did so, the exertion or the fresh air seemed to make him feel better, at least for the time being.) He lost his appetite, and he was always irritable with his children. He grumbled at Mike for being out so much on his bicycle, and he grumbled at Judy for being at home. Her investigations no longer amused him at all. Judy had pointed out that his illness seemed to vary with the weather; fine days made it worse. She wondered why. Her father said he'd give her *why*, if she weren't careful.

At last Mrs. Cook burst out that she could stand this no longer. "Arthur, you *must* go to the doctor." As though he had only been waiting for someone to insist, Mr. Cook agreed.

The doctor listened carefully to Mr. Cook's account of his symptoms and examined him thoroughly. He asked whether he smoked and whether he ate enough roughage. Reassured on both these points, the doctor said he thought Mr. Cook's condition might be the result of nervous tension. "Anything worrying you?" asked the doctor.

"Of course, there is!" exploded Mr. Cook. "I'm ill, aren't I? I'm worried sick about that!"

The doctor asked if there was anything else that Mr. Cook worried about. His wife? His children? His job?

"I lie awake in the morning and worry about them all," said Mr. Cook. "And about that huge garden in that awful state . . ."

"What garden?"

"Our garden. It's huge and it's been let go wild and I ought to get it in order, I suppose, and—oh, I don't know! I'm no gardener."

"Perhaps you shouldn't have a garden that size," suggested the doctor. "Perhaps you should consider moving into a house with no garden or at least a really manageable one. Somewhere, say, with just a patio, in Walchester."

"That's what we moved *from*," said Mr. Cook. "Less than six months ago."

"Oh, dear!" said the doctor. He called Mrs. Cook into the surgery and suggested that her husband might be suffering from overwork. Mr. Cook was struck by the idea; Mrs. Cook less so. The doctor suggested a week off, to see what *that* would do.

That week marked the climax of Mr. Cook's illness; it drove Mrs. Cook nearly out of her wits and Judy to urgent inquiries.

The week came at the very beginning of June, an ideal month in which to try to recover from overwork. Judy and Mike were at school all day, so that everything was quiet at home for their father. The sun shone, and Mr. Cook planned to sit outside in a deck chair and catch up on lost sleep. Then, when the children came home, he would go to bed early with the portable television set. (He assumed that rest would be dealing with fogginess of vision.)

Things did not work out like that at all. During that week Mr. Cook was seized with a terrible restlessness. It seemed impossible for him to achieve any repose at all. He tried only once to watch television, and Judy noticed that thereafter he seemed almost—yes, he seemed afraid. He was a shadow of his former self when, at the end of the week, he went back to work.

After he had left the house that morning, Mrs. Cook spoke her fears: "It'll be the hospital next, I know. And once they begin injecting and cutting up— Oh, why did we ever come to live here!"

"You think it's something to do with the house?" asked Judy. Mike had already set off to school; she lingered.

"Well, your dad was perfectly all right before. I'd say there was something wrong with the drains here, but there's no smell, and anyway, why should only he fall ill?"

"There is something wrong with the house," said Judy. "I couldn't ask the Johnsons about it, so I asked the Cribbles."

"The Cribbles! That we bought the house from?"

"Yes. They live the other side of Walchester. I went there—"

"Oh, Judy!" said her mother. "You'll get yourself into trouble with your questions, one of these days."

"No, I shan't," said Judy (and she never did). "I went to ask them about this house. I rang at the front door, and Mrs. Cribble answered it. At least, I think it must have been her. She was quite nice. I told her my name, but I don't think she connected me with buying the house from them. Then I asked her about the house, whether *they* had noticed anything."

"And what did she say?"

"She didn't say anything. She slammed the door in my face."

"Oh, Judy!" cried Mrs. Cook, and burst into tears.

Her mother's tears decided Judy. She would beard Mr. Biley himself, of Ketch, Robb, and Biley. She was not so innocent as to suppose he would grant her, a child, an official interview. But if she could buttonhole him somewhere, she might get from him at least one useful piece of information.

After school that day, Judy presented herself at the offices of Ketch, Robb, and Biley in Walchester. She had her deception ready. "Has my father been in to see Mr. Biley yet?" she asked. That sounded respectable. The receptionist said that Mr. Biley was talking with a client at present and that she really couldn't say.

"I'll wait," said Judy, like a good girl.

Judy waited. She was prepared to wait until the offices shut at half past five, when Mr. Biley would surely leave to go home, but much earlier than that, Mr. Biley came downstairs with someone who was evidently rather an important client. Mr. Biley escorted him to the door, chatting in the jovial way that Judy remembered so well. They said good-bye at the door and parted, and Mr. Biley started back by the way he had come.

Judy caught up with him, laid a hand on his arm. "Mr. Biley, please!"

Mr. Biley turned. He did not recognize Judy. He smiled. "Yes, young lady?"

"We bought Southcroft from the Cribbles," she began.

Mr. Biley's smile vanished instantly. He said, "I should make clear at once that Ketch, Robb, and Biley will not, under any circumstances, handle that property again."

"Why?" asked Judy. She couldn't help asking.

"The sale of the same property three times in eighteen months may bring income to us, but it does not bring reputation. So I wish you good day."

Judy said, "*Please*, I only need to ask you one thing, really." She gripped the cloth of his sleeve.

The receptionist had looked up to see what was going on, and Mr. Biley was aware of that. "Well? Be quick," he said.

"Before the Cribbles and the Johnsons, there were the Baxters. When old Mr. Baxter died, where did Mrs. Baxter move to?"

"Into Senior House, Waddington Road." He removed Judy's fingers from his coat sleeve. "Remember to tell your father *not* to call in Ketch, Robb, and Biley for the resale of the property. Good-bye."

It was getting late, but Judy thought she should finish the job. She found a telephone booth and the right money and rang her mother to say she was calling on Mrs. Baxter in the old people's apartments in Waddington Road. She was glad that her telephone time ran out before her mother could say much in reply.

Then she set off for Waddington Road.

By the time she reached the apartments, Judy felt tired, thirsty, hungry. There was no problem about seeing Mrs. Baxter. The porter told her the number of Mrs. Baxter's apartment and said Mrs. Baxter would probably be starting her tea. The residents had just finished seeing a film on mountaineering in the Alps and—as he put it—would be brewing up late.

Judy found the door and knocked. A delicious smell of hot-buttered toast seemed to be coming through the keyhole. A thin little voice told her to come in. And there sat Mrs. Baxter behind a teapot with a cozy on it, in the act of spreading honey on a piece of buttered toast.

"Oh," said Judy, faintly.

Mrs. Baxter was delighted to have a visitor. "Sit down, dear, and I'll get another cup and saucer and plate."

She was such a nice little old woman, with gingery gray hair—she wore a gingery dress almost to match—and rather dark popeyes. She seemed active but a bit slow. When she got up in a slow, plump way to get the extra china, Judy was reminded of a hamster she had once had, called Pickles.

Mrs. Baxter got the china and some biscuits and poured out another cup of tea. All this without asking Judy her name or her business.

"Sugar?" asked Mrs. Baxter.

"Yes, please," said Judy. "I'm Judy Cook, Mrs. Baxter."

"Oh, yes? I'll have to get the tin of sugar. I don't take sugar myself, you know."

She waddled over to some shelves. She had her back to Judy, but Judy could see the little hamster hands reaching up to a tin marked SUGAR.

"Mrs. Baxter, we live in the house you used to live in, Southcroft."

The hamster hands never reached the sugar tin but stayed up in the air for as long as it might have taken Judy to count ten. It was as though the name Southcroft had turned the little hamster woman to stone.

Then the hands came down slowly, and Mrs. Baxter waddled back to the tea table. She did not look at Judy; her face was expressionless.

"Have a biscuit?" she said to Judy.

Judy took one. "Mrs. Baxter, I've come to ask you about Southcroft."

"Don't forget your cup of tea, dear."

"No, I won't. Mrs. Baxter, I must ask you several things—"

"Just a minute, dear."

"Yes?"

"Perhaps you take sugar in your tea?"

"Yes, I do, but it doesn't matter. I'd rather you'd let me ask you—"

"But it does matter," said Mrs. Baxter firmly. "And I shall get the sugar for you. I don't take it myself, you know."

Judy had had dreams when she had tried to do something and could not because things—the same things—happened over and over again to prevent her. Now she watched Mrs. Baxter waddle over to the shelves, watched the little hamster hands reach up to the sugar tin and—this time—bring it down and bring it back to the tea table. Judy sugared her tea, and took another biscuit, and began eating and drinking. She was trying to steady herself and fortify herself for what she now realized was going to be very, very difficult. Mrs. Baxter had begun telling her about mountaineering in the Alps. The little voice went on and on, until Judy thought it must wear out.

It paused.

Judy said swiftly, "Tell me about Southcroft, please. What was it like to live in when you were there? Why is it so awful now?"

"No, dear," said Mrs. Baxter hurriedly. "I'd rather go on telling you about the Matterhorn."

"I want to know about Southcroft," cried Judy.

"No," said Mrs. Baxter. "I never talk about it. Never. I'll go on about the Matterhorn."

"Please. You must tell me about Southcroft." Judy was insisting, but she knew she was being beaten by the soft little old woman. She found she was beginning to cry. "Please, Mrs. Baxter. My dad's ill with living there."

"Oh, no," cried the little hamster woman. "Oh, no, he couldn't be!"

"He is," said Judy, "and you won't help!" Stumblingly she began to get up.

"Won't you stay, dear, and hear about the Matterhorn?"

"No!" Judy tried to put her cup back on the dainty tea table, but couldn't see properly for her tears. China fell, broke, as she turned from the table. She found the handle of the door and let herself out.

"Oh, dear, oh, dear, oh, dear!" the little voice behind her was crying, but whether it was about the broken china or something else it was impossible to say.

Judy ran down the long passages and past the porter, who stared at her tear-wet face. When she got outside, she ran and ran and then walked and walked. She knew she could have caught a bus home, but she didn't want to. She walked all the way, arriving nearly at dusk, to find her mother waiting anxiously for her. But instead of questioning Judy at once, Mrs. Cook drew her into the kitchen, where they were alone. Mike was in the sitting room, watching a noisy television program.

Mrs. Cook said, "Your dad telephoned from Walchester soon after you did. He said he wasn't feeling very well, so he's spending the night with your aunt Edie."

They stared at each other. Mr. Cook detested his sister Edie. "He'd do anything rather than come here," said Judy. "He's afraid."

Mrs. Cook nodded.

"Mum, we'll just have to move from here, for Dad's sake."

"I don't know that we can, Judy. Selling one house and buying another is very expensive; moving is expensive."

"But if we stay here . . ."

Mrs. Cook hesitated. Then: "Judy, what you were doing this afternoon—your calling on old Mrs. Baxter—was it any use, any help?"

"No."

Mrs. Cook groaned aloud.

Judy's visit to Mrs. Baxter had not led to the answering of any questions, but there was an outcome.

The next day, in the afternoon, Judy and Mike had come home from school and were in the kitchen with their mother. It was a gloomy tea. There was no doubt at all that their father would come home this time—after all here were his wife and his children that he loved—but the homecoming seemed likely to be a grim and hopeless one.

From the kitchen they heard the click of the front gate. This was far too early to be Mr. Cook himself, and besides, there'd been no sound of a car. Mike, nearest to the window, looked out. "No one we know," he reported. "An old lady." He laughed to himself. "She looks like a hamster."

Judy was at the front door and opening it before Mrs. Baxter had had time to ring. She brought her in and introduced her to the others, and Mrs. Cook brewed fresh tea while the children made her comfortable in the sitting room. Besides her handbag, Mrs. Baxter was carrying a dumpy zip-up case which seemed heavy; she kept it by her. She was tired. "Buses!" she murmured.

Mrs. Cook brought her a cup of tea.

"Mrs. Baxter doesn't take sugar, Mum," said Judy.

They all sat round Mrs. Baxter, trying not to stare at her, waiting for her to speak. She sipped her tea without looking at them.

"Your husband's not very well, I hear," she said at last to Mrs. Cook.

"No."

"Not home from work yet?"

"Not yet."

Mrs. Baxter was obviously relieved. She looked at them all now. "And this is the rest of the family. . . ." She smiled timidly at Mike. "You're the baby of the family?"

Mike said, "I'm younger than Judy. Mum, if it's okay, I think I'll go out on my bike with Charlie Feather." He took something to eat and went.

Mrs. Baxter said, "We never had children."

"A pity," said Mrs. Cook.

"Yes. Everything would be different, if it had been different." Mrs. Baxter paused. "Do you know, I've never been back to this house—not even to the village—since Mr. Baxter died."

"It was very sad for you," said Mrs. Cook, not knowing what else to say.

"It's been a terrible *worry*," said Mrs. Baxter, as though sadness was not the thing that mattered. Again she paused. Judy could see that she was nerving herself to say something important. She had been brave and resolute to come all this way at all.

Mrs. Cook could also see what Judy saw. "You must be tired out," she said.

But Judy said gently, "Why've you come?"

Mrs. Baxter tried to speak, couldn't. Instead, she opened the zip-up bag and dragged out of it a large, heavy book: *The Vegetable and Fruit Grower's Encyclopaedia and Vade-Mecum.* She pushed it into Mrs. Cook's lap. "It was Mr. Baxter's," she said. "Give it to your husband. Tell him to use it and work hard in the garden, and I think things will right themselves in time. You need to humor him."

Mrs. Cook was bewildered. She seized upon the last remark. "I humor him as much as I can, as it is. He's been so unwell."

Mrs. Baxter tittered. "Good gracious, I didn't mean *your* husband; I meant mine. Humor Mr. Baxter."

"But—but he's dead and gone!"

Mrs. Baxter's eyes filled with tears. "That's just it; he isn't. Not both. He's dead but not gone. He never meant to go. I knew what he intended; I knew the wickedness of it. I told him, I begged him on his deathbed, but he wouldn't listen. You know that bit of the burial service 'We brought nothing into this world, and it is certain that we can carry nothing out'? Well, there was something he'd dearly have liked to have taken out. He couldn't, so he stayed in this world with it: his garden. We were both good churchgoers, but I believe he set his vegetable garden before his God. I know that he set it before me." She wept afresh.

"Oh, dear, Mrs. Baxter!" said Mrs. Cook, much distressed.

"When he was dying," said Mrs. Baxter, after she had blown her nose, "I could see there was something he wanted to say. I'd been reading the Twenty-third Psalm to him — you know, about the valley of the shadow of death. He was trying to speak. I leant right over him, and he managed to whisper his very last words. He said, 'Are the runner beans up yet?' Then he died."

Nobody spoke. Mrs. Baxter recovered herself and went on.

"I knew — I *knew* he wouldn't leave that garden after he'd died. I just hoped the next owners would look after it as lovingly as he'd done, and then in time he'd be content to go. That's what I hoped and prayed. But the first lot of people were going to cover it with dog kennels, and I heard that the second lot were going to lay it out with artificial streams and weeping willows and things. Well, he made their lives a misery, and they left. And now your husband . . ."

"He's just never liked gardening," said Mrs. Cook.

The two women stared at each other bleakly.

"Why can't Dad be allowed to watch TV?" asked Judy. Then, answering herself: "Oh, I see, he ought to be working in the garden every spare minute in daylight and fine weather."

"Mr. Baxter quite enjoyed some of the gardening programs, sometimes," Mrs. Baxter said defensively.

There was a long silence.

"It's lovely soil," said Mrs. Baxter persuasively. "Easy to work. Grows anything. That's why we came to live here, really. All my married life, I never had to buy a single vegetable. Fruit, too — raspberries, strawberries, gooseberries, all colors of currants. So much of everything, for just the two of us, that we had to give a lot of stuff away. We didn't grow plums or pears or apples—except for the Bramleys—because Mr. Baxter wouldn't have trees shading the garden. But all those vegetables—you'd find it a great saving, with a family."

"It seems hard on my husband," said Mrs. Cook.

"It's hard on mine," said Mrs. Baxter. "Look at him!" Startled, Mrs. Cook and Judy looked where Mrs. Baxter was looking, through the French windows and down the length of the garden. The sun fell on the weedy earth of the garden, on nothing else.

Mrs. Cook turned her gaze back into the room, but Judy went on looking, staring until her eyes blurred and her vision was fogged with a kind of brown fogginess that was in the garden. Then suddenly she was afraid.

"But *look!*" said Mrs. Baxter, and took Judy's hand in her own little paw, which had grown soft and smooth from leisure in Senior House. "*Look!*" Judy looked where she pointed, and the brown fogginess seemed to concentrate itself and shape itself, and there dimly was the shape of an old man dressed in brown from his brown boots to his battered brown hat, with a piece of string tied around the middle of the old brown waterproof he was wearing. He stood in an attitude of dejection at the bottom of the garden, looking at the weeds.

Then Mrs. Baxter let go of Judy's hand, and Judy saw him no more.

"That was his garden mac," said Mrs. Baxter. "He would wear it. When all the buttonholes had gone, as well as the buttons, and I wouldn't repair it anymore, then he belted it on with string."

"He looked so miserable," said Judy. She had been feeling sorry for her father; now she began to feel sorry for Mr. Baxter.

"Yes," said Mrs. Baxter. "He'd like to go, I've no doubt of it, but he can't leave the garden in that state." She sighed. She gathered up her handbag and the other empty bag.

"Don't go!" cried Mrs. Cook and Judy together.

"What more can I do? I've told you; I've advised you. For *his* sake, too, I've begged you. No, I can't do more."

She would not stay. She waddled out of the house and down the front path, and at the front gate met Mr. Cook. He had just got out of the car. She gave him a scared little bob of a good-day and scuttled past him and away.

Mr. Cook came in wearily; his face was grayish. "Who was that old dear?" he asked. But he did not really want to know.

His wife said to him, "Arthur, Judy is going to get your tea—won't you, love?—while I explain a lot of things. Come and sit down and listen."

Mrs. Cook talked, and Mr. Cook listened, and gradually his face began to change. Something lifted from it, leaving it clear, almost happy, for the first time for many weeks. He was still listening when Judy brought his tea. At the end of Mrs. Cook's explanation, Judy added hers: she told her father what—*whom*—she had seen in the garden when Mrs. Baxter had held her hand. Mr. Cook began to laugh. "You saw him, Judy? An old man all in brown with a piece of string tied round his middle—oh, Judy, my girl! When I began really seeing him, only the other day, I was sure I was going off my rocker! I was scared! I thought I was seeing things that no one else could see, things that weren't there at all! And you've seen him, too, and he's just old man Baxter!" And Mr. Cook laughed so much that he cried, and in the end he put his head down among the tea things and sobbed and sobbed.

It was going to be all right after all.

In Mr. Baxter's old-fashioned mind, the man of the family was the one to do all the gardening. That was why, in what Judy considered a very unfair way, he had made a dead set at her father. But now all Mr. Cook's family rallied to him. Even Mike, when the need was explained, left his bicycle for a while. They all helped in the garden. They dug and weeded and made bonfires of the worst weeds and began to build a compost heap of harmless garden rubbish. They planted seeds if it were not too late in the season and bought plants when it was. Mr. Cook followed the advice of the *Encyclopaedia* and occasionally had excellent ideas of his own. When Judy asked him where he got them, he looked puzzled at himself and said he did not know. But she could guess.

Every spare moment that was daylight and fine, Mr. Cook worked in the garden, and his illness was cured. His appetite came back, he slept like a top, and he would have enjoyed television again except that in the middle of programs he so often fell asleep from healthy exhaustion.

Well over a year later, on a holiday jaunt in Walchester, Judy was passing one of the cinemas. An audience mainly of senior citizens was coming out from an afternoon showing of *Deadly Amazon*. Judy felt a touch on her arm, soft yet insistent, like the voice that spoke, Mrs. Baxter's: "My dear, how—how is he?"

"Oh, Mrs. Baxter, he's much, much better! Oh, thank you! He's really all right. My mum says my dad's as well as she's ever known him."

"No, dear, I didn't mean your father. How is *he*—Mr. Baxter?"

Judy said, "We think he's gone. Dad hasn't seen the foggiest wisp of him for months, and Dad says it doesn't *feel* as if he's there anymore. You see, Dad's got the garden going wonderfully now. We've had early potatoes and beans and peas—oh, and raspberries—and Dad plans to grow asparagus—"

"Ah," said Mrs. Baxter. "No wonder Mr. Baxter's gone. Gone off pleased, no doubt. That *is* nice. I don't think you need worry about his coming back. He has enough sense not to. It won't be long before your father can safely give up gardening, if he likes."

"I'll tell him what you say," Judy said doubtfully.

But of course, it was too late. Once a gardener, always a gardener. "I'll never give up now," Mr. Cook said. "I'll be a gardener until my dying day."

"But not after that, Arthur," said his wife. "Please."

A Christmas Pudding
Improves with Keeping ❖

*I*t was boiling hot weather. The tall old house simmered and seethed in a late heat wave. The Napper family shared the use of the garden, but today it was shadier and cooler for them to stay indoors, in their basement flat. There they lay about, breathless.

"I wish," said Eddy, "I wish—"

"Go on," said his father. "Wish for a private swimming pool, or a private ice-cream fountain, or a private—" He gave up, too hot.

"I wish," said Eddy, and stopped again.

"Go to the park, Eddy," said his mother. "Ask if the dog upstairs would like a walk and take him to the park with you. See friends there. Try the swings for a bit of air."

"No," said Eddy. "I wish I could make a Christmas pudding."

His parents stared at him, too stupefied by heat to be properly amazed. He said, "I know you always buy our Christmas pudding, Mum, but we could make one. It wouldn't be too early to make one now. We could. I wish we could."

"Now?" said his mother faintly. "In all this heat? And why? The bought puddings have always been all right, haven't they?"

"I remember," said Mr. Napper, "my granny always made her own Christmas puddings. Always."

"You and your granny!" said Mrs. Napper.

"She made several at once. I remember them boiling away in her kitchen for hours and hours and hours. She made them early and stored them. When Christmas came, she served a pudding kept from the year before." He sighed, smacked his lips. "A Christmas pudding improves with keeping."

Mrs. Napper had closed her eyes, apparently in sleep, but Eddy was listening.

"We used to help with the puddings," said Mr. Napper. "We all had a turn at stirring the mixture. You wished as you stirred, but you mustn't say what your wish was. And the wish came true before the next Christmas."

"Yes!" cried Eddy. "That's it! I want to stir and to wish—to wish—"

"Well," said his mother with her eyes shut, "if we ever make our own Christmas pudding, it won't be during a heat wave."

"I just wish—" Eddy began again.

"Stop it, Eddy!" said his mother, waking up to be sharp. "Go to the park. Here's money for ice cream."

When Eddy had gone, his father said, "That settled him!"

His mother said, "The ideas they get! Come and gone in a minute, though . . ." They both dozed off.

But the idea that had come to Eddy did not go. Not at all.

The Nappers had moved into their basement flat in the spring of that year. Once, long before, the whole house had been one home, for one well-off family, with servants, or a servant, in the basement kitchen. Later the house had been split up into flats, one floor to a flat, for separate families. Nowadays one family lived on the first floor, where the bedrooms had been. Another family lived on the ground floor, where the parlor and dining room had been. (And this family owned a dog and shared the garden with the Nappers.) And the Nappers themselves lived in the basement.

The conversion of the house into flats had been done many years before, but this was the first time since then—although the Nappers were not to know it—that a child had lived in the basement. Eddy was that child.

From their very first moving into the basement, Eddy had had strange dreams. One dream, rather, and not a dream that his dreaming eyes saw but something that he dreamed he heard. The sound was so slight, so indistinct, that at first even his dreaming self did not really notice it. *Swish—wish—wish!* it went. *Swish, wish, wish!* The dream sound, even when he came to hear it properly, never woke him up in fright. Indeed, it did not frighten him at all. To begin with, he did not even remember it when he woke up.

But *swish—wish—wish!*—the sound became more distinct as time passed, more insistent. Never loud, never threatening, however, but coaxing, cajoling, begging, begging and imploring.

"Please," said Eddy to his mother, "oh, *please!* It's not a heat wave now; it's nearly Christmas. And it's Saturday tomorrow; we've got all day. Can't we make our own Christmas pudding tomorrow? Please, please!"

"Oh, Eddy! I'm so busy!"

"You mean we can't?" Eddy looked as if he might cry. "But we must! Oh, Mum, we must!"

"No, Eddy! And when I say no, I mean no!"

That evening, as they sat round the gas fire in their sitting room, there was an alarming happening: a sudden rattle and clatter that seemed to start from above and come down and that ended in a crash, a crash not huge but evidently disastrous, and it was unmistakably in their own basement flat, in their own sitting room.

And yet it wasn't.

Mrs. Napper had sprung to her feet with a cry: "Someone is trying to break in!" Her eyes stared at the blank wallpapered wall from which the crashing sound had seemed to come. There was nothing whatsoever to be seen, and now there was dead silence—except for the frantic barking of the dog upstairs. (The dog had been left on guard, while his family went out, and he hadn't liked what he had just heard, any more than the Nappers had.)

Suddenly Eddy rushed to the wall and put his hands flat upon it. "I wish—" he cried. "I wish—"

His father pulled him away. "If there's anybody—or anything— there," he said, "I'll get at him." He knocked furiously on the wall several times. Then he calmed himself and began rapping and tapping systematically, listening intently for any sound of hollowness and swearing under his breath at the intrusive barking of the dog upstairs.

"Ah!" he said. "At last!" He began scrabbling at the wallpaper with his pocketknife and his fingernails. Layer upon layer of wallpaper began to be torn away.

"Whatever will the landlord say?" asked Mrs. Napper, who had recovered her courage and some of her calm.

Mr. Napper said, "Eddy, get my toolbox. I don't know what may be under here." While Eddy was gone, Mrs. Napper fetched dust sheets and spread them out against the mess.

What lay underneath all the ancient wallpaper was a small, squarish wooden door let into the wall at about waist level; its knob was gone, but Mr. Napper prized it open without too much difficulty. The dog upstairs was still barking, and as soon as the little door was open, the sound came down to them with greater clearness.

With one hand Mr. Napper was feeling through the doorway into the blackness inside. "There's a shaft in here," he said. "It's not wide or deep from front to back, but it seems to go right up. I need the torch, Eddy."

Even as Eddy came back with the torch, Mr. Napper was saying cheerfully, "We've been making a fuss about nothing. Why, this is just an old-fashioned service lift, from the time our sitting room was part of a big kitchen."

"A lift?" Eddy repeated.

"Only a miniature one, for hauling food straight up from the kitchen to the dining room and bringing the dirty dishes down again. It was worked by hand."

Mrs. Napper had not spoken. Now she said, "What about all that rattling—and the crash?"

Mr. Napper was shining his torch into the shaft of the service lift. "The ropes for hauling up and down were rotten with age. They gave way at last. Yes, I can see the worn-out ends of the cords."

"But why should they choose to rot and break now?" asked Mrs. Napper. "Why *now*?"

"Why not now?" asked Mr. Napper, closing that part of the discussion. He was still peering into the shaft. "There was something on the service shelf when it fell. There are bits of broken china and—this."

He brought out from the darkness of the square hole an odd-looking, dried-looking, black-looking object that sat on the palm of his hand like an irregularly shaped large ball.

"Ugh!" said Mrs. Napper instantly.

Mr. Napper said, "It's just the remains of a ball of something, a composite ball of something." He picked at it with a fingernail. "Tiny bits all stuck and dried together . . ." He had worried out a fragment, and now he crumbled it in his hand. "Look!"

Mrs. Napper peered reluctantly over his shoulder. "Well, I must say—"

"What is it?" asked Eddy. But suddenly he knew.

His mother had touched the crumblings and then immediately wiped her fingers on a corner of dust sheet. "It looks like old, old sultanas and raisins and things. . . ."

"That's what I think," said Mr. Napper. "It's a plum pudding. It *was* a plum pudding."

Eddy had known: a Christmas pudding.

"But what was it doing there, in that service lift thing?" asked Mrs. Napper. "Did someone leave it there deliberately, or was it just mislaid? Was any of it eaten, do you think?"

"Hard to tell," said Mr. Napper.

"And why did the workmen leave it there, when they sealed up the shaft, to make the separate flats?" She was worrying about this mystery. "Perhaps it was between floors and they didn't see it."

"Or perhaps they didn't like to touch it," said Eddy.

"Why do you say that?" his mother asked sharply.

"I don't know," said Eddy.

They cleared up the mess as well as they could. The ancient pudding was wrapped in newspaper and put in the wastebin under the kitchen sink.

Then it was time for Eddy to go to bed.

That night Eddy dreamed his dream more clearly than ever before. *Swish—wish—wish!* went whatever it was, round and round. *Swish—wish—wish!* In his dream he was dreaming the sound, and in his dream he opened his eyes and looked across a big old shadowy kitchen, past a towering dresser hung with jugs and stacked with plates and dishes on display, past a little wooden door to a service lift, past a kitchen range with saucepans and a kettle on it.

His gaze reached the big kitchen table. Someone was standing at the table, with his back to Eddy: a boy, just of Eddy's age and height, as far as he could tell. In fact, for an instant, Eddy had the strangest dream sensation that he, Eddy, was standing there at the kitchen table. He, Eddy, was stirring a mixture of something dark and aromatic, with a long wooden spoon in a big earthenware mixing bowl, stirring round and round, stirring, stirring. *Swish—wish—wish . . . Swish—wish—wish . . .*

Wish! whispered the wooden spoon as it went round the bowl. *Wish! Wish!* But Eddy did not know what to wish. His not knowing made the boy at the table turn toward him. And when Eddy saw the boy's face, looked into his eyes, he knew. He knew everything, as though he were inside the boy, inside the boy's mind. He knew that this boy lived here in the basement; he was the child of the servant of the house. He helped his mother to cook the food that was put into the service lift and hauled up to the dining room upstairs. He helped her to serve the family who ate in the dining room, and sat at their ease in the parlor, and slept in the comfortable bedrooms above. He hated the family that had to be served. He was filled with hatred as a bottle can be filled with poison.

The boy at the table was stirring a Christmas pudding for the family upstairs, and he was stirring into it his hatred and a wish. . . .

Wish! whispered the wooden spoon. *Wish! Wish!* And the boy at the table smiled at Eddy, a secret and deadly little smile: They were two conspirators, or one boy. Either way, they were wishing, wishing. . . .

Someone screamed, and at that Eddy woke. And the screamer was Eddy himself. He tore out of his bed and his bedroom to where he could see a light in the little kitchen of the basement flat. There were his parents in their dressing gowns, drinking cups of tea. The kitchen clock said nearly three o'clock in the morning.

Eddy rushed into his mother's arms with a muddled, terrified account of a nightmare about a Christmas pudding. His mother soothed him and looked over his head to his father. "You said it was just coincidence that neither of us could sleep tonight for bad dreams. Is Eddy part of the coincidence, too?"

Mr. Napper did not answer.

Mrs. Napper said, "That hateful, *hateful* old corpse of a pudding, or whatever it is, isn't going to spend another minute in my home." She set Eddy aside so that she could go to the wastebin under the sink.

"I'll take it outside," said Mr. Napper. "I'll put it into the dustbin outside." He was already easing his feet into his gardening shoes.

"The dustbin won't be cleared for another five days," said Mrs. Napper.

"Then I'll put it on the bonfire, and I'll burn it in the morning."

"Without fail?"

"Without fail."

Mr. Napper carried the Christmas pudding, wrapped in old newspaper, out into the garden, and Eddy was sent back to bed by his mother. He lay awake in bed until he heard his father's footsteps coming back from the garden and into the flat. Eddy didn't feel safe until he had heard that.

Then he could go to sleep. But even then he slept lightly, anxiously. He heard the first of the cars on the road outside. Then he heard the people upstairs letting their dog out into the garden, as usual. The dog went bouncing and barking away into the distance, as it always did. Then he heard his parents getting up. And then, because he wanted to see the bonfire's first burning—to *witness it*—Eddy got up, too.

So Eddy was with his father when Mr. Napper went to light the bonfire. Indeed, Eddy was ahead of him on the narrow path, and he was carrying the box of matches.

"Whereabouts did you put the—the thing?" asked Eddy.

"The plum pudding? I put it on the very top of the bonfire."

But it was not there. It had gone. There was a bit of crumpled old newspaper, but no pudding. Then Eddy saw why it had gone, and where. It had been dragged down from the top of the bonfire, and now it lay on the ground, on the far side of the bonfire, partly eaten, and beside it lay the dog from the ground-floor flat. Eddy knew from the way the dog lay, and the absolute stillness of its body, that the dog was dead.

Mr. Napper saw what Eddy saw.

Mr. Napper said, "Don't touch that dog, Eddy. Don't touch anything. I'm going back to tell them what's happened. You can come with me."

But Eddy stayed by the bonfire because his feet seemed to have grown to the ground, and his father went back by himself. Alone, Eddy began to shiver. He wanted to cry; he wanted to scream. He knew what he wanted to do most of all. With trembling fingers he struck a match and lit the bonfire in several places. The heap was very dry and soon caught. It blazed merrily, forming glowing caves of fire within its heart. Eddy picked up the half-eaten Christmas pudding and flung it into one of the fiery caverns, and blue flames seemed to leap to welcome it and consume it.

Then Eddy began really to cry and then felt his father's arms round him, holding him, comforting him, and heard the voice of his mother and then the lamentations of the family of the ground-floor flat, whose dog had been poisoned by what it had eaten.

And the bonfire flamed and blazed with flames like the flames of hell.

Samantha and
the Ghost ❖

*T*his was the first time that Samantha
had climbed her grandparents' apple tree, and at the top she found the
Ghost. After expressions of surprise on both sides, they settled sociably
among the branches.

"Nice to have someone to chat to, for once," said the Ghost.

"But oughtn't you to be groaning or clanking chains?" asked
Samantha.

"I'm not the groaning kind, and I haven't chains to clank," said the
Ghost. "Although I do have something else, for moonlight nights."

"What?"

But the Ghost slid away from that point; he was evasive. All that
Samantha could see of him in the sunlight was a wide shimmer of air
over one of the outermost apple branches. If she looked directly, she
could hardly be sure that he was there at all. If she focused her gaze to
one side on, say, the chimney pots of her grandparents' bungalow,
then, out of the corner of her eye, she could see him more clearly. Not
his face, not his clothing, but an impression of a wide body and limbs.

His hands seemed to be resting on his knees; was he holding something across them?

"I've never thought of an apple tree being haunted," Samantha remarked. She remembered something. "My grandfather says this tree never bears any fruit, never has any blossom even. He says it's unnatural. Well, perhaps it's because you live here."

"Possibly," said the Ghost, not interested. Samantha thought he would be interested all right if she revealed to him that her grandfather was seriously thinking of cutting down this unsatisfactory tree, to make room for raspberry canes. But she decided not to tell him that.

The Ghost said, "This tree is not my real haunt, not my original one. I was already haunting here when it was planted. You see, my bedchamber, where I first began to haunt, was here."

"Here?"

"*Here*, where the top of this apple tree now is. Our mansion was ten times the size of any of these low cottages"—he meant the bungalows, Samantha realized—"and it stood handsomely where they have now been built. My bedchamber, naturally, was on the first floor, at exactly this level, here—*here*." The ghostly shimmer moved around in the top of the apple tree and beyond it, apparently pacing out the dimensions of a long-ago bedroom.

"And the mansion has gone—completely gone?" Samantha asked wonderingly.

"I suppose I overhaunted it," the Ghost admitted. "I made life impossible for the inhabitants."

"But, if you don't groan or clank chains or anything . . ."

"I didn't say I didn't do anything." The shimmer was seated again, and the hands moved—yes, holding something. "At first I haunted thoroughly—much more thoroughly than I have ever had the heart to do since. I haunted that house to the top of my ability. Nobody could go on living in it. Nobody. Soon the house stood empty, neglected. Woodworm abounded; dry rot set in. In the end the thing had to be pulled down completely—razed to the ground—to make room for lesser dwellings."

"Leaving you stranded in midair," said Samantha.

"Exactly. Most awkward. There must be quite a few unfortunate spirits in my plight, up and down the country." (Samantha suddenly remembered a piercingly cold pool of air always to be passed through on a certain staircase of her school—an old ghost built into a new building, perhaps?)

The Ghost was going on: "I can tell you, I was glad when the apple tree grew up to bedchamber level. Something solid to put my feet up on at last."

"Why do you haunt a bedroom?" asked Samantha.

"I was a permanent invalid."

"I'm so sorry." Samantha had quite a tender heart. "Not bedridden, though?"

"Not entirely, but confined to the bedchamber." The Ghost sighed. "I died there."

A sad little silence, in which they heard from below the sound of the opening of the French windows of the bungalow.

Samantha's grandmother stepped into the garden. "Samantha!" She looked all round, but not upward, and Samantha made no sound. "Tea, Samantha!" She added enticingly, "And something special for tea!" She did not wait for an answer, partly because she was rather deaf and knew it. She went back indoors, confident of Samantha's following her.

"What's special for tea?" the Ghost asked eagerly.

"I think it'll be fried sausages and bacon today." Samantha was already beginning to clamber down the tree. She paused to sniff the air. "Yes, sausages and bacon."

The Ghost was also sniffing, in a different way. He was crying, Samantha realized. Between sobs he whimpered, "Fried sausages and bacon! How I used to adore fried sausages and bacon! Bacon all curled and crisp, and sausages bursting out of their little weskits . . ." Samantha had no idea how you comforted a ghost or lent one a handkerchief. And she hadn't a handkerchief, anyway, and she was not really sure how sympathetic she felt toward a shimmer crying its heart out over fried sausages and bacon. And her tea was waiting for her. . . .

She hardened her heart against the Ghost and jumped the last few feet to the ground. She heard, from behind her and above, the Ghost's pleading: "Come again, please, come again. . . ."

She went indoors.

After tea, Samantha spent the evening as usual with her grandparents, watching TV and playing cards. When they played, the room seemed very quiet, except for the wind moaning in the chimney and shrieking and screeching round the bungalow. "The wind's up again," said Samantha. "Like last night."

Her grandmother went on counting knitting stitches, but her grandfather began his usual complaint. He was not really a grumbler, Samantha knew, but the sound of the wind got on his nerves. He said so. "It's a ghastly sound," he said, "and it's against all reason and nature. How can the wind wail and moan and shriek *when there isn't any wind*? Time and time again, when that row starts, I've gone outside, and the air is still—still. It's unnatural."

"Unnatural . . ." Samantha repeated to herself, and remembered the barrenness of the apple tree and remembered the Ghost. . . . Suddenly it dawned on her that almost certainly she knew what object the Ghost held in his hands. She flushed with indignation.

The next morning she climbed the apple tree and tackled the Ghost. "You may not have chains to clank, but you have a violin and you play it at night. You play it shockingly, *horribly* badly, don't you?"

The Ghost actually seemed pleased. "So you heard my fiddling last night?"

"We couldn't help hearing you. You made my grandfather's evening a misery. Need you?"

"It's a very important part of the haunt," the Ghost said.

Before she could stop him, he had tucked the misty instrument into position under his misty chin and had drawn the bow across the strings. A long, thin screech tore the morning quiet. Down in the bungalow garden, Samantha's grandfather dropped his trowel with an exclamation of agony and clapped his hands to his ears.

"I'm sure you've no right to do that in the daytime," Samantha said sternly to the Ghost. "And why do it at all?"

"I played in life. I must do so after death."

"But why? I mean, why did you play in life? You play so abominably you can't ever have enjoyed it."

"No," said the Ghost. "But I didn't mind it. I'm not in the least musical, you see."

"Then why—*why?*"

"I was an invalid. I needed constant attention. Constant. But after some years I found that people were losing interest in me; they were beginning to neglect to answer my bell. That's when I got myself a fiddle and began fiddling. Oh, my! They came soon enough then!" He chuckled. "They rushed to beg me to stop. I got into the habit of fiddling instead of ringing the bell."

Samantha was looking at the Ghost with new eyes. "What was your illness?" she asked.

Again the Ghost was pleased. "Nobody knew, ever. The doctors, one and all, were baffled. Every medicine and drug and linctus and embrocation and inhalant and tablet and pill—they tried everything. In vain, in vain."

"What were the symptoms of the illness?"

"Difficult to define," said the Ghost. "Certainly lassitude."

"Lassitude?"

"Well, lethargy."

"Lethargy?"

"Don't repeat so, dear girl! Manners, manners! Yes, lassitude and lethargy. The mere notion of activity, work of any description, produced faintness, prostration, collapse. So, lassitude, lethargy—"

"Laziness," Samantha said under her breath.

"I beg your pardon?"

"Nothing. How old were you when you died?"

"A medical triumph, I suppose. I was eighty-nine. A frail eighty-nine, of course."

"How much did you weigh?"

"I really cannot see what—two hundred and thirty-eight pounds, actually."

Samantha drew a deep breath. She shouted, "You were a great, fat, lazy old pig!"

The Ghost shimmered violently with anger. "You're an ill-bred, uppish, rude little girl!"

Samantha disregarded him as though he had not spoken. "You're selfish and unkind, and you've just got to stop making my grandfather's life a misery with your horrible fiddling!"

"Who says?"

"I say!"

They glared at each other.

"Get out of my tree!" said the Ghost.

"Your tree!"

"As long as my bedchamber is at the top!"

"I wouldn't stay anywhere near your silly bedroom or your stupid violin, so there!" And Samantha slid rapidly down through the branches to the ground and ran indoors. Nor did she emerge again.

That evening the screaming and shrieking round the bungalow reached an almost unbelievable pitch. Even Samantha's deaf grandmother seemed to notice it, and her grandfather grew very pale.

Samantha flung down her hand of cards and shouted: "You'll have to move house, won't you?"

"No, dear," said her grandmother.

"No," said her grandfather. "At our age, on our pensions, we can't afford to move house all over again."

"And perhaps we'll cut down the apple tree next spring," said Grandmother, "and perhaps that'll make a difference. Wind whistles through trees."

"This isn't wind," said Grandfather.

"I'm glad you'll cut the tree down, anyway," Samantha declared with savagery.

"But only if the poor thing still doesn't have any fruit blossoms next spring," said her grandmother.

They resumed their cards, playing with stony determination. Then Samantha went to bed, where she fell asleep at last to the infuriated raging of a badly played violin.

The next day was the last of Samantha's visit. Deliberately she went nowhere near the apple tree. She and her grandmother went by bus to the shops. Gently it rained.

That night they all went to bed early. There had been only a little moaning and wailing down the chimney—nothing violent. To Samantha's surprise, even this sound had died to silence. She wondered why.

Late into the night Samantha stayed awake, wondering. Almost she was worrying. At last she got up, put on her dressing gown, tiptoed through the bungalow to the French windows and out.

There was the apple tree, sharply defined in the moonlight, and there was the Ghost. By moonlight he and his ghostly surroundings were much more visible. He seemed to be leaning out of a window at the top of the apple tree. He was looking down at her. She was taken aback. He was, indeed, grossly fat, and very old, too, with floating white hair. But he had a babyish look that, without being exactly attractive, was at least pitiful.

"Please," he whispered down to her, "please—please come up. . . ." Samantha had, of course, been warned against strangers with strange invitations, but this one was still not very much more than a shimmer up a tree. He was no danger. She climbed up to him, and they sat together, as they had done on that first—friendly—afternoon, talking. Samantha perched on a branch; the Ghost, in a long, flowered dressing gown, sat in his rocking chair by an open fire, which gave out an uncozy blaze. Round the Ghost, foggily, Samantha could see the bedchamber itself: tall windows, one of them still open; a four-poster bed; and a table whose top was crammed with medicine bottles and old-fashioned pillboxes.

"You didn't visit me today," the Ghost said reproachfully.

"I thought we'd quarreled."

"My dear girl, in life I was used to quarrels. What I never got used to—can never get used to—is being alone. Loneliness . . ." He shed tears.

With an effort Samantha said, "I'm sorry."

"You'll visit me again tomorrow?"

"I'm afraid not. I'm going home tomorrow morning."

He burst into sobs.

Samantha could contain herself no longer. "*You* cry because you have to put up with not having a visitor, but what about my poor grandfather, who has to put up with your awful, awful fiddling night after night? What about that?"

"I'd stop playing, I'd stop playing forever," wailed the Ghost, "if only I didn't have to haunt here alone, all alone. Alone for hundreds and hundreds of years . . ."

"I'm sorry," Samantha repeated. "I go home tomorrow."

The Ghost said wistfully, "Do you think anyone else will ever climb this apple tree for a chat?"

"No."

"No?"

"Because my grandfather's going to have it chopped down next spring unless it has blossom then. And it won't do that, as long as you stay here, will it?"

"I can see what you're hinting at," said the Ghost. "You think I should leave."

Samantha said nothing.

"But how could I leave this?" He waved his arm round the misty bedroom. "I'm not fond of it, but it's all I have of home."

"Do you know," said Samantha, "you're not only a ghost, but you're haunting the mere ghost of a bedroom? That's not worthy of you."

"Isn't it?"

"No. If I were you, I'd get away. I'd go."

"But where could I go?"

"Places," Samantha said crisply.

"Have a good time, you mean? But *alone*?"

"Not alone. You said there must be lots of ghosts like yourself, stranded in midair, made more or less homeless. Go and find them. Join up with them. Make up a party and go places."

"Really?" He was becoming excited. "Cut a dash?"

"That's it. Leave this dreary ghost of a room and all this dreary rubbish." Samantha reached forward and swept her hand dramatically over the surface of the medicine table, but her hand went through it all without effect, leaving it undisturbed.

"Allow me!" The Ghost heaved himself from his chair and waddled the few steps toward the table. He was carrying his violin in his left hand, the bow in his right. With vicious dabs of his bow, the Ghost sent bottles and boxes flying off the table in an irregular rain of medication. Samantha saw that not one of them reached the floor, because they melted into nothingness even as they fell.

The Ghost threw the bow after the bottles and boxes, and that vanished, too.

A few more waddling steps, and the Ghost was at the window. With surprising agility, he clambered up, stood on the sill.

Samantha gasped at the peril of it. But then, what peril to a ghost?

"Never again!" cried the Ghost, and flung the violin from him in a great arc. For a moment Samantha saw its shape in the moonlight; then it faded, vanished.

"And I'm off!" The Ghost flung himself forward through the window. He did not fall, he did not fly, and he certainly did not vanish. He went. He hurried through the air until he was lost to Samantha's sight. Pleasure seeking.

Samantha was left at the top of the apple tree. Round her, every trace of that ghostly bedroom had vanished with the going of the Ghost himself. She climbed down and went to bed.

The next day Samantha went home. She wrote to her grandparents to thank them for her visit, and in time she had a letter back. They reported that, oddly, the screeches and moanings round the house and down the chimney had stopped.

Samantha nodded to herself.

In the spring she visited the bungalow again. The apple tree was full of fruit blossom—a picture, as Samantha's grandmother said—and there was no question now of chopping it down.

That autumn the tree bore its first crop, a bumper one. Samantha went to help pick the apples. Her grandfather was not allowed to climb ladders, so Samantha climbed and picked. She climbed to the very top of the tree and perched there for a moment.

"What's it like up there?" called her grandfather, from below.

"Nice," said Samantha. "But a bit lonely."

A Prince in Another Place ❖

J was caretaker at our school at the time, but I was not—I repeat, *not*—responsible for the damage done to the school playground. People said the asphalt looked as if it had boiled up under quite extraordinary heat; how could I be held responsible for that?

I'll begin at the beginning, and the beginning was when poor young Mr. Hartley hanged himself.

Mr. Hartley was one of the three teachers at Little Pawley Church of England Primary School; the other two were Mr. Ezra Bryce, the headmaster, and Mrs. Salt, in charge of Infants. The vicar, old Mr. Widdington, came into school sometimes to help with assembly and religious instruction.

Mr. Hartley was very young, very timid, and very inexperienced, and he had just recovered from an illness, I believe. This was his first teaching job and, as it turned out, his last. Mr. Bryce did for him. Mr. Bryce bullied him and harried him and sneered at him and jeered at him and altogether made Mr. Hartley's life so appalling (as only Mr.

Bryce knew how) that the poor young man decided to leave it. He committed suicide in his lodgings on the second day of his second term at the school.

Of course, anyone in the village could make a good guess at what lay behind that death, but Bully Bryce was sly as well as a bully, and he could always cover up after himself. At different times the police and the education people came round asking questions, but he was able to explain everything. He said that poor young Hartley had been far too highly strung to be a teacher—and he was in delicate health, too. So, in spite of all the fatherly support that he, Mr. Bryce, had tried to give him, the young man had cracked under the strain. Such a pity! said Mr. Bryce. (I can imagine the tears coming to his eyes as he spoke.)

After the inquest the funeral took place far away, in Mr. Hartley's home parish. His only family was a widowed mother and an elder brother, who came home from abroad for the funeral. That seemed to be the end of Mr. Hartley.

The day after the funeral, a new teacher turned up at the school to take over Mr. Hartley's work there. This was Mr. Dickins. He was just a stopgap, of course, a supply teacher sent by the education people; he wouldn't be staying long, he said. For a teacher, he was rather a remarkable-looking man. He had a head of really flaming red hair. And he smiled to himself a good deal, and when he laughed, you saw he had excellent teeth, strong-looking and rather pointed, almost sharp. He had very small feet. I must have said something about them to him once; he was an easy chap and often had a word with me. I remember he said he had the greatest difficulty in getting shoes to fit. "The trouble is my odd-shaped feet, Mr. Jackson," he said. But at least he was nimble enough, as far as I could see.

At first, everyone wondered how the new teacher would stand up to his headmaster. For indeed, it was possible to stand up to Bully Bryce. Mrs. Salt, of Infants, had been doing it for years, by being deaf as a post whenever her headmaster addressed her, and she defended her Infants as a tigress defends her cubs. And the Juniors were able to look after themselves, chiefly by banding together in self-defense. I've heard them chanting outside the headmaster's window:

> Bully B, Bully B,
> My dad will come
> If you touch me!

As for me, I could stand up to Mr. Bryce, or I wouldn't have been school caretaker for so long. But if I'd been young and frightened, like poor Mr. Hartley—oh! There's no doubt of it: Mr. Bryce knew how to pick his victims.

But it was soon plain that Mr. Dickins wouldn't need to stand up to Mr. Bryce: he became his friend instead, his bosom friend. They were always together: in school hours, they consulted together and took their cups of tea and their dinners together. In the evening, they would go for a drink together in the pub.

For some reason, old Mr. Widdington, the vicar, became very much upset at this friendship. He was worrying about it one day when he met me in the village street. "And there's another thing, Mr. Jackson," he said. "Is this Mr. Dickins really suitable as a teacher, even for a short time? You've a grandchild in the Juniors; what does she say?"

"Well, Vicar," I said, "I think our Susie quite enjoys being taught by him."

"We must look for more than *pleasure*," he said, shaking his reverend gray locks. He was an old-fashioned chap in his ideas. "What does he *teach* them?"

"The usual things, I suppose," I said, "even if he teaches them in these unusual, funny ways they do nowadays."

"Unusual? Funny?" Mr. Widdington said quite sharply. "What do you mean?"

"Well, Susie says her class was doing number work or arithmetic or new math, or whatever they call it nowadays. Mr. Dickins wanted to show them five and five. So he lit all the fingers and thumb of one hand, like candles. And then, with his flaming fingers and thumb, he lit all the fingers and thumb of his other hand, so that he had five and five—ten candles."

After a little pause, Mr. Widdington said, "That was a conjuring trick."

"I suppose it must have been," I said.

"Anything else?" asked Mr. Widdington.

"Well, Susie says he's told them that he's really a prince in another place."

"Where?"

"He didn't say. In another place. Those were his words, according to Susie. But I said to Susie, 'He can't be one of our princes from Buckingham Palace, and there aren't many princes about elsewhere, as there used to be, even abroad.'"

"I don't like it," said Mr. Widdington. "'A prince in another place'—no, I don't like it at all. I shall get in touch with the Education Authority to check up on the man's background and qualifications." (I thought to myself, And a nice long time that'll take!) "And in the meantime," said Mr. Widdington, "I shall make a point of having a private word with Mr. Bryce about his Mr. Dickins."

"You'll be lucky, Vicar," I said. "You'll find it hard to get Bryce without Dickins; it's like a man and his shadow, nowadays."

"I'll get Bryce to come into the church for a chat," said the vicar. The church and the churchyard are right next to the school, with only a wall between them and a door in the wall.

I don't know why the vicar thought he could get Mr. Bryce into the church without Mr. Dickins coming, too; the plan didn't seem a particularly good one to me. But the vicar thought it was, and oddly, he was proved right.

The next day, just after school, the vicar caught Mr. Bryce and asked him to come into the church to look at some arrangements there for the next Children's Harvest Festival. Mr. Bryce could be quite obliging, if it suited him, and he agreed to go at once. "Coming, Nick?"

he said over his shoulder to Mr. Dickins. Mr. Dickins hesitated for a moment, then followed them through the door into the churchyard.

I pretended to be clearing rubbish in the playground, so that I could watch the three of them, over the wall.

They were going through the churchyard by a path so narrow that you could only walk single file. Mr. Widdington led the way, and Mr. Dickins came last, and Mr. Bryce was in the middle, between the two of them. They rounded the corner of the church and so came to the main south door. Mr. Widdington was just leading the way into the church, and Mr. Bryce following, when I heard Mr. Dickins give a cry of pain, and they turned back to him. I couldn't hear what was said, but it was plain from the tones of voice and the gestures that Mr. Dickins had twisted his ankle or hurt it in some way. He wanted to rest it, while the other two went into the church. So they went in, and he stayed outside, sitting on one tombstone with his foot up on another.

I was watching Mr. Dickins, but I didn't realize that he was also watching me. He never missed much. Now he waved to me in a very cheery way from his tombstone. I had the feeling that if I'd been near enough, I should have seen him wink.

Mr. Widdington and Mr. Bryce were a long time talking in the church, but I didn't think the talk went the way that Mr. Widdington had hoped. When they came out of the church, they didn't come out together. Mr. Bryce burst out first and rushed up to Mr. Dickins as if he'd been longing to get back to him. He seized him by the hand and hauled him to his feet, paying no attention to the hurt done to Mr. Dickins's ankle, and really it didn't seem as if there could ever have been much wrong with it, anyway. They went striding off together, the two of them, arm in arm. And a little later the vicar came shuffling out of the church, by himself. He looked his age then, old, and dejected. Somehow defeated. Yes, as if he'd failed.

And now Mr. Bryce and Mr. Dickins seemed closer than ever. They took to staying on at the school, after the children and Mrs. Salt had gone home, and Mr. Dickins would play his fiddle. He may have played well, but his tunes were strange, and I didn't like to hear them.

And now I noticed that Susie and her friends had a new little ditty for playtime. They'd dance in a ring and chant:

> Bully B, Bully B,
> Where are you going,
> And what do you see?

It wasn't just a few children, either. That nonsense chant became a kind of craze. All the children were singing the same song in playtime, dancing round in rings of five or six or seven. The playground was giddy with the whirling and singing. Once I saw Mr. Bryce at his window staring out on it all and, at his elbow, just behind him, Mr. Dickins smiling quietly to himself, as usual.

All this was in the summer term. The weather was fine, dry, but there was no sultriness, no hint of storms building up. Yet, perhaps there was a strange feeling in the air, or was I just imagining it? Certainly old Mr. Widdington was fussing more than usual and more anxiously. He dropped into the school almost every day now, on one excuse or another. The dancing and singing of the children in the playground worried him. Why did they do it? he asked. He got me to ask Susie that: where the words and the dancing came from, who started it, or who had taught them all. But Susie didn't know. She said they had all just begun doing it; that was all.

I told Mr. Widdington what Susie had said, and he looked even more upset. I said, "Well, have you had an answer to that letter you wrote to the education people, about Mr. Dickins?"

"Not yet. But I've also written to—to someone else."

I didn't want to seem inquisitive. As it turned out, I learned soon enough who "someone else" was.

Playtime was just over that day. The rings of dancing, singing children had broken up; they were all going back to their classrooms. I had been by the school gate, watching them. I heard footsteps coming up behind me, but I paid no attention. Then a voice: "Excuse me. Is Mr. Widdington about?"

And the voice was the voice of poor young Mr. Hartley, who killed himself. . . .

I turned round because I was too frightened not to, if you see what I mean, and there was Mr. Hartley looking at me! For two awful seconds, that's what I thought, and then I realized that this man was very like our Mr. Hartley, but older, more solid-looking, and sunburned from foreign lands. He could see what I had been thinking. He said, "I am the brother of Timothy Hartley, who used to teach here. And you must be Mr. Jackson." We shook hands. He explained that the vicar had asked him to meet him here; he was a little early. Then he said, "Mr. Widdington has asked me to see Mr. Bryce, to talk to him."

I said, "If it's for the sake of your poor brother, Mr. Hartley, it'll be a waste of your breath. It will, really."

"It's not for his sake; it's for Mr. Bryce's own sake."

I could only stare at him. He went on: "Mr. Jackson, I would never, never have consented to come here to see that man, except that your Mr. Widdington asked me to—implored me to. He said the matter was very urgent, indeed." I still stared at Mr. Hartley, and now he looked aside in an embarrassed way and said, "Mr. Widdington mentioned Mr. Bryce's immortal soul."

From the school the fiddle playing of Mr. Dickins had started up; Mr. Dickins had never played his tunes in school hours before.

The elder Mr. Hartley heard the fiddling. He said, "I'm not waiting for Mr. Widdington after all. I'm going to Mr. Bryce now. Now."

"Through that door then," I said, and pointed across the playground.

When he had gone into the school, everything was very quiet and still, except for the fiddling. That went on for a while. Then the door from the churchyard into the playground clicked, and I looked that way and saw the vicar coming through. He hesitated on the edge of the playground, looking round him. I was just going over to him when things began to happen.

The school door through which Mr. Hartley had gone opened again, and he came out. He had not looked to me a man to be easily scared, but now his face was chalky white, his eyes were staring, and he walked altogether like a sleepwalker in a nightmare. He came across the deserted playground toward the gate, and I came forward a little to meet him.

Behind him, in the doorway, appeared Mr. Bryce. His face was dark, and he was shouting foul abuse after Mr. Hartley—abuse not only of him but of the poor young man who had hanged himself. And behind Mr. Bryce smiled the face of Mr. Dickins.

Mr. Bryce stood in the doorway, nearly filling it, for he was a big man. I've not yet told you what he looked like. Bullies can be fat or thin or medium-sized; Bully Bryce was the heavy, bull-like kind. He filled his clothes almost to bursting, and his head seemed to have burst up out of his collar, and his eyes seemed to be bursting from his head. They were bloodshot eyes, as well as bulging, and they glared now, and when he bellowed his abuse across the playground, the spittle flew from his mouth at every word.

Mr. Hartley had reached me, and I was partly supporting him, while he tried to recover himself. So we stood on the edge of the playground, and I was facing it. Mr. Hartley had his back to it at first, but pretty soon he turned his head to see what was fixing my attention. And the vicar, too, also on the edge of the playground, was staring, and Mrs. Salt, of the Infants, now stood in her doorway to the playground, gazing distractedly and crying, "Children! Children! Stop, stop!"

For all the children of the school were coming out of it, onto the playground. The Infants were climbing out of the low windows of their classroom, one after another, and holding hands as they danced away across the playground, while Mrs. Salt called to them in vain, "Whatever are you doing? Stop, stop!" The Juniors, too, had come streaming out of the building and, hand in hand, ran and danced and joined up with the Infants in one long skein of children that moved to and fro in ceaseless meander over the playground.

Now Mr. Bryce was advancing into the playground, always with Mr. Dickins at his elbow. At first I thought he was coming to put a stop to what was going on, but this was not so. He had stopped storming and shouting; he was quite silent. He walked slowly, perhaps reluctantly, step after step, into the middle of the playground, and the skein of dancing children kept clear of him as he moved. I saw that Mr. Dickins had tucked his fiddle under one arm and now had the other hooked into Mr. Bryce's. They were arm in arm, as so often, but this time they were not walking equally. Mr. Dickins was urging Mr. Bryce forward, positively pulling him along. They reached the middle of the playground and went no further. And the children were running mazily about them, chanting now:

> Bully B, Bully B,
> Where are you going,
> And what do you see?

The long line of children wavered about the playground until the two ends of it came together and joined. Suddenly there was one irregularly shaped ring of children, with Mr. Bryce and Mr. Dickins in the middle of it.

The children still ran, and as they ran, they pulled outward—outward—to form a proper circle round the two men. When they had achieved this, more or less, they stopped running and changed to dancing on the spot, still chanting as they danced:

> Bully B, Bully B,
> Where are you going,
> And what do you see?

And the air in the playground seemed to tighten, so that there was hardly room to breathe, and we, the witnesses—the vicar, Mr. Hartley, Mrs. Salt, and myself—stood stock-still and staring—

> Bully B, Bully B,
> Where are you going,
> And what—

—and there was a sound such as I hope never to hear again on earth—a deafening *crack!*—and at the same time an upward burst of flaming light against which—instantaneously—my eyes closed. But against the inside of my eyelids was printed the image of Mr. Dickins and Mr. Bryce, entwined, and they seemed to be all on fire, inside my eyelids, and I heard a howl that was more than any human being could make, and yet it was human, and I knew that it had been made by Mr. Bryce.

I put my hands up to my shut eyes, as though I had been blinded, and I fell to my knees.

When I opened my eyes again, the playground was in confusion. The children were no longer holding hands, or dancing, or chanting; they ran aimlessly, or stood, or sat, some sobbing or weeping, others laughing hysterically. Mrs. Salt was trying to control them and get them back to their classrooms. The vicar was leaning against the wall of the churchyard, as though he had been flattened there by the blast of an explosion. Mr. Hartley was lying on the ground beside me, half out of his senses for the time being.

The middle of the playground was empty: no Mr. Bryce, no Mr. Dickins. Where they had stood, there was a huge bubbled scar in the asphalt, like two lips that had opened widely once—perhaps to swallow some tasty morsel—and then closed again in a dreadful sneer.

That's really all. Mr. Bryce and Mr. Dickins were never seen again. Nobody knew where they'd gone. Mrs. Salt said they couldn't just have vanished, as we seemed to think; that was against common sense and reason. She was sure they'd slipped away, under our very noses and escaped to an enemy power, for whom they had been spying in this country.

"An enemy power . . ." Mr. Widdington said thoughtfully.

We had trouble with the education people. They had never answered Mr. Widdington's letter because they hadn't been able to trace Mr. Dickins in their records. Certainly, they had never sent us a Mr. Dickins as a supply teacher. They denounced Mr. Dickins as an impostor.

When they heard of the mysterious disappearance of two of our staff—well, one, because, of course, they wouldn't count Mr. Dickins—they went so far as to send an official in person to make inquiries. He found out no more than I've already told you, but just before he was leaving, he noticed the damage in the playground. He said to me, "What the hell's been going on here?"

I didn't answer him. I didn't think that kind of language was suitable for an education person, in a primary school playground; I wouldn't have liked Susie to hear him.

The Road It Went By ❖

He looked down into a deep, dark, oblong hole, my mother and I. Aunt Cass, who stood beside us, said, "He wanted to be buried in the weedy part of the cemetery. That's what he said. 'The weedy part . . . ' "

"It's weedy all right, Aunt Cass," said my mother.

The gravedigger's spade had shorn through a tangle of greenery into the earth and then through the tangle of roots there. All kinds of roots, from the hairlike roots of grass to the rank, yellow roots that must be nettle, but, among all the others and more than any other, wriggled pale roots that looked like unpicked white knitting wool. I recognized ground elder. Then the spade had dug deeper still until it reached the barrenness and darkness of the subsoil of my uncle Percy's grave.

"Yes," said Aunt Cass, and sighed and turned away, and we followed. The funeral was not until the next day; my mother could not attend, and I would not. I had not even wanted to come down with her to see Aunt Cass. But now, suddenly, I felt sorry about Uncle Percy; I had known him so well when I was a small boy, and I remembered the times when he had been kind to me, and gentle.

I had often been sent to stay with my aunt and uncle; they were really my great-aunt and great-uncle, and elderly. They had never had children of their own, and in their quiet, slow way, they welcomed me. For myself, I was happy to go to them and to be in a place that was still nearly the country, with big gardens round about where my uncle Percy worked in his retirement.

Uncle Percy now did jobbing gardening, and he often took me with him on his jobs.

Mainly, my uncle Percy dug, and of course, he weeded as he dug. By far the worst weed in the gardens we visited was ground elder. (Dog elder, my uncle called it.) And the worst place for ground elder was Mrs. Hartington's herbaceous border.

Mrs. Hartington was rather grand. On no account was her jobbing gardener to come up the front drive to reach the garden, which lay at the back of the house. Instead, he must come by the lane that ran along the bottom of the garden and use the door in the fence there. Mrs. Hartington always unlocked the door just before my uncle's arrival.

So Uncle Percy and I entered Mrs. Hartington's garden by the door in the fence at the bottom, went past the rubbish heap and the vegetable patch, and so arrived at the lawn and that overgrown border.

Mrs. Hartington popped out of the house at once to give her orders to her jobbing gardener: "Percy, I want you to get on with the digging of the border."

"Yes, Mrs. Hartington, ma'am."

"And you're always forgetting to light that bonfire. Don't forget again."

"No, Mrs. Hartington, ma'am."

She went back indoors.

My uncle Percy began to dig and weed, while I unpacked from my Mickey Mouse suitcase my spacemen and spacewomen and space vehicles and various rubbery monsters. Then I started to build their headquarters and habitations out of stones and twigs and mud. Sometimes I had tried to tell my uncle of the amazing exploits being carried out so close to his feet. Mostly he did not hear me—he was deaf—but if his hearing aid was working, he still paid little attention to what he dismissed mildly as my "rambling on." The truth is, my uncle had no fancy, no imagination. He was incapable of believing in anything he could not see or hear or touch or smell or of inventing such a thing. I have always been quite convinced of that.

Besides, later, I had my own experience.

My uncle dug steadily on, weeding as he dug. This was all that was ever expected of him; this was the limit of his gardening skill. He was not clever with plants; really, he was not clever at all, or enterprising. At home, they had only a small back garden that had been entirely paved over for many years. Aunt Cass grew tomatoes in great pots, but Uncle Percy went there only in summer to take his Sunday nap in a deck chair. He was not exactly a lazy man, but he was slow.

He was also, as I have said, gentle in his speech and in all his ways.

This afternoon I was prattling to him as he dug. Suddenly he said, "Hush!" and ceased work to bend almost tenderly over the mess of earth and root and stems that he was handling. (This was not the first time he had behaved oddly in Mrs. Hartington's garden. Before now I had wondered what my uncle was hearing or hoped to hear, when he screwed his hearing aid so firmly into his ear as he weeded. Young as I was, I had decided that he was not really preparing to listen to me or to the birds or perhaps to any ordinary thing in the garden.)

And this was the moment when Mrs. Hartington chose to come out onto her garden doorstep with a mug of tea to be fetched by her jobbing gardener. (Nothing for me, ever.)

"Percy!" she called.

He was listening to something else; he did not move his head; he did not move at all.

"Percy!" she called again, more sharply.

He ignored her.

She set off across the lawn with an angry briskness, walked straight through my mud and twig structures, smashing them, and so reached my uncle. "Percy!" she said very loudly. "Your tea!"

Without lifting his head, my uncle said, "Shut up!"

Mrs. Hartington was so startled that she slopped the hot tea from the mug onto the earth of the border. This time he rounded on her and shouted, "You silly old hen! You'll hurt it!"

My uncle never spoke like that to anyone—let alone to Mrs. Hartington. Never.

Mrs. Hartington stared at him, dumbstruck with amazement. Only slowly did the words come to her that she judged right.

Meanwhile, "*It?*" I said, and peered at the earth of the border where the tea had splashed. There was nothing to be seen but ground elder, rooted or uprooted.

Mrs. Hartington had begun speaking. "*Please,*" she said to my uncle—and she sounded the word like a plunging dagger—"*please,* remember my instructions that a fire should be lit on the rubbish heap at least once a week. You have persistently disobeyed my order in this respect."

My uncle Percy did not answer her; he had turned back to his work, and his hearing aid now dangled free. It seemed insolently to sneer at her.

Mrs. Hartington raised her voice. "*Please,* obey my orders. Otherwise the *few* weeds that you have *managed* to dig out of my border will reinvade my garden."

She wheeled round and went back to the house, still carrying the mug, and my uncle resumed his digging and weeding.

But—*it?*

I stared at the earth and then peeped at my uncle, a little fearfully. I did not question him, partly because his hearing aid was still disconnected. In the end I went back to my play. I had to repair the destruction caused by recent interplanetary attack.

At the end of that afternoon, I walked beside my uncle as he barrowed his weed load down to Mrs. Hartington's rubbish heap. Then I realized the truth of her complaint; he had not lit a fire there for a long time.

And he was not going to do so now.

He began to empty his fresh barrow load onto the heap. Instead of tipping it all out in one go, he was moving it piecemeal, handful by slow handful. There was something unusual—lingeringly attentive, even loving—in the way he spread his fingers among the roots of the ground elder.

I dared to ask him now, "What is it, Uncle Percy?"

He told me, and I'm sure he told me only because I was just a child; I didn't count. He said, "There's the root of that dog elder, and then there's another thing, like another root, but it's not a root. That other thing winds and twines round the dog elder root, like ivy climbing a tree. It uses dog elder; dog elder root is the road it goes by. It never comes above the earth. I don't know where it comes from, or where it's going, or why, at all. But it sings. No, it doesn't sing, and it doesn't speak. Something else, it does. . . . I can feel it sometimes. . . ." He moved his fingers gently among the roots. "And sometimes I think I can hear it on my whajamacallit. . . ."

And he screwed his hearing aid into his ear and bent his head over his recent weedings.

"Can I listen on your hearing aid, Uncle?"

"No."

"What's it like? Is it music then?"

"No. Not that, either, but it sounds all the time in the earth. . . ."

After a while he gave a sharp sigh that made me realize that he had been holding his breath. Then he put his handful onto the rubbish heap, and after that, he did tip all the rest of the barrow load onto the rubbish heap. Then he gathered up some good soil from the ground and spread it protectively over the newly dug roots.

Then we were ready to go home.

The next day a brief note arrived from Mrs. Hartington for my uncle Percy. Mrs. Hartington would not be requiring my uncle's services again in her garden. She would be making other, more satisfactory arrangements. His pay to date was enclosed in the envelope.

My aunt Cass was indignant on my uncle's account, but he did not say much. He started at once on an extraordinary task. He began taking

up all the paving stones in their back garden. It was a heavy job for an
old man, but he worked steadily at it. Aunt Cass fluttered round him,
begging him for reasons and explanations. He gave none.

By the afternoon of the next day, all the paving stones were stacked
in one corner of the little garden, exposing an area of bare, sour-looking
earth.

"That won't grow anything but weeds," said my aunt Cass.

"Yes," said Uncle Percy.

That evening Uncle Percy went very early to bed. Aunt Cass told
me to play quietly, because my uncle was resting. She thought he was
resting after his efforts in the back garden; she did not realize that he
was resting before further effort.

What happened next was a shock to everyone.

In the very early hours of the morning, the police station received
an urgent call from Mrs. Hartington. She had heard footsteps on the
gravel of her front drive and by the side of the house, and she had
glimpsed a figure carrying what she thought was a sack.

The police came at once and, searching Mrs. Hartington's garden,
found . . . my uncle Percy! He would give no explanation of his presence there at that hour. His sack was empty, and there was no clue as
to what, if anything, he had intended to put into it. There was no sign
of his being about to break into Mrs. Hartington's house, in spite of
Mrs. Hartington's conviction that that had been "what he was up to."

In the end, in the face of my uncle's gloomy, unbroken silence, the
police decided that the old fellow was a bit off his head. Perhaps the
shock of Mrs. Hartington's abrupt dismissal had been too much for
him. Probably he had had no criminal intention that night, perhaps no
clear intention at all. He had always been a bit of an odd old fellow,
but at least, in all his life, he had never been anything but law-abiding.
Everyone agreed on that. No one in the village had a bad word for Old
Perce—except, of course, Mrs. Hartington.

The police managed in the end to persuade Mrs. Hartington to let
the matter drop. At the same time, they suggested to Aunt Cass, who
was terribly upset, of course, that she have a chat with the doctor about

Uncle Percy. They also suggested that in future, she should keep a very sharp watch on him between sunset and sunrise. This she began to do.

In the daytime my uncle Percy still went jobbing gardening, although, of course, never at Mrs. Hartington's. At first people looked at him a little wonderingly; Mrs. Hartington had put her story about, no doubt. But nobody liked Mrs. Hartington much or believed her.

I still went gardening with my uncle, but things were different now. In his slow, silent way, Uncle Percy was unhappy. He dug ground elder from other flower beds and vegetable plots, but—no, it was not the same. One afternoon, as he finished work, he said to me, "You're off home tomorrow, boy. Did you know that?"

"Yes, Uncle."

"Before that, I've something I want you to do."

"What, Uncle?"

"I'll show you," he said.

He took me a roundabout way homeward, going by the lane at the bottom of Mrs. Hartington's garden. ("She's out," he said; I don't know how he knew that.) He tried the door in the fence, but of course, it was locked. The fence was too high for anyone to climb easily, and barbed wire lay along the top. The slats of the fence were set too close for anyone to squeeze through, even a child. But as we dawdled along the fence, my uncle pulled gently at each slat. All resisted.

Sometimes there was a passerby in the lane. Whenever anyone appeared, my uncle Percy was just taking a stroll with his great-nephew. At the end of Mrs. Hartington's fence, my uncle turned me round, and we walked slowly back along it. Again he tested the slats, pulling a little more strongly this time. And this time he found one that was loose—only very slightly loose—at the bottom. He pulled and shook until the slat was a great deal looser. He brought out a pair of pliers and managed to extract a fastening nail from the bottom of the slat, and another. Now the slat hung only from the top. It looked perfectly in position, like all the other slats, but in fact, it could be swung to one side or the other to make a narrow gap in the fencing, a narrow entrance into Mrs. Hartington's garden.

"You're small enough," said my uncle. "You could get through there."

"But—but—"

"After dark—it would have to be after dark." I was appalled.

"You'll easily get through there and get it for me," he said.

"It?" But I knew what he meant. I began to cry.

He caught me by the shoulders so roughly that it hurt, and he swung me round to face him, and he bent right down to my level. He stared at me with his blue, blue eyes. He stared and stared. I was too frightened to go on crying. He said, "I must have it."

"It?"

"I must have it, and you must get it for me. Tonight." He was whispering, but he might as well have been shouting, yelling, screaming, shrieking. I cowered from the sound of his voice. I had no will of my own against his. Only a child as young as I could get through that narrow gap in the fence, yet I knew I was far too young to be made to undertake such a venture, at night, alone. Yet I should have to do it.

Late that night, on the excuse to my aunt that he was going to the toilet, Uncle Percy came to my room and roused me. My aunt became aware that more was going on than she knew of.

"What is it?" she called sleepily from their bedroom.

"Little chap's wakeful," my uncle called back. He helped me quickly to dress. Then I took my Mickey Mouse suitcase, empty, as I had been told. As I crept down the stairs, I heard my uncle getting back into bed beside my aunt.

It wasn't far to the lane at the bottom of Mrs. Hartington's garden, and I knew the way, and there was some starlight. But I was terribly frightened, even if I were frightened of nothing. I was a very little boy then, remember. I longed for my mother to be there, or at least for someone safe to meet me and ask, "What's a little fellow like you doing out all alone in the middle of the night?" But the village street was deserted at such a time.

I reached the lane, the fence, the slat that moved. I swung the slat aside, as I had been shown how, and squeezed myself and my little suitcase through into Mrs. Hartington's garden.

The garden was even more frightening than the street and the lane, because of the dark, motionless shapes of the bushes and tall plants— or because those shapes looked as if at any second they might cease to be motionless. And here, rearing up almost to my own height, was the rubbish heap. I put my suitcase down.

Now I had to follow my uncle's instructions very carefully. I had to face the side of the heap where he had discharged the last load of weeds. I had to thrust my hand into the heap and count slowly to twenty. If, during that time, I did not feel anything particular, I was to try again in another place. ("What kind of *particular* feeling, Uncle?" "You'll know, soon enough.")

The first place I tried: nothing. I moved my hand and tried again, noticing how cold my hand was and how it trembled, even inside the earthy heap. Nothing, again. I'll try three times and then stop, I thought. Three times, and then I go back.

How dark it was in the garden, how still, how quiet—

By now I was shuddering all over with cold and with fear. I thrust my hand in for the third time, in a third place, and counted up to twenty, and more.

Nothing. So now I could go home.

But I was afraid to go back without what my uncle wanted so much. I remembered the violence of his hands on my shoulders; I remembered the glare of his blue eyes.

I thrust my hand into the heap again and counted, and before I reached twenty, I began to feel it.

It . . .

I did not know whether I felt by touch or whether in some way I heard whatever was there, among the roots of the ground elder, clasping, twining, winding, climbing round the roots of the ground elder. Whatever it was, awareness of it flowed into me, for as long as I held my hand there. Was it pain or pleasure that I felt? Whatever it was, I ceased to be frightened, or anxious, or even conscious of what had to be done next. I stood there like a boy enchanted into a statue.

Then some little creature—a field mouse, I think it must have been—ran over my left foot and roused me.

I closed my hand on what it already touched inside the rubbish heap, and I withdrew a handful of roots and earth. I put the handful into my Mickey Mouse case. Then I took another handful and another and another, until the case was full. Then I shut the case and fastened it and made my way with it back through the fence, along the lane and the village street and in through the front door of my great-uncle's house, which I had left unlatched.

I had been told by my uncle to carry the case through to the garden at the back and leave it there. By the starlight I could just see the raw earth of the garden and, in the middle of it, an oblong blackness—a hole that was just about the size of my Mickey Mouse suitcase. My uncle had told me nothing, but I knew at once that this was a hole he had dug to receive the roots that were to grow and spread and flourish and fill this little garden.

I left my case by the hole and went indoors again and upstairs to bed. I knew that Aunt Cass was asleep, by the particular pitch of her snore. I could not hear Uncle Percy's snore. Of course, he could have been sound asleep without snoring, but I did not think so.

I got into bed and put my head under the bedclothes. I gave a gasp, and then I began to cry. I cried and cried. I cried for the fearfulness of that night's lonely, dark journey, and I cried because I had held something in my hand and then had had to let it go. I cried myself to sleep.

The next morning—the morning of my departure—I found my Mickey Mouse suitcase waiting for me downstairs, emptied and clean. I put my space people and my monsters back into it.

There was no oblong hole now to be seen in the middle of the back garden.

That day I went home, and I never came back by myself again. I refused absolutely to go another visit alone to my uncle Percy and aunt

Cass, and I refused to explain why I would not go. My mother guessed, I think, that something had frightened me badly, but she could never find out what it was.

So my mother went down by herself, very occasionally, just for the day. She reported that Uncle Percy was becoming odd in his behavior—odd and oddly happy. He was always digging in the little back garden, she said—digging *with his bare hands*. But never weeding. The garden had become a paradise for weeds, especially ground elder. Ground elder was king there.

When Uncle Percy died at last, my mother persuaded me to go with her to see Aunt Cass. In the end I was glad I did go. But I've told you all that.

And after it was all over, Mrs. Hartington spread a cruel tale that Aunt Cass had cared so little for her husband that she never planted or even weeded his grave. She may not have weeded it, but I'm sure that she must have planted it—with roots from their own back garden. Uncle Percy would have made her promise to do that. I'm certain of it.

Auntie ❖

*U*p to the day she died, Auntie could thread the finest needle at one go. She did so on that last rainy day of her life. And by the end of her life her long sight had grown longer than anyone could possibly have expected.

Auntie's exceptional eyesight had been no particular help to her in her job: she was a file clerk in a block of offices, forever sorting other people's dull letters and dull memoranda. Boring, but Auntie was not ambitious, nor was she ever discontented.

Auntie's real interest—all her care—was for her family. She never married, but by the time of her retirement from work, she was a great-aunt—although she was never called that—and she liked being one. She baby-sat and took children to school and helped with family expeditions. She knitted and crotcheted and sewed; above all, she sewed. She mended and patched and made clothes. She sewed by hand when necessary; otherwise she whirred the handle of an ancient sewing machine that had been a wedding present to her mother long before.

Unfortunately, she was not particularly good at making clothes. Little Billy, her youngest great-nephew, was her last victim. "Do I *have* to wear this blazer thing?" he whispered to his mother, Auntie's niece. (He whispered because—even in his bitterness—he did not want Auntie to overhear.) "Honestly, Mum, no one at school ever wears anything looking like this."

"Hush!" said his mother. Then: "Auntie's very kind to take all that trouble and to save us money, too. You should be grateful."

"I'm not!" said little Billy, and he determined, when he was old enough, he wouldn't be at Auntie's mercy anymore. Meanwhile Auntie, who doted on Billy as the last child of his generation, was perplexed by the feeling that something she had done was not quite right.

Auntie was not a thinker, but she had common sense and—more and more—foresight. She knew, for instance, that nobody can live forever. One day she said, "I wonder when I shall die? And how? Heart, probably. My old dad, your granddad, died of that."

She was talking to the niece, Billy's mother, with whom Auntie now lived. The niece said, "Oh, Auntie, don't *talk* so!"

Auntie said, "My eyesight's as good as ever—well, better, really— but my hands aren't so much use." She looked at her hands, knobbling with rheumatism. "I can't use 'em as I once did."

"Never *mind*!" said the niece.

"And the children are growing up. Even Billy." Auntie sighed. "Growing too old for me."

"The children *love* their auntie!" said the niece angrily. This was true, in its way, but that did not prevent great-nephews and great-nieces from becoming irritated when Auntie babied them and fussed over their clothing or over whatever they happened to be doing.

Auntie did not continue the argument with her niece. She was no good at discussion or argument, anyway. That wasn't her strong point.

Her eyesight was her strong point and yet also her worry. In old age she sat for long periods by her bedroom window, looking out over rooftops to distant church spires and tower blocks. "I don't like seeing so far," she said once. "What's the use to me? Or to anyone else?"

"You're lucky," said her nephew-in-law, Billy's father. "Some people would give their eyes to—well, they'd give a lot to have your eyesight at your age."

"It's—it's *wrong*," said Auntie, trying to explain something.

"If it happens that way, then it's natural," said her nephew.

"Natural!" said Auntie, and she took to sitting at her bedroom window with her eyes closed.

One day: "Asleep?" her niece asked softly.

"No." Auntie's eyes opened at once. "Just resting my eyes. Trying to get them not to go on with all this looking and looking, seeing and seeing . . ." Here Auntie paused, again attempting to sort out some ideas. But the ideas and what lay behind them could not be as easily sorted and filed into place as those documents in the office where she had worked years ago.

"Ah," said the niece, preparing to leave it at that.

But Auntie had something more to say. "When I'm in bed and asleep, I dream, and I know dreams are rubbish, so I needn't pay any attention to them. But when I sit here, wide-awake, with my eyes open or even with my eyes closed, then—"

The niece waited.

Auntie said carefully, "Then I think, and thinking must be like seeing. I see things."

"What things?"

"Things a long way off."

"That's because you're longsighted, Auntie."

"I wouldn't mind that. But the things a long way off are coming nearer."

"Whatever do you mean?"

"How should I know what I mean? I'm just telling you what *happens*. I see things far away, and they're coming close. I don't understand it. I don't like it."

"Perhaps you're just having daydreams, Auntie."

"You mean, it's all rubbish?"

"Well, is it?"

Auntie moved restlessly in her chair. She hated to be made to think in this way, but there were some things you had to think of with your mind, when you couldn't straightforwardly see them with your eyes and then straightforwardly grasp them with your hands, to deal with them then and there.

There were these other things.

"No," said Auntie crossly. "They're not rubbish. All the same, I don't want to think about them. I don't want to talk about them."

So there was no more talk about the far things that were coming nearer, but as for thinking—well, Auntie couldn't help doing that, in her way. Her life was uneventful, so that what she thought about naturally was what she saw with her eyes or in her mind's eye.

One day the married niece asked if she could use Auntie's old sewing machine to run up some curtains; her own machine had broken down.

"So has mine," said Auntie. "The needle's broken."

"You have several spare needles, Auntie," said the niece. "I think I could put one in."

The niece went downstairs to where the ancient sewing machine was kept. When she had unlocked and taken off the wooden lid, she found that the needle was not broken after all. It did not need replacing. She sighed to herself and smiled to herself at Auntie's mistake, and then she set to work with Auntie's sewing machine.

She threaded up the machine with the right cotton for her curtains, arranged the material in the right position under the needle, and began to turn the handle of the machine. The stitching began, but the curtain material was very thick, and the needle penetrated it with difficulty. . . .

With more difficulty at every stitch . . .

The needle broke.

So, after all, the niece had to change the needle, to finish sewing her curtains. Later on she said to Auntie, "Your machine's all right now, but the needle broke."

"I told you so," said Auntie.

"No, Auntie. You said the needle *had* broken; you ought to have said, 'The needle will break.' " The niece laughed jollily.

"I don't want to say things like that," said Auntie. She spoke sharply, and her niece saw that she was upset for some reason.

So she said, "Never mind, Auntie. It was just a funny thing to have happened, after what you said. A coincidence. Think no more of it."

The niece thought no more of it, but Auntie did. She brooded over the strangeness of her long sight, over the seeing of faraway things that came nearer. She now kept that strangeness private to herself, secret, but sometimes something popped into a conversation before she could prevent it.

One family teatime, when Auntie had been sitting silent for some time, she said, "It's lucky there's never anyone left in those offices at night."

"Which offices?"

"Where I used to work, of course."

"Oh—" Nobody was interested, except for little Billy. He was always curious. "Why is it lucky, Auntie?"

But already Auntie regretted having spoken; one could see that. "No reason," she said. "Nothing . . . I was just thinking, that's all. . . ."

The next morning, with Auntie's early cup of tea, the niece brought news.

"You'll never guess, Auntie!"

"Those old offices are burned out."

"Why, you *have* guessed! Yes, it was last night after you'd gone to bed early. An electrical short started the fire, they think. Nobody's fault, and nobody hurt—nobody in the building."

"No," said Auntie. "Nobody at all . . ."

"But you should have seen the blaze! You were asleep, so we didn't wake you, but we took little Billy to see. My goodness, Auntie! The smoke there was!"

"Yes," said Auntie. "The smoke . . ."

"And the flames—huge flames towering up!"

"Yes." said Auntie. "The whole place quite gutted . . ."

"And all the fire engines wailing up!"

"Yes," said Auntie. "Five fire engines . . ."

Her niece stared at her. "There *were* five fire engines, but how did you know?"

Auntie was flustered, and the niece went on staring. Auntie said, "Well, a big blaze like that would *need* five fire engines, wouldn't it?"

Her niece said nothing more, but later she reported the conversation to her husband. He was not impressed. "Oh, I daresay she woke up and saw the fire through her bedroom window. With her long sight she saw the size of the fire, and—well, she realized it would need at least five fire engines. As she said, more or less."

"That's *just* possible as an explanation," said his wife, "if it weren't for one thing."

"What thing?"

"Auntie's bedroom window doesn't look in that direction at all. Her old office block is on the other side of the house."

"Oh!" said Auntie's nephew-in-law.

In the time that followed, Auntie was very careful indeed not to talk about her sight, long sight, or foresight. Even so, her niece sometimes watched her intently and oddly, as she sat by her bedroom window. And once her nephew-in-law sought her out to ask whether she would like to discuss with him the forthcoming Derby and which horse was likely to win the race. Auntie said she had never been interested in horse racing and disapproved of it because of the betting. So that was that.

One afternoon in early spring—not cold, but dreary and very overcast—Auntie was restless. She went downstairs to her sewing machine and fiddled with it. She did a little hand sewing on a pair of Billy's trousers, where a seam had come undone. (That was the last time that she threaded a needle.)

Then she went upstairs and came down again in her coat and hat.

"You're not thinking of going out, Auntie?" cried her niece. "Today of all days? It's just beginning to rain!"

"A breath of fresh air, all the same," said Auntie.

"It's not suitable for you, Auntie. So slippery underfoot on the pavements."

Auntie said, "I thought I'd go and meet Billy off the school bus."

"Oh, Auntie! Billy's too old to need meeting off the bus nowadays. He doesn't need it, and he wouldn't like it. He'd hate it."

Auntie sighed, hesitated, then slowly climbed up the stairs to her bedroom again.

Five minutes later she was coming downstairs again, almost hurriedly, still hatted and coated. She made for the stand where her umbrella was kept.

"Auntie!" protested the niece.

Auntie patted the handbag she was carrying. "An important letter I've written—and must get into the post."

Her niece gaped at her. Auntie never wrote important letters; she never wrote letters at all.

"About my pension," Auntie explained. "Private," she added, as she saw that her niece was about to speak.

Her niece did speak, however. She had quite a lot to say. "Auntie, your letter *can't* be all that urgent. And if it is, Billy will be home soon, and he'll pop to the letter box for you. It's really ridiculous— *ridiculous*—of you to think of going out in this wet, gray, slippery, miserable weather!"

Suddenly Auntie was different. She was resolved, stern in some strange determination. "*I must go*," she said, in such a way that her niece shrank back and let her pass.

So Auntie, her umbrella in one hand and her handbag in the other, set out.

The weather had worsened during the short delay. She had to put up her umbrella at once against the rain. She hurried along toward the letter box—hurried, but with care, because the pavement and road surfaces were slippery, just as her niece had said.

The letter box lay a very little way beyond the bus stop where Billy's school bus would arrive. There was a constant to-and-fro of traffic, but no bus was in sight. Instead of going on to the letter box, Auntie hesitated a moment, then took shelter from the rain in the doorway of a gent's outfitter's, just by the bus stop. From inside the shop, an assistant, as he said later, observed the old lady taking shelter and observed all that happened afterward.

Auntie let down her umbrella, furled it properly, and held it in her right hand, her handbag in her left.

The shop assistant, staring idly through his shop window, saw the school bus approaching its stop, through almost blinding rain.

The old lady remained in the doorway.

The school bus stopped. The children began to get off. The traffic swirled by on the splashing road.

The old lady remained in the doorway.

The shop assistant's attention was suddenly caught by something happening out on the road, in the passing traffic. A car had gone out of control on the slippery road. It was swerving violently; it narrowly missed another car and began skidding across the road, across the back of the school bus. Nearly all the children were away from the bus by now—except for one, slower than the rest. In a moment of horror, the shop assistant saw him, unforgettably: a little boy, wearing a badly made blazer, who was going to be run over and killed.

The assistant gave a cry and ran to the door, although he knew he would be too late.

But someone else was ahead of him, from that same doorway. The old lady darted—no, flung herself, *flew*—forward toward the child.

There were two—perhaps three?—seconds for action before the car would hit the child. The old lady wouldn't reach him in that time, but the assistant saw her swing her right arm forward, the hand clutching a furled umbrella by its ferrule. The crook of the umbrella hooked inside the front of the little boy's blazer and hooked him like a fish from water out of the path of the skidding car. The old lady fell over backward on the pavement with the child on top of her, and the car skidded past them, crashed into the bus stop itself, and stopped. The driver sat stupefied inside, white-faced, shocked, but otherwise uninjured.

Nobody was injured, except Auntie. She died in the ambulance, on her way to the hospital. Heart, the doctors said. No wonder, at her age, and in such extraordinary circumstances.

Much later, after the funeral, Billy's mother looked for the letter that Auntie had written to the pension people. "It should have been in her handbag, because the shopman said she didn't go on to the letter box to post anything. But it wasn't in her handbag."

"She must have left it behind by mistake," said Billy's father. "She was getting odd in old age. It'll be somewhere in her bedroom."

"No, I've searched. It isn't there."

"Why on earth do you want it, anyway?" said Billy's father. "All that pension business ceases with her death."

"I don't want the letter," said his wife. "I just want to know whether there ever was one."

"What are you driving at?"

"Don't you see? The letter was an excuse."

"An excuse?"

"She wanted an excuse to be at that bus stop when Billy got off because she knew what was going to happen. She foresaw."

They stared at each other. Then the nephew said, "Second sight— that's what you mean, isn't it? But it's one thing to foresee, say, which horse is going to win the Derby. And it's quite another thing to foresee what's going to happen and then deliberately to prevent its happening. That's altering the course of things. . . . That's altering everything. . . ."

The niece said, "But you don't understand. She foresaw that Billy would be in danger of being killed, so she went to save him. But she also foresaw that very thing—I mean, she foresaw that she would go to save him. That she *would* save him. Although it killed her."

The nephew liked a logical argument, even about illogical things. He said, "She could still have altered that last part of what she foresaw. She could have decided *not* to go to the bus stop, because she foresaw that it would all end in her death. After all, nobody wants to die."

"You still don't understand," his wife said. "You don't understand Auntie. She knew she would save Billy, even if she had to die for it.

She had to do it, because it was her nature to do it. Because she was Auntie. Don't you *see?*"

The nephew, seeing something about Auntie he had never properly perceived before, said quite humbly, "Yes, I see. . . ."

And the niece, leaning on his shoulder, wept again for Auntie, whom she had known so well since she had been a very little girl. Known so well, perhaps, that she had not known Auntie truly for what she really was, until then.

As for Billy, he never said much about that rainy day, the last of Auntie's life. He hadn't gone to Auntie's funeral—children often don't—but he wore his horrible, homemade blazer until he grew out of it. And he never, never forgot Auntie.

His Loving Sister ❖

When I was a child, my best friend lived next door. He was Steve Phillips, and he had an elder brother and a little sister. After they were all killed, my mother used to hug me and say, "There but for the grace of God . . ." Meaning that I might have been killed, too.

My mother had known Mrs. Phillips—Lizzie Phillips—all her life. Ours was that sort of village in those days. Our family got on very well with all the Phillips family—except for one thing. My parents didn't like Lizzie Phillips's brother, Billy Peterman, who ran the only garage in the village and lived over it. He was much younger than his sister, and he was the kind of man who always would look young: rosy cheeks and innocent blue eyes and fair, tousled hair.

In fact, my father couldn't bear Billy Peterman.

My father used to get angry about quite a lot of things, and he said that most garages were crooked somewhere, but the Daffodil Garage was run by a crook. My mother said that Billy Peterman wasn't really a crook—just weak and lazy. He always had been, even as a little boy. Then my father asked her: where had Billy Peterman got the money to run a garage, anyway, unless he'd sponged on his sister and her family? My mother didn't answer that, but she would wind up the argument by saying that Lizzie Phillips really loved Billy. She had brought him — and his sister — up when their mother had died. The sister had married young and gone to Canada. That left just Lizzie and Billy. When Lizzie married and had children, she still loved Billy and cared for him as if he were another, older child, and Billy let her.

My father snorted. The only dealings with the Daffodil Garage that my father would allow himself were for petrol and oil. He always checked his change carefully afterward.

We knew the Phillipses so well that every morning in term time Mr. Phillips drove me with his own children to school in Ponton. He worked in Ponton, and he dropped us off at school on the way. I used to sit with Steve and Lily in the backseat of the car, and Peter, the eldest of their three children, sat in the front with his father.

Of course, the Phillipses had to use the Daffodil Garage, because of the family connection. Mr. Phillips never talked much, anyway, and he didn't grumble, but my father said he must often have been fed up. Sometimes their car had to go back over and over again for the same thing to be put right. And once — and this is where the story really starts — the repairs dragged on for so long that Billy Peterman had to lend another car, one of his own, to the family. On the very day that happened, I started with whooping cough.

I was in bed upstairs, and my mother was downstairs. My mother could always be at home in the mornings. She worked afternoons, and Lizzie worked mornings, in the same shop in the village. You can see what a useful arrangement that was when we were little: always one mother at home if anything went wrong, in either family.

Well, Mrs. Phillips had gone off to work, and all the rest of the Phillipses had gone off to Ponton in the car from the Daffodil Garage. My father had gone to work, and there was just my mother and me.

It was quiet and very peaceful. My coughing had tired me, so I was glad just to lie back on the pillows. My mother had drawn my bed forward so that I could see out of the window and into the street outside.

She thought I might be interested to watch the passersby. But there hadn't really been any that morning.

But now a police car came cruising slowly down the street. To my amazement, it stopped quite near our house. A policewoman got out and went up the path to the Phillipses' front door and rang the bell. There was no answer, of course.

After a while the policewoman came down the path again and into the road and had a word with the police driver. Then she stood and looked thoughtfully at the Phillipses' house and at the houses on either side. You could almost see her wondering which of the two neighbors to try next.

She decided on our house. She opened the front gate and walked up the path. Then I lost sight of her under the front porch, but I heard the bell ring, and my mother stopped vacuuming and went to answer it.

It all seemed very odd to me because the policewoman came right into the house at once, and my mother took her into the sitting room and shut the door. By this time, in spite of the whooping cough, I was out of bed and at the bedroom door, listening. All I could hear were two voices—mostly the policewoman's—talking in low tones. It was quite a while before my mother showed the policewoman out. She went back to her police car and was driven away.

I nipped back into bed and called to my mother to come and tell me about whatever it was. She didn't answer. There was a long, long silence from downstairs. I didn't know why, but I was frightened.

Then I heard my mother's feet coming slowly up the stairs. She came into my bedroom. I had never, never seen her looking like that before. Her face was quite white, with staring eyes, from which rolled down tears and tears and tears.

She wasn't seeing me at all, and then suddenly she was. She made a strange, huge leap across the room to me, almost like a kangaroo, and she clutched me in her arms and hugged me there until I could hardly breathe. That was when she first said, "There but for the grace of God . . ."

Yes, all three children had been killed outright, and their father.

They had been driving down the hill from our village to join the main road to Ponton at the T junction. Ours was a minor road; the Ponton road was a major one. So the Ponton traffic on it had the right-of-way, and when I had been with them, Mr. Phillips often had to wait at the T junction. He was a careful, good driver.

That morning one of those huge container lorries was going along the main road at a moderate pace and coming up to the T junction. The driver saw the Phillipses' car approaching from a distance. He expected to see it beginning to slow up to stop, but he saw it was still coming on quite fast. He still expected it to stop, and then, the lorry driver said, he caught a glimpse through the windscreen of the other driver's face—Mr. Phillips's face. Even at the distance that still separated them, he saw the horror on it. *The car couldn't stop.* The lorry driver put on his brakes and swerved, but too late. The car from the Daffodil Garage crashed into the side of the lorry, and everyone in it was killed.

The lorry driver was all right, but terribly shaken. The accident hadn't been his fault at all, of course. But whose fault was it then? "I tell you, I saw his face," the lorry driver kept saying. "He *couldn't* stop. I saw his face. . . ."

What was left of the car was towed to the nearest garage, which was the Daffodil. In due course the police examined it carefully but found nothing wrong.

My father, at home, exploded. "Nothing wrong! Of course there was nothing wrong by the time that crook, Billy Peterman, had seen to it. But the brakes must have failed, mustn't they? He ought never to have let that car out of his garage with brakes in that condition. He killed the four of them, and then, to save his own skin, he tinkered and put things right, before the police got on to him!"

"Hush!" said my mother. "Hush, hush, hush! Don't say such things, even if they're true. Suppose Lizzie ever heard you?"

"Heard me?" cried my father. "Don't you think she *knows* her brother killed them?"

As I look back now, that time of my childhood seems to have been dark and muddled and strange. Suddenly I hadn't a best friend any-more. My father was angry for a lot of the time. My mother cried a lot of the time, and she slept at nights in the Phillipses' house, so that Lizzie Phillips should not be quite alone.

I suppose there was a funeral, or four funerals. Lizzie Phillips's sister flew over from Canada. She stayed with Lizzie, and she was very brisk and businesslike. She told us that Lizzie had agreed to go back to Canada with her and settle there.

"Will she like that?" my mother asked doubtfully.

"There's nothing for her *here*," said the brisk Canadian.

"There's nothing for her anywhere," said my mother sadly.

We saw Lizzie go. Her face was a strange pale color; her eyes were dead. She kissed my mother good-bye, but my mother said afterward that she had felt as if she were kissing a statue of somebody. Lizzie drove away with her sister.

"I wonder if she'll be able to stick it out there," said my father. "I think she'll come back."

"No," said my mother. "I don't think she cares enough about any-thing now. I don't think she will."

But as it turned out later, my father was the one who was right.

What about Billy Peterman all this time? Of course, we didn't know all the ins and outs of the family's affairs, but we knew that Lizzie had absolutely refused to see him after the accident. She left for Canada without having said good-bye to him.

Billy Peterman went on running his Daffodil Garage, apparently just as usual.

For a long time, I was remembering—when I least wanted to—two faces: my mother's face on that whooping cough morning, running over with tears, and Lizzie Phillips's face when she came to say good-bye, like carved stone. And I missed Steve terribly. One afternoon, without telling anybody, I walked all the way from our village down the hill to the T junction with the main road to Ponton. I stood there, just looking, for a long time. Dusk was beginning to fall, and there were already lights on the cars and lorries as they came and went along the main road. I wished Steve weren't dead. I wished he were alive to play with me again. Suddenly I was frightened that I would call him back.

He would come: his ghost . . .

I turned tail and fled up the hill again. I never went back alone on foot to that T junction again.

Meanwhile, as people do, we began to live ordinary lives once more. Another family moved into the house next door, and we got on well with them, although not quite as well as with the Phillipses. I played with the children sometimes.

I think now that my mother must have missed Lizzie's friendship very much indeed. After all, they had known each other since they were little girls together. She wrote several times to Canada, but there was no reply.

My father recovered more easily. He still had a hate against the Daffodil Garage, but occasionally he would drop in for petrol if his tank was empty. After such a call, he came home to us quite excited. "I told you so! Lizzie Phillips is back! She couldn't stand Canada and that bossy sister."

"Where is she?" cried my mother. "Where's she staying? Why hasn't she come to us?"

"I suppose she's staying with Billy; I saw her in Billy's office at the garage, standing by his cash desk. She wasn't actually talking to him, but there she was."

My mother was startled. "She couldn't be staying with him!" she said. "Not after what he did! Never!" (That was really the only time my mother let slip that she knew my father was right about Billy Peterman's responsibility for the accident.)

"Well, you always used to say she was a loving sister," said my father. "Anyway, wherever she's staying, she's sure to be round here soon to see you."

But Lizzie Phillips didn't call.

My mother waited a day; she waited two. She felt hurt that such an old friend as Lizzie should be in the same village and not come to see her. In the end, she decided to go herself and call on Lizzie at the Daffodil Garage—if that were really where she was staying. She took me with her. I think she was nervous and wanted the company even of a child.

As we walked into the forecourt of the garage, my mother said, "Surely, yes, there she is!" I thought I saw the figure of a woman slipping away out of sight. My mother called, "Lizzie! Lizzie! Please!"

But no one came forward to her.

My mother went on to where Billy Peterman was sitting in his little office, just sitting. He was a lazy young man, as my mother always said, but he didn't exactly look as if he were lazing comfortably at his desk now. He would always look a young man, but now he suddenly looked an old young man. The roses in his cheeks had faded; his fair hair looked dull and dusty; his blue eyes gazed vacantly at my mother. He had seen her coming, he must have done, and he must have heard her calling. But he made no move.

My mother went quite close to him. "Lizzie's here now, isn't she?"

"Yes," he said.

"I want to see her," my mother said.

"Well," he said, in a flat voice, "you have seen her, haven't you? She's always here now. With me."

"I want to see her and talk to her," my mother insisted.

He shook his head.

"What do you mean, Billy Peterman? You can't keep her to yourself!"

He laughed in a strange, flat way. Then he said, "Lizzie died in Canada ten days ago. The letter said she didn't want to live any longer. They said she died of a broken heart."

My mother stared and stared at him. She had never really liked Billy Peterman; none of us did. But she had known him as a little boy, and she was easily touched to pity. Now she said, as if she really meant it, "Poor, poor Billy . . ."

He turned his head aside, so that we should not see his face.

Very soon after that, Billy Peterman sold the Daffodil Garage and moved away. No one knew where he went or ever heard of him again.

What I have often wondered since is this: Did his loving sister go with him?

Mr. Hurrel's Tallboy ❖

I was only a child at the time, so—just to please me, I suppose—I had been given the job of listening for the knocks on the party wall. (My bedroom-playroom was right against the wall that divided us from our next-door neighbors, the Hurrels. And in fact, I could hear much more than deliberate knocking through that thin wall. But all that comes later.)

The knocking came: a cheerful *rat-tat-tat*!

I rushed downstairs, where my mother and father were already waiting. We trooped through our front door and down our front path, through our front gate, sharp right for a step or two, and then sharp right again through the Hurrels' gate and up their path to their front door.

The door stood open, with Mrs. Hurrel—tiny, frail, gasping with excitement—welcoming us in. The ground floor of their house was Mr. Hurrel's workshop, with all his tools and timber; he was a retired furniture restorer and cabinetmaker. We were taken upstairs to their living room, which was the room next to mine, with the party wall between.

Against this wall stood the tallboy.

I was prepared—I had been prepared by my parents' explanations—for the appearance of the tallboy. I knew that it was so very tall
only because it was really two chests of drawers, made to fit with beautiful exactitude one on top of the other. The lower section had three
long drawers and stood on four elegant, little, splayed-out legs. The
upper section had three long drawers and, at the very top, a pair of
short ones.

All that was no surprise to me. What I was not prepared for was the
awe-inspiring magnificence, the *majesty* of the tallboy. Its surface of
polished wood glowed richly; its head reared almost to the ceiling. It
dwarfed into insignificance the figure of Mr. Hurrel, who stood beside
it. Yet he had made it; it was his. It was as if, all those years, ordinary-
looking, ordinary-sized Mr. Hurrel had had this tallboy inside him,
imprisoned, cramped, struggling to get out. Now it was out, and it
stood there in its full splendor, a masterpiece of furniture.

The tallboy was Mr. Hurrel's masterpiece; it was also his whim.
Nobody, really, made tallboys nowadays—hadn't done so, seriously,
for well over a hundred years. But in his job, Mr. Hurrel had had the
repairing of antique tallboys, and the dazzling idea had come to him of
making one of his own. He had worked on it in his spare time for several years, and now, in retirement, he had finished it at last.

Mr. Hurrel stood by his tallboy, smiling only a little. He said nothing, because he had nothing to say. His tallboy spoke for him.

My mother was exclaiming at the number of drawers: "The storage
space!"

The Hurrels' grown-up son, Denis, who had taken time off from
his job in Scotland for the occasion, said, "Mum has to stand on a
chair to reach the top drawers!"

"Yes, just fancy!" said Mrs. Hurrel breathlessly. Her son put an arm
affectionately round her shoulder and laughed.

The only other person in the room was the Hurrels' daughter,
Wendy. She was much older than her brother, unmarried, and working in London. She came home sometimes, but we never felt that we
knew her well. She was pale, insignificant-looking, silent.

Mrs. Hurrel was pulling out one of the drawers of the tallboy, to show my mother the quantity of sheets, tablecloths, and other things she was able to keep there. The drawer pulled out smoothly, smoothly, and when it was pushed back, there was a tiny puff of air—a sigh of air escaping at the last moment. (I had very sharp ears in those days; I heard it.) So perfect was the fit.

My father was respectfully questioning Mr. Hurrel about the making of the tallboy, and Mr. Hurrel, after all, was taking pleasure in answering him; you could see that. He spoke of mortise and tenon and dowel pegging and the dovetailing—the finest—of the fronts and backs of all the drawers; of canted front corners and dentil molding and cross-grained banding and cock-beading. He spoke of the woods he had used: pine for the back and for the cornice framing; oak for the drawers; but everywhere else, solid mahogany or mahogany veneer. "Honduras mahogany," said old Mr. Hurrel. "Only the best . . ."

I was gazing at the wooden handles of the drawers; from the center of each knob a little star twinkled at me. "Are they really gold?" I asked, because the tallboy deserved only the best.

Mr. Hurrel did not laugh at me. "Not gold," he said. "Brass. I've always fancied that decoration. And wooden handles for the drawers — they were my fancy, too."

While we were talking, Denis had brought a bottle of champagne out of the fridge, and his mother had brought glasses. My father said jovially that someone ought to smash the bottle against the side of the tallboy, to launch it, as they used to do with oceangoing liners. Mr. Hurrel shuddered, and his wife said quickly, "Nobody's ever going to hurt your tallboy, Edward." And, indeed, when Denis opened the champagne bottle, he was careful to turn away from the tallboy, so that the cork flew out in the opposite direction.

Then we all drank our glasses of champagne, toasting the new tallboy, and Mr. Hurrel, its maker, and Mrs. Hurrel, his wife. We wished them health and long life. It was the first time I had ever tasted champagne. It seemed to explode in my mouth in rockets of liquid excitement. To my mind, the champagne and the tallboy went together: both dizzyingly splendid. Sublime.

But our champagne wishes did not, alas, come true.

Mrs. Hurrel had always been delicate, and not long after our celebrations she had to take to her bed. There was even talk of her going into the hospital, but she wouldn't have that. So old Mr. Hurrel nursed her and did the housekeeping as best he could. And the arrangement was that he would knock on the party wall if he needed help urgently. Twice he did that and woke me, and I woke my mother, and she went round, even in the middle of the night.

Wendy came for a weekend and helped, and Denis came for another weekend. He suggested taking his mother back to Scotland with him, and his father, too, of course. He had a house in Scotland and was marrying a Scottish girl, so there would be a home for them. The old people wouldn't hear of it.

Denis Hurrel came round to talk to my parents. You could see that he was worried. He'd been talking to Wendy on the telephone; he thought she would come down to help again.

"Just for the weekend?"

"No." He looked uncomfortable. "I didn't suggest anything to her, I promise you, and anyway, it's not ideal. But she's likely to come for good."

My parents were startled and very doubtful. "Give up her job? Leave all her friends in London?"

"She hasn't any friends," Denis said quickly. "So she says. And she's always had this idea she'd like to queen it at home, be housekeeper for my dad. She never really got on with Mum for that very reason, I think. She wanted Dad to herself, always."

"But, Denis, it's your mother she'll have to care for. Constant attention."

"Wendy'll manage that, and in return, she'll have the running of the house for Dad."

"Well, I don't know. I'm sure . . ." my mother said.

"Look! If you get worried, ring me in Scotland. I'll come."

"There!" said my father. "That sounds all right to me."

And so it was, for a long time. Wendy did the shopping and the cooking and housecleaning and nursed her mother. Old Mrs. Hurrel became a permanent invalid, but she was fairly cheerful. How long she would live was another matter, people said.

Mr. Hurrel never seemed to notice Wendy and all that she was doing for him. She might not have been there, for the attention he paid to her. He cared only for his furniture—his tallboy particularly. He was always polishing it. It was his darling, his magnificent child.

And Wendy? Nobody knew what she thought of life with her parents.

And then one day, suddenly, one of those parents died. No, not invalid Mrs. Hurrel, but Mr. Hurrel. He died in his sleep—heart disease, according to the doctor. His wife was terribly upset, of course, and so was Denis, when he came for the funeral. Again, he tried to persuade his mother to move up to Scotland; she refused. "I stay here," she said, "where he made his beautiful tallboy. Wendy will look after me."

As for Wendy herself, if she had been rather taciturn before, she was almost speechless now. You felt that the death of her father had embittered her. I was frightened of her because I had this feeling that now she was bottling something up inside her. Something larger than herself. And dark. And very frightening.

"I don't think Denis should have left Wendy in sole charge of the old lady," my mother said uneasily. "I've a good mind to ring Scotland and tell him so." But she didn't.

At first there seemed nothing particular to worry about, except that Mrs. Hurrel told us that Wendy no longer spoke to her at all. Nor did she acknowledge our greetings in the street. Nor did she greet us with even a word whenever we rang at the Hurrels' front door.

"Cooped up in that house for most of the time, not talking," said my mother. "It's not natural. She'll begin to go off her head."

My father said, "She'll begin talking to the furniture."

"She does," I said, pleased to add an item of solid fact to the conversation. "I can hear her through the wall. She bangs about a lot, and she talks to the furniture."

They stared at me. *"Talks to the furniture?"*

I didn't realize until then that my father had only been joking. No one is supposed literally to talk to furniture.

"Or perhaps she talks just to the tallboy," I suggested, trying in some way to make the whole thing sound more likely.

They came to my room that evening, put their ears to the party wall, and listened. You couldn't distinguish the words, but you could recognize the voice; it was Wendy all right. Her tone was bitter and furiously accusing, and as well as talking, she was violently banging about, as I had said.

My father whispered, "She really is going off her head."

My mother whispered back, "She shouldn't be looking after that poor old dear, helpless in bed."

They went downstairs at once, to telephone to Scotland.

If they had not gone off so promptly, I should have asked them to wait and to go on listening, with more care still. In the pauses in Wendy's raving and banging, there was something else one could just hear, a sound that was not exactly a voice, and yet, goaded, it spoke, as it seemed: It *replied*.

On the telephone Denis Hurrel promised my mother to come home that very weekend.

That Friday evening my mother gave my father his tea and then went out to call on a friend. I was upstairs. I felt easier in my room than usual, because there was no sound from the other side of the party wall. Wendy was elsewhere in the Hurrels' house or perhaps out of the house altogether, but that was very seldom nowadays.

Our front doorbell rang. I paid no attention to the caller; my dad was there to deal with whoever it was.

Later my mother came back, and soon after, I came downstairs to be with them. Wendy had started up again, on the other side of the party wall, worse than ever before. . . .

Downstairs, my father was telling my mother about the visitor. "I was taken aback. I mean, Wendy's never called round before."

"Was it about her mother?"

"No, and I didn't have time to ask about her. Wendy was in such a hurry—such a state—to borrow our ax."

"To borrow *what?*"

"Our ax, our hatchet." My father's voice faltered as he saw my mother's expression. "It's all right. Really. She only wanted it to chop wood for their fire."

My mother said, "The Hurrels haven't an open fire anywhere in that house." My father's jaw dropped. My mother was crying, "Oh, that poor old thing in bed! Oh, my God! And you lent her an ax!"

My mother had started for the front door, but my father passed her. I followed them out of the house; I was too frightened to be left behind, alone.

We ran down to our front gate, in through the Hurrels', and up to their front door. As we came up the path, we could see the light in Mrs. Hurrel's bedroom, upstairs, and we could hear Wendy's voice, raised high.

My father rang the doorbell and, at the same time, lifted the flap of the letter box, to call through it. He never did so, because the lifting of the flap allowed us to hear more clearly what was going on upstairs. Wendy was now shouting at the top of her voice. "I'll kill you!" she howled. "I'll kill you!"

No one had ever thought of my father as a particularly strong man; I do not think he thought that of himself. But instantly he had drawn back and then run at the door like a battering ram, and we flung ourselves upon the door at the same time. The door fastenings broke, and we all fell inside.

At the same time, from above, came a woman's scream, with a great crash. My father and mother tore upstairs to Mrs. Hurrel's bedroom. I hid under the stairs, too terrified to follow them this time. So I know only what they chose to tell me later.

They found old Mrs. Hurrel sitting on the edge of her bed, white-faced and shivering, trying to stand up, trying to walk. She kept saying that she must go to Wendy. Wendy was in the living room; something terrible had happened to Wendy.

They went into the living room.

Wendy lay on the floor, dead—a glance was enough to confirm that—with the tallboy on top of her. She still held in her grip the ax, our ax. She had evidently been attacking the tallboy with the ax, particularly chopping at its legs. In her fury, she did not foresee the consequences, or perhaps she did not care. She had severed one front leg completely; the other one was splintered and had broken. The tallboy had tottered, and the upper section had fallen forward, all its drawers shooting out ahead of it in their smooth, their deadly way. She had not sprung back in time to escape, and the upper drawers had caught her about the head and face and neck, and the fall of the upper casing upon her had completed the tallboy's counterassault, or self-defense. The contents of the drawers lay in confusion all about the body, white cotton and linen stained with Wendy's blood.

All this I learned only bit by bit, and much later; I was a child, to be shielded from nightmares. I was sent to stay for some time with a school friend living on the other side of town. When I was finally allowed home, a great deal had happened in my absence: the inquest and the funeral, for instance. Old Mrs. Hurrel was to live with Denis and his new wife in Scotland, and meanwhile he was clearing the house and putting it up for sale.

"What about the—" My father could not get the word out.

My mother said, "What about the tallboy, Denis? Your father could have repaired it, if he were still alive. Perhaps another craftsman as clever as he was . . ."

"No," said Denis. "No." He looked strangely at them and then told some story about a dog that at first seemed to me to have nothing to do with the tallboy and its ruination. He said the dog, a big, beautiful creature, a pedigree, belonged to a master with a vicious streak in him. The man tormented and beat the dog cruelly, and one day the dog turned on the man and savaged him, so that the man died.

"It wasn't really the dog's fault," said Denis. "You could say he was under extreme provocation. You could say he was acting in self-defense. But they shot the dog afterward. They had to shoot the dog."

My father covered his eyes with his hands, and my mother cried, "But, Denis, the tallboy is just a piece of furniture, and your father . . ."

Denis said, "My father's not here; but I think he would agree about what should be done with the tallboy. Although it would have broken his heart."

Early next morning, before most people were about, Denis built a bonfire in the Hurrels' back garden. When it was going well, he fetched the tallboy: first the drawers, one by one; then the upper casing; then the lower, with its mutilated legs.

Watching from our back window, I saw the remains of the tallboy, as Denis carried them. You could see that it had once been big and beautiful, a pedigree thing, as Denis had said. But it wasn't just that the legs had been hacked and broken. Everywhere the surface of the wood had been bruised and broken, the veneer splintered off. Regularly Wendy must have kicked at it and battered it, with whatever object came to her hand as a weapon. Those were the bangings I had heard, between her cursings, through the party wall.

Denis put all the pieces onto the blazing bonfire, and they caught fire quickly and burned, and burned utterly away. By the next day the bonfire was nothing but a heap of white wood ash, and Denis Hurrel had gone back to Scotland with his old mother.

And that evening, at dusk, when nobody was noticing, I climbed our fence and went to the bonfire. I sifted through the wood ash with my fingers, and in the end I found three of those little brass stars that had winked at me from the center of the tallboy's wooden drawer knobs. They were blackened from the fire, but I pocketed them up, and later I cleaned them and polished them, till they shone like gold. And I have them still.

That's really the end of the story, I suppose. New people moved into the Hurrels' house next door, and I could hear them sometimes through the party wall. But when everything had gone quiet next door—in the middle of the night, for instance—I used to think I could hear something else: the ghost of a voice, or perhaps the voice of a ghost. Not the voice of old Mr. Hurrel, returned to this world to lament the death of his beloved tallboy, not the voice of Wendy, murderous-sounding with jealousy and hatred, but another voice that was hardly a voice at all—an undertone that implored mercy, that pleaded for its life . . .

I heard that voice, or thought I heard it, for as long as we lived in that house. I wonder if anyone, later, ever heard it. Or whether, anyway, with the passage of time, the voice failed and fell into silence, as do the voices of all things to which life has been given, or even lent.

The Hirn ❖

*T*his was a new motorway, and Mr. Edward Edwards liked that. He liked new things—things newly designed and newly made. He drove his powerful car powerfully, just at the speed limit, eating up the miles, as the saying is—eating up as an impatient boa constrictor might swallow its unimportant prey.

The new motorway sliced through new countryside. (Old countryside, really, but new to motorway travelers, and that was what mattered.) Open it was, with huge fields, mostly arable. Mr. Edwards approved the evident productivity.

He drove well, looking ahead at the road, keeping an eye on the rearview mirror, and at the same time sparing casual glances toward the landscape on the right and on the left.

Something snagged in Mr. Edwards's mind, suddenly: there was an unexpected and unwelcome catching of his attention, as though on some country walk a hanging bramble had caught on his sleeve, on his arm. (But he had not gone on any country walk for many years.)

He glanced sharply to his left again.

To his left the gentle rise and fall of farmland was perhaps familiar. . . .

And that house . . .

That farmhouse . . .

Instantly Mr. Edward Edwards had looked away from the farmhouse, but he could not prevent himself from remembering. He was driving his car as fast and as well as before, but he remembered. They say that in the moment of drowning, a man may remember the whole of his past life, *see* it. In the moment of driving past Mortlock's, Mr. Edward Edwards remembered everything, saw everything in his mind's eye, from long ago.

The farmhouse and farmlands had belonged to the Mortlocks for several generations, but in the last generation there had been no children. The heir was young Edward Edwards, from London, whose grandmother happened to have been a Mortlock.

After the funeral of his last elderly cousin, young Edward stayed on at Mortlock's to see exactly what his inheritance consisted of—and what further might be made of it. He knew nothing of farming, but already he knew about money and its uses. Already he knew what was what.

Above all, he was clever enough to know his own ignorance. He certainly did not intend—at least at first—to try farming on his own. He might, however, put in an experienced farm manager—but keep an eye on him, too.

He suspected that a good deal could be done to improve on Mortlock methods of farming. He understood, for instance, that up-to-date farmers were grubbing up hedges to make larger, more economic fields. That was an obvious increase in efficiency. No land should be wasted; every acre—only he thought modernly in hectares—ought to be utilized. Total efficiency would be his aim—or rather, the aim of his farm manager.

Meanwhile, he had just a farm foreman, old Bill Hayes.

Bill Hayes was old only in the dialect of the countryside; in actuality, he was young middle-aged. That local inaccuracy of speech annoyed Edward Edwards. And anyway, although Bill Hayes was not old in age, young Edward suspected him of being old in ideas.

In the company of his farm foreman, young Edward tramped purposefully over his fields, trying to understand what he saw and to assess its value. Often, of course, he was baffled; then Bill Hayes would do his best to explain. Sometimes young Edward was satisfied. Sometimes, however, he made a suggestion or a criticism, which Bill Hayes would invariably show to be impractical, even foolish.

Edward Edwards began to dislike old Bill Hayes.

The only time he was certain of his opinion against the foreman's was over the Hirn. This was an area of trees, using up about a third of a hectare of land, in the middle of one of the best fields.

"What is it?" asked young Edward Edwards, staring across the stub-bled earth to that secretive-looking clump of trees.

And old Bill had answered, "It's Hirn."

"Just some trees?"

"Well, there's water, too, in the middle," said old Bill. "You could call it a pond."

"But what's the point of it?"

And old Bill Hayes had repeated, "It's Hirn."

Somehow his careless omission, twice, of the "the" that so obviously should have been there irritated young Edward. Again, there was that stupid suggestion of dialect, old worldness, and the rest. "Well," he said, "the Hirn will have to justify its existence if it's to remain. Otherwise, it goes."

"Goes?"

"The land must be reclaimed for better use."

"Better use? For Hirn?"

Young Edward thought: the fellow has an echo chamber where his brains should be! Aloud, he said, "If we get rid of the trees and fill in this pond place, then we can cultivate the land with the rest of the field."

"I shouldn't do that, sir."

"Why not?"

Old Bill Hayes did not answer.

"What's so special about the Hirn, then?"

Bill Hayes said, "Well, after all, it is Hirn. . . ."

Young Edward could get no further than that. But at least this senseless conversation made plain to him that he must get rid of old Bill Hayes as soon as possible. He needed a thoroughly rational, modern-minded farm manager; that was certain. This business of the Hirn was typical of what must have been going on, unchecked, during the Mortlock years.

Young Edward was pretty certain that the Hirn must be dealt with—and the sooner the better, of course. But he was not impulsive, not foolhardy. He would examine the site carefully for himself—and by himself—before coming to a decision. After all, there might even be valuable timber among those trees. (He was pleased with himself for the thought. Surely, he was already learning.)

So the next day he set off alone in his car—not at all a car of the make, age, or condition that, in later years, he would care to have been seen driving. He knew the nearest point of access to the Hirn, a side road, along which had been built a line of small houses. Just beyond the last house, on the same side, was a field gate, and by this he parked. Through the gate, in the distance, he could already see the Hirn.

He climbed the gate and set off across the fields, passing by the side of the back garden of the last small house. A woman was pegging out her washing, and a toddler played about beside the washing basket. The toddler stopped playing to stare, but his mother went on with her work. Yet young Edward felt that she, too, was watching him. No wonder, perhaps. This little colony of houses was remote from most comings and goings.

A little later, as he was crossing the furrows, he looked back, to mark the gateway where he had left the car and to see whether—yes, the two in the garden were now both openly staring after him. The woman held the child in her arms, and an old man had also come out of the house next door. He stood just on the other side of the hedge from the woman and child, staring in the same direction.

Edward Edwards reached the Hirn. Even he could see that the woodland had been disgracefully neglected; no one had laid a finger on it for many, many years—perhaps ever, it seemed. The trees grew all anyhow—some strangled by ivy; some age-decayed and falling; some crippled by the fall of others; some young, but stunted and deformed in the struggle upward to the sunlight. The space between the trees was dense with undergrowth.

It was very still, but no doubt there would be birds and other wild creatures. Young Edward peered about him. He could see no movement at all, but he supposed that beady bird eyes would be watching him.

He began to push his way through the undergrowth between the trees, to find the water of which Bill Hayes had spoken.

He came to a small clearing—so it seemed—among the trees: open, green, and almost eerily even. Absolutely flat. He hesitated at the edge of the clearing and then, with a shock, realized that this was the water. Mantled by some overspreading tiny plant life, it had seemed to him to be solid, turfy land. He had almost fallen into the pond, almost walked into it.

There was no knowing how deep the water was.

The water was unmoving, except perhaps at its edges, where he thought he saw, out of the corner of his eye, a slight stirring. Perhaps tadpoles? But was this the season for tadpoles? He tried to remember, but he had never been much of a tadpole boy, even with the few opportunities that London offered. He had always hated that dark wriggliness.

He decided to complete his examination by walking round the edge of the pond. This turned out to be difficult because of the thickly growing vegetation. At one place a bush leaned in a straggly way over the water; it bore clusters of tiny dark purple berries. He thought that these must be elderberries, and he knew you could eat elderberries. He stretched out a hand to pick some and then thought that perhaps these were not elderberries, perhaps another kind of fruit, perhaps poisonous. He drew his hand back sharply. He felt endangered.

And then he saw the amazing oak. The trunk must have been at least two meters across at its base, but the tree was quite hollow, with some other younger tree boldly growing up in the middle of it. All the same, the oak was not dead: from its crust of bark, twigs and leaves had spurted. And at some time someone—apparently to keep this shell of a tree from falling apart—had put a steel cable round it.

"Pointless," said young Edward to himself. Because of the elder-berries—if they had been elderberries—he had felt afraid, and that still angered him. Now the sight of the giant oak, whose collapse was thus futilely delayed, angered him even more.

He pushed his way out of the little piece of woodland to its far side and the open field beyond. From there the small houses were not visible. The Hirn lay between.

The shortest way back to the field gate and his car would have been by the path his pushing and trampling had already made through the woodland. But he decided not to reenter the Hirn. He preferred to take the long way round the outside, until he was in view of the houses, the gate, the car.

When he could see the houses, he could see that the woman and child were still in their garden, also the old man in his. When they saw him coming, they went indoors.

"I don't know what they thought they were going to see," young Edward said to himself resentfully. "Something—oh, *very* extraordinary, no doubt!"

He went straight back to the car and then home. His examination of the Hirn had been quick but thorough enough. There had been nothing much to see, and frankly, he did not like the place.

The next day he tackled old Bill Hayes and told him that the Hirn must be obliterated. He did not use the word, but it was in his mind as he gave the order. After all, he was owner and master.

Old Bill Hayes looked at him. "But it's Hirn," he said.

"So you mentioned before," said young Edward, knowing that his sarcasm would be wasted on Bill's dullness. "All the same, see that what I want is done."

Old Bill Hayes made no further objection, but neither did he do anything in the days that followed.

Then, realizing that his wishes had been ignored, Edward gave the order again.

Again, nothing happened.

This time, his blood up, young Edward acted for himself, without consulting or even informing old Bill Hayes. He made the right inquiries and was able to arrange for an outside firm to do the clearance job. They said it would take several days. They would start by cutting down all the trees. The timber—valueless, of course—and the brushwood would then be cleared. Remaining tree stumps and roots must all be grubbed up; otherwise they would grow again, even more strongly. Finally, the pond would be filled in, and the whole site leveled.

In only a short time all trace of the Hirn would have disappeared.

On the first day of the operation young Edward Edwards had a morning appointment with the manager of the local bank where the Mortlocks had always done business. There were financial matters still to be sorted out. But on top of these, the manager annoyed young Edward with unwanted advice. He strongly urged him not to take on the Mortlock farm on his own account, even with a farm manager. It would be more sensible (the manager said) to sell the farm and farmhouse and use the money in some business that he was more likely fully to understand.

Young Edward was furious.

His fury lasted into the afternoon, when he decided that he was in just the mood to inspect the destruction of the Hirn. Besides, he somehow felt that he ought to be there—perhaps as a witness to the execution.

He drove his car to the same place as before and set off again across the fields. It was easy to see where the gang had been before him, with their heavily loaded vehicles, and he could already see where they had been at work: the treed area of the Hirn was now only about a tenth of its original size. The other nine-tenths had been roughly cleared, leaving freshly cut tree stumps sticking up everywhere like jagged teeth.

The gang themselves had gone home. He was disappointed—and disapproving—that they had chosen to stop work so early.

Once, before he reached what was left of the Hirn, young Edward looked back over the fields to the houses. No one at all in the gardens. No lights yet in any windows, as there would be soon, but he was aware of something, a pallor behind a window glass: a face looking out in his direction. From more than one window he fancied that they watched him.

He was soon picking his way among the many tree stumps, making for the few trees that were left standing near the pond. The dying oak had been left standing. It survived. He stared at it. Unwillingly, he came to the decision that he wanted to touch it. He went right up to it and laid the flat of his hand against the bark. For the first time it occurred to him to wonder how old the tree might be. People said that oaks could live for hundreds of years . . . hundreds and hundreds of years. . . .

He decided that he had seen enough of the Hirn. He turned away from the oak, to get out of this tiny remnant of woodland. Tiny it might be, but it was thick—thicker than he had noticed on his coming. He had to push his way through the undergrowth—perhaps because this was not the way he had come but a new way? Certainly it had been much easier for him to reach the oak than now it was for him to get away from it.

The end of the afternoon was coming; the light was failing.

He came to the pond. The water looked almost black now. To his surprise he saw that there were still trees and bushes crowding the banks around it; he had thought, as he came over the fields, that they had been cut down.

He turned away from the water in the direction—he thought—of the houses and his parked car. He must have made a mistake, however, for he reentered untouched woodland again.

He was angered at how long it was taking him to get out of this wretched grove of trees.

He came to the oak again and turned from it abruptly to struggle on through the undergrowth in the direction he supposed to be the right one. The only sound was the sound of his crashing about and his own heavy breathing, and then he thought—or perhaps he imagined?—he was hearing something else. He stopped to listen carefully. . . .

(Driving fast along the motorway, Mr. Edwards remembered standing still to listen so carefully, so very carefully. As he drove, his hands tightened on the driving wheel until his knuckles whitened. . . .)

Young Edward Edwards listened. . . .

It was very quiet. Everywhere round him was now still and very,

very quiet. But all the same, he thought there was something—not a sound that began and ended but a sound that was there, as the wood was there. The sound enclosed him, as the wood enclosed him.

The sound was of someone trying not to laugh—of someone privately amused, quietly and maliciously amused.

Young Edward made a rush forward and reached the pond again.

He stood there, and the sound was there with him, all around him. He stared at the blackness of the water until he could feel his eyes beginning to trick him. He watched the water, and the water seemed to watch him. The surface of the blackness seemed to shiver, to shudder; the edges of the water seemed to crinkle. The mantle of black on the surface of the water seemed to be gathering itself up, as a woman's garments are gathered, before the woman herself rises. . . .

(Along the motorway, Mr. Edwards drove fast, trying to think of nothing but the motorway, but he had to remember. . . .)

Young Edward ran; he was trying to run; he was trying to escape. The sound was still round him, and round him now, everywhere, trees stood in his way and the undergrowth spread wide to catch him. They all baited him, for someone's private amusement. He fought to run: a bramble snagged in his sleeve and then tried to drag the coat from his back; an elder branch whipped him across the face; a sly tree root tripped him.

He tripped. He was falling.

He knew that he was falling among tall trees and thickets of undergrowth, and that he was lost—forever lost! He gave a long scream, but a blow on the head finished the scream and also finished young Edward Edwards for the time being.

In the houses they heard the long scream that suddenly stopped, and a little party set off hurriedly to find young Mr. Edwards. They had been waiting for something to happen. They were not callous people, only very fearful; otherwise they might have gone earlier.

They found him lying among the tree stumps of the cleared part of the woodland. He had fallen headfirst onto one of them. Later, in the hospital, he was told that he had been very lucky. He might so easily have split his whole head open on that jagged tree stump. Killed himself.

And later still, in London (where he had insisted on going, straight from the hospital), he had instructed the bank to arrange for the immediate sale of Mortlock's, farmhouse and farm, the lot. That had been done, most profitably, and he had never seen the place again—until today, from the motorway.

As he drove, he ventured another quick glance to his left. The farmhouse was no longer in sight. His spirits lifted. These must still be Mortlock fields, but they would soon be passed, too.

Then he saw the houses—and recognized them. . . .

Then the big field . . .

Then, in the middle, green and flourishing, a coppice of trees. . . .

He had been warned that unless they were grubbed up by the roots, the tree stumps would sprout and grow even more strongly. Yes, they had grown, and now, as once before, thick woodland hid from sight that mantled water. And he began to think he heard—borne on some unlikely wind—the faintest sound of unkind laughter.

Mr. Edwards brought his gaze back strictly to the motorway ahead, turned the car radio on to full volume, accelerated well over the speed limit, and so passed beyond further sight of the trees that were Hirn.

He put view and sound, and remembrance of both, behind him for good. He had made up his mind, for good: he would not drive this way again. There were always other roads and other modes of travel—rail, air. He would never use this motorway again.

He never did.

The Yellow Ball ❖

*T*he ladder reached comfortably to the branch of the sycamore they had decided on, and its foot was held steady by Lizzie, while her father climbed up. He carried the rope— nylon, for strength—in loops over his shoulder. He knotted one end securely round the chosen branch and then let the other end drop. It fell to dangle only a little to one side of where Con held the old motor tire upright on the ground. Really, of course, there was no need for the tire to be held in that position yet, but something had to be found for Con to do, to take his mind off the cows in the meadow. He was nervous of animals, and cows were large.

Their father prepared to descend the ladder.

And then—how exactly did it happen? Why did it happen? Was Con really the first to notice the knothole in the tree trunk, as he later claimed? Or did Lizzie point it out? Would their father, anyway, have reached over sideways from the ladder—as he now did—to dip his fingers into the cavity?

"There's something in here. . . . Something stuck . . ." He teetered a little on the ladder as he tugged. "Got it!"

And as he grasped whatever was in the hole, the air round the group in the meadow tightened, tautened with expectancy.

Something was going to happen. . . .

Going to happen . . .

To happen . . .

"Here we are!" He was holding aloft a dingy, spherical object. "A ball—it's a ball! A chance in a thousand. Someone threw a ball high, and it happened to lodge here! No, a chance in a million for it to have happened like that!"

He dropped the ball. Lizzie tried to catch it but was prevented by the ladder. Con tried but was prevented by the tire he held. The ball bounced, but not high, rolled out a little way over the meadow, came to rest.

And something invisibly in the meadow breathed again, watchful, but relaxed. . . .

The two children forgot the ball, because their father was now down from the ladder; he was knotting the free end of the rope round the tire, so that it cleared the ground by about half a meter. It hung there, enticingly.

While their father put his ladder away, the children began arguing about who should have first go on the tire. He came back, sharply stopped their quarreling, and showed them how both could get on at the same time: they must face each other, with both pairs of legs through the circle of the tire, but in opposite directions. So they sat on the lowest curve of the tire, gripping the rope from which it hung, and their father began to swing them, higher and higher, wider and wider.

As they swung up, the setting sun was in their eyes, and suddenly they saw the whole of the meadow, but tilted, tipped, and they saw the houses on the other side of the meadow rushing toward them, and then as they swung back again, the houses were rushing away, and the meadow, too.

Swinging, swinging, swinging, they whooped and shrieked for joy.

Their mother came out to watch for a little and then said they must all come in for tea. So all three went in, through the little gate from the meadow into the garden and then into the house. They left the tire still swaying; they left the dirty old ball where it had rolled and come to rest and been forgotten.

As soon as he had finished his tea, Con was eager to be in the meadow, to have the tire to himself while there was still daylight. Lizzie went on munching.

But in a few moments, he was indoors again, saying hesitantly, "I think—I think there's someone in the meadow waiting for me."

Their father said, "Nonsense, boy! The cows will never hurt you!"

"It's not the cows at all. There's someone waiting. For me."

Their mother looked at their father. "Perhaps . . ."

"I'll come out with you," he said to Con, and so he did, and Lizzie followed them both.

But Con was saying, "I didn't say I was afraid. I just said there was someone in the meadow. I thought there was. That's all." They went through the garden gate into the meadow.

"Man or woman?" Con's father asked him. "Or boy or girl?"

"No," said Con. "It wasn't like that."

His father had scanned the wide meadow thoroughly. "No one at all." He sighed. "Oh, Conrad, your *imagination*! I'm going back before the tea's too cold. You two can stay a bit longer, if you like. Till it begins to get dark."

He went indoors.

Lizzie, looking beyond the tire and remembering after all, said, "That ball's gone."

"I picked it up." Con brought it out of his pocket, held it out to Lizzie. She took it. It was smaller than a tennis ball, but heavier, because solid. One could see that it was yellow under the dirtiness, and it was not really so very dirty after all. Dirt had collected in the tiny, shallow holes with which the surface of the ball was pitted. That was all.

"I wonder what made the holes," said Lizzie.

Con held out his hand for the ball again. Lizzie did not give it up. "It's just as much mine as yours," he said. They glared at each other, but uneasily. They did not really *want* to quarrel about this ball; this ball was for better things than that.

"I suppose we could take turns at having it," said Lizzie. "Or perhaps you don't really want the ball, Con?"

"But I do—I do!" At the second "do" he lunged forward, snatched the ball from his sister, and was through the gate with it, back toward the house—and Lizzie was after him. The gate clicked shut behind them both.

Suddenly they both stopped and turned to look back. Oh! They knew that something was coming—

High, and over—

They saw it—or rather, they *had* seen it, for it happened so swiftly.

A small, dark shape, a shadow had leaped the shut gate after them—elegant as a dancer in flying motion—eager.

Con breathed: "Did you see him?"

"Her," Lizzie whispered back. "A bitch. I saw the teats, as she came over the gate."

"Her ears lifted in the wind. . . ."

"She had her eyes on the ball—oh, Con! It's *her* ball! Hers! She wants it; she wants it!"

Though nothing was visible now, they could feel the air of the garden quivering with hope and expectancy.

"Throw it for her, Con!" Lizzie urged him. "Throw it!"

With all his strength Con threw the yellow ball over the gate and out into the meadow, and the shadow of a shape followed it in another noble leap and then a long darting movement across the meadow, straight as an arrow after the ball, seeming to gain on it, to be about to catch up with it, to catch it.

But when the ball came to rest, the other movement still went on, not in a straight line anymore, but sweeping to and fro, quartering the ground, seeking, seeking.

"It's her ball. Why doesn't she find it and pick it up?" Con asked wonderingly. "It's there for her."

Lizzie said, "I think—I think it's because it's a real ball, and she's not a real dog. She can't pick it up, poor thing; she's only some kind of ghost."

A ghost! Con said nothing but drew closer to his sister. They stood together in the garden, looking out into the meadow, while they accustomed their minds to what they were seeing. They stood on the solid earth of the garden path; behind them was their house, with the lights now on and their father drinking his cups of tea; in front of them lay the meadow with the sycamore tree; in the far distance, the cows.

All real, all solid, all familiar.

And in the middle of the meadow—to and fro, to and fro—moved the ghost of a dog.

But now Con moved away from his sister, stood stalwartly alone again. An ordinary ghost might have frightened him for longer; a real dog would certainly have frightened him. But the ghost of a dog—that was different!

"Lizzie," he said, "let's not tell anyone. Not anyone. It's our private ghost. Just ours."

"All right."

They continued gazing over the meadow until they could no longer see through the deepening dusk. Then their mother was rapping on the window for them to come indoors, and they had to go.

Indoors, their parents asked them, "Did you have a good swing on the tire?"

"The tire?" They stared and said, "We forgot."

Later they went into the meadow again with a flashlight to look for the yellow ball. They were on the alert, but there was now nobody, nothing that was waiting—even when Con, holding the ball in his hand, pretended that he was about to throw it. No ardent expectation. Nothing now but the meadow and the trees in it and the unsurprised cows.

They brought the ball indoors and scrubbed it as clean as they could with a nailbrush, but there would always be dirt in the little holes. "Those are tooth marks," said Con.

"Hers," said Lizzie. "This was her own special ball that she used to carry in her mouth when she was alive, when she was a flesh-and-blood dog."

"Where did she live?" asked Con. But of course, Lizzie didn't know. Perhaps in one of the houses by the meadow; perhaps even in their own, before ever they came to it.

"Shall we see her tomorrow?" asked Con. "Oh, I want to see her again tomorrow!"

The next day they took the yellow ball into the meadow before school, but with no result. They tried again as soon as they got home: nothing. They had their teas and went out to the tire again with the yellow ball. Nobody—nothing—was waiting for them. So they settled themselves on the tire and swung to and fro, but gently, and talked to each other in low voices, and the sun began to set.

It was almost dusk, and they were still gently swinging, when Lizzie whispered, "She's here now, I'm sure of it!" Lizzie had been holding on to the nylon rope with one hand only, because the other held the yellow ball; it was her turn with it today, they had decided. Now she put her feet down to stop the swinging of the tire and stepped out from it altogether.

"Here, you!" she called softly, and, aside to Con: "Oh, I wish we knew her name!"

"Don't bother about that," said Con. "Throw the ball!"

So Lizzie did. They both saw where it went; also, they glimpsed the flashing speed that followed it. And then began the fruitless searching, to and fro, to and fro. . . .

"The poor thing!" said Lizzie, watching.

Con was only pleased and excited. He still sat on the tire, and now he began to push hard with his toes, to swing higher and higher, chanting under his breath, "We've got a ghost—a ghooooost! We've got a ghost—a ghooooost!" Twice he stopped his swinging and chanting and left the tire to fetch the ball and throw it again. (Lizzie did not want to throw.) Each time they watched the straight following of the ball and then the spreading search that could not possibly have an end. But when darkness began to fall, they felt suddenly that there was no more ghost in the meadow, and it was time for them to go indoors, too.

As they went, Con said, almost shyly, "Tomorrow, when it's really my turn, do you think if I held the ball out to her and sort of *tempted* her with it, that she'd come close up to me? I might touch her. . . ."

Lizzie said, "You can't touch a ghost. And besides, Con, you're frightened of dogs. You know you are. Else we might have had one of our own—a real one—years ago."

Con simply said, "This dog is different. I like this dog."

This first evening with the ghost dog was only a beginning. Every day now they took the yellow ball into the meadow. They soon found that their ghost dog came only at sunset, at dusk. Someone in the past had made a habit of giving this dog a ball game in the evening, before going indoors for the night. A ball game—that was all the dog hoped for. That was why she came at the end of the day, whenever a human hand held the yellow ball.

"And I think I can guess why Dad found the ball where he did, high up a tree," said Lizzie. "It was put there deliberately, after the dog had died. Someone—probably the person who owned the dog—put it where no one was ever likely to find it. That someone wanted the ball not to be thrown again, because it was a haunted ball, you might say. It would draw the dog—the ghost of the dog—to come back to chase it and search for it and never find it. Never find it. Never."

"You make everything sound so sad and wrong," said Con. "But it isn't, really."

Lizzie did not answer.

They had settled into a routine with their ghost dog. They kept her yellow ball inside the hollow of the tire and brought it out every evening to throw it in turns. Con always threw in his turn, but Lizzie often did not want to for hers. Then Con wanted to have her turn for himself, and at first she let him. Then she changed her mind: she insisted that on her evenings, neither of them threw. Con was annoyed ("Dog in the manger," he muttered), but after all, Lizzie had the right.

A Saturday was coming when neither of them would throw, for a different reason. There was going to be a family expedition to the zoo, in London; they were all going on a cheap day excursion by train, and they would not be home until well after dark.

The day came, and the visit to the zoo went as well as such visits do, and now at last they were on the train again, going home. All four were tired, but only their parents were dozing. Con was wide-awake and excited by the train. He pointed out to Lizzie that all the lights had come on inside the railway carriage; outside, the view was of darkening land-scapes and the sparkling illumination of towns, villages, and highways.

The ticket inspector came round, and Lizzie nudged their father awake. He found the four tickets of the family, and they were clipped.

"And what about the dog?" said the ticket inspector with severity.

"Dog?" Their father was still half asleep, confused.

"Your dog. It should have a ticket. And why isn't it in the baggage compartment?"

"But there's no dog! We haven't a dog with us. We don't own a dog."

"I saw one," said the inspector grimly. He stooped and began look-ing under the seats, and other passengers began looking, too, even while they all agreed that they had seen no dog.

And there really was no dog.

"Sorry, sir," said the ticket inspector at last. His odd mistake had shaken him. "I could have sworn I saw something move that was a dog." He took off his glasses and worried at the lenses with his hand-kerchief and passed on.

The passengers resettled themselves, and when their own parents were dozing off again, Lizzie whispered to Con, "Con, you little demon! You brought it with you—the yellow ball!"

"Yes!" He held his pocket a little open and toward her, so that she saw the ball nestling inside. "And I had my hand on it, holding it, when the ticket man came to us. And it worked! It worked!" He was so pleased with himself that he was bouncing up and down in his seat.

Lizzie said in a furious whisper, "You should never have done it! Think how terrified that dog must have been to find herself on a train—a *train*! Con, how could you treat a dog so?"

"She was all right," Con said stubbornly. "She can't come to any harm, anyway. She's not a dog; she's only the ghost of one. And anyway, it's as much my yellow ball as yours. We each have a half share in it."

"You never asked my permission about my half of the ball," said Lizzie. "And don't talk so loud; someone will hear."

They talked no more in so public a place, nor when they got home. They all went straight to bed, and all slept late the next morning, Sunday.

All except for Lizzie; she was up early, for her own purposes. She crept into Con's room, as he slept, and took the yellow ball from his pocket. She took the yellow ball down the garden path to her father's work shed, at the bottom. She and the yellow ball went inside, and Lizzie shut the door behind them.

Much later, when he was swinging on the tire in the morning sunshine, Con saw Lizzie coming into the meadow. He called to her, "All right! I know you've taken it, so there. You can have it today, anyway, but it's my turn tomorrow. We share the yellow ball. Remember?"

Lizzie came close to him. She held out toward him her right hand, closed; then she opened it carefully, palm upward. "Yours," she said. On her flattened palm sat the domed shape of half the yellow ball. She twisted her hand slightly, so that the yellow dome fell on its side; then Con could see the sawed cross section—black except for the outer rim of yellow.

For a moment Con was stunned. Then he screamed at her, "Wherever you hide your half, I'll find it! I'll glue the halves together! I'll make the yellow ball again and I'll throw it—I'll throw it and I'll throw it and I'll throw it!"

"No, you won't," said Lizzie. This time she held out toward him her cupped left hand; he saw a mess of chips and crumbs and granules of black, dotted with yellow. It had taken Lizzie a long time in her father's workshop to saw and cut and chip and grate her half ball down to this. She said flatly, "I've destroyed the yellow ball forever." Then, with a gesture of horror, she flung the ball particles from her and burst into a storm of sobbing and crying.

Only the shock of seeing Lizzie crying in such a way—she rarely cried at all—stopped Con from going for her with fists and feet and teeth as well. But the grief and desolation that he saw in Lizzie made him know his own affliction; grief at loss overwhelmed his first rage, and he began to cry, too.

"Why did you have to do that to the yellow ball, Lizzie? Why didn't you just hide it from me? Up a tree again—I might not have found it."

"Somebody would have found it, someday. . . ."

"Or in the earth. You could have dug a deep hole, Lizzie."

"Somebody would have found it. . . ."

"Oh, it wasn't fair of you, Lizzie!"

"No, it wasn't fair. But it was the only way. Otherwise she'd search forever for something she could never find."

"Go away," said Con.

Lizzie picked up the half ball from the ground, where she had let it fall. She took it back with her to the house, to the dustbin. Then she went indoors and upstairs to her bedroom and lay down on her bed and cried again.

They kept apart all day, as far as possible, but in the early evening, Lizzie saw Con on the tire, and she went out to him, and he let her swing him gently to and fro. After a while he said, "We'll never see her again, shall we?"

"No," said Lizzie, "but at least she won't be worried and disappointed and unhappy again, either."

"I just miss her so," said Con. "If we can't have the ghost of a dog, I wish we had a real dog."

"But, Con—"

"No, truly, I wouldn't be frightened if we had a dog like her—just like her. It would have to be a bitch—she was black, wasn't she, Lizzie?"

"I thought so. A glossy black. I remember, her collar was red. Red against black; it looked smart."

"A glossy black bitch with a whippy tail and those big, soft ears that flew out. That's what I'd like."

"Oh, Con!" cried Lizzie. She had always longed for them to have a dog, and it had never been possible because of Con's terrors. Until now . . .

Con was still working things out: "And she must be a jumper and a runner, and she must *love* running after a ball. And we'll call her—what ought we to call her, Lizzie?"

"I don't know. . . ."

"It must be exactly the right name—*exactly* right. . . ."

He had stopped swinging; Lizzie had stopped pushing him. They remained quite still under the sycamore tree, thinking.

Then they began to feel it: something was going to happen. . . .

For one last time, a quittance for them . . .

The sun had already set; daylight was fading. "What is it? What's happening?" whispered Con, preparing to step out of the tire, afraid.

"Wait, Con. I think I know." Thinking, foreseeing, Lizzie knew. "The ball's destroyed; it's a ghost ball now, a ghost ball for a ghost dog. Look, Con! It's being thrown!"

"*Being thrown?*" repeated Con. "But—but—*who's* throwing it?"

"I don't know, but look—oh, look, Con!"

They could not see the thrower at all, but they thought they could see the ghost of a ball, and they could certainly see the dog. She waited for the throw and then—on the instant—was after the ball in a straight line of speed, and caught up with it, and caught it, and was carried onward with the force of her own velocity, but directed her course and began to come back in a wide, happy, unhurried curve. The yellow ball was between her teeth, and her tail was up in triumph—a thing they had never seen before. She brought the ball back to the thrower, and the thrower threw again, and again she ran, and caught, and came loping back. Again, and again, and again.

They could not see the thrower at all, but once the ghost of a voice—and still, they could not tell: man, woman, boy, or girl?—called to the dog.

"Listen!" whispered Lizzie, but they did not hear the voice again.

They watched until darkness fell and the throwing ceased.

Con said, "What was her name? Nellie? Jilly?"

Lizzie said, "No, Millie."

"Millie?"

"It's short for Millicent, I think. An old name, Millicent."

"I'm glad now about the yellow ball," said Con. "And we'll call her Millicent—Millie for short."

"Her?"

"You know, our dog."

They left the tire under the sycamore and went indoors to tackle their parents.

About the Author ❖

*P*hilippa Pearce was born in 1920 and grew up in a millhouse in the village of Great Shelford in England. The millhouse, the river, the garden—all of these settings have played important parts in Ms. Pearce's books.

The Daily Telegraph recently described Philippa Pearce as "possibly the greatest living British writer for children." She is the author of many books, several of which are considered classics both in the United States and in her native England. Her award-winning titles include *Tom's Midnight Garden,* which won the Carnegie Medal and is an ALA Notable Book, *The Battle of Bubble and Squeak,* which won the Whitbread Award, and *Mrs. Cockle's Cat,* which won the Kate Greenaway Medal. Three of her books—*Minnow on the Say, The Battle of Bubble and Squeak,* and *The Shadow Cage and Other Tales of the Supernatural*—received Carnegie Commendations. She lives in Cambridgeshire, England.

Story Credits ❖

"Still Jim and Silent Jim," copyright © 1959 by Philippa Pearce, was first published in 1959 by Basil Blackwell and Mott Ltd.

"What the Neighbors Did," copyright © 1967 by Philippa Pearce, was first published in *Twentieth Century*, First Quarter 1967, and subsequently adapted for broadcasting in the BBC School Broadcasting series *Living Language*.

"Return to Air," copyright © 1969 by Philippa Pearce, was originally written for the BBC School Broadcasting series *Over to You* in 1964, and first published, in a slightly different form, in *The Friday Miracle and Other Stories*, edited by Kaye Webb, published in 1969 by Penguin Books Ltd.

"In the Middle of the Night," "The Tree in the Meadow," "Fresh," "The Great Blackberry Pick," and "Lucky Boy," copyright © 1972 by Philippa Pearce, were first published in *What the Neighbors Did and Other Stories*, published in 1972 by Longman.

"Bluebag," copyright © 1976 by Philippa Pearce, was first published under the title "The Nest" in *Cricket*, vol. 3, no. 2, August 1976.

"The Shadow Cage," "Miss Mountain," "Guess," "At the River Gates," "Her Father's Attic," "The Running Companion," "Beckoned," "The Dear Little Man with His Hands in His Pockets," "The Dog Got Them," and "The Strange Illness of Mr. Arthur Cook," copyright © 1977 by Philippa Pearce, were first published in *The Shadow Cage and Other Tales of the Supernatural*, published in 1977 by Kestrel Books.